It Starts with Us

It Starts with Us

A Novel

Colleen Hoover

ATRIA PAPERBACK

NEW YORK LONDON TORONTO SYDNEY NEW DELHI

ATRIA
PAPERBACK

An Imprint of Simon & Schuster, Inc.
1230 Avenue of the Americas
New York, NY 10020

First Atria Paperback edition October 2022

ATRIA PAPERBACK and colophon are trademarks of Simon & Schuster, Inc.

For information about special discounts for bulk purchases, please contact Simon & Schuster Special Sales at 1-866-506-1949 or business@simonandschuster.com.

The Simon & Schuster Speakers Bureau can bring authors to your live event. For more information or to book an event, contact the Simon & Schuster Speakers Bureau at 1-866-248-3049 or visit our website at www.simonspeakers.com.

Manufactured in China

1   3   5   7   9   10   8   6   4   2

Library of Congress Control Number: 2022942782

ISBN 978-1-6680-0122-6
ISBN 978-1-6680-0123-3 (ebook)

This book is for the brave and bold Maria Blalock

Dear reader,

This book is a sequel to *It Ends with Us* and begins right where the first book concluded. For the best reading experience, *It Starts with Us* should be read second in the two-book series.

After releasing *It Ends with Us*, I never imagined I would one day be writing a sequel. I also never imagined that the book would be received as it has been by so many. I am so grateful to all of you who found Lily's story to be as empowering as I find my own mother's.

After *It Ends with Us* gained momentum on TikTok, I was inundated with requests for more Lily and Atlas. And how could I possibly deny a community that has changed my life? This novel was written as a thank-you for the tremendous support, and because of that, I wanted to deliver a much lighter experience.

Lily and Atlas deserve it.

I hope you enjoy their journey.

All my love,
Colleen Hoover

It Starts with Us

Chapter One
Atlas

The way *ass whole* is misspelled in red spray paint across the back door of Bib's makes me think of my mother.

She would always insert a brief pause between syllables, making it sound like two separate words. I wanted to laugh every time I heard it, but it was hard to find the humor in it as a child when I was always the recipient of the hurled insult.

"Ass . . . whole," Darin mutters. "Had to be a kid. Most adults know how to spell that word."

"You'd be surprised." I touch the paint, but it doesn't stick to my fingers. Whoever did this must have done it right after we closed last night.

"Do you think the misspelling was intentional?" he asks. "Are they suggesting you're so much of an asshole that you're a whole *entire* ass?"

"Why do you assume they were targeting *me*? They could have been targeting you or Brad."

"It's your restaurant." Darin takes off his jacket and uses it to pry a large shard of exposed broken glass out of the window. "Maybe it was a disgruntled employee."

"Do I have disgruntled employees?" I can't think of a single person on payroll who would do something like this.

The last person I'd had quit was five months ago, and she left on good terms after getting a college degree.

"There was that guy who did the dishes before you hired Brad. What was his name? He was named after some kind of mineral or something—it was super weird."

"Quartz," I say. "It was a nickname." I haven't thought about that guy in so long. I doubt he's holding a grudge against me after all this time. I fired him right after we opened because I found out he wasn't washing the dishes unless he could actually see food on them. Glasses, plates, silverware—anything that came back to the kitchen from a table looking fairly clean, he'd just put it straight on the drying rack.

If I wouldn't have fired him, he would have gotten us shut down by the health department.

"You should call the police," Darin says. "We'll have to file a report for insurance."

Before I object, Brad appears at the back door, his shoes crunching the broken glass beneath his feet. Brad has been inside taking inventory in order to see if anything was stolen.

He scratches the stubble on his jaw. "They took the croutons."

There's a confused pause.

"Did you say 'croutons'?" Darin asks.

"Yeah. They took the whole thing of croutons that were prepared last night. Nothing else seems to be missing, though."

That wasn't at all what I was expecting him to say. If someone broke into a restaurant and didn't take appliances or anything else of value, they probably broke in because they were hungry. I know that kind of desperation firsthand. "I'm not reporting this."

Darin turns to me. "Why not?"

"They might catch whoever did it."

"That's the point."

I grab an empty box out of the dumpster and start picking up shards of glass. "I broke into a restaurant once. Stole a turkey sandwich."

Brad and Darin are both staring at me now. "Were you drunk?" Darin asks.

"No. I was hungry. I don't want anyone arrested for stealing croutons."

"Okay, but maybe food was only the beginning. What if they come back for appliances next time?" Darin says. "Is the security camera still broken?"

He's been on me to get that repaired for months now. "I've been busy."

Darin takes the box of glass from me and starts to pick up the remaining pieces. "You should go work on that before they come back. Heck, they might even try to hit up Corrigan's tonight since Bib's was such an easy target."

"Corrigan's has working security. And I doubt whoever it was will vandalize my new restaurant. It was a matter of convenience, not a targeted break-in."

"You *hope*," Darin says.

I open my mouth to respond, but I'm interrupted by an incoming text message. I don't think I've ever reached for my phone faster. When I see the text isn't from Lily, I deflate a little.

I ran into her this morning while I was running errands.

It was the first time we've seen each other in a year and a half, but she was late for work and I had just received the text from Darin informing me we had a break-in. We parted somewhat awkwardly on the promise that she would text me once she got to work.

It's been an hour and a half since then, and I still haven't heard from her. An hour and a half is nothing, but I can't ignore the nagging in my chest that's trying to convince me she's having doubts about everything that was said between us in that five-minute exchange on the sidewalk.

I'm definitely not having doubts about what *I* said. I might have gotten caught up in the moment—in seeing how happy she looked and finding out she's no longer married. But I meant every word I said to her.

I'm ready for this. *More* than ready.

I pull up her contact info in my phone. I've wanted to text her so many times over the last year and a half, but the last time I spoke to her, I left the ball in her court. She had so much going on, I didn't want to complicate her life even more.

She's single now, though, and she made it sound like she was finally ready to give whatever could be between us a chance. However, she's had an hour and a half to think about our conversation, and an hour and a half is plenty of time to form regrets. Every minute that passes without a text is going to feel like a whole damn day.

She's still listed as Lily Kincaid in my phone, so I edit her contact info and change her last name back to Bloom.

I feel Darin hovering, looking over my shoulder at my phone screen. "Is that *our* Lily?"

Brad perks up. "He's texting Lily?"

"'*Our* Lily'?" I ask, confused. "You guys met her once."

"Is she still married?" Darin asks.

I shake my head.

"Good for her," he says. "She was pregnant, right? What did she end up having? A boy or a girl?"

I don't want to discuss Lily because there's nothing to discuss yet. I don't want to make it more than what it might be. "A girl, and that's the last question I'm answering." I focus on Brad. "Theo coming in today?"

"It's Thursday. He'll be here."

I head inside the restaurant. If I'm going to discuss Lily with anyone, it'll be Theo.

Chapter Two
Lily

My hands are still shaking, even though it's been almost two hours since I ran into Atlas. I can't tell if I'm shaking because I'm flustered or because I've been too busy to eat since I walked in the door. I've barely had five seconds of peace to process what happened this morning, much less eat the breakfast I brought with me.

Did that actually just happen? Did I really ask Atlas a series of questions so awkward, I'll be mortified well into next year?

He didn't seem awkward, though. He seemed very happy to see me, and then when he hugged me, it felt like a part of me that had been dormant suddenly sprang to life.

But this is the first moment I've had to even take a bathroom break, and after looking at myself in the mirror just now, I kind of want to cry. I'm splotchy, I have carrots smeared across my shirt, my nail polish has been chipped since, like, January.

Not that Atlas expects or wants perfection. It's just that I've imagined running into him so many times, but not one of those fantasies starred me bumping into him in the middle of a hectic morning, half an hour after being the target of an eleven-month-old with a handful of baby food.

He looked so good. He smelled so good.

I probably smell like breast milk.

I'm so rattled by what our chance encounter might mean, it took me twice as long to organize everything for the delivery driver this morning. I haven't even checked our website for new orders today. I give myself one last look in the mirror, but all I see is an exhausted, overworked single mom.

I make my way out of the bathroom and back to the register. I pull an order from the printer and begin making out the card. My mind has never been more in need of a distraction, so I'm glad it's been a busy morning.

The order is for a bouquet of roses for someone named Greta from someone named Jonathan. The message reads, *I'm sorry about last night. Forgive me?*

I groan. Apology flowers are my least-favorite kind of bouquets to assemble. I always end up obsessing over what they're apologizing for. Did he miss their date? Did he come home late? Did they fight?

Did he hit her?

Sometimes I want to write the number for the local domestic violence shelter on the cards, but I have to remind myself that not every apology is attached to something as awful as the things that were attached to the apologies I used to receive. Maybe Jonathan is Greta's friend and he's trying to cheer her up. Maybe he's her husband and he took a prank a little too far.

Whatever the reason for the flowers, I hope they mean something good. I tuck the card into the envelope and stick it into the bouquet of roses. I set them on the delivery shelf and am pulling up the next order when I receive a text.

I lunge for my phone as if the text is about to self-destruct and I only have three seconds to read it. I shrink when I look at the screen. It's not from Atlas, but rather from Ryle.

Can she eat French fries?

I shoot a quick response. **Soft ones.**

I drop my phone onto the counter with a thud. I don't like for her to have French fries too often, but Ryle only has her one to two days a week, so I try to make sure she gets more nutritious foods when she's with me.

It was nice not thinking about Ryle for a few minutes, but his text has reminded me that he exists. And as long as he exists, I fear that any type of relationship, or even a friendship between me and Atlas, *can't* exist. How will Ryle take it if I start seeing Atlas? How would he act if they ever had to be around each other?

Maybe I'm getting ahead of myself.

I stare at my phone, wondering what I should say to Atlas. I told him I would text him after I opened the store, but customers were waiting before I even unlocked the door. And now that Ryle has texted, I've gone and remembered Ryle exists in this scenario, too, which makes me hesitant to text Atlas at all.

The front door opens, and my employee Lucy finally walks in. She always seems so put-together, even when I can tell she's in a bad mood.

"Good morning, Lucy."

She flicks hair out of her eyes and sets her purse on the counter with a sigh. "Is it?"

Lucy isn't at her friendliest in the morning. It's why my other employee Serena or I usually work the register until at least eleven, while Lucy puts arrangements together in the back. She's much better with customers after a cup or five of coffee.

"I just found out our place cards never arrived because they were discontinued, and it's too late to order more. The wedding is in less than a *month*."

So much has gone wrong leading up to this wedding, I have half a mind to tell her not to go through with it. But I'm not superstitious. Hopefully she isn't, either.

"Homemade place cards are in style," I offer.

Lucy rolls her eyes. "I hate crafting," she mutters. "I don't even want a wedding now. It feels like we've been planning it for longer than we even dated." *That's accurate.* "Maybe we'll just call it off and go to Vegas. You eloped, right? Do you regret it?"

I don't know which part of all that to address first. "How can you hate crafting? You work at a flower shop. And I'm divorced; of course I regret eloping." I hand her a small stack of orders I haven't gotten to yet. "But it *was* fun," I admit.

Lucy goes to the back and starts on the rest of the orders, and I go back to thinking about Atlas. *And Ryle.* And Armageddon, which is what the two of them in my brain at the same time feels like.

I have no idea how this is expected to work. When Atlas and I ran into each other, it was as if everything else faded away, including Ryle. But now Ryle is beginning to seep back into my thoughts. Not in the way thoughts of Ryle *used* to occupy my mind, but more in a way that feels like a roadblock. My love life has finally been on a straight path with no bumps or curves, basically because it's been nonexistent for well over a year and a half, but now it feels like there's nothing but rough terrain and obstacles and cliffs ahead.

Is it worth it? Of course *Atlas* is worth it.

But are *we* worth it? Is us potentially becoming a thing worth the stress it would inevitably bring to all the other areas of my life?

I haven't felt this conflicted in so long. Part of me wants to call Allysa and tell her about seeing Atlas, but I can't. She knows how Ryle still feels about me. She knows how he'd feel if I brought Atlas into the picture.

I can't talk to my mother because she's my mother. As close as we've become lately, I'd still never freely discuss my dating life with her.

There's really only one woman I feel comfortable talking to about Atlas.

"Lucy?"

She appears from the back, pulling an earbud out of her ear. "Did you need me?"

"Can you cover me for a while? I need to go run an errand. I'll be back in an hour."

She makes her way behind the counter, and I grab my purse. I don't get a lot of alone time now that I have Emerson, so I occasionally steal an hour here and there during the workweek when I have someone to back up my absence at the shop.

Sometimes I like to sit in my thoughts, and it's impossible to do that in the presence of a child because even when she's asleep I'm in mom mode. And with the constant flow of traffic at work, it's rare that I can find a stretch of peace without being interrupted.

I've found that being alone in my car with my music on, and occasionally a slice of dessert from the Cheesecake Factory, is sometimes all it takes to sort through the knots in my brain.

Once I'm parked with a clear view of Boston Harbor, I lean my seat back and grab the notepad and pen I brought with me. I don't know if this will help as much as dessert sometimes does, but I need to release my thoughts in the same way I've done in the past. This method has helped before when I need things to fall neatly into place. Although this time, I'm just hoping it helps things not to fall completely apart.

Dear Ellen,

> *Guess who's back?*
> *Me.*
> *And Atlas.*
> *Both of us.*
> *I ran into him on my way to meet Ryle with Emmy this morning. It was so good to see him. But as reaffirming as it was to see him and to know where we both stand at this point in our lives, it ended a bit awkwardly. He was having a minor emergency with his restaurant and was in a hurry; I was late opening the store. We parted on the promise that I would text him.*
> *I want to text him. I do. Especially because seeing him reminded me of how much I miss the feeling I get when I'm around him.*
> *I didn't realize how lonely I'd been feeling until those few minutes with him this morning. But since Ryle and I divorced . . . oh, wait.*

Wow. I haven't told you about the divorce.

It's been way too long since I've written to you. Let me back up.

I decided my separation from Ryle should be permanent after giving birth to Emmy. I asked him for a divorce right after she was born. I wasn't attempting to be cruel in my timing, I just didn't know which choice I was going to make until I held her in my arms and knew with every fiber of my being that I would do whatever it took to break the cycle of abuse.

Yes, asking for a divorce hurt. Yes, I was heartbroken. But no, I don't regret it. My choice helped me realize that sometimes the hardest decisions a person can make will most likely lead to the best outcomes.

I can't lie and say I don't miss him, because I do. I miss what we sometimes were. I miss the family we could have been for Emerson. But I know I made the right decision, even though I sometimes get overwhelmed by the weight of it. It's difficult because I still have to interact with Ryle. He still possesses all the good qualities I fell in love with, and now that I'm no longer in a relationship with him, it's rare I see the negative side that ultimately ended our marriage. I think that has to do with the fact that he's on his best behavior. He had to be agreeable and not put up too much of a fight because he knew I could have reported him for all the incidents of domestic violence I experienced at his hands. He could have lost a lot more than his wife, so when it came to the custody arrangement, things were more amiable than I expected them to be.

That may have been more because I put up less of a

fight than he did. My lawyer was very straightforward when I said I wanted sole custody. Unless I was willing to drag the dirtiest parts of our rock bottom into a courtroom, there wasn't much I could do to prevent Ryle from getting visits with Emerson. And even if I were to bring up the domestic violence, my lawyer said it's very rare that a willing, successful father without a record, who provides financial support, would have any sort of rights removed.

I was looking at two options. I could choose to press charges and drag this through the courts, only to be met with a very possible joint custody arrangement. Or I could attempt to work an agreement out with Ryle that would satisfy us both, while preserving our coparenting relationship.

I guess you could say we came to a compromise, even though there isn't an agreement in the world that would make me feel comfortable with sending my daughter off with someone I know possesses a temper. But all I can do is choose the lesser of two evils when it comes to custody and hope that Emmy never sees that side of him.

I want Emmy to bond with her father. I've never wanted to keep her from him. I just want to ensure she's safe, which is why I begged Ryle to agree to day visits for the first couple of years. I never told him outright it's because I don't know that I fully trust him with her. I think I might have blamed it on my breastfeeding situation and the fact that he's on call all the time, but deep down I'm sure he knows why I've never wanted her to stay with him overnight.

The past abuse is something we don't talk about. We

talk about Emmy, we talk about work, we plaster on smiles when we're in the presence of our daughter. Sometimes it feels forced and fake, at least on my end, but it's better than what this could have been had I taken him to court and lost. I'll fake a smile until she's eighteen if it means I don't have to share custody and potentially expose my daughter to the worst parts of her father on a more regular basis.

It's been working out okay so far, if you don't count the occasional gaslighting and unwanted flirtation from him. As clear as I've made my feelings during this divorce, he still has hope for us. He says things sometimes that indicate he hasn't fully let go of the idea of us. I fear that a huge part of Ryle's cooperation rests on the notion that he'll eventually win me back if he's good enough for long enough. He has it in his head that I'll soften over time.

But life isn't going to happen his way, Ellen. I'm ultimately going to move on, and if I'm being honest, I hope I end up moving on in Atlas's direction. It's too soon to know if that's a possibility, but I know for a fact I'll never move back in Ryle's direction, no matter how much time passes.

It's been almost a year since I asked Ryle for the divorce, but it's been almost nineteen months since the fight that ultimately caused our separation. Which means I've been single for over a year and a half.

A year and a half of separation between potential relationships seems like plenty of time, and maybe it would be if it were anyone other than Atlas. But how can I possibly make this work? What if I text Atlas and he invites me to lunch? And then lunch goes wonderful, which I'm sure it would, and lunch leads to dinner? And dinner leads to us falling right back into step with where we left off when we were younger? And then we're both happy and we fall back in love and he becomes a permanent part of my life?

I know it sounds like I'm getting ahead of myself, but it's Atlas we're talking about here. Unless he had a personality transplant, I think you and I both know how easy Atlas is for me to love, Ellen. That's why I'm so hesitant, because I'm scared it will work out.

And if it works out, how will Ryle feel about my new relationship? Emerson is almost a year old, and we've gone this whole year without too much drama, but I know that's because we've found a good flow that nothing has interrupted. So why does it feel like any mention of Atlas will cause a tsunami?

Not that Ryle deserves the concern I'm currently feeling over this situation, but he has the potential to make my dating life a living hell. Why does Ryle still occupy an entire wall in my many layers of thoughts? That's what it feels like—as if these wonderful things happen, but as they start to sink in, they eventually reach a part of me that is still making decisions based on Ryle and his potential reactions.

His reactions are what I fear the most. I want to hope that he wouldn't be jealous, but he will be. If I start dating Atlas, he'll make it difficult for everyone. Even though I know divorce was the right choice, there are still consequences to that choice. And one of those consequences is that Ryle will always look at Atlas like he's the thing that broke up our marriage.

Ryle is the father of my daughter. No matter what man

comes and goes in my life from this point forward, Ryle is the one constant that I'll always have to appease if I want the most peaceful experience for my daughter. And if Atlas Corrigan is back in my life—Ryle will never be appeased.

I wish you could tell me what decision to make. Do I sacrifice what I know will make me happy for the sake of avoiding the inevitable disruption Atlas's presence would cause?

Or will I always have an Atlas-shaped hole in my heart unless I allow him to fill it?

He's expecting me to text him, but I think I need more time to process this. I don't even know what to say to him. I don't know what to do.

I'll let you know if I figure it out.

Lily

Chapter Three
Atlas

"'We finally reached the *shore*'?" Theo says. "You actually *said* that to her? Out loud?"

I shift uncomfortably on the couch. "We bonded over *Finding Nemo* when we were younger."

"You quoted a *cartoon*." Theo's head roll is dramatic. "And it didn't work. It's been over eight hours since you ran into her, and she still hasn't texted you."

"Maybe she got busy."

"Or maybe you came on too strong," Theo says, leaning forward. He clasps his hands between his knees and refocuses. "Okay, so what happened after you said all the cheesy lines?"

He's brutal. "Nothing. We both had to get to work. I asked if she still had my number, and she said she had it memorized, and then we said good—"

"Hold up," Theo interrupts. "She has your number *memorized*?"

"Apparently so."

"Okay." He looks hopeful. "This means something. No one memorizes numbers anymore."

I was thinking the same thing, but I also wondered if she memorized my number for other reasons. Back when I wrote it down and put it in her phone case, it was for an emergency. Maybe part of her feared the day she'd need it, so she memorized it for reasons that had nothing to do with me.

"So, what do I do? Text her? Call her? Wait until she reaches out to me?"

"It's been eight hours, Atlas. Calm down."

His advice is giving me whiplash. "Two minutes ago, you acted like eight hours without a text was too long. Now you're telling me to calm down?"

Theo shrugs and then kicks my desk to make his chair spin. "I'm twelve. I don't even have a phone yet, and you want my opinion on texting etiquette?"

It surprises me that he doesn't have a phone yet. Brad doesn't seem like he would be a strict father. "Why don't you have a phone?"

"Dad says I can have one when I turn thirteen. Two more months," he says wistfully.

Theo has been coming to the restaurant a couple of days a week after school since Brad's promotion six months ago. Theo told me he wanted to be a therapist when he grows up, so I let him practice on me. At first, the talks we would have were intended for his benefit. But lately, I feel like I'm the one benefiting.

Brad peeks his head into my office in search of his son. "Let's go. Atlas has work to do." He motions for Theo to stand up, but Theo just keeps spinning in my desk chair.

"Atlas is the one who called me in here. He needed advice."

"I'll never understand whatever this is," Brad says, pointing between me and Theo. "What advice do you get from my son? How to avoid your chores and win at *Minecraft*?"

Theo stands up and stretches his arms over his head. "Girls, actually. And winning isn't the point of *Minecraft*, Dad. It's more of a sandbox game." Theo looks over his shoulder at me as he's leaving my office. "Just text her." He says that like it's the obvious solution. Maybe it is.

Brad yanks him away from the door.

I settle back into my desk chair and stare at my blank phone screen. *Maybe she memorized the wrong number.*

I open her contact and hesitate. Theo could be right. I could have come on too strong this morning. We didn't say much when we ran into each other, but what we did say had meaning and intent. Maybe that scared her.

Or . . . maybe I'm right and she memorized the wrong number.

My fingers hover over my phone's keyboard. I want to text her, but I don't want to pressure her. However, she and I both know our lives would have turned out so different if I hadn't made so many missteps with her in the past.

I spent years making excuses for why my life wasn't good enough for her to be a part of it, but Lily always fit. She was a perfect fit. I refuse to let her walk away this time without a little more effort on my part. I'll start with making sure she has my correct number.

It was good seeing you today, Lily.

I wait to see if she's going to text me back. When I see the three dots pop up, I hold my breath in anticipation.

You too.

I stare at her response for way too long, hoping it'll be accompanied by another text. But it isn't. That's all I'm getting.

It's only two words, but I can read between the lines.

I sigh in defeat and drop my phone onto my desk.

Chapter Four
Lily

Mine and Ryle's situation has been an unconventional one since Emerson was born. I don't think many couples file divorce papers at the same time they sign their newborn's birth certificate.

As much as I was disappointed in Ryle for being the thing that forced me to have to make the decision to end our marriage, I didn't want to prevent him from bonding with our daughter. I cooperate with him as much as I can since his schedule is so hectic. I sometimes even take her to his work to visit him on his lunch break.

He's also had a key to my place since before Emerson was born. I only gave it to him because I lived alone and was afraid I'd go into labor and he'd need access to the apartment. But he never gave the key back after her birth, even though I've been meaning to ask him for it. He sometimes uses it on the rare occasions he has a late surgery and has extra time to spend with Emmy in the mornings after I head to work. That's why I haven't asked for it back. But lately, he's been using the key to bring Emmy home.

He texted me just before I closed the shop earlier and told me Emmy was tired, so he was taking her to my place to put her to bed. The frequency he's been using the key lately is making me wonder if Emmy is the only one he's trying to spend more time with.

My front door is unlocked when I finally make it to my apartment. Ryle is in the kitchen. He glances up at me when he hears the front door shut.

"I grabbed dinner," he says, holding up a bag from my favorite Thai place. "You haven't eaten, have you?"

I don't like this. He's been making himself more and more comfortable here. But I'm emotionally drained from the day already, so I shake my head and decide to confront the issue at a different time. "I haven't. Thank you." I set my purse on the table and pass the kitchen, heading for Emmy's room.

"I just laid her down," he warns.

I pause right outside her door and press my ear to it. It's quiet, so I back away from the door and head into the kitchen without waking her.

I feel awful about my short response to Atlas earlier, but this interaction with Ryle is confirming all my concerns. How am I supposed to start something with someone new when my ex still brings me dinner and has a key to my apartment?

I need to set firm boundaries with Ryle before I can even begin to entertain the idea of Atlas.

Ryle chooses a bottle of red wine from my tabletop wine rack. "Mind if I open this?"

I shrug as I spoon pad thai onto my plate. "Go ahead, but I don't want any."

Ryle puts the bottle back and opts for a glass of tea. I grab a water out of the fridge, and we both take a seat at the table.

"How was she today?" I ask him.

"A little cranky, but I had a lot of errands to run. I think she just got tired of going in and out of the car seat. She was better when we went over to Allysa's."

"When's your next day off?" I ask him.

"Not sure. I'll let you know." He reaches forward and uses his thumb to wipe something off my cheek. I flinch a little, but he doesn't notice. Or maybe he pretends not to. I'm not sure if he realizes the reaction I have anytime his hand comes near me is a negative one. Knowing Ryle, he probably thinks I flinched because I felt a spark.

After Emmy was born, there were moments here and there when I *would* feel a spark between us. He'd do or say something sweet, or he'd be holding Emmy while he sang to her, and I would feel that familiar desire for him bubbling up inside of me. But I somehow found it within me to pull myself out of the moment every time. It only takes one bad memory to immediately dull any fleeting feelings I have in his presence.

It's been a long, bumpy road, but those feelings are finally nonexistent.

I attribute that to the list I wrote of all the reasons why I chose to divorce him. Sometimes, after he leaves, I go to my bedroom and read it to reiterate that this arrangement is the best one for all of us.

Well. Maybe not this *exact* arrangement. I'd still like my key returned to me.

I'm about to take another bite of noodles when I hear a muffled ping come from my purse across the table. I drop my fork and quickly reach for my phone before Ryle does.

Not that he would read my texts, but the last thing I want right now is for him to even try to be polite by handing me my phone. He might see that the text is from Atlas, and I'm not prepared for the storm that would bring.

The text isn't from Atlas, though. It's from my mother. She's sending pics of Emmy she took earlier this week. I set the phone down and pick up my fork, but Ryle is staring at me.

"It was my mother," I say. I don't know why I even say that. I don't owe him an explanation, but I don't like the way he's staring at me.

"Who were you *hoping* it would be? You practically lunged across the table for your phone."

"No one." I take a drink. He's still staring. I have no idea how well Ryle can read me, but it looks like he knows I'm lying.

He spins his fork in his noodles and looks down at his plate with a hardened jaw. "Are you seeing someone?" There's an edge to his voice now.

"Not that it's any of your business, but no."

"Not saying it is my business. Just having a casual conversation."

I don't respond to that because it's a lie. Any recently divorced husband asking his ex-wife if she's seeing someone is making anything but casual conversation.

"I do think we need to have a more serious conversation at some point about dating," he says. "Before either of us brings other people around Emerson. Maybe lay some ground rules."

I nod. "I think we need to lay ground rules for a lot more than just that."

His eyes narrow. "Like what?"

"Your access to my apartment." I swallow. "I'd like my key back."

Ryle stares stoically before he responds. Then he wipes his mouth and says, "I can't put my daughter to bed?"

"That's not what I'm saying at all."

"You know my schedule is crazy, Lily. I hardly get to see her as it is."

"I'm not saying I want you to see her any less. I just want my key back. I value my privacy."

Ryle's expression is tight. He's upset with me. I knew he would be, but he's making this into more than it is. It has nothing to do with how much I want him to see Emmy. I just don't want him having easy access to my apartment. I moved out and divorced him for a reason.

It's not going to be a huge change, but it's one that needs to happen, or we'll be stuck in this unhealthy routine forever.

"I'll just start keeping her overnight, then." He says it with such conviction while eyeing me for a reaction. I know he can feel the discomfort I'm suddenly drowning in.

I keep my voice calm. "I don't think I'm ready for that."

Ryle drops his fork on his plate with a thud. "Maybe we need to modify the custody arrangement."

Those words infuriate me, but I somehow prevent my rage from boiling over. I stand and pick up my plate. "Really, Ryle? I ask for the key to *my* apartment back and you threaten me with court?"

We agreed to this arrangement, but he's acting like that was for *my* benefit rather than his. He knows I could have taken him to court for sole custody after everything he put me through. Hell, I never even had him arrested. He should be grateful I've been as generous as I have.

When I get to the kitchen, I set down my plate and grip the edges of the counter, allowing my head to drop between my shoulders. *Calm down, Lily. He's just reacting.*

I hear Ryle sigh regretfully, and then he follows me into the kitchen. He leans against the counter while I rinse my plate. "Can you at least give me a timeline?" His voice is lower when he speaks. "When will I get overnights with her?"

I press my hip against the counter and face him. "When she can talk."

"Why then?"

I hate that he even needs me to say this out loud. "So she can tell me if something happens, Ryle."

When the full meaning of what I've just said sinks in, he chews on his bottom lip with a small nod. I can see the frustration in the veins that rise in his neck. He pulls his keys out of his pocket and removes my apartment key. He tosses it on the counter and walks away.

When he grabs his jacket and disappears out the front door, I feel that familiar twinge of guilt creeping into my chest. The guilt is always followed by doubts like, *Am I being too hard on him?* and *What if he really has changed?*

I know the answers to these questions, but sometimes it feels good to read the reminders. I go to my room and pull the list out of my jewelry box.

1) He slapped you because you laughed.
2) He pushed you down a flight of stairs.
3) He bit you.

4) He tried to force himself on you.

5) You had to get stitches because of him.

6) Your husband physically hurt you more than once.

   It would have happened again and again.

7) You did this for your daughter.

I run my finger over the tattoo on my shoulder, feeling the small scars he left there with his teeth. If Ryle did these things to me at the highest points of our relationship, what would he be capable of at the lowest?

I fold the list and put it back in my jewelry box for the next time I might need a reminder.

Chapter Five
Atlas

"It was definitely targeted," Brad says, staring at the graffiti.

Whoever vandalized Bib's two nights ago decided to hit up my newest restaurant last night. Corrigan's has two damaged windows, and there's another message spray painted across the back door.

Fuck u Atlass.

They added an *s* and underlined *ass* in my name. I catch myself wanting to laugh at the cleverness, but my mood isn't making space for humor this morning.

Yesterday, the vandalism barely fazed me. I don't know if it was because I had just run into Lily and was still riding that high, but this morning I woke up stuck on her apparent avoidance of me. Because of that, the damage to my newest restaurant feels like it's cutting a little deeper.

"I'll check the security footage." I'm hoping it reveals something useful. I still don't know if I want to go to the police. Maybe if it's someone I know, I can at least confront them before I'm forced to resort to that.

Brad follows me into my office. I power on the computer and open the security app. I think Brad can feel my frustration, because he doesn't speak while I search the footage for several minutes.

"There," Brad says, pointing to the lower left-hand corner of the screen. I slow down the footage until we see a figure.

When I hit play, we both stare in confusion. Someone is curled up on the back steps, unmoving. We watch the screen for about half a minute, until I hit rewind again. According to the time stamp on the footage, the person remains on the steps for over two hours. Without a blanket, in a Boston October.

"They *slept* here?" Brad says. "They weren't too worried about getting caught, were they?"

I rewind the footage even more until it shows the person walking into the frame for the first time, a little after one in the morning. Because it's dark, it's hard to make out facial features, but they seem young. More like a teenager than an adult.

They snoop around for a few minutes—dig through the dumpster. Check the lock on the back door. Pull out the spray paint and leave their clever message.

Then they use the can of spray paint to attempt to break the windows, but Corrigan's windows are triple-paned, so the person eventually gets bored, or grows tired of trying to make a big enough hole to fit through like they did at Bib's. That's when they proceed to lie down on the back steps, where they fall asleep.

Just before the sun rises, they wake up, look around, and then casually walk away like the entire night never happened.

"Do you recognize him?" Brad asks.

"No. You?"

"Nope."

I pause the footage on what may be the clearest visual we can get of the person, but it's grainy. They're wearing jeans and a black hoodie with the hood pulled tight so that their hair isn't visible.

There's no way we would be able to recognize whoever this is if we saw them in person. It isn't a clear enough picture, and they never looked straight at the camera. The police wouldn't even find this footage useful.

I send the file to my email anyway. Right when I hit send, a phone pings. I glance at mine, but it's Brad who received a text.

"Darin says Bib's is fine." He pockets his phone and heads toward my office door. "I'll start cleaning up."

I wait for the file to finish sending to my email, then I start the footage over again, feeling more pity than irritation. It just reminds me of the cold nights I spent in that abandoned house before Lily offered me the shelter of her bedroom. I can practically feel the chill in my bones just thinking about it.

I have no idea who this could be. It's unnerving that they wrote my name on the door, and even more unnerving that they felt comfortable enough to hang out and take a two-hour nap. It's like they're daring me to confront them.

My phone begins to vibrate on my desk. I reach for it, but it's a number I don't recognize. I normally don't answer those, but Lily is still in the back of my mind. She could be calling me from a work phone.

God, I sound pathetic.

I raise the phone to my ear. "Hello?"

There's a sigh on the other end. A female. She sounds relieved that I answered. "Atlas?"

I sigh, too, but not from relief. I sigh because it isn't Lily's voice. I'm not sure whose it is, but anyone other than Lily is disappointing, apparently.

I lean back in my office chair. "Can I help you?"

"It's me."

I have no idea who "me" is. I think back to any exes that could be calling me, but none of them sound like this person. And none of them would assume I would know who they were if they simply said, *It's me.*

"Who's speaking?"

"*Me*," she says again, emphasizing it like it'll make a difference. "Sutton. Your *mother.*"

I immediately pull the phone away from my ear and look at the number again. This has to be some kind of prank. How would my mother get my phone number? Why would she *want* it? It's been years since she made it clear she never wanted to see me again.

I say nothing. *I have nothing to say.* I stretch my spine and lean forward, waiting for her to spit out the reason she finally put forth the effort to contact me.

"I . . . um." She pauses. I can hear a television on in the background. It sounds like *The Price Is Right.* I can almost picture her sitting on the couch, a beer in one hand and a cigarette in the other at ten in the morning. She mostly worked nights when I was growing up, so she'd eat dinner and then stay up to watch *The Price Is Right* before going to sleep.

It was my least-favorite time of day.

"What do you want?" My voice is clipped.

She makes a noise in the back of her throat, and even though it's been years, I can tell she's annoyed. I can tell in that one release of breath that she didn't *want* to call me. She's doing it because she *has* to. She's not reaching out to apologize; she's reaching out because she's desperate.

"Are you dying?" I ask. It's the only thing that would prevent me from ending this call.

"Am I *dying*?" She repeats my question with laughter as if I'm absurd and unreasonable and an *ass . . . whole*. "No, I'm not *dying*. I'm perfectly fine."

"Do you need money?"

"Who doesn't?"

Every ounce of anxiety she used to fill me with returns in just these few seconds on the phone with her. I immediately end the call. I have nothing to say to her. I block her number, regretful that I gave her as long as I did to speak. I should have ended the call as soon as she told me who she was.

I lean forward over my desk and cradle my head in my hands. My stomach is churning from the unexpectedness of the last couple of minutes.

I'm surprised by my reaction, honestly. I thought this might happen one day, but I imagined myself not caring. I assumed I'd feel as indifferent toward her returning to my life as I did when she forced me to leave hers. But back then, I was indifferent to a lot of things.

Now I actually *like* my life. I'm proud of what I've accomplished. I have absolutely no desire to allow anyone from my past to come in and threaten that.

I run my hands over my face, forcing down the last few

minutes, then I push back from my desk. I walk outside to help Brad with the repairs and do my best to move beyond this moment. It's hard, though. It's like my past is crashing into me from all directions, and I have absolutely no one to discuss this with.

After a few minutes of both of us working in silence, I say to Brad, "You need to get Theo a phone; he's almost thirteen."

Brad laughs. "You need to get a therapist who's closer to your age."

Chapter Six
Lily

"Have you decided what you're doing for Emerson's birthday?" Allysa asks.

Allysa and Marshall threw a first birthday party for their daughter, Rylee, that was so big, it was worthy of a Sweet Sixteen. "I'm sure I'll just let her have a smash cake and give her a couple of presents. I don't have room for a big party."

"We could do something at our place," Allysa offers.

"Who would I invite? She'll be one; she has no friends. She can't even talk."

Allysa rolls her eyes. "We don't throw kids' parties for our *babies*. We throw them to impress our friends."

"You're my only friend, and I don't need to impress you." I hand Allysa an order from the printer. "Are we doing dinner tonight?"

We get together for dinner at least twice a week at their place. Ryle occasionally pops by, but I purposefully plan my visits on nights he's on call. I don't know if Allysa has ever noticed. If she has, she probably doesn't blame me. She says it's painful watching Ryle when I'm around because she also suspects he still has hope for us. She prefers to spend time with him when I'm not present.

"Marshall's parents are coming into town today, remember?"

"Oh yeah. Good luck with that." Allysa likes Marshall's parents, but I don't think anyone truly looks forward to hosting their in-laws for an entire week.

The front door chimes, and Allysa and I both look up at the same time. I doubt her world starts to spin like mine does, though.

Atlas is walking toward us.

"Is that . . ."

"Oh, God," I mutter under my breath.

"Yes, he *is* a god," Allysa whispers.

What is he doing here?

And why *does* he look like a god? It makes the decision I've been weighing that much more difficult. I can't even find my voice long enough to say hello to him. I just smile and wait for him to reach us, but the walk from the door to the front counter seems like it's expanded by a mile.

He doesn't take his eyes off me as he makes his way over. When he reaches us, he finally acknowledges Allysa with a smile. Then he looks back at me as he sets a plastic bowl with a lid on the counter. "I brought you lunch," he says casually, as if he brings me lunch every day and I should have been expecting it.

Ah, that voice. I forgot how far it reaches.

I grab the bowl, but I don't know what to say with Allysa hovering next to me, watching us interact. I glance at her and give her the look. She pretends not to notice, but when I don't stop staring at her, she eventually yields.

"Fine. I'll go flower the . . . *flowers*." She walks away, giving us privacy.

I turn my attention back to the lunch Atlas brought. "Thank you. What is it?"

"Our weekend special," Atlas says. "It's called *why are you avoiding me* pasta."

I laugh. Then I cringe. "I'm not avoid . . ." I shake my head with a quick sigh, knowing I can't lie to him. "I *am* avoiding you." I lean my elbows onto the counter and cover my face with my hands. "I'm sorry."

Atlas is quiet, so I eventually look up at him. He seems sincere when he says, "Do you want me to leave?"

I shake my head, and as soon as I do, his eyes crinkle a little at the corners. It's barely a smile, but it causes a warmth to tumble down my chest.

Yesterday morning when I ran into him, I said so much. Now I'm too confused to speak. I don't know how I'm supposed to have a full-on conversation with him about everything that's been going through my mind over the last twenty-four hours when I feel so tongue-tied around him.

He had the same impact on me when I was younger, but I was more naïve back then. I didn't know how rare men like Atlas were, so I didn't know how lucky I was to have him in my life.

I know now, which is why it terrifies me that I might screw this up. Or that *Ryle* might screw this up.

I lift the bowl of pasta he brought. "It smells really good."

"It *is* good. I made it."

I should laugh at that, or smile, but my reaction doesn't fit the conversation. I set the bowl aside. When I look at him again, he can see the war in my expression. He counters with a reassuring look. Not much is said between us, but the nonverbal cues we're trading are saying enough. My eyes are apologizing for my silence over the last twenty-four hours, he's silently telling me it's okay, and we're both wondering what comes next.

Atlas slides his hand slowly across the counter, closer to mine. He lifts his index finger and skims it down the length of my pinkie. It's the smallest, most tender move, but it makes my heart flip.

He pulls his hand back and clenches his fist as if he might have felt the same thing I did. He clears his throat. "Can I call you tonight?"

I'm about to nod when Allysa suddenly bursts through the door to the back, wide-eyed. She leans in and whispers, "Ryle is almost here."

My blood feels like it freezes in my veins. *"What?"* I don't say that so she'll repeat it. I say it because I'm shocked, but she repeats herself anyway.

"Ryle is pulling in. He just texted." She waves a hand toward Atlas. "You have ten seconds to hide him."

I'm sure Atlas can see the absolute fear in my expression when I look at him, but he very calmly says, "Where do you want me?"

I point to my office and rush him in that direction. Once we're in the office, I second-guess myself. "He might come in here." I cover my mouth with a shaky hand while I think, and then point to my office supply closet. "Can you hide in there?"

Atlas looks at the closet and then looks at me. He points at the door. "In the closet?"

I hear the front door chime, and I'm filled with even more urgency. "Please?" I open the closet door. It isn't the most ideal place to hide an actual human, but it's a walk-in closet. He'll fit just fine.

I can't even look him in the eye when he moves past me and into the closet. I could die right now. This is so mortifying. All I can do is murmur, "I'm so sorry," as I close the door.

I do my best to compose myself. Allysa is chatting with Ryle when I exit my office. He greets me with a nod, but his attention is back on Allysa. She's digging through her purse for something.

"They were in here earlier," she says.

Ryle is tapping his fingers impatiently.

"What are you looking for?" I ask her.

"Keys. I accidentally brought them with me, and Marshall needs the SUV to get his parents from the airport."

Ryle looks irritated. "Are you sure you didn't set them aside when I told you I was coming to get them?"

I tilt my head, focusing on Allysa. "You knew he was coming?" How could she forget to tell me he was on his way here when Atlas showed up?

She reddens a little. "I got sidetracked by . . . unexpected events." She holds up her hand in victory. "Found them!" She drops them in Ryle's palm. "Okay, bye, you can leave now."

Ryle makes a move like he's about to go, but then he turns and sniffs the air. "What smells so good?"

His and Allysa's eyes meet the bowl at the same time. Allysa pulls it to her, cradling it. "I cooked lunch for me and Lily," she lies.

Ryle raises an eyebrow. "*You* cooked?" He reaches for the bowl. "I have to see this. What is it?"

Allysa hesitates before handing him the bowl. "Yeah, it's chicken . . . baraba doula . . . meat." She looks at me and her eyes are wide. *She is such a horrible liar.*

"Chicken *what*?" Ryle opens the bowl and inspects it. "It looks like shrimp pasta."

Allysa clears her throat. "Yeah, I cooked the shrimp in . . . chicken stock. That's why it's called chicken barabadoulameat."

Ryle puts the lid back on and looks at me with concern as he slides the bowl across the counter back to Allysa. "I'd order pizza if I were you."

I force a laugh, but so does Allysa. Both of us laughing makes our reaction seem way too compulsory for a joke that wasn't even funny.

Ryle's expression narrows. He takes a couple of steps back, a suspicious look in his eye. He must be used to the two of us having inside jokes that he isn't a part of, because he doesn't even question us. He spins and walks out of the flower shop in a rush to get the keys to Marshall. Allysa and I both stand as still as statues until we're sure he's left the building and is way out of earshot. Then I look at her incredulously.

"Chicken barba*what*? Did you just completely make up a new language?"

"I had to say *something*," she says defensively. "You stood there like a lump! You're welcome."

I wait a couple of minutes to make sure Ryle has had time to leave. I walk out front to ensure Ryle's car is gone.

Then I regretfully walk into my office and head to the supply closet to inform Atlas he's in the clear. I exhale before opening the door.

Atlas is waiting patiently, his arms crossed as he leans against a shelf, as if being hidden in a closet doesn't bother him in the least.

"I'm so sorry." I don't know how many apologies it will take to make up for what I just asked Atlas to do, but I'm prepared to say it a thousand more times.

"Is he gone?"

I nod, but rather than exit the closet, Atlas grabs my hand, pulls me in and closes the door.

Now we're both in the closet.

The *dark* closet. But not so dark that I can't see the flicker in his eyes that indicates he's holding back a smile. *Maybe he doesn't absolutely hate me for this.*

He releases my hand, but it's so cramped in here for the two of us, parts of him are grazing parts of me. My stomach knots, so I press my back into the shelf behind me in an attempt not to press into him, but it feels like he's draped over me like a warm blanket. He's so close, I can smell his shampoo. I very calmly try to breathe through my nerves.

"Well? Can I?" he asks, his voice a whisper.

I have no idea what he's asking me, but I want to answer with a confident *yes.* Rather than blurt out my consent to a question I don't even know, I silently count to three. Then I say, "Can you what?"

"Call you tonight."

Oh. He jumped right back into the conversation we were having out front, as if Ryle never even interrupted us.

I pull in my bottom lip and bite down on it. I want to say *okay* because I want Atlas to call me, but I also want Atlas to know that me hiding him from Ryle inside of this closet is probably on par with how the rest of our interactions will go since Ryle is always going to be in the picture, considering we share a child.

"Atlas . . ." I say his name like something awful is about to follow it up, but he interrupts me.

"Lily." He says my name with a smile, like nothing I could possibly add to his name would be awful.

"My life is complicated." I don't intend for it to come out like a warning, but it does.

"I want to help you uncomplicate it."

"I'm scared your presence is going to complicate it even more."

He raises an eyebrow. "I'll complicate *your* life or *Ryle's* life?"

"His complications become *my* complications. He's the father of my child."

Atlas dips his head ever so slightly. "Exactly. He's her father. He's not your husband, so you shouldn't allow your concern for his feelings to persuade you to give up what could be the second-best thing to ever happen to you."

He says that with such conviction, my heart feels like it's tumbling down my rib cage like a Plinko chip. *The second-best thing to ever happen to me?* I wish his confidence in us were contagious. "What's the *first*-best thing to ever happen to me?"

He looks at me pointedly. "Emerson."

Hearing him call my daughter the best thing to ever happen to me makes me damn near melt. I hug myself and hold back my smile. "You're going to make this difficult for me, huh?"

Atlas slowly shakes his head. "Difficult is the last thing I want to be for you, Lily." He moves and the door begins to open, spilling light into the closet. He faces me with one hand on the door and the other on the wall. "When's a good time to call you tonight?" He seems so at ease with this conversation, it makes me want to pull him back into the closet and kiss him so that maybe some of his assurance and patience will seep into me.

My mouth feels like cotton when I say, "Whenever."

His eyes settle on my lips for a beat, and I feel the look all the way to my toes. But then Atlas closes the door, shutting me alone inside the closet.

I deserved that.

A mixture of embarrassment, nervousness, and maybe even a little bit of desire is flooding my cheeks. I remain unmoving until I hear the faint chime of the front door being opened.

I'm fanning myself when Allysa opens the closet door moments later. I quickly drop my hands to my hips to hide what Atlas's presence does to me.

Allysa folds her arms across her chest. "You hid him in the closet?"

My shoulders fall with my shame. "I know."

"*Lily.*" She sounds disappointed in me, but what would she rather I have done? Reintroduced them to one another? "I mean, I'm glad you did it, because I'm not sure how that would have turned out, but . . . you hid him in the *closet*. You just shoved him in here like an old coat."

Her rehashing the moment isn't helping me recover from it. I move toward the front of the store with Allysa on my heels. "I had no choice. Atlas is the one guy on this earth Ryle would never approve of me dating."

"I hate to break it to you, but there's only one guy on this earth Ryle would approve of you dating, and that's Ryle."

I don't respond to that because I'm terrified that she's right.

"Wait," Allysa says. "Are you and Atlas *dating*?"

"No."

"But you just said he's the one guy Ryle would never approve of you dating."

"I said that because if Ryle had seen him here, that's what he would have assumed."

Allysa folds her arms over the counter and looks crestfallen. "I'm feeling very left out right now. There's a huge gap you need to fill in."

"Gap? What do you mean?" I try to look busy by pulling a vase toward me and moving some of the flowers around. Allysa takes the vase from me.

"He brought you lunch. Why did he bring you lunch if the two of you aren't actively talking? And if you're actively talking, why didn't you tell *me* about it?"

I pull the vase back from her. "We ran into each other yesterday. It was nothing. I haven't even spoken to him since before Emmy was born."

Allysa grabs the vase again. "I run into old friends every day. They don't bring me lunch." She slides the vase back to me. We're using it like a conch shell, as if we need it for permission to speak.

"Your friends probably aren't chefs. That's what chefs do: They cook people lunch." I slide the vase back to her, but she says nothing. She's concentrating so hard, it's like she's attempting to read my mind to get past all the lies she thinks I'm spewing. I pull the vase back from her. "It's honestly nothing. *Yet.* You'll be the first to know if anything changes."

She looks momentarily satisfied by that response, but there's a flicker of something in her face before she looks away. I can't tell if it's concern or sadness. I don't ask her, because I know this is hard for her. I imagine the idea of *any* man bringing me lunch who isn't Ryle probably makes her a little sad.

In Allysa's idea of a perfect world, she would have a brother who never hurt me, and I would still be her sister-in-law.

Chapter Seven
Atlas

"When you're working with flounder, always hold your knife like this." I demonstrate how to start with the dull end at the tail, but Theo looks away as soon as I begin to scale the fish.

"Gross," he mutters, covering his mouth. "I can't." Theo moves to the other side of the counter, putting space between himself and the cooking lesson.

"I'm only scaling it. I haven't even cut it open yet."

Theo makes a gagging sound. "I have no interest in working with food. I'll stick to being your therapist." Theo pushes himself onto the counter. "Speaking of, did you ever text Lily?"

"I did."

"She text you back?"

"Sort of. It was a short text, so I decided to take her lunch today to see where her head is at."

"That was a bold move."

"I've spent my life not making bold moves when it comes to her. I wanted to make sure she knew where I stood this time."

"Oh no," Theo says. "What cheesy thing did you say to her about fish and beaches and shores?"

I never should have told him what I said to Lily about

finally reaching the shore. I'm not going to hear the end of it. "Shut up. You've probably never even spoken to a girl; you're twelve."

Theo laughs, but then I notice an awkwardness settle over him when he thinks I'm not looking. He grows quiet, despite the ruckus going on around us. There are at least five other people in the kitchen right now, but everyone is so focused on their work, no one is paying attention to the conversation I'm having with Theo.

"You like someone?" I ask him.

He shrugs. "Kinda."

The discussions I have with Theo are usually one-sided. As much as he likes to ask questions, he doesn't answer very many, so I tread carefully. "Oh yeah?" I try to act casual with my response so he'll expand. "Who is she?"

Theo is looking down at his hands. He's picking at his thumbnail, but I can see his shoulders sink a little after my question, like I did something wrong.

Or *said* something wrong.

"Or *he*," I clarify. I whisper it to be sure he's the only one who hears it.

Theo's eyes dart up to mine.

He doesn't have to confirm or deny anything. I can see the truth written in the fear that's resting behind his eyes. I give my attention back to the fish I'm preparing, and as nonchalantly as possible, I say, "Do you go to school with him?"

Theo doesn't immediately answer. I'm not sure if I'm the first person he's admitted this part of himself to, so I want to make sure to treat that with the care it deserves. I want him to know he has an ally in me, but I also hope he's aware he has an ally in his father, too.

Theo looks around to make sure no one is hovering long enough to follow along with our conversation. "He's been in math club with me all year." His words are quick and concise, like he wants to release them and never say them again.

"Does your dad know?"

Theo shakes his head. I watch as he swallows what look like nervous thoughts.

I put down my knife when I'm done scaling the fish and move to the sink closest to Theo to wash my hands. "I've known your dad for a long time. He's one of my best friends for a reason. I don't surround myself with people who aren't good." I can see the reassurance settle in him when I say that, but I can also tell he's uncomfortable and probably wants to change the subject. "I would say you should text this person you like, but you're probably the only twelve-year-old left on earth without a cell phone. You'll never date anyone at this rate. You'll probably be single and phoneless forever."

Theo is relieved I'm ribbing him. "I'm so glad you decided to be a chef and not a therapist. You suck at advice."

"I take offense to that. I give good advice."

"Okay, Atlas. Whatever you say." He seems to loosen up. He follows me as I head back to my station. "Did you ask Lily out on a date when you went to her work?"

"No. I will tonight. I'm calling her when I get home." I walk by Theo and ruffle his hair on my way to the freezer.

"Hey, Atlas?"

I pause. His eyes are filled with concern, but one of the waiters pushes through the doors and walks between us, preventing Theo from saying whatever it was he was about to say. He doesn't have to say it, though.

"Not saying a word, Theo. Client confidentiality goes both ways."

That seems to reassure him. "Good, because if you said something to my dad, I would tell him how cheesy you are with your pickup lines." Theo mockingly presses his palms to his cheeks. "We finally reached the beach, my little whale."

I glare at him. "That's not at all how it went."

Theo points across the kitchen. "Look! It's sand—we've reached land!"

"Stop."

"Lily, what the heck, our boat is wrecked!"

He's still following me around the kitchen making fun of me when his dad's shift ends. I've never been happier to see him leave.

Chapter Eight
Lily

It's almost 9:30 at night, and I have no missed calls. Emerson has been asleep for an hour and a half, and she's usually awake by six in the morning. I go to bed around ten because if I don't get at least eight hours of sleep, I function at the capacity of a zombie. But if Atlas doesn't call before ten, I'm not sure I'll be able to sleep at all. I'll wonder if I should have apologized seventy more times for hiding him in a closet today.

I walk to the bathroom sink to start my nightly skin-care routine, and I take my phone with me. I've carried it with me every step since he showed up at lunchtime today and told me he'd call me tonight. I should have clarified what *tonight* meant.

To Atlas, *tonight* could mean eleven.

To me, it could mean eight.

We probably have two completely different definitions for what morning and night even mean. He's a successful chef who gets home to unwind after midnight, and I'm in my pajamas by seven in the evening.

My phone makes a noise, but it isn't a ringtone. It's making a noise like someone is trying to FaceTime me.

Please don't be Atlas.

I am not prepared for a video chat; I just put face scrub on. I look at the phone and sure enough, it's him.

I answer it and quickly flip the phone around so that he can't see me. I leave it on my sink while I speed up the cleansing process. "You asked if you could *call* me. This is a video chat."

I hear him laugh. "I can't see you."

"Yeah, because I'm washing my face and getting ready for bed. You don't need to see me."

"Yes, I do, Lily."

His voice makes my skin feel tingly. I flip the camera around and hold it up with an *I told you so* expression. My wet hair is still wrapped in a towel, I'm wearing a nightgown my grandmother probably used to own, and my face is still covered in green foam.

His smile is fluid and sexy. He's sitting up in bed, wearing a white T-shirt, leaning against a black wooden headboard. The one time I went to his house, I never went into his bedroom. His wall is blue, like denim.

"This was definitely worth the decision to video-chat," he says.

I set the phone back down, facing me this time, and finish rinsing. "Thanks for lunch today." I don't want to give him too much praise, but it was the best pasta I've ever had. And it was two hours old before I even had a chance to take a lunch break and eat it.

"You liked the *why are you avoiding me* pasta?"

"You know it was great." I walk to my bed once I'm finished in the bathroom. I prop my phone on a pillow and lie on my side. "How was your day?"

"It was good," he says, but he's not very convincing with the way his voice drops on the word *good*.

I make a face to let him know I don't believe him.

He looks away from the screen for a second, like he's processing a thought. "It's just one of those weeks, Lily. It's better now, though." His mouth curls into a slight grin, and it makes me smile, too.

I don't even have to make small talk. I'd be happy just staring at him in complete silence for an hour.

"What's your new restaurant called?" I already know it's his last name, but I don't want him to know I googled him.

"Corrigan's."

"Is it the same kind of food as Bib's?"

"Sort of. It's fine dining, but with an Italian-inspired menu." He rolls onto his side, propping his phone on something so that he's mirroring my position. It feels like old times when we'd stay up late chatting on my bed. "I don't want to talk about me. How are you? How's the floral business? What's your daughter like?"

"That's a lot of questions."

"I have a lot more, but let's start with those."

"Okay. Well. I'm good. Exhausted most of the time, but I guess that's what I get for being a business owner and a single mother."

"You don't look exhausted."

I laugh. "Good lighting."

"When does Emerson turn one?"

"On the eleventh. I'm going to cry; this first year went so fast."

"I can't get over how much she looks like you."

"You think so?"

He nods, and then says, "But the flower shop is good? You're happy there?"

I move my head from side to side and make a face. "It's okay."

"Why just okay?"

"I don't know. I think I'm tired of it. Or tired in general. It's a lot, and it's tedious work for not very much financial return. I mean, I'm proud that it's been successful and that I did it, but sometimes I daydream about working in a factory assembly line."

"I can relate," he says. "The idea of being able to go home and not think about your job is tempting."

"Do you ever get bored of being a chef?"

"Every now and then. It's why I opened Corrigan's, honestly. I decided to take more of an ownership role and less of a chef role. I still cook several nights a week, but a lot of my time goes to keeping them both running on the business side."

"Do you work crazy hours?"

"I do. But nothing I can't work a date night around."

That makes me smile. I fidget with my comforter, avoiding eye contact because I know I'm blushing. "Are you asking me out?"

"I am. Are you saying yes?"

"I can free up a night."

We're both smiling now. But then Atlas clears his throat, like he's preparing for a caveat. "Can I ask you a difficult question?"

"Okay." I try to hide my nerves over what he's about to ask.

"Earlier today you mentioned your life was complicated. If this . . . *us* . . . becomes something, is it really going to be an issue for Ryle?"

I don't even hesitate. "Yes."

"Why?"

"He doesn't like you."

"Me specifically or any guy you might potentially date?"

I scrunch up my nose. "You. Specifically you."

"Because of the fight at my restaurant?"

"Because of a lot of things," I admit. I roll onto my back and move my phone with me. "He blames most of our fights on you." Atlas is clearly confused, so I elaborate without making things too uncomfortable. "Remember when we were teenagers and I used to write in my journal?"

"I do. Even though you never let me read anything."

"Well, Ryle found the journals. And he read them. And he didn't like what he read."

Atlas sighs. "Lily, we were kids."

"Jealousy doesn't have an expiration date, apparently."

Atlas presses his lips into a thin line for a moment, like he's attempting to push down his frustration. "I really hate that you're stressing over his potential reaction to things that haven't even happened yet. But I get it. It's the unfortunate position you're in." He looks at me reassuringly. "We'll take it one step at a time, okay?"

"One very *slow* step at a time," I suggest.

"Deal. Slow steps." Atlas adjusts the pillow beneath his head. "I used to see you writing in those journals. I always wondered what you wrote about me. *If* you wrote about me."

"Almost everything was about you."

"Do you still have them?"

"Yeah, they're in a box in my closet."

Atlas sits up. "Read me something."

"No. *God*, no."

"Lily."

He looks so hopeful and excited at the possibility, but I can't read my teenage thoughts out loud to him over Face-Time. I'm growing red just thinking about it.

"Please?"

I cover my face with a hand. "No, don't beg." I'll give in to those blue puppy-dog eyes if he doesn't stop looking at me like he is.

He can see he's wearing me down. "Lily, I have ached since I was a teenager to know what you thought of me. One paragraph. Just give me that much."

How can I say no to that? I groan and toss the phone on the bed in defeat. "Give me two minutes." I walk to my closet and pull down the box. I carry it over to my bed and begin flipping through the journals to find something that won't embarrass me too much. "What do you want me to read? My retelling of our first kiss?"

"No, we're going slow, remember?" He says that teasingly. "Start with something from the beginning."

That's much easier. I grab the first journal and flip through it until I find something that looks short and not too humiliating. "Do you remember the night I came to you crying because my parents were fighting?"

"I remember," he says. He settles into his pillow and puts one arm behind his head.

I roll my eyes. "Get comfy while I mortify myself," I mutter.

"It's me, Lily. It's *us*. There's nothing to be embarrassed about."

His voice still has that same calming effect it's always had. I sit cross-legged and hold the phone with one hand and my journal in the other, and I begin to read.

A few seconds later the back door opened and he looked behind me, then to the left and right of me. It wasn't until he looked at my face that he saw I was crying.

"You okay?" he asked, stepping outside. I used my shirt to wipe away my tears, and noticed he came outside instead of inviting me in. I sat down on the porch step and he sat down next to me.

"I'm fine," I said. "I'm just mad. Sometimes I cry when I get mad."

He reached over and tucked my hair behind my ear. I liked it when he did that and I suddenly wasn't nearly as mad anymore. Then he put his arm around me and pulled me to him so that my head was resting on his shoulder. I don't know how he calmed me down without even talking, but he did. Some people just have a calming presence about them and he's one of those people. Completely opposite of my father.

We sat like that for a while, until I saw my bedroom light turn on.

"You should go," he whispered. We could both see my mom standing in my bedroom looking for me. It wasn't until that moment that I realized what a perfect view he has of my bedroom.

As I walked back home, I tried to think about the entire

time Atlas has been in that house. I tried to recall if I'd walked around after dark with the light on at night, because all I normally wear in my room at night is a T-shirt.

Here's what's crazy about that, Ellen: I was kind of hoping I had.

—Lily

Atlas isn't smiling when I finish reading. He's staring at me with a lot of feeling, and the heaviness in his eyes is making my chest tight.

"We were so young," he says. His voice carries a little bit of ache in it.

"I know. Too young to deal with the stuff we dealt with. Especially you."

Atlas isn't looking at his phone anymore, but he's moving his head in agreement. The mood has shifted, and I can tell he's thinking about something else entirely. It brings me back to what he tried to brush off earlier when he said it's been *one of those weeks*.

"What's bothering you?"

His eyes return to his phone. He seems like he might brush it off again, but then he just sighs and readjusts himself so that he's sitting higher up against his headboard. "Someone vandalized the restaurants."

"Both of them?"

He nods. "Yeah, it started a few days ago."

"You think it's someone you know?"

"It's not anyone I recognize, but the security footage wasn't very clear. I haven't reported it to the police yet."

"Why haven't you?"

His eyebrows furrow. "Whoever it is seems younger—maybe in their teens. I guess I'm worried they might be in a similar situation to the one I was in back then. Destitute." The tension in his eyes eases a bit. "And what if they don't have a Lily to save them?"

It takes a few seconds for what he says to register. When it does, I don't smile. I swallow the lump in my throat, hoping he can't see my internal reaction to that. It's not the first time he's mentioned I saved him back then, but every time he says it, I want to argue with him. I didn't save him. All I did was fall in love with him.

I can see *why* I fell in love with him. What owner is more concerned about the situation of the person vandalizing their business than they are with the actual damage being done? "Considerate Atlas," I whisper.

"What was that?" he says.

I didn't mean to say that out loud. I slide a hand over the heat moving across my neck. "Nothing."

Atlas clears his throat, leaning forward. A subtle smile materializes. "Back to your journal," he says. "I wondered if you knew I could see into your bedroom window back then, because after that night, you left that light on a hell of a lot."

I laugh, glad he's lightening the mood. "You didn't have a television. I wanted to give you something to watch."

He groans. "Lily, you *have* to let me read the rest."

"No."

"You locked me in a closet today. Letting me read your journals would be a good way to apologize for that."

"I thought you weren't offended."

"Maybe it's a delayed offense." He begins to nod slowly. "Yeah . . . starting to feel it now. I'm *really* offended."

I'm laughing when Emmy begins to work up a cry across the hall. I sigh because I don't want to hang up, but I'm also not the mom who can let her child cry it out. "Emmy's waking up. I have to go. But you owe me a date."

"Name the time," he says.

"I'm off on Sundays, so a Saturday night might be good."

"Tomorrow is Saturday," he says. "But we're going slow."

"I mean . . . that's pretty slow if we're counting from the first day we met. That puts a lot of years between meeting you and going on a first date with you."

"Six o'clock?"

I smile. "Six is perfect."

As soon as I say that, Atlas squeezes his eyes shut for two seconds. "Wait. I can't tomorrow. *Shit.* We're hosting an event; they need me at the restaurant. Sunday?"

"I have Emmy Sunday. I'd rather wait before bringing her around you."

"I get that," Atlas says. "Next Saturday?"

"That'll give me time to line up someone to watch her."

Atlas grins. "It's a date, then." He stands up and begins walking through his bedroom. "You're off on Sundays, right? Can I call you this Sunday?"

"When you say 'call,' do you mean video chat? I want to be prepared this time."

"You couldn't be unprepared if you tried," he says. "And yes, it'll be a FaceTime. Why would I waste time with a phone call when I can look at you?"

I like this flirty side of Atlas. I have to bite my bottom lip for two seconds in order to hold back my grin. "Goodnight, Atlas."

"'Night, Lily."

Even the way he makes such intense eye contact while saying goodbye makes my stomach flip. I end the call and press my face into my pillow. I squeal like I'm sixteen again.

Chapter Nine
Atlas

"Let me see a picture," Theo says. He's sitting on the back steps watching me pick up shattered glass and several bags of trash from the third incident, which occurred last night. Brad called this morning to let me know Bib's was hit again. He and Theo met me here to clean it up, even though I told him not to worry about coming. I hate when my employees have to show up for anything on the only day of the week we're closed.

"I don't have a picture of her," I say to Theo.

"So she's ugly?"

I toss the box of glass into the dumpster. "She's gorgeous and way out of my league."

"Ugly would still be out of your league," he deadpans. "She doesn't have social media?"

"She does, but it's set to private."

"You aren't her friend on anything? Facebook? Instagram? Do you even have a Snapchat?"

"What do you know about Snapchat? You don't even have a phone."

"I have my ways," he says.

His dad comes back outside with a trash bag. He holds it open, and we start throwing some of the scattered garbage in it while Theo remains on the steps. "I would help, but I just took a shower," he says.

"You showered yesterday," Brad says.

"Yeah, and I'm still clean." Theo focuses on me again. "Do you have social media?"

"No, I don't have time for that."

"Then how do you know her stuff is set to private?"

I've occasionally attempted to look her up online, and as much as I don't want to admit that, I'm not sure there's a person on this planet who hasn't done a few Google searches on people from their past. "I've looked her up before. You have to have a profile and follow her to see her stuff."

"So make a profile and follow her," Theo says. "I swear, sometimes you make things harder than they need to be."

"It's complicated. She has an ex-husband who doesn't like me, and if he saw that we were friends online it might become an issue for her."

"Why doesn't he like you?" Theo asks.

"We got into a fight. Here at the restaurant, actually," I say, nudging my head toward the building.

Theo's eyebrows lift slightly. "Seriously? Like a real fight?"

Brad straightens up. "Wait. That guy was Lily's *husband*?"

"I thought you knew that," I say.

"None of us knew who he was, or why you were fighting him. That was the only time we've ever seen you kick someone out of the restaurant, though. Makes so much sense now."

I guess this is the first time I've talked about it since it happened. I remember I left for the night right after that fight with Ryle, so no one had a chance to ask me about it. When I came back to work the following Monday, people could probably read my mood and see that I still didn't want to talk about it.

"What did you get into a fight about?" Theo asks.

I glance at Brad, because he's aware of what Lily went through. Lily told him and Darin at my house. But Brad looks like he's leaving it up to me whether or not I'm honest with Theo. I usually am about almost anything, but it's not my place to share Lily's business.

"I don't even remember," I mutter.

I do think this could be a good teaching moment with Theo about how never to treat a partner, but it's a part of Lily's life I don't feel comfortable talking about without her present. It's also a part of her life I shouldn't have interfered with, even though I wouldn't take it back if given the chance. As immature as my reaction might have been that night when I hit Ryle, I was holding back. I wanted to do more than just punch him. I had never been that angry at another human—not even my mother or stepfather. Not even Lily's father.

It's one thing to dislike someone for how they treat me, but it's an entirely different kind of anger when the person I admire the most in this world is mistreated.

My phone begins to buzz in my pocket. I quickly pull it out and see that Lily is attempting to return my FaceTime from an hour ago. She was driving and said she would call me when she got home.

We've exchanged several texts since our chat on Friday, but I've been anxious to talk to her face-to-face again.

"Is that her?" Theo asks, perking up.

I nod and try to pass him on the steps, but he stands up and follows me into the restaurant.

"Seriously?" I ask, facing him.

"I want to see what she looks like."

I have to answer it before I miss the call, so I slide my finger across the screen while trying to shut Theo outside. "I'll screenshot it for you. Go help your dad." The video connects, and Theo is still trying to push his way inside. "Hey," I say, smiling at Lily on the screen.

"Hey," Lily says.

"Let me see," Theo whispers, snaking his arm around the door in an attempt to snatch my phone.

"Give me a second, Lily." I hold the phone to my chest so that she can't see anything, and then I open the back door far enough to press my palm against Theo's face. I guide him back down the top step. "Brad, get your child."

"Theo, come here," Brad says. "Help me with this."

Theo's shoulders slump, but he finally relents and turns toward his father. "But I'm *clean*," he mumbles.

I close the door and pull the phone away from my chest. Lily is laughing. "What was that?"

"Nothing." I walk to my office and close and lock the door for privacy. "How's your day?" I take a seat on the couch.

"Good. We just got back from lunch with my mother and her boyfriend. Went to a little sandwich shop on Borden; it was cute."

"How is your mother?" We haven't talked about her parents at all, other than her mentioning her father passed away.

"She's really good," Lily says. "She's been dating a guy

named Rob. He makes her happy, although it's a little weird seeing her giddy over a man. I like him, though."

"She lives in Boston now?"

"Yeah, she moved here after my father died to be closer to me."

"That's good. I'm glad you have family here."

"What about you? Does your uncle still live in Boston?"

My uncle?

Oh. I did tell her that. I squeeze the back of my neck and wince. "My uncle." I can't remember the exact lie I told her back then—it's been so long. "My uncle died when I was nine, Lily."

Her eyebrows wrinkle in confusion. "No, you moved in with an uncle when you were eighteen. It's why you left."

I sigh, wishing I could go back and redo most of our time together back then, and the things I told her or failed to tell her in order to spare her feelings. But wouldn't we all go back if we could redo our teenage years? "I lied to you. I didn't have an uncle in Boston at that point."

"What?" She's still shaking her head, trying to make it make sense. She doesn't seem angry, though. More confused than anything. "Then who did you go live with?"

"No one. I couldn't keep sneaking into your bedroom forever. I knew it wouldn't end well, and other than you, there was nothing in that town that could help me better my situation. Boston had shelters and resources. I told you my uncle was still alive so you wouldn't worry about me."

Lily's head falls back against her headboard and she closes her eyes for a bit. "Atlas." She says my name with sympathy. When she opens her eyes again, it looks like she's attempting not to tear up. "I don't know what to say. I thought you had family."

"I'm sorry I lied. I wasn't trying to be malicious, I just wanted to spare—"

"Don't apologize," she says, interrupting me. "You did the right thing. Winter was about to hit, and you might not have survived it in that house." She wipes at a tear. "I can't imagine how hard that was. Moving to Boston at that age with nothing. No one."

"It worked out," I say, flashing a grin. "It all worked out." I'm attempting to pull her out of the mood I just sunk her in. "Don't think about where we used to be; just think about where we are."

She smiles. "Where are you right now? Is that your office?"

"It is." I spin the phone around so she can get a glimpse of it. "It's small. Just a couch and a computer, but I'm rarely in here. I spend most of my time in the kitchen."

"Are you at Bib's?"

"Yeah. Both restaurants are closed on Sundays—I'm just here cleaning up."

"I can't wait to visit Corrigan's. Is that where we're going on our date next Saturday?"

I laugh. "No way am I bringing you to either of my restaurants on a date. The people I work with are too curious about my personal life."

She grins. "Funny, because I'm curious about your personal life, too."

"I'm an open book for you. What do you want to know?"

She contemplates that for several seconds, and then

comes back with, "I want to know who the people in your life are. You didn't really have anyone when we were teenagers, but you're an adult now, with businesses and friends and a whole life I know very little about. Who are your people, Atlas Corrigan?"

I don't know how to respond to that with anything but laughter.

She doesn't smile in return, though, which makes me think she's asking the question more out of concern for me than curiosity. I look at her gently, hoping to ease some of that worry. "I have friends," I say. "Some of them you met a while back at my house. I don't have family, but it's not a void I feel. I like my career, and my life." I pause, and then say something completely honest. "I'm happy, if that's what you're wondering."

I see the corner of her mouth lift. "Good. I was always curious about where you ended up. I tried to find you on social media, but I didn't have any luck."

That makes me laugh, considering Theo and I just had this conversation. "I don't use social media much." If I told her I'd use it every day if her pages weren't private, Theo might say that confession would scare her off. "I have profiles for the restaurants, but two of my employees manage them." I let my head fall back against the couch. "I'm too busy for it. I downloaded TikTok a few months ago, but that was a mistake. Sucked me in for hours one night, and I missed a meeting the next morning. I deleted the app later that day."

Lily laughs. "I would do just about anything to watch you make TikTok videos."

"Never gonna happen."

Lily's attention is stolen away for a moment, and then she starts to lift up on her bed, but pauses. "Hold on a second. I need to set my phone down." She drops the phone, but I don't think she realizes it catches on something and flips so that it's at an angle. The camera is on her, and I see her adjust Emerson from one breast to another. It's only a few seconds, almost too quick for me to realize what's happening before it's over. I don't think she meant for the camera to be pointed at her.

When she notices the phone, her eyes go wide for a second, and then the screen goes black as soon as her hand meets it. When it's pointed at her face again, she's covering her eyes with splayed fingers. "I am so sorry."

"For what?"

"I think I just flashed you."

"You did, but it's not something you should apologize for. I should thank you."

She laughs, appearing to appreciate that comment. "Nothing you haven't seen before," she says with an adorably embarrassed shrug. She adjusts a pillow under the arm she's using to hold Emerson while she breastfeeds. "I'm trying to wean her, since she's about to turn one. We were down to once a day, but Sundays are hard because I'm with her all day." She scrunches up her nose. "I'm sorry. I doubt you want to know breastfeeding details."

"I can't think of a single subject you could discuss that would bore me."

"Oh, I bet I can think of one before our date," she says, treating my comment like it's a challenge. She glances away from her phone screen. I can't see Emerson, but I can tell

Lily's looking down at her because she gets this smile on her face that I only see when she's talking about or looking at her daughter. It's a smile born from pride, and one of my favorite expressions to see flash across Lily's face.

"She's falling asleep," Lily whispers. "I should go."

"Yeah, I should probably go, too." I don't want to leave Brad and Theo to clean up the majority of the damage outside without me.

"I might call you later tonight, if that's okay," Lily says.

"Of course it is." I remember what Theo said about wanting to see a picture of Lily, so before she ends the call, I take a quick screenshot. It makes an obvious screenshot noise, and Lily tilts her head curiously.

"Did you just take a—"

"I wanted a picture of you," I say quickly. "Bye, Lily." I end the call before I let myself be too embarrassed by that. I had no idea it would make that noise and that she would be able to hear it. Theo better appreciate this.

I open my office door and find Brad sweeping the kitchen. I'm confused, because the kitchen is cleaned after closing, and the damage done to the restaurant overnight was contained to the outside. "Did they not clean the floors last night?"

"Kitchen's fine—I'm just pretending to sweep," he says. Brad clocks the confusion on my face, so he elaborates. "I wanted Theo to have to clean up most of the mess outside since he hates doing it so much. It's a dad thing."

"Oh. Makes sense." It makes *no* sense, but I leave Brad to fake-sweep and head back outside.

Theo is grimacing as he uses his thumb and index finger

to barely lift a piece of trash. "This is so gross," he mutters, dropping it into the bag. "You need to hire a private security guard or something; this is getting out of hand."

That's not a bad idea.

I hold my phone in front of Theo's face so he can see the picture of Lily I just screenshotted.

He pulls his neck back, surprised. "That's Lily?"

"That's Lily." I slide my phone into my pocket and take the trash bag from Theo.

"That explains it." He drops down onto the top step.

"Explains what?"

"Why you get so tongue-tied around her and say the stupid stuff you say."

I disagree with his belief that the things I say to her are stupid, but he's right about one thing. She's so beautiful, I do sometimes feel tongue-tied around her. "I can't wait until you start dating," I say. "I'm going to give you so much shit."

Chapter Ten
Lily

"Mom, it's fine. Really." I'm holding the phone between my cheek and my neck. "I'm already at Allysa's; it's not an inconvenience at all."

"Are you sure? Rob said he could watch her."

"No, Rob needs to take care of you."

"Okay. Tell Emmy her nannie is sorry."

"Nannie? Is that what you're going by now?"

"I'm trying it out," she says. "I didn't like *grandma*."

She's referred to herself as a grandmother in four different ways since Emmy was born, but none of them have stuck yet. "Love you, Mom. Hope you feel better."

"Love you, too."

I end the call and then grab Emmy out of her car seat. I'm relieved to see Ryle's car isn't in his assigned spot. I wasn't planning on coming to the building where he and Allysa both have apartments, but my mother and Emmy came down with the same illness this week.

When I picked her up from my mother's yesterday, Emmy had a slight fever. It peaked around two in the morning, and nothing I did helped. It was gone by the time I had to get ready for work today, though. But then it hit my mother this afternoon with a vengeance, and I had to go pick up Emmy in the middle of the workday. I had a little bit of a panic moment because tonight is my date with Atlas. I thought I was going to have to cancel, but Allysa saved the day.

I didn't tell her why I needed a sitter. I texted her and asked if she could watch Emmy for a few hours this afternoon and into tonight, and she responded with one word. **Gimme.**

I warned her that Emmy had a fever last night, but Emmy and Rylee spend so much time together, we stopped worrying about one getting the other sick months ago, since it happens every other week. Emmy probably got the fever from Rylee to begin with.

I knock on Allysa's door, and when she opens it, she's immediately grabbing for Emerson. "Come here," she says. She pulls Emerson to her and squeezes her. "She smells so good. Rylee doesn't smell like a baby anymore. Makes me sad." She pushes the door open to invite me in, and when I walk inside holding the diaper bag, Allysa finally registers my outfit. "Hold up," she says. She points a finger up and down my body. "What's this? Why am I babysitting?"

I really don't want to tell her where I'm going, but it's Allysa. She reads me better than anyone. She can see the hesitation on my face and takes it for exactly what it is. "Is this a *date* outfit?" She whispers it and then closes the front door. "Is it the Greek god?"

"Atlas. Yes. Please don't tell your brother."

Right when I say that, I notice Marshall standing close by in the living room. He immediately covers his ears and says, "I heard nothing. I see nothing. Lalalalalala." He walks through the foyer and disappears into the kitchen.

Allysa brushes his presence off with a wave. "He's so good at being neutral; don't worry about him." She motions for me to follow her into the living room. Rylee is in a playpen, so Allysa walks Emmy over to her. "Rylee, look who's here!"

Rylee smiles when she sees Emmy. The girls are starting to show excitement in each other's presence. I love that they're not too far apart in age. The six-month gap feels smaller and smaller the older Emmy gets.

"Where is he taking you?"

I smooth my hands down my outfit, and then flick off a piece of lint. "To dinner, but I've never been to this place. I hope I'm not overdressed."

"Is this your first date with him? You seem nervous."

"It is our first date, and I *am* nervous. But it's a different kind of nervous. A good nervous. I know him so well already, so I don't feel like I'm about to have to spend an evening with a stranger."

Allysa studies me for a moment with gentle eyes. "You seem excited. I've missed this side of you."

"Yeah. Me too." I bend to give both Emmy and Rylee kisses. "I won't be out too late. I have to get back to the shop and close up for Lucy, so he's picking me up there. I should be back around nine thirty, so try to keep her up until then if you don't mind."

"Why are you coming back so early? That's lame."

"I didn't sleep last night. I'm exhausted. But I don't want to cancel the date, so I'm going to power through."

"Ugh. Motherhood," Allysa says, rolling her eyes. "I'll keep her awake—go have fun. Drink a coffee or a five-hour or something."

I've lost count of the number of coffees I've had today. "Love you. Thanks for saving the day," I say on my way out the door.

"That's what I'm here for," she singsongs.

Chapter Eleven
Atlas

I wanted the day to go by faster, so I decided to help out in the kitchen at Bib's even though I prepared for the night with a full staff. Now I smell like garlic. This is the third time I've tried scrubbing the smell off, to no avail. But if I don't leave now, I'll be late meeting her.

We're taking it slow, so I'm picking her up at her work rather than her apartment. I have no idea where she lives now, or if she still lives in the apartment building I showed up at almost two years ago when she needed help. For whatever reason, where we live is something that hasn't come up in our conversations. She probably doesn't even know I sold my house and moved into the city earlier this year. I'm curious how far apart we live from each other now.

"I smell cologne," Darin says after he passes me. He stops walking toward the freezer and turns to give me a once-over. "Why are you wearing cologne? Why are you dressed up?"

I sniff my hands. "I don't smell like garlic?"

"No, you smell like you're going out. Are you leaving?"

"I *am* leaving. I'll be back around closing time, though. I think I might stay the night here and see if I can catch whoever is vandalizing the restaurants." There were several days of a quiet stretch between incidents, but we got hit for a fourth time last night. It wasn't too costly, though. This time they just scattered the trash everywhere again. That's a lot easier to clean up than repainting has been. That may be because Brad keeps bringing Theo to help. I should probably give Theo a heads-up that the more he complains about a chore, the more likely he's going to be made to do that chore.

I plan to confront whoever is doing the damage tonight and see if I can't figure out their motive and talk them down before I get the police involved. I'm confident most things can be handled with a simple, honest conversation rather than a dramatic intervention, but I have no idea who I'm dealing with.

Darin leans in and quietly says, "Who you going out with? Lily?"

I dry my hands on a towel and nod once.

Darin smiles and walks away. I like that my friends like Lily. They brought her up a couple of times after our poker night, but I think they could tell it bothered me. I didn't like discussing Lily when she wasn't a part of my life.

But now it looks like there's a possibility she's back in the picture. Maybe. This might be why I'm so nervous: because I know what a huge risk Lily is taking by going out with me tonight. If things progress with us, that could impact her life in negative ways. Which might be why I started to feel the immense pressure two hours ago of making sure this date is worth it for her.

But I smell like I'm terrified of vampires, so it's already not going my way.

•   •   •

I pull into the parking lot at five minutes to six. Lily must have been waiting for me, because she exits her store and locks the door behind her before I'm even out of my car.

As soon as I lay eyes on her, I get even more nervous. She looks incredible. She's wearing a black jumpsuit and heels. She pulls on her jacket and meets me in the middle of the parking lot.

I lean in and greet her with a quick kiss on her cheek. "You look stunning." I swear she reddens a little after I say that.

"Do I? I didn't sleep last night. I feel like I look ninety."

"Why didn't you sleep?"

"Emmy ran a fever all night. She's better now, but . . ." Lily yawns. "I'm sorry. I just drank coffee. It'll hit in a minute."

"It's okay. I'm not tired, but I do smell like garlic."

"I like garlic."

"Good thing."

Lily leans back on her heels and looks down at her outfit. "I wasn't sure what to wear since I've never been to this restaurant."

"I've never been there, either, so I have no idea. But I have a feeling you'll be fine." I chose a new restaurant I've been wanting to try. It's about a forty-five-minute drive, but I figured that would give us time to catch up on the way over.

"I have a present for you," she says. "It's in my car. Let me grab it."

I follow her to her car and watch her retrieve something from the console. When she hands it to me, I can't hold back a smile. "Is this your journal?" She read another quick passage to me last night, but she was so embarrassed reading it out loud, she refused to give me more.

"That's one of them. We'll see how tonight goes before I give you the other one."

"No pressure or anything." I walk her to my car and open the passenger door for her. She starts to yawn again as I'm closing her door.

I feel bad, like maybe she's too exhausted for this date. I have no idea what it's like to raise a child. I feel kind of selfish that I'm not offering to reschedule, so before I back out of the parking lot, I speak up. "If you'd rather go home and sleep, we can do this next weekend."

"There's nothing else I'd rather do than this, Atlas. I'll sleep when I'm dead." She clicks her seat belt. "You actually do smell like garlic."

I think she's kidding. Lily used to joke all the time when we were younger. It's one of the things I loved most about her—that she always seemed to be in a good mood despite all the bad things surrounding her. It's that same strength I admired in her in the days I was with her after she found out she was pregnant in the emergency room. I know that was one of the lowest points of her life, but she was able to smile through it all, and even spent an entire evening impressing my friends with her humor during a poker night.

Everyone handles stress differently, and none of those ways is necessarily wrong, but Lily handles it with grace. And grace just happens to be the quality I find the most attractive in people.

"How'd you manage to get away on a Saturday night?" Lily asks.

I hate that I'm driving because I want to look at her while I respond. I've never seen her look this . . . womanly?

Is that a compliment? I don't even know. I probably shouldn't say it out loud in case it isn't, but when Lily and I fell in love, neither of us were what we would now consider adults. But it's different tonight. We're grown-ups with careers, and she's a mother and a boss and independent. *It's sexy as hell.*

The only other time I've spent with her as adults was when she was technically still with Ryle, so it felt wrong thinking of her the way I am now. *Like I want her.*

I keep my focus on the road and try not to create a lull in our conversation, but I think I might be a little flustered. That surprises me.

"How did I manage getting away?" I say, pretending like I'm mulling over the question rather than obsessing about how much I want to stare at her. "I hire dependable people."

Lily smiles at that. "Do you always work on weekends?"

I nod. "I usually only take off Sundays, when we're closed. The occasional Monday."

"What do you enjoy the most about your job?"

She's full of questions tonight. I give her a sidelong glance and smile. "Reading the reviews."

She makes a noise like she's shocked. "I'm sorry," she says. "Did you say *reviews*? You read your restaurant reviews?"

"Every single one."

"*What?* Oh my God, you must not have a single insecurity. I make Serena run our social media so I can *avoid* reviews."

"Your reviews are great."

She practically turns her entire body toward me in the seat. "You read *my* reviews?"

"I read reviews for anyone I know who owns a business. Is that weird?"

"It's not *not* weird."

I flip on my blinker. "I like reading reviews. I feel like business reviews are a reflection of the owner, and I want to know what people think of my restaurants. The constructive criticism helps. I haven't had the kitchen experience a lot of chefs have, and critics are some of the best teachers."

"What do you get out of reading reviews about *other* people's businesses?"

"Nothing, really. I just find it entertaining."

"Do I have any bad ones?" Lily looks away from me, half turning so that she's facing forward again. "Never mind, don't answer that. I'm just going to pretend they're all good and that everyone loves my flowers."

"Everyone *does* love your flowers."

She presses her lips together in an attempt to suppress her smile. "What's your *least*-favorite part of your job?"

I love that she's asking me such random questions. It reminds me of all the nights we would stay up late, and she would pepper me with questions about myself. "Up until last week, it was health inspections," I admit. "They're extremely stressful."

"Why up until last week? What changed?"

"The vandalism."

"Did it happen again?"

"Yeah, twice this week."

"And you still have no idea who it is?"

I shake my head. "No clue."

"Do you have any angry ex-girlfriends?"

"Nah, I doubt it. They don't seem the type."

Lily kicks off her heels and pulls one of her legs into her seat, making herself more comfortable. "How many serious relationships have you had?"

She's going there. Okay. "Define 'serious.'"

"I don't know. More than two months?"

"One," I say.

"How long were you together?"

"A little more than a year. I met her while I was in the military."

"Why'd you break up?"

"We moved in together."

"That's why you broke up?"

"I think living together escalated the realization that we were incompatible. Or maybe we were just at different points in our lives. I was focused on my career, and her focus was on which outfits to wear to the clubs I was too tired to go to with her. When I got out of the military and moved back to Boston, she stayed behind and moved into a loft with two of her friends."

Lily laughs. "I cannot picture you in a club."

"Yeah. That's why I'm single, I guess." My phone rings with an incoming call from Corrigan's, interrupting us before I'm able to throw her own question back at her. "I have to take this," I say.

"Go ahead."

I answer the call over Bluetooth. It ends up being a freezer issue that requires me to make two more phone calls before I've got it sorted out and a repair technician on the way there. When I'm finally able to give my attention back to

Lily, I glance over at her and find her asleep, her head limp against her shoulder. I hear a dainty snore coming from her.

The coffee never kicked in, I guess.

I let her sleep all the way to the restaurant. We pull in about ten minutes to seven. It's dark, and the restaurant looks crowded, but we have a few minutes before I have to check in for our reservation, so I let her rest.

Her snore is as endearing as she is. It's delicate, almost too light to hear. I take a quick video I can use to tease her with later, and then I reach into the backseat and grab her journal. I know she said not to read it in front of her, but technically I'm not. She's asleep.

I open it to the first page and begin reading.

I read the first entry, completely captivated. I feel like I'm breaking a rule reading this, but she's the one who brought it.

I read the second entry. Then the third. Then I log into my reservation app and cancel our reservation because unless I wake her up this very second, we're going to be late. I'd rather our table go to someone else, because Lily looks like she's been needing this sleep for a while.

And I want to read another entry. I'll take her somewhere else for dinner once she wakes up.

Every word she wrote is taking me right back to when we were teenagers. There are so many times I want to laugh at the things she says and how she says them, but I stifle my laughter so that I don't startle her.

I eventually read a passage that I'm almost positive is leading up to our first kiss. I look at the clock and we've already been sitting here for half an hour, but Lily is still sound asleep, and I can't stop in the middle of this entry. I keep reading, hoping she stays asleep long enough for me to get to the end of this one.

"I need to tell you something," he said.

I held my breath, not knowing what he was going to say.

"I got in touch with my uncle today. My mom and I used to live with him in Boston. He told me once he gets back from his work trip I can stay with him."

I should have been so happy for him in that moment. I should have smiled and told him congratulations. But I felt all of the immaturity of my age when I closed my eyes and felt sorry for myself.

"Are you going?" I asked.

He shrugged. "I don't know. I wanted to talk to you about it first."

He was so close to me on the bed, I could feel the warmth of his breath. I also noticed he smelled like mint, and it made me wonder if he uses bottled water to brush his teeth before he comes over here. I always send him home every day with lots of water.

I brought my hand up to the pillow and started pulling at a feather sticking out of it. When I got it all the way out, I twisted it between my fingers. "I don't know what to say, Atlas. I'm happy you have a place to stay. But what about school?"

"I could finish down there," he said.

I nodded. It sounded like he had already made up his mind. "When are you leaving?"

I wondered how far away Boston is. It's probably a few hours, but that's a whole world away when you don't own a car.

"I don't know for sure that I am."

I dropped the feather back onto the pillow and brought my hand to my side. "What's stopping you? Your uncle is offering you a place to stay. That's good, right?"

He tightened his lips together and nodded. Then he picked up the feather I'd been playing with and he started twisting it between his fingers. He laid it back down on the pillow and then he did something I wasn't expecting. He moved his fingers to my lips and he touched them.

God, Ellen. I thought I was gonna die right then and there. It was the most I'd ever felt inside my body at one time. He kept his fingers there for a few seconds, and he said, "Thank you, Lily. For everything." He moved his fingers up and through my hair, and then he leaned forward and planted a kiss on my forehead. I was breathing so hard, I had to open my mouth to catch more air. I could see his chest moving just as hard as mine was. He looked down at me and I watched as his eyes went right to my mouth. "Have you ever been kissed, Lily?"

I shook my head no and tilted my face up to his because I needed him to change that right then and there or I wasn't gonna be able to breathe.

Then—almost as if I were made of eggshells—he lowered his mouth to mine and just rested it there. I didn't know what to do next, but I didn't care. I didn't care if we just stayed like that all night and never even moved our mouths, it was everything.

His lips closed over mine and I could kind of feel his hand shaking. I did what he was doing and started to move my lips like he was. I felt the tip of his tongue brush across my lips once and I thought my eyes were about to roll back in my head. He did it again, and then a third time, so I finally did it, too. When our tongues touched for the first time, I kind of smiled a little, because I'd thought about my first kiss a lot. Where it would be, who it would be with. Never in a million years did I imagine it would feel like this.

He pushed me on my back and pressed his hand against my cheek and kept kissing me. It just got better and better as I grew more comfortable. My favorite moment was when he pulled back for a second and looked down at me, then came back even harder.

I don't know how long we kissed. A long time. So long, my mouth started to hurt and my eyes couldn't stay open. When we fell asleep, I'm pretty sure his mouth was still touching mine.

We didn't talk about Boston again.

I still don't know if he's leaving.

—*Lily*

Wow.

Wow.

I close the journal and look over at Lily. She wrote our first kiss with so much detail, it makes me feel inferior to my teenage self.

Did it actually happen that way?

I remember that night, but I was a hell of a lot more

nervous than Lily described me to be. It's funny how, when you're a teenager, you think you're the only inexperienced, nervous human on the planet. You think almost every other teenager has life figured out way better than you do, but it isn't that way at all. We were both scared. And infatuated. And in love.

I had fallen in love with her long before our first kiss, though. I loved her more than I had ever loved anyone before that moment. I think I loved her more than I've ever loved anyone *after* that moment.

I think I still might.

There's so much Lily doesn't know about that part of my life. So much I want to tell her now that I've read her version of some of our time together. It's obvious she has no clue how instrumental she was in my life back then. At a time when everyone was turning their backs to me, Lily was the only one who stepped up.

She's still sound asleep, so I pull out my phone and open a blank note. I start typing, detailing what my life was like before she entered it. I don't mean to write as much as I do, but I guess I have a lot I want to say to her.

It's another twenty minutes before I finally finish typing everything, and another five minutes before Lily finally begins to rouse.

I set my phone in the cupholder, unsure if I'm going to allow her to read what I just wrote. I might wait a few days. A few weeks. She wants to take things slow, and I'm not sure what I said toward the end of that letter matches her idea of "slow."

Her hand goes up, and she scratches her head. She's facing the window, so I don't see her face when her eyes open, but I can tell when she's awake because she sits straight up. She stares out her window for a beat, then swings her head in my direction. A few strands of hair are stuck to her cheek.

I'm leaning against my door, watching her casually, as if this is completely normal first-date behavior.

"Atlas." She says my name like it's an apology and a question at the same time.

"It's okay. You were tired."

She grabs her phone and looks at the time. "Oh my *God.*" She leans forward, pressing her elbows into her thighs and her face into her palms. "I can't believe this."

"Lily, it's fine. Really." I hold up the journal. "You kept me company."

She eyes the journal and then groans. "This is *mortifying.*"

I toss the journal into the backseat. "I personally found it enlightening."

Lily hits me playfully on my shoulder. "Stop laughing. I feel too bad for it to be funny."

"Don't feel bad, you're exhausted. And probably hungry. We could grab a burger on the drive back."

Lily falls dramatically against her seat. "Let the fancy chef take the girl for fast food since she slept through her date. Why not?" She flips the visor down and notices the hair stuck to her cheek. "Wow, I am such a *mom.* Is this our last date? It is. Did I ruin this already? I wouldn't blame you."

I put the car in reverse. "Not even close after everything I just read. Not sure anything could top this date."

"You have very low standards, Atlas."

I find her self-deprecation adorably attractive. "I have a question about your journal."

"What?" She's wiping away a smear of mascara. Everything about her seems so defeated now that she thinks she ruined our date. I can't stop smiling, though.

"The night of our first kiss . . . did you put the blankets in the washer on purpose? Was that a trick to get me to sleep in your bed?"

She scrunches up her nose. "You read that far?"

"You were asleep for a long time."

She contemplates my question, and then nods an admission. "I wanted you to be my first kiss back then, and that wouldn't have happened if you kept sleeping on the floor."

She's probably right about that. And it worked.

It's *still* working, because reading her description of our first kiss brought back every feeling she pulled out of me that night. She could sleep the entire way back home, and I'd still think this was the best date I've ever been on.

Chapter Twelve
Lily

"I can't believe you let me sleep for that long." It's been ten minutes, and my stomach is still rolling from embarrassment. "Did you finish reading the whole journal?"

"I stopped after I read about our first kiss."

That's good. That's not too embarrassing. But if he would have read about the first time we had sex while I was sleeping in the seat next to him, I'm not sure I could have recovered.

"This is so not fair," I mutter. "You have to do something mortifying so the scales even out, because right now I feel like I've completely ruined our night."

Atlas laughs. "You think me doing something to mortify myself will make you feel better about tonight?"

I nod. "Yes, that's the law of the universe. Eye for an eye, humiliation for humiliation."

Atlas taps his thumb on his steering wheel as he massages his jaw with his free hand. Then he nudges his head toward his phone, which is sitting in the cupholder. "Open the Notes app on my phone. Read the first one."

Oh, wow. I was kidding, but I snatch up his phone so fast. "What's your password?"

"Nine five nine five."

I enter the numbers and then glance over his home screen while I have it open. Every app is tucked neatly into a folder. He has zero unread texts and one unread email. "You're a neat freak. Who has *one* unread email?"

"I don't like clutter," he says. "Side effect of the military. How many unread emails do you have?"

"Thousands." I open the Notes app and click on the most recent one. As soon as I see the two words at the top, I drop the phone, pressing it facedown on my thigh. *"Atlas."*

"Lily."

I can feel my embarrassment being swallowed up by a warm wave of anticipation falling over me. "You wrote me a *Dear Lily* letter?"

He nods slowly. "You were asleep for quite a while." When he glances at me, his smile falters, like he's worried about whatever it is he wrote. He faces forward again, and I can see the roll of his throat.

I lean my head against the passenger window and begin to read silently.

Dear Lily,

You're going to be mortified when you wake up and realize you fell asleep on our first date. I'm a little too excited for your reaction. But you seemed so tired when I picked you up, it actually makes me happy to see you getting some rest.

This past week has been surreal, hasn't it? I was beginning to think I may never be a part of your life in any significant way, and then poof, you show up.

I could go on and on about what that run-in meant to me, but I promised my therapist I'd stop saying cheesy shit to you. Don't worry, I plan on breaking that promise many times, but you asked if we could take things slow, so I'll give it a few more dates.

Instead, I think I'm going to steal a page from your playbook and talk about our past. It's only fair. You let me read some of your most intimate thoughts at such a vulnerable point in your life, I figure it's the least I can do to give you some insight into my life at that time.

My version is a little grittier, though. I'll try to spare you the worst of the details, but I'm not sure you can fully know what your friendship meant to me without knowing what I went through before you came along.

I told you some of it—about how I ended up in the position I was in, living in that abandoned house. But I had felt homeless a lot longer than that. My whole life, really, even though I had a house and a mother and, occasionally, a stepfather.

I don't remember what things were like when I was young. I have this fantasy that maybe she was a good mother once upon a time. I do remember a day trip we took to Cape Cod where we tried coconut shrimp for the first time, but if she was a decent mother outside of that one day, that one meal, that part of her never became a core memory for me.

My core memories were stretches of time spent alone, or just trying to stay out of her way. She was quick to anger and quick to respond. For the first ten or so years of my life, she was stronger and faster than me, so I spent the better part of a decade hiding from her hand, from her cigarettes, from the lash of her tongue.

I know she was stressed. She was a single mother working nights to try and provide for me, but as many excuses as I made for her back then, I've seen my fair share of single mothers navigate life just fine without resorting to the things my mother did.

You've seen my scars. I won't go into the details, but as bad as it was, it got even worse when she was on her third marriage. I was twelve when they met.

Little did I know, the age of twelve would be my only peaceful year. She was always gone because she was with him, and when she was home, she was actually in a decent mood because she was falling in love. Funny how love for a partner can make or break how some people treat their own children.

But twelve turned into thirteen turned into Tim moving in with us, and the next four years of my life were hell on earth. When I wasn't making my mother angry, I was making Tim angry. When I was home, I was being yelled at. When I was at school, the house was being destroyed by their fights, and I'd be expected to clean up after them when I got home.

Life with them was a nightmare, and by the time I was finally strong enough to take up for myself, that's when Tim decided he didn't want to live with me anymore.

My mother chose him. I was forced to leave. They didn't have to ask twice; I was more than ready to go, but that's because I had somewhere to go.

Until I didn't. I was gone three months before the

friend I was staying with moved with his family to Colorado.

At that point, I had no one and nowhere else to go, and no money to get there if I did, so I was forced to go back to my mother and ask if I could come back home.

I still remember the day I showed back up to that house. I had barely been gone three months, and the place was already falling apart. The yard hadn't been mowed since the last time I'd done it before being kicked out. All the window screens were missing, and there was a gaping hole where the doorknob used to be. By the looks of the place, you would think I'd been gone for years.

My mother's car was in the driveway, but Tim's wasn't. It looked like her car had been there for a while. The hood was propped open, and there were tools scattered near it, along with at least thirty beer cans someone had shaped in the form of a pyramid against the garage door.

Even the newspapers had piled up on the cracked concrete walkway. I remember picking them up and setting them on one of the old iron chairs to dry out before I knocked on the door.

It felt weird knocking on the door of a house I had lived in for years, but on the off chance Tim was home, I wasn't about to open the door without permission. I had a house key still, but Tim had made it very clear that he'd turn me in for trespassing if I ever tried to use it.

I couldn't have used it even if I wanted to. There was no doorknob.

I could hear someone making their way across the living room. The curtain on the small window at the top half of the front door moved, and I saw my mother peek outside. She stared for a few seconds, unmoving.

She eventually opened the door a few inches. Far enough that I could see that, at two o'clock in the afternoon, she was still in her pajamas, which were an oversized Weezer T-shirt one of her exes had left behind. I hated that shirt because I liked that band. Every time she wore it, she ruined them a little more for me.

She asked what I was doing there, and I didn't immediately want to give her my reasons. Instead, I asked her if Tim was home.

She opened the door a bit more and folded her arms so tightly together, it made one of the band members on her shirt look decapitated. She told me Tim was at work and asked what I wanted.

I asked her if I could come inside. She contemplated my question and then looked over my shoulder, her eyes scanning the street. I don't know what she was checking for. Maybe she was afraid a neighbor would witness her allowing her own son to visit.

She left the door open for me while she went to her bedroom to change. The house was eerily dark, I remember. All the curtains were drawn, creating a sense of confusion on what time of day it was. It didn't help that the clock on the stove was blinking, and the time was off by over eight hours. If I still lived there, that's something else I would have fixed.

If I still lived there, the curtains would have been open. The kitchen counters wouldn't have been covered with dirty dishes. There wouldn't have been a missing doorknob, or an unkempt yard, or days' worth of soggy newspapers pil-

ing up. I realized in that moment that I was the one who had been keeping that house together all the years I was growing up.

It gave me hope. Hope that maybe they realized I was an asset rather than an inconvenience, and they would allow me to return home until I finished high school.

I saw a doorknob kit on the kitchen table, so I picked it up and inspected it. The receipt was beneath it. I looked at the date on the receipt, and it was purchased over two weeks prior.

The doorknob was the right fit for the front door. I didn't know why Tim hadn't installed it if he'd had it for two weeks, so I found the tools in a kitchen drawer and opened the package. It was several minutes before my mother came out of her room, but by the time she did, I already had the new doorknob in place on the front door.

She asked what I was doing, so I twisted the knob and opened the door a little to show her it worked.

I'll never forget her reaction. She sighed and said, "Why do you do shit like this? It's like you want him to hate you." She snatched the screwdriver out of my hand and said, "Maybe you should go before he realizes you were here."

Part of the reason I could never get along with anyone in that house was because their reactions always seemed misplaced. When I would help out around the house without being asked, Tim would say it was because I was antagonizing him. When I wouldn't help with something, he'd say it was because I was lazy and ungrateful.

"I'm not trying to upset Tim," I said. "I fixed your doorknob. I was just trying to help."

"He was going to do it as soon as he had the time."

Part of Tim's problem was that he always had the time. He never kept a job more than six months and spent more time gambling than he did with my mother.

"Did he get a job?" I remember asking her.

"He's looking."

"Is that where he is right now?"

I could see in her expression that Tim wasn't out job hunting. Wherever he was, I was sure it was putting my mother even more in debt than she already was. Her debt was probably the straw that broke the camel's back and got me kicked out in the first place. When I found a stash of maxed-out, past-due credit card bills in her name, I confronted Tim about them.

He didn't like being confronted. He preferred the preteen version of me he met to the near adult I grew into. He liked the version of me he could push around without being pushed back. The version of me he could manipulate without me calling him out.

That version of me left between the ages of fifteen and sixteen. Once Tim realized he couldn't threaten me physically anymore, he tried ruining my life in other ways. One of those ways was leaving me without a place to live.

I eventually swallowed my pride and came right out with it. I told my mother I had nowhere to go.

My mother's expression wasn't just void of empathy, it was full of annoyance. "I hope you aren't asking to move back in after everything you did."

"Everything I did? You mean when I called him out because his gambling addiction put you in debt?"

That's when she called me an asshole. Or ass whole, rather. She always said that word wrong.

I attempted to plead with her, but she quickly resorted to the person I was used to. She hurled the screwdriver at me. It was so sudden and unexpected because we weren't even arguing at that point, so I wasn't able to duck in time. It hit me right above my left eye, in the center of my eyebrow.

I rubbed my fingers across the cut, and they came away smeared with blood.

All I did was ask to move home. I didn't disrespect her. I didn't curse at her. I simply showed up and fixed her front door and tried to reason with her, and I ended up with a bloody gash.

I remember staring at my fingers, thinking, "Tim didn't do this. My mother did this."

For so long, I had blamed Tim for everything that went wrong in that household, but everything wrong with that household started with her. Tim simply amplified what was already an awful environment.

I remember thinking that I would rather be dead than back with her. Up until that moment, there was a part of me that still held something for her. I don't know if it was a sliver of respect, but I was somehow able to appreciate that she had kept me alive when I was younger. But isn't that the most basic thing a parent should do when they decide to bring a child into the world?

I realized at that point I had been giving her too much credit. I always blamed our lack of a bond on her being a single mother, but there were a lot of busy single mothers out there who somehow still bonded with their children. Mothers who took up for their children when they were being mistreated. Mothers who wouldn't look the other way when their thirteen-year-old came away from a punishment with a black eye and a busted lip. Mothers who didn't allow their husbands to force their school-aged child into homelessness. Mothers who didn't throw screwdrivers at their children's heads.

Despite realizing what an uncaring human she truly was, I made one last attempt to pull humanity out of her. "Can I at least get some of my stuff before I leave?"

"You don't have anything," she said. "We needed the space."

I couldn't look at her after that. It was as if she wanted nothing more than to erase me from her life, so I vowed in that moment to help her do just that.

The blood was dripping into my eye when I was walking away from the house.

I can't tell you what the rest of that day was like. To feel so incredibly unwanted, unloved, alone. I had no one. Nothing. No money, no belongings, no family.

Just a wound.

We're impressionable when we're younger, and when you're told you are nothing for years on end by everyone you should mean something to, you start to believe it. And you slowly start to become nothing.

But then I met you, Lily. And even though I was nothing, when you looked at me, you somehow saw something. Something I couldn't see. You were the first person in my life to show an interest in who I was as a human. No one

96 | **Colleen Hoover**

had ever asked me questions about myself the way you did. After those few months I spent getting to know you, I stopped feeling like I was nothing. You made me feel interesting and unique. Your friendship gave me worth.

Thank you for that. Even if this date leads nowhere and we never speak again, I will always be grateful to you for somehow seeing something in me that my own mother was blind to.

You're my favorite person, Lily. And now you know why.

Atlas

My throat is so thick with burgeoning tears, I can't even verbally respond to what I just read. I set the phone on my leg and wipe at my eyes. I hate that he's driving right now, because if we were parked, I'd throw my arms around him and hug him tighter than he's ever been hugged. I'd probably kiss him, too, and pull him into the backseat, because no one has ever said such heartbreakingly sad things in such a sweet way to me before.

Atlas reaches across the seat and grabs his phone. He drops it back into the cupholder, but then he reaches for my hand. He threads his fingers through mine and squeezes my hand while staring straight ahead. That move causes a commotion in my chest. I wrap my other hand over the top of his, and holding hands like this reminds me of all the bus rides when we'd just sit in silence, sad and cold, holding on to each other.

I stare out the window, and he stares straight ahead, and neither of us says a word on our drive back to the city.

* * *

We stop and grab to-go burgers just two miles from my flower shop. Atlas knows I don't want Emerson to be up too far past her bedtime, so we eat in the parking lot of Lily Bloom's. Our conversation since getting back into the city and ordering burgers has been much lighter. It isn't lost on me that I'm not mortified anymore. Him being vulnerable with me seemed to be the reset button I needed for our date to get back on track.

We've been discussing all the places we've traveled. He has me beat by a long shot, considering the time he spent in the Marines. He's been to five different countries, and the only place I've been outside of the country is Canada.

"You've never even been to Mexico?" Atlas asks.

I wipe my mouth with a napkin. "Never."

"Did you and Ryle not have a honeymoon?"

Ugh. I hate the sound of his name in the middle of this date. "No, we eloped in Vegas. Didn't have time for a honeymoon."

Atlas takes a sip of his drink. When he looks at me, his eyes are piercing, like he's hoping to unpack the thoughts I'm not saying. "Did you want a wedding?"

I shrug. "I don't know. I knew Ryle never wanted to get married, so when he said we should go to Vegas and get married, I saw it as a window of opportunity that might close. I guess I felt like eloping was better than not marrying him at all."

"What if you get married again? You think you'll do it differently?"

I laugh at that question, and nod immediately. "Absolutely. I want it all. Flowers and bridesmaids and shit." I pop a fry into my mouth. "And romantic vows, and an even more romantic honeymoon."

"Where would you go?"

"Paris. Rome. London. I have no desire to sit on a hot beach somewhere. I want to see all the romantic places in Europe and make love in every city and take pictures kissing in front of the Eiffel Tower. I want to eat croissants and hold hands on trains." I drop my empty container of fries into the sack. "What about you?"

Atlas reaches for my free hand, and he holds it. He doesn't answer me. He just smiles at me and squeezes my hand, like what he wants is a secret that's too soon to spill.

Holding his hand feels like such a natural thing. Maybe because we used to do this so much as teenagers, but sitting in this car with him and *not* holding his hand feels more out of place than holding hands does.

Even with the hitch I put into our date by falling asleep, the entire night has felt easy and comfortable. Being near him is second nature. I trace a finger over the top of his wrist. "I need to go."

"I know," he says, rubbing his thumb over mine. Atlas's phone pings, so he reaches for it with his free hand and reads the incoming text. He sighs quietly, and the way he drops his phone back into the cupholder makes me think he's irritated with whoever just texted him.

"Everything okay?"

Atlas forces a smile, but it's a pathetic attempt. I see right through it, and he knows it. He breaks eye contact and looks down at our hands. He flips mine over until it's faceup, and he begins to trace the lines in my palm. His finger feels like a lightning rod, zapping electricity from my hand throughout the rest of my body. "My mother called me last week."

That confession takes me aback. "What did she want?"

"I don't know, I ended the call before she could tell me, but I'm pretty sure she needs money."

I thread our hands together again. I don't know what to say to him. That has to be hard, not hearing from your mother for almost fifteen years, and then she finally reaches out when she needs something. It makes me so grateful that my mother is a huge part of my life.

"I didn't mean to drop that on you when you're in a hurry. We should save some conversation for our second date." He smiles at me, and it instantly flips the mood. It's remarkable how his smile can dictate the feelings occurring inside my own chest. "Come on, I'll walk you to your car."

I laugh because my car is literally two feet away. But Atlas rushes around the front of his car and opens my door, then helps me out. And then, with one step each, we're at my car.

"Fun walk," I tease.

He flashes a brief smile, and I don't know if he means for it to be seductive, but I'm suddenly warm all over, despite the cold weather. Atlas peeks over my shoulder, nudging his head toward my car. "Do you have more journals in there?"

"Just had the one on me."

"Shame," he says. He leans a shoulder against my car, so I do the same, facing him.

I have no idea if we're about to kiss. I wouldn't object,

but I also just ate onions after sleeping for over an hour, so I doubt my mouth is at its most appealing right now.

"Do I get a redo?" I ask.

"A redo of what?"

"This date. I'd like to be awake for the next one."

Atlas laughs, but then his laugh dissipates. He stares at me for a beat. "I forgot how fun it is being around you."

His words confuse me because *fun* is not what I would call our time together back then. It was sad, at best. "You think those times were fun?"

He lifts a shoulder in a half shrug. "I mean, it was the lowest point of my life, sure. But my memories with you from back then are still some of my favorites."

His compliment makes me blush. I'm glad it's dark.

But he's right. It was a low point in both of our lives, but being with him was still somehow the highlight of my teenage years. I guess *fun* is the perfect way to describe what we made of it. And if we somehow had fun together at such a low point in both of our lives, it makes me wonder what we could be like at our highest.

It's the exact opposite of the thoughts I had about Ryle last week. I've experienced the lowest of lows with Atlas, and he has never been anything but incredible and respectful to me. Yet, the man I chose to be my husband somehow disrespected me in ways no one deserves . . . all while we were at such a high point in our lives.

I'm grateful for Atlas because I know he's the standard I now hold people to. He's the standard I should have held Ryle to from the very beginning.

There's a convenient gust of cold air that sweeps between

us. It would be the perfect excuse for Atlas to pull me to him, but he doesn't. Instead, the quietness builds between us until there's only one thing left to do. Either kiss or say goodnight.

Atlas brushes a strand of my hair from my forehead. "I'm not going to kiss you yet."

I hope my disappointment isn't obvious, but I know it is. I practically deflate in front of him. "Is it my punishment for falling asleep?"

"Of course not. I'm just feeling inferior after reading about our first kiss."

I sputter laughter. "Inferior to *who*? Yourself?"

He nods. "Teenage Atlas through your eyes was quite the charmer."

"So is adult Atlas."

He groans a little, like he already wants to change his mind about the kiss. The groan makes things feel a little more serious. He moves fluidly away from the car until he's standing right in front of me. I press my back against my car door and look up at him, hoping he's about to kiss the hell out of me.

"Also, you asked me to take things slow, so . . ."

Dammit. I did do that. I said *very* slow, if I remember correctly. *I hate myself.*

Atlas leans forward, and I close my eyes. I feel his breath scattering across my cheek right before he presses a quick kiss against the side of my head. "Goodnight, Lily."

"Okay."

Okay? Why did I say "okay"? I'm so flustered.

Atlas laughs softly. When I open my eyes, he's backing away from me, heading to the driver's side of his car. Before he leaves, he rests his arm on the roof of the car and says, "I hope you get some sleep tonight."

I nod, but I don't know if that's going to be possible. I feel like every bit of caffeine I've consumed today has just kicked in all at once. I won't be able to sleep after this date. I'm going to be thinking about the letter he let me read. And when I'm not thinking about that, I'm going to be replaying our first kiss in my head all night long, wondering what part two is going to feel like.

•   •   •

"*Just keep swimming, swimming, swimming . . .*"

The familiar sounds of *Finding Nemo* are coming from Allysa and Marshall's living room when I open the door to their apartment.

When I pass by the kitchen, Marshall is standing in front of the refrigerator with both doors wide open. He nods a greeting, and I wave, but I don't make small talk with him because I'm aching to hug Emerson.

When I enter the living room, I'm shocked to find Ryle on the sofa. He didn't mention he would be off work tonight. Emerson is asleep on his chest, and Allysa is nowhere around.

"Hey."

Ryle doesn't look up to greet me, but he doesn't have to look up for me to know something is bothering him. I can see the firm set of his jaw—a dead giveaway that he's angry. I want to pick up Emerson, but she looks peaceful, so I leave her on Ryle's chest. "How long has she been asleep?"

Ryle is still staring at the television, one of his hands

protectively on Emmy's back, the other behind his head. "Since this movie started."

I recognize the scene, which lets me know it's been about an hour.

Allysa finally walks into the room, breathing life into it. "Hey, Lily. I'm sorry she's asleep; we tried so hard to keep her awake." We give each other a two-second glance. She silently apologizes that Ryle is here. I silently tell her it's okay. They're siblings—I can't expect him not to show up when he knows she's babysitting his daughter.

Ryle motions for Allysa. "Can you put Emerson on her pallet? I need to talk to Lily."

The curtness in his voice alarms both me and Allysa. We give each other another look as she pries Emerson off Ryle's chest. The ache to hold her only grows wider as Allysa lays her on the pallet.

Ryle stands up, and for the first time since I walked in, he makes eye contact with me. He gives me a once-over, noticing the outfit and the heels I'm wearing. I can see the slow roll of his throat. He nudges his head upward, indicating he wants to speak to me on the rooftop balcony.

Whatever conversation this is, he wants complete privacy.

He exits the apartment to head to the roof, and I look toward Allysa for guidance. Once Ryle is out of earshot, she says, "I told him you had an event tonight."

"Thanks." Allysa swore she wouldn't tell Ryle about my date, but I can't figure out why he's so angry if he doesn't know where I've been. "Why is he upset?"

Allysa shrugs. "No idea. He seemed fine when he showed up an hour ago."

I know better than anyone how Ryle can seem fine one second and absolutely the opposite of fine the next. But I usually know what's setting him off.

Did he find out I went on a date? *Did he find out it was with Atlas?*

Once I'm on the roof, I locate Ryle leaning over the ledge, looking down. My stomach is already in knots. My heels click against the floor as I make my way over to him.

Ryle glances at me briefly. "You look . . . *nice.*" He says it in a way that makes it seem like an insult rather than a compliment. Or maybe that's just my guilt.

"Thank you." I lean against the ledge, waiting for him to speak up about whatever is bothering him.

"Did you just get back from a date?"

"I had an event." I go along with Allysa's lie. There's no point in being honest with him, because it's too soon to know if this thing with Atlas is going anywhere yet, and the truth would only upset Ryle more. I press my back against the ledge and fold my arms over my chest. "What is it, Ryle?"

He waits a beat before he finally speaks. "I've never seen that cartoon before tonight."

Is he just trying to make small talk or is he angry about something? I'm confused by this whole conversation.

Until I'm not.

I swear, I can be such an idiot sometimes. *Of course he's upset.* He once read all my journal entries. He knows how much that movie means to me after having read everything I wrote about it, but I guess now that he's finally seen it, he's connected the dots. And by the looks of it, he's added some dots of his own.

He turns now, facing me with an expression full of betrayal. "You named our daughter *Dory*?" He takes a step closer. "You chose my daughter's middle name because of your connection with *that man*?"

I feel an immediate pulsing in my temples. *That man.* I break eye contact with him while I think of how to properly communicate this. When I chose the name Dory as Emerson's middle name, I didn't do it for Atlas. That movie meant something to me long before Atlas came into the picture, but I probably should have thought twice about it before going through with naming her that.

I clear my throat, making room for the truth. "I chose that name because the character inspired me when I was younger. It had nothing to do with anyone else."

Ryle releases an exasperated, disappointed laugh. "You're a real piece of work, Lily."

I want to argue with him, to further prove my point, but I'm getting nervous. His demeanor is bringing back every fear of him I've ever held. I try to defuse the situation by escaping it.

"I'm going home now." I start to head toward the stairs, but he's faster than me. He moves past me, and then he's in between me and the door to the stairwell. I take a nervous step back. I slip my hand in my pocket in search of my phone in case I need to use it.

"We're changing her middle name," he says.

I keep my voice firm and steady when I respond. "We named her Emerson after your brother. That's your connection to her name. Her middle name is *my* connection. It's only fair. You're reading too much into it."

I try to sidestep around him, but he moves with me.

I glance over my shoulder to measure the distance between myself and the ledge. Not that I feel like he'd throw me over it, but I also didn't think he'd be capable of shoving me down a flight of stairs.

"Does he know?" Ryle asks.

He doesn't have to say Atlas's name for me to know exactly who he's talking about. I feel the guilt swallowing me, and I'm worried Ryle can sense it.

Atlas does know Emerson's middle name is Dory, because I made it a point to tell him. But I honestly didn't name my daughter for Atlas. I named her for *me*. Dory was my favorite character before I even knew Atlas Corrigan existed. I admired her strength, and I only named her that because strength is the one trait I hope my daughter has more than anything else.

But Ryle's reaction is making me want to apologize, because *Finding Nemo* does mean something to both Atlas and me, and I knew it when I ran after Atlas on the street to tell him about her middle name.

Maybe Ryle deserves to be angry.

Therein lies our issue, though. Ryle can be angry, but that doesn't mean I deserve everything that accompanies his anger. I'm falling back into that same trap of forgetting that nothing I could do would warrant his extreme past reactions.

I may not be perfect, but I don't deserve to fear for my life every time I make a mistake. And this may have been a mistake that deserves more discussion, but I don't feel comfortable having a conversation about it with Ryle on a rooftop without witnesses.

"You're making me nervous. Can we please go back downstairs?"

Ryle's entire demeanor changes as soon as I say that. It's like he punctures against the sharp insult. "Lily, *come on.*" He moves away from the door and walks all the way to the other side of the balcony. "We're arguing. People argue. *Christ.*" He spins away from me, giving me his back now.

Here comes the gaslighting. He's attempting to make me feel crazy for being scared, even though my fear is more than warranted. I stare at him for a moment, wondering if the argument is over or if he has more to say. I want it to be over, so I open the door to the stairwell.

"Lily, wait."

I pause because his voice is much calmer, which leads me to believe he might be capable of a verbal disagreement rather than an explosive fight tonight. He walks back over to me with a pained expression. "I'm sorry. You know how I feel about anything related to him."

I do know, which is precisely why I've had such conflicting feelings about Atlas potentially being a part of my life again. The simple idea of having to confront Ryle with that information makes me want to vomit. Especially now.

"It upset me to find out that our daughter's middle name might have been something you chose to deliberately hurt me. You can't expect something like that not to affect me."

I lean against the wall and fold my arms over my chest. "It had nothing to do with you or Atlas and everything to do with me. I swear." Just mentioning Atlas's name out loud seems to get it stuck in the air between us, like it's a tangible thing Ryle can reach out and punch.

Ryle nods once with a tight expression, but it appears that he accepts that answer. I honestly don't know if he should. Maybe I did do it subconsciously to hurt him. I don't even know at this point. His anger is making me question my intentions.

This all feels so grossly familiar.

We're both quiet for a while. I just want to go to Emerson, but Ryle seems to have more to say, because he moves closer, placing a hand on the wall beside my head. I'm relieved that he doesn't look angry anymore, but I'm not sure I like the look in his eye that has replaced the anger. It's not the first time he's looked at me this way since our separation.

I feel my entire body stiffen at his gradual change in demeanor. He moves a couple of inches closer, *too* close, and dips his head.

"Lily," he says, his voice a scratchy whisper. "What are we *doing*?"

I don't respond to him because I'm not sure why he's asking that. We're having a conversation. One he started.

He lifts a hand, fingering the collar of my jumpsuit, which is peeking out beneath my coat. When he sighs, his breath moves through my hair. "Everything would be so much easier if we could just . . ." Ryle pauses, maybe to think about the words he's about to say. The words I don't want to hear.

"Stop," I whisper, preventing him from finishing.

He doesn't complete his thought, but he also doesn't back away. If anything, it feels like he moves even closer. I've done nothing in the past that would make him think it's okay to move in on me like this. I do nothing that gives him hope for us other than foster a civil coparenting relationship. He's the one always trying to push my boundaries and straddle the line of what I'm okay with, and I'm honestly tired of it.

"What if I've changed?" he asks. "*Really* changed?" His eyes are full of a mixture of sincerity and sorrow.

It does nothing for me. *Absolutely nothing.* "I don't care if you've changed, Ryle. I hope you *have*. But it's not my responsibility to test that theory."

Those words hit him hard. I see it when he has to take a moment to swallow whatever unkind response he knows he shouldn't give me right now. He stops talking, stops looking at me, stops hovering.

He huffs, frustrated, and then backs away and makes his way toward the stairs, hopefully to his own apartment. He slams the door shut behind him.

I don't immediately follow, for obvious reasons. I need space. I need to process.

This isn't the first time he's asked me what we're doing— like our divorce is some long game I'm playing. Sometimes he'll say it in passing, sometimes in a text. Sometimes he makes it a joke. But every time he suggests how senseless our divorce is, I recognize it for what it is. A manipulation tactic. He thinks if he treats our divorce like we're being silly, I'll eventually agree with him and take him back.

His life would be easier if I took him back. Allysa's and Marshall's lives might even be made easier by it, because they wouldn't have to dance around our divorce and their relationship with him.

But *my* life wouldn't be easier. There's nothing easy about fearing for your safety any time you make a misstep.

Emerson's life wouldn't be easier. I've lived her life. There's nothing easy about living in that kind of household.

I wait for my anger to dissipate before heading back downstairs, but it doesn't. It just builds and builds with every step I descend. I feel like the reaction I'm having is too big for what just happened, or maybe that's just how I've conditioned myself to feel when I'm around Ryle. Maybe it's a combination of that and my lack of sleep. Maybe it's the date with Atlas that I almost ruined. Whatever it is that's making me react so intensely catches up with me right outside of Allysa's apartment door.

I need a moment to collect my emotions before being near my daughter, so I sit on the floor of the hallway to cry it out. I like to shed tears in private. Happens quite regularly, unfortunately, but I've been finding myself getting overwhelmed a lot. Divorce is overwhelming; being a single mother is overwhelming; running a business is overwhelming; dealing with an ex-husband who still scares you is overwhelming.

And then there's that splinter of fear that creeps into my conscience when Ryle says something to suggest our divorce was a mistake. Because sometimes I do wonder if my life wouldn't be so overwhelming if I still had a husband who shared some of the burdens of raising his child. And sometimes I wonder if I'm overreacting by not allowing my daughter to have overnights with her own father. Relationships and custody agreements don't come with a blueprint, unfortunately.

I don't know if every move I make is the right one, but I'm doing my best. I don't need his manipulation and gaslighting on top of that.

I wish I were at home; I would walk straight to my jewelry box and pull out the list of reminders. I should take a picture of it so I always have it on my phone in the future. I definitely underestimate how difficult and confusing interactions with Ryle can be.

How do people leave these cycles when they don't have the resources I had or the support from their friends and family? How do they possibly stay strong enough every second of the day? I feel like all it takes is one weak, insecure moment in the presence of your ex to convince yourself you made the wrong decision.

Anyone who has ever left a manipulative, abusive spouse and somehow stayed that course deserves a medal. A statue. A freaking *superhero* movie.

Society has obviously been worshipping the wrong heroes this whole time because I'm convinced it takes less strength to pick up a building than it does to permanently leave an abusive situation.

I'm still crying a few minutes later when I hear Allysa's door open. I look up to find Marshall exiting the apartment carrying two bags of trash. He pauses when he sees me sitting on the floor.

"Oh." His eyes dart around, as if he's hoping someone else will help me. Not that I need help. I just needed a moment of respite.

Marshall sets the bags on the floor and walks over. He takes a seat across from me and stretches out his legs. He scratches uncomfortably at his knee. "I'm not sure what to say. I'm not good at this."

His discomfort makes me laugh through my tears. I toss

up a frustrated hand. "I'm fine. I just need to cry sometimes when Ryle and I fight."

Marshall pulls up a leg like he's about to stand up and go after Ryle. "Did he hurt you?"

"No. No, he was fairly calm."

Marshall relaxes back to the floor, and I don't know why, maybe it's because he's the unlucky one in front of me right now, but I unload all my thoughts on him.

"I think that's the problem—that he actually had a *right* to be mad at me this time, and he was relatively calm about it. Sometimes we can argue, and it doesn't lead to anything more than a disagreement. And when that happens, I start to question whether I overreacted by asking for a divorce. I mean, I know I didn't overreact. I *know* I didn't. But he has this way of planting seeds of doubt in me, like maybe things could have gotten better if I just gave him more time to work on himself." I feel bad that I'm laying all this on Marshall. It's not fair to him because Ryle is his best friend. "I'm sorry. This isn't your issue."

"Allysa cheated on me."

Marshall's words stun me silent for a good five seconds. "Wh-what?"

"It was a long time ago. We worked through it, but dammit, it hurt like hell. She broke my heart."

I'm shaking my head in an attempt to process this information. He keeps talking, though, so I try to keep up.

"We weren't in a good place. We were going to different colleges and trying to make long distance work, and we were young. And it wasn't even anything big. She had a drunk make-out with some guy at a party before she remembered how amazing I am. But when she told me . . . I've never been so angry in my life. Nothing had ever cut me like that did. I wanted to retaliate: I wanted to cheat on her, so she'd know how it felt; I wanted to slash her tires and max out her credit cards and burn all her clothes. But no matter how mad I was, when she was standing right in front of me, I never, not for one second, thought about physically hurting her. If anything, I just wanted to hug her and cry on her shoulder."

Marshall looks at me with sincerity. "When I think about Ryle hitting you . . . I get absurdly angry. Because I love him. I do. He's been my best friend since we were kids. But I also hate him for not being better. Nothing you have done and nothing you could do would excuse any man's hands on you out of anger. Remember that, Lily. You made the right choice by leaving that situation. You should never feel guilty for that. Pride is the only thing you should feel."

I had no idea how heavily any of this was weighing on me, but Marshall's words lift so much weight off me, I feel like I could float.

I'm not sure those words could mean more coming from anyone else. There's something about getting validation from someone who loves Ryle like a brother that's reaffirming. Empowering.

"You're wrong, Marshall. You're pretty damn good at this."

Marshall smiles and then helps me to my feet. He picks up his trash bags and I head back inside their apartment to find my daughter and hug her so tight.

Chapter Thirteen
Atlas

It's amazing how a night can go from being something I've been hoping would happen for years, to something I've been dreading would happen for years.

If I hadn't received that text just as I was dropping off Lily, I absolutely would have kissed her. But I want our first kiss as adults to be free from distraction.

The text was from Darin, informing me that my mother is at Bib's. I didn't tell Lily about the text because I hadn't yet told her my mother was attempting to work her way back into my life. And then as soon as I told her about my mother calling me, I regretted it. The date was going so well, and I was risking that by ending it on such a somber note.

I didn't text Darin back because I didn't want to interrupt my time with Lily. But even after the date ended and we drove away in separate cars, I still didn't text Darin back. I drove around for half an hour trying to figure out what to do.

I'm hoping my mother got tired of waiting for me. I took my time arriving back to the restaurant, but I'm here now, and I guess I need to confront this. She seems adamant about speaking with me.

I park in the alley behind Bib's so that I can go through the back door in case she's waiting in the restaurant lobby, or at a table. I'm not sure she would recognize me if she saw me, but I'd rather have the advantage by approaching her on my terms.

Darin notices me enter through the back door and immediately makes his way over.

"You get my text?"

I nod and remove my coat. "I did. Is she still here?"

"Yeah, she insisted on waiting. I sat her at table eight."

"Thanks."

Darin looks at me cautiously. "Maybe I'm overstepping, but . . . I swear you said your mother was dead."

That almost makes me laugh. "I never said *dead*. I said she was gone. There's a difference."

"I can tell her you aren't coming in tonight." He must sense the storm brewing.

"It's okay. I have a feeling she isn't going away until I talk to her."

Darin nods and then spins to head back to his station in the kitchen.

I'm glad he's not asking too many questions, since I have no idea why she's here, or who she even is now. She probably wants money. Hell, I'd give it to her if it means I don't have to deal with her calling or showing up again.

I should prepare for that outcome. I go to my office and grab a handful of cash out of the safe and then I make my way through the kitchen doors, out into the restaurant. I hesitate before glancing at table eight.

When I do, I'm relieved to see her back is to me.

I calm myself with a deep breath and then I make my way over to her. I don't want to have to hug her or fake niceties, so I let no time lag between us making eye contact and me taking a seat directly across from her.

She has the same unaffected expression she's always had when she looks across the table at me. There's a small frown playing at the corner of her mouth, but it's always there. She's constantly, albeit inadvertently, frowning.

She looks worn. It's only been about thirteen or so years since I've seen her last, but there are decades' worth of new lines that have formed around her eyes and mouth.

She takes me in for a moment. I know I look vastly different from the last time she saw me, but she makes no indication that she's surprised by that. She's completely stoic, as if I'm the one who should speak first. I don't.

"Is this all yours?" she finally asks, waving a hand around the restaurant.

I nod.

"Wow."

To anyone else watching us, they might think she's impressed. But they don't know her like I know her. That one word was meant as a putdown, as if she's saying, *Wow, Atlas. You're not smart enough for something like this.*

"How much do you need?"

She rolls her eyes. "I'm not here for money."

"What is it, then? You need a kidney? A *heart*?"

She leans back against her seat, resting her hands in her lap. "I forgot how hard it is to have a conversation with you."

"Then why do you keep trying?"

My mother's eyes narrow. She's only ever known the version of me that was intimidated by her. I'm no longer intimidated. Just angry and disappointed.

She huffs, and then brings her arms back up to the table, folding them together. She looks at me pointedly. "I can't find Josh. I was hoping you've talked to him."

I know it's been a long time since I've seen my mother, but I can't for the life of me place anyone named Josh. *Who the hell is Josh? A new boyfriend she thinks I should know about? Is she still using drugs?*

"He does this all the time but never for this long. They're threatening to file truancy charges on me if he doesn't show back up to school."

I am so lost. "Who is Josh?"

Her head falls back as if she's irritated that I'm not following along. "*Josh.* Your little brother. He ran away again."

My . . . *brother?*

Brother.

"Did you know parents can go to jail for truancy violations? I'm looking at *jailtime*, Atlas."

"I have a *brother?*"

"You knew I was pregnant when you ran away."

I absolutely didn't know . . . "I didn't run away—you kicked me out." I don't know why I clarify that; she's fully aware of that fact. She's just trying to deflect blame. But her kicking me out when she did makes so much more sense now. They had a baby on the way, and I no longer fit into the picture.

I bring both arms up and clasp my hands behind my head, frustrated. Shocked. Then I drop them to the table again and lean forward for clarity. "I have a *brother?* How old is he? Who's his . . . Is he Tim's son?"

"He's eleven. And yes, Tim is his father, but he left years ago. I don't even know where he lives now."

I wait for this to fully hit. I was expecting anything and everything *but* this. I have so many questions, but the most important thing right now is to figure out where this kid is. "When was the last time you saw him?"

"About two weeks ago," she says.

"And you reported it to the police?"

She makes a face. "No. Of course not. He's not missing, he's just trying to piss me off."

I have to squeeze my temples to refrain from raising my voice. I still don't understand how she found me or why she thinks an eleven-year-old kid is trying to teach her a lesson, but I'm laser focused on finding him now. "Did you move back to Boston? Did he go missing here?"

My mother makes a confused face. "Move back?"

It's like we're speaking two different languages. "Did you move back here or do you still live in Maine?"

"Oh, God," she mutters, attempting to remember. "I came back, like, ten years ago? Josh was just a baby."

She's lived here for ten years?

"They're going to arrest me, Atlas."

Her child has been missing for two weeks, and she's more worried about being arrested than she is about him. *Some people never change.* "What do you need me to do?"

"I don't know. I was hoping he reached out to you and that maybe you knew where he was. But if you didn't even know he existed—"

"Why would he reach out to me? Does he know about me? What does he know?"

"Other than your name? Nothing; you were never around."

My adrenaline is rushing through me so fast, I'm shocked I'm still sitting across from her. My whole body is tense when I lean forward. "Let me get this straight. I have a little brother I never knew about, and he thinks I didn't care that he *existed*?"

"I don't think he actively thinks about you, Atlas. You've been absent his whole life."

I ignore her dig because she's wrong. Any kid that age would think about the brother they believed abandoned them. I'm sure he hates the idea of me. Hell, he's probably the one who has been—*Shit. Of course.*

This explains so much. I would bet both of my restaurants that he's the one who has been vandalizing them. And why the misspelling reminded me of my mother. The kid is eleven; I'm sure he's capable of googling my information.

"Where do you live?" I ask her.

She practically squirms in her seat. "We're in between houses, so we've been staying at the Risemore Inn for the past couple of months."

"Go back there in case he shows up," I suggest.

"I can't afford to stay there anymore. I'm in between jobs, so I'm staying with a friend for a couple of days."

I stand up and pull the money out of my pocket. I drop it on the table in front of her. "The number you called me on the other day—is that your cell?"

She nods, sliding the money off the table and into her hand.

"I'll call you if I find out anything. Go back to the hotel and try to get the same room. He needs you to be there if he comes back."

My mother nods, and for the first time, she looks somewhat ashamed. I leave her to sit in that feeling without saying goodbye. I'm hoping she's feeling at least a fraction of what she made me feel for years. What she's likely making my little brother feel right now.

I can't believe this. She went and made a whole human and didn't think to tell me?

I walk straight through the kitchen and out the back door. No one is in the alley right now, so I take a moment to pull myself together. I'm not sure I've ever been this stunned.

Her child is out there running the streets of Boston all alone and she waits two goddamn weeks before doing anything about it? I don't know why it surprises me. This is who she is. It's who she's always been.

My phone begins to ring. I'm so on edge, I want to throw it at the dumpster, but when I see it's Lily attempting to Face-Time me, I steady myself.

I slide my finger across the screen, prepared to tell her it isn't a good time, but when her face pops up, it feels like the perfect time. I'm relieved to hear from her, even though it's only been an hour since I last saw her. I'd give anything to reach through the phone and hug her.

"Hey." I try to keep my voice stable, but there's a sharpness to it that cuts through. She can tell because her expression grows concerned.

"Are you okay?"

I nod. "Things sort of went south after I went back to work. I'm fine, though."

She smiles, but it's kind of sad. "Yeah, my night went south, too."

I didn't notice at first, but it looks like she's been crying. Her eyes are glassy and a little puffy. "Are *you* okay?"

She forces another smile. "I will be. I just wanted to say thank you for tonight before I went to sleep."

I hate that she's not standing in front of me right now. I don't like seeing her sad; it reminds me too much of all the times I saw her sad when we were younger. At least back then I was close enough to hug her. *Maybe I still can.*

"Would a hug make you feel better?"

"Obviously. I'll be fine after I get some sleep, though. Talk tomorrow?"

I have no idea what happened between our date and this phone call, but she looks completely defeated. She looks very similar to how I feel.

"Hugs take two seconds, and you'll sleep so much better. I'll be back here before they even know I've left. What's your address?"

A small grin peeks through her gloom. "You're going to drive five miles just to give me a hug?"

"I'd *run* five miles just to give you a hug."

That makes her smile even bigger. "I'll text you my address. But don't knock too loud; I just put Emmy down."

"See you soon."

Chapter Fourteen
Lily

I've been out of the dating loop for a while, so if *hug* is code for something else, I have no idea.

Surely a hug still just means a hug.

I can barely work social media, much less keep up with slang. I swear, I'm the most out-of-touch millennial I know. It's as if I skipped right over Gen X and into Boomer territory. I'm a Boomer millennial. A *boollennial*. Hell, my mother is a Boomer and probably knows more about these things than I do. She's the one with a new boyfriend. I should call her and ask for pointers.

I brush my teeth, just in case a hug is a *kiss*. And then I change clothes twice, until I end up back in the pajamas I had on when I FaceTimed him. I'm trying way too hard to look like I'm not trying too hard. Sometimes being a woman is so dumb.

I'm pacing my apartment, anxious for his knock. I don't know why I'm so nervous; I just spent three hours with him.

Well, one and a half if I don't count the nap I took in the middle of our date.

Several dozen paces later, there's a light tap on my apartment door. I know it's Atlas, but I glance through the peephole anyway.

He even looks good all distorted through a peephole. I smile when I noticed he changed, too. Just his jacket, but still. He was wearing a thick black coat when we went out earlier, but now he's wearing a simple gray hoodie.

Dear God. I like it so much.

I open the door, and Atlas leaves zero seconds between our first moment of eye contact and when his arms sweep me in for a hug.

He holds me so tight, it makes me want to ask him what was so bad about the last hour, but I don't. I just quietly hug him back. I settle my cheek against his shoulder and revel in the comfort of him.

Atlas didn't even step inside my apartment. We're just standing in the doorway, as if a hug still just means a hug. His cologne is nice. It reminds me of summer, like he's defying the cold. He seemed so concerned about smelling like garlic earlier, but all I could smell was this same cologne.

He lifts a hand to the back of my head and rests it there gently. "You okay?"

"I am now." My response is muffled against him. "You?"

He sighs, but he doesn't say he's okay. He just leaves his answer hanging in his exhale, until he slowly releases me. He lifts a hand and runs his fingers down a piece of my hair. "I hope you get some sleep tonight."

"You too," I say.

"I'm not going home, I'm staying at the restaurant tonight." He shakes that sentence off like he shouldn't have said anything. "It's a long story, and I need to get back. I'll catch you up on everything tomorrow."

I want to invite him in and make him give me all the details right now, but I feel like he'd offer them up if he were in the mood. I'm certainly not in the mood to talk about what happened with Ryle, so I'm not going to force him to talk about whatever put a damper on *his* night. I just wish there was a way I could make it better.

I perk up when I think of something that might do the trick. "Do you need more reading material?"

His eyes glint with a twinge of excitement. "I do, actually."

"Wait here." I head to my bedroom and look in my box of things, searching for the next journal. When I find it, I take it back to him. "This one is a little more graphic," I tease.

Atlas takes the journal with one hand and then slides his other arm around my lower back and tugs me against him. Then, quickly, he steals a peck. It's so soft and fast, it doesn't even fully register that he kissed me until it's over.

"Goodnight, Lily."

"Goodnight, Atlas."

Neither of us moves. It feels like it might hurt if we separate. Atlas pulls me even tighter against him and then he lowers his lips to the spot near my collarbone where my tattoo is hidden beneath my shirt. The tattoo he doesn't even know is there. He kisses it unknowingly, and then, sadly, he leaves.

I close the door and press my forehead against it. I feel all the familiar feelings of a crush, but this time those feelings are accompanied by worry and hesitation, even though it's Atlas, and Atlas is one of the good ones.

I blame Ryle for that. He took what little trust I had left in men thanks to my father, and he stripped me of it.

But I think this crush is a sign that Atlas might be able to give back what my father and Ryle took from me. My stomach moves from the flutters Atlas left me with to what feels like a six-foot drop on that thought, because I know how that would make Ryle feel.

The more joy I get from my interactions with Atlas, the more dread I feel about having to break the news to Ryle.

Chapter Fifteen
Atlas

When I was in the military, I was stationed with a friend who had family from Boston. His aunt and uncle were getting ready to retire and wanted to sell their restaurant. It was called Milla's, and when I visited it on leave one year, I absolutely fell in love with the place. I can say it was the food, or the fact that it was located in Boston, but the truth is, I fell in love with it because of the preserved tree growing in the center of the main dining room.

The tree reminded me of Lily.

If anything is going to remind someone of their first love, trees are probably the last thing you want as a reminder. They're everywhere. Which is probably why I've thought about Lily every day since I was eighteen, but that could also be because I still, to this day, feel like I owe her my life.

I'm not sure if it was the tree, or the fact that the restaurant came almost fully stocked and staffed, but I felt a pull to buy it when it became available. It wasn't my goal to own a restaurant right out of the military. I had planned to work as a chef to gain experience, but when this opportunity presented itself, I couldn't walk away from the prospect. I used the money I saved up from my time as a Marine, and I secured a business loan, bought the restaurant, changed the name, and created a whole new menu.

Sometimes I feel guilty for the success Bib's has had—like I haven't paid my dues. I didn't just inherit the staff, who already knew what they were doing, but I inherited customers as well. I didn't build it from the ground up, which is why I feel a heavy amount of imposter syndrome when people congratulate me on the success of Bib's.

That's why I opened Corrigan's. I don't know that I was trying to prove anything to anyone other than myself, but I wanted to know that I could do it. I wanted the challenge of creating something from nothing and watching it flourish and grow. Like what Lily wrote in her journal about why she liked growing things in her garden when we were teenagers.

Maybe that's why I feel more protective of Corrigan's than I do over Bib's, because I created it from nothing. That might also be the reason I put more effort into protecting it. Corrigan's has a working security system and is a hell of a lot harder to break into than Bib's.

Which is why I chose to spend tonight at Bib's, even though Corrigan's is due to be broken into if we're going by the rotating schedule this kid has developed. The first night was Bib's, the second night was Corrigan's, he took a few days off, and then the third and fourth incidents were at Bib's. I may be wrong, but I have a feeling he'll show up here again before going back to Corrigan's, simply because he's had more success getting into the less secure of the two places. I just hope tonight isn't one of the nights he decides not to show up.

He'll definitely show up here if he's hungry. Bib's is his

better bet for food, which is why I'm hiding on the far side of the dumpster, waiting. I pulled over one of the tattered chairs the smokers use on their breaks, and I've been passing time by reading. Lily's words have kept me company. A little too well, because there have been several times I've been so engrossed in this journal, I forget that I'm supposed to be on alert.

I don't know for certain if the kid who has been vandalizing my restaurants is the same kid who shares a mother with me, but the timing makes sense. And the targeted insults that he's been spray painting make sense if they're coming from a kid who despises me. I can't think of anyone else who would have a good reason to be angry with me more than a little boy who feels abandoned by his older brother.

It's almost two in the morning. I check the security app on my phone for Corrigan's, but there's nothing new happening over there, either.

I go back to reading the journal, even though the last couple of entries have been painful to read. I didn't realize how much my leaving for Boston impacted Lily when she was younger. In my mind at that age, I felt like an inconvenience in her life. I had no idea how much she felt I *brought* to her life. Reading the letters she wrote back then has been a lot more difficult than I expected it to be. I thought it would be fun to read her thoughts, but when I started reading them, I remembered how cruel our childhoods were to us. I don't think about it much anymore because I'm so far removed from the life I lived back then, but I'm being thrown back into those moments from every angle this week, it seems. The information in the journal entries, my mother, finding out I have a brother—it all feels like everything I've tried running from has formed a slow leak that's threatening to sink me.

But then there's Lily and her impeccable timing being back in my life. She always seems to show up when I need a lifeline.

I flip through the rest of the journal and see that I'm already halfway through the last entry she made. I have very little recollection of that night because of the dreadful way it ended. Part of me doesn't even want to experience it from her point of view, but I can't not know how I left her feeling for all those years.

I open the last entry and pick up where I left off.

> *He took my hands in his and told me he was leaving sooner than he planned for the military, but that he couldn't leave without telling me thank you. He told me he'd be gone for four years and that the last thing he wanted for me was to be a sixteen-year-old girl not living my life because of a boyfriend I never got to see or hear from.*
>
> *The next thing he said made his blue eyes tear up until they looked clear. He said, "Lily. Life is a funny thing. We only get so many years to live it, so we have to do everything we can to make sure those years are as full as they can be. We shouldn't waste time on things that might happen some-day, or maybe even never."*
>
> *I knew what he was saying. That he was leaving for the military and he didn't want me to hold on to him while he was gone. He wasn't really breaking up with me be-cause we weren't ever really together. We'd just been two*

people who helped each other when we needed it and got our hearts fused together along the way.

It was hard, being let go by someone who had never really grabbed hold of me completely in the first place. In all the time we've spent together, I think we both sort of knew this wasn't a forever thing. I'm not sure why, because I could easily love him that way. I think maybe under normal circumstances, if we were together like typical teenagers and he had an average life with a home, we could be that kind of couple. The kind who comes together so easily and never experiences a life where cruelty sometimes intercepts.

I didn't even try to get him to change his mind that night. I feel like we have the kind of connection that even the fires of hell couldn't sever. I feel like he could go spend his time in the military and I'll spend my years being a teenager and then it will all fall back into place when the timing is right.

"I'm going to make a promise to you," he said. "When my life is good enough for you to be a part of it, I'll come find you. But I don't want you to wait around for me, because that might never happen."

I didn't like that promise, because it meant one of two things. Either he thought he might never make it out of the military alive, or he didn't think his life would ever be good enough for me.

His life was already good enough for me, but I nodded my head and forced a smile. "If you don't come back for me, I'll come for you. And it won't be pretty, Atlas Corrigan."

He laughed at my threat. "Well, it won't be too hard to find me. You know exactly where I'll be."

I smiled. "Where everything is better."

He smiled back. "In Boston."

And then he kissed me.

Ellen, I know you're an adult and know all about what comes next, but I still don't feel comfortable telling you what happened over those next couple of hours. Let's just say we both kissed a lot. We both laughed a lot. We both loved a lot. We both breathed a lot. A lot. And we both had to cover our mouths and be as quiet and still as we could so we wouldn't get caught.

When we were finished, he held me against him, skin to skin, hand to heart. He kissed me and looked straight in my eyes.

"I love you, Lily. Everything you are. I love you."

I know those words get thrown around a lot, especially by teenagers. A lot of times prematurely and without much merit. But when he said them to me, I knew he wasn't saying it like he was in love with me. It wasn't that kind of "I love you."

Imagine all the people you meet in your life. There are so many. They come in like waves, trickling in and out with the tide. Some waves are much bigger and make more of an impact than others. Sometimes the waves bring with them things from deep in the bottom of the sea and they leave those things tossed onto the shore. Imprints against the grains of sand that prove the waves had once been there, long after the tide recedes.

That was what Atlas was telling me when he said "I

love you." He was letting me know that I was the biggest wave he'd ever come across. And I brought so much with me that my impressions would always be there, even when the tide rolled out.

After he said he loved me, he told me he had a birthday present for me. He pulled out a small brown bag. "It isn't much, but it's all I could afford."

I opened the bag and pulled out the best present I'd ever received. It was a magnet that said "Boston" on the top. At the bottom in tiny letters, it said, "Where everything is better." I told him I would keep it forever, and every time I look at it I'll think of him.

When I started out this letter, I said my sixteenth birthday was one of the best days of my life. Because up until that second, it was.

It was the next few minutes that weren't.

Before Atlas had shown up that night, I wasn't expecting him, so I didn't think to lock my bedroom door. My father heard me in there talking to someone, and when he threw open my door and saw Atlas in bed with me, he was angrier than I'd ever seen him. And Atlas was at a disadvantage by not being prepared for what came next.

I'll never forget that moment for as long as I live. Being completely helpless as my father came down on him with a baseball bat. The sound of bones snapping was the only thing piercing through my screams.

I still don't know who called the police. I'm sure it was my mother, but it's been six months and we still haven't talked about that night. By the time the police got to my *bedroom and pulled my father off of him, I didn't even recognize Atlas, he was covered in so much blood.*

I was hysterical.

Hysterical.

Not only did they have to take Atlas away in an ambulance, they also had to call an ambulance for me because I couldn't breathe. It was the first and only panic attack I've ever had.

No one would tell me where he was or if he was even okay. My father wasn't even arrested for what he'd done. Word got out that Atlas had been staying in that old house and that he had been homeless. My father became revered for his heroic act—saving his little girl from the homeless boy who manipulated her into having sex with him.

My father said I'd shamed our whole family by giving the town something to gossip about. And let me tell you, they still gossip about it. I heard Katie on the bus today telling someone she tried to warn me about Atlas. She said she knew he was bad news from the moment she laid eyes on him. Which is crap. If Atlas had been on the bus with me, I probably would have kept my mouth shut and been mature about it like he tried to teach me to be. Instead, I was so angry, I turned around and told Katie she could go to hell. I told her Atlas was a better human than she'd ever be and if I ever heard her say one more bad thing about him, she'd regret it.

She just rolled her eyes and said, "Jesus, Lily. Did he brainwash you? He was a dirty, thieving homeless kid who was probably on drugs. He used you for food and sex and now you're defending him?"

She's lucky the bus stopped at my house right then. I grabbed my backpack and walked off the bus, then went inside and cried in my room for three hours straight. Now my head hurts, but I knew the only thing that would make me feel better is if I finally got it all out on paper. I've been avoiding writing this letter for six months now.

No offense, Ellen, but my head still hurts. So does my heart. Maybe even more right now than it did yesterday. This letter didn't help one damn bit.

I think I'm going to take a break from writing to you for a while. Writing to you reminds me of him, and it just all hurts too much. Until he comes back for me, I'm just going to keep pretending to be okay. I'll keep pretending to swim, when really all I'm doing is floating. Barely keeping my head above water.

—Lily

I close the journal after reading the last page.

I don't know what to feel because I feel everything. Rage, love, sadness, happiness.

I've always hated that I couldn't remember most of that night no matter how hard I tried to think back on every word that was said between us. The fact that Lily wrote it all down is a gift—albeit a sad one.

There were so many things about that time in my life that I was afraid she was too fragile to hear. I only wanted to protect her from the negative stuff going on in my life, but reading her words has shown me that she didn't need protecting from it. If anything, she could have helped me through it.

It makes me want to write her another letter, but even more, it makes me want to be in her presence, talking about these things face-to-face. I know we're taking things slow, but the more I'm around her, the more impatient I am to be around her again.

I stand up to take the journal inside and to grab something to drink for the wait, but I pause as soon as I come to a stand. There's a streetlight at the other end of the alley creating a spotlight on the building, and there's a shadow moving across the light. The shadow travels across the building in the other direction, as if whatever is casting the shadow is coming my way. I back up a step so that I can remain hidden.

Someone eventually comes into view. A kid closes in on the back door.

I don't know if this kid is my brother, but it's definitely the same person I saw on the security footage at Corrigan's. The same clothes, the same hoodie tightened around their face.

I remain hidden and watch them, becoming more and more convinced by the second that it's exactly who I think it is. He's built like me. He even moves like me. I'm filled with anxious energy because I want to meet him. I want to tell him that I'm not angry and that I know what he's going through.

I'm not sure I was even angry at whoever was doing this before I knew it could potentially be my brother. It's hard to be angry at a kid, but it's especially hard to be angry at one who was raised by the same woman who attempted to raise me. I know what it's like to have to do what you can to survive. I also know what it's like when you'd do anything to get someone's attention. *Anyone's.* There were times in my childhood I just wanted to be noticed, and I have a feeling that's exactly what's going on here.

He's hoping to be caught. This is more a cry for attention than anything.

He walks right up to the back door of the restaurant without an ounce of hesitation. This place has become familiar to him. He checks the back door to see if it's locked. When it doesn't open, he pulls a new can of spray paint out of his hoodie. I wait for him to lift it, and that's when I decide to make my presence known.

"You're holding it wrong." My voice startles him. When he spins around and looks up at me and I see how young he really is, my heartstrings stretch so tight, it feels like they're about to pop. I try to imagine Theo out here alone in the middle of the night like this.

There's still a youthfulness to the fear in his eyes. When I start walking toward him, he backs up a step, looking around for a quick escape. But he doesn't attempt to run.

I'm sure he's curious about what's going to happen. Isn't this why he's been showing up here night after night?

I hold out my hand for the can of spray paint. He hesitates, but then hands it to me. I demonstrate how to hold it the proper way. "If you do it like this, it won't drip. You hold it too close."

Every emotion is running across his face as he studies me, from anger to fascination to betrayal. The two of us are quiet as we take in just how much we look alike. We both took after our mother. Same jawline, same light eyes, same mouths, down to the unintentional frown. It's a lot for me to take in. I've been resigned to the idea that I had no family, yet here he is in the flesh. It makes me wonder what he's feeling while he looks back at me. Anger, obviously. Disappointment.

I lean a shoulder against the building, looking down at him with complete transparency. "I didn't know you existed, Josh. Not until a few hours ago."

The kid shoves his hands into the pockets of his hoodie and looks at his feet. "Bullshit," he mutters.

The hardness in him at such a young age makes me sad. I ignore the anger in his response and pull my keys out to unlock the back door to the restaurant. "You hungry?" I hold the door open for him.

He looks like he wants to run, but after a moment of indecision, he ducks his head and walks inside.

I flip on the lights and make my way into the kitchen. I grab the ingredients to make him a grilled cheese and I start cooking while he walks around slowly, taking everything in. He touches things, opens drawers, cabinets. Maybe he's taking inventory for the next time he decides to break in. Or maybe his curiosity is a cover for his fear.

I'm plating his food when he finally speaks up. "How do you know who I am if you didn't know I existed?"

This feels like it could lead to a lengthy conversation, and I'd rather have it while he's more comfortable. There isn't a table back here with seating, so I motion toward the doors that lead into the dining room. There's enough light from the exit signs that I don't have to power up the dining room lights.

"Sit here." I point to table eight and he takes a seat in the exact spot our mother sat in earlier tonight. He starts eating as soon as I set his food down. "What do you want to drink?"

He swallows, and then shrugs. "Whatever."

I go back to the kitchen and pour him a glass of ice water and then slide into the booth across from him. He drinks half of it in one gulp.

"Your mother showed up here tonight," I say. "She's looking for you."

He makes a face that indicates he doesn't care, and then he continues eating.

"Where have you been staying?"

"Places," he says with a mouthful.

"Are you in school?"

"Not lately."

I let him get in a few more bites before I continue. The last thing I want to do is run him off with too many questions. "Why did you run away?" I ask. "Because of her?"

"Sutton?"

I nod. I wonder what kind of relationship they have if he doesn't even call her "Mom."

"Yeah, we got in a fight. We always fight over the stupidest shit." He eats his last bite, then downs the rest of his water.

"And your dad? Tim?"

"He left when I was little." His eyes roam around the room, landing on the tree. When he looks back at me, he tilts his head. "Are you rich?"

"If I was, I wouldn't tell you. You've tried to rob me several times now."

I can see a smirk playing across his lips, but he refuses to release it. He relaxes into the booth more, pulling his hoodie away from his face. Strands of greasy brown hair fall forward, and he pushes them back. His hair holds the shape of a cut that's long overdue, with sides that have grown out too long and uneven to be intentional.

"She told me you left because of me. She said you didn't want a brother."

I have to hold back my irritation. I pull his empty plate of food and his glass toward me, and I stand up. "I didn't know about you until today, Josh. I swear. I would have been around if I had."

He eyes me from his seat, studying me. Wondering if he can trust me. "You know about me now." He says that like it's a challenge to do better. To prove his low expectations of the world wrong.

I nudge my head toward the doors to the kitchen. "You're right. Let's go."

He doesn't immediately get out of the booth. "Where to?"

"My house. I have a room for you as long as you stop cussing so much."

He raises an eyebrow. "What are you, some kind of religious nutjob?"

I motion for him to stand up. "An eleven-year-old muttering cuss words all the time seems desperate. It's not cool until you're at least fourteen."

"I'm not eleven, I'm twelve."

"Oh. She said you were eleven. *Still.* Too young to be cool."

Josh stands up and starts to follow me through the kitchen.

I spin and face him as I push back through the doors.

"And for future reference, you spelled *asshole* wrong. There's no *w*."

He looks surprised. "I thought that looked funny after I wrote it."

I put his dishes in the sink, but it's almost three in the morning and I'm not in the mood to wash them. I flip out the lights and have Josh lead the way out the back door. When I'm locking it, he says, "Are you going to tell Sutton where I am?"

"I don't know what I'm going to do yet," I admit. I start walking down the alley, and he rushes to catch up with me.

"I'm thinking of going to Chicago, anyway," he says. "I probably won't stay more than one night at your place."

I laugh at the idea that this kid thinks I'm going to allow him to run off to another city now that I know he exists. *What am I getting myself into?* I have a feeling my day-to-day responsibilities have just doubled. "Do we have any other siblings I don't know about?" I ask him.

"Just the twins, but they're only eight."

I stop in my tracks and look at him.

He grins. "I'm kidding. It's just the two of us."

I shake my head and grab the back of his hoodie, pulling it down over his head. "You're something."

He's smiling when we make it to my car. I'm smiling, too, until I feel a sharp stab of worry in the center of my gut.

I've known him for half an hour. I've known *of* him for a fraction of a day. Yet I suddenly feel like I'll be protective of him for a lifetime.

Chapter Sixteen
Lily

You lose your mornings after having children.

I used to open my eyes and lie in bed for several minutes before grabbing my phone and catching up on everything I might have missed while I slept. I'd have a cup of coffee, and then mentally map out my day while I showered.

But now that I have Emmy, her early morning cry rips me out of bed, and I become her gopher before I even have time to pee. I rush to change her, rush to clothe her, rush to feed her. By the time I'm finished with morning mother duties, I'm late for work and barely have time to do those things for myself.

It's why I cherish Sunday mornings. It feels like the only day of the week I get any sense of calm. When Emmy wakes up on Sundays, I always bring her back to bed with me. We lie together and I listen to her babble and there's absolutely no rush to get up or be somewhere.

Sometimes, like right now, she falls back to sleep, and I just stare at her for long stretches of time—marveling at the wonder that is motherhood.

I grab my phone and take a picture of her to text to Ryle, but I hesitate before hitting send. I don't miss Ryle at all, but it does make me sad in moments like this that Ryle doesn't get to do this with us, or that I don't get to share in the joys *they* have together. There's nothing better than adoring the child you made with the person you made them with, which is why I always try to text him pictures and videos. But I'm still upset about last night and don't really feel like reaching out yet. I save the picture for a more peaceful day.

Fucking Ryle.

Divorce is difficult. I knew it would be, but it's so much harder than I anticipated. And navigating divorce with a child in the mix is a million times trickier. You're stuck interacting with that person for the remainder of your life. You have to either figure out a way to plan birthday parties together or figure out a way to be okay with having separate celebrations. You have to plan on which holidays each of you get to spend with your child, which days of the week, down to which hours of the day sometimes.

You can't snap your fingers and be done with the person you married and divorced. You're stuck with them. Forever.

I'm stuck dealing with Ryle's feelings forever, and frankly, I'm growing tired of always feeling sorry for him, worried for him, fearful of him, *considerate* of his feelings.

How long am I supposed to wait before I start dating someone else without Ryle being justified in his jealousy? How long do I have to wait before I tell him I'm dating Atlas if Atlas and I become a thing? How long until I get to start making decisions about my own life without worrying about his feelings?

My phone vibrates. It's my mother calling. I slide softly out of the bed to walk to the living room before answering it.

"Hey."

"Can I have Emerson today?"

I laugh at her blatant disregard for her daughter now that she has a granddaughter. "I'm good, how are you?" My mother loves Emmy as much as I do—I'm convinced of that. When Emmy turned six weeks old, my mother started taking her for a few hours at a time while I worked. She actually stayed at her house overnight last month—it was Emmy's first night away from me since she'd been born. She had fallen asleep at my mother's, and neither of us wanted to wake her, so I went back for her the next morning.

"Rob and I are close by; we could come pick her up in twenty minutes. We're going to the botanical gardens; I thought it would be fun to get her out. I'm sure you could use the break."

"Yeah, sure. I'll get her dressed."

.   .   .

Half an hour later, there's a knock at my door. I open it and let my mother and Rob inside. My mother beelines across the living room, straight to Emmy, who is on a pallet on the floor.

"Hi, Mom." I say it teasingly.

"Look at this adorable outfit," my mother says, picking her up. "Did I buy her this?"

"No, it's a hand-me-down from Rylee, actually." It's nice that Rylee is six months older. We haven't had to buy Emmy many clothes because Allysa gives me more than enough of Rylee's. And they're always in great condition because I don't think Rylee ever wears an outfit twice.

Emmy is wearing the outfit Rylee wore at her first birthday party. I was hoping it would eventually be passed down to Emmy, because it's adorable. It's a pair of pink leggings with green whole watermelons on them, and a green long-sleeved top with a pink slice of watermelon in the center of it.

My mother has bought almost everything else Emmy wears, including the blue jacket I'm putting on her right now.

"That doesn't match her outfit," my mother says. "Where's the pink jacket I bought her?"

"It's too little, and it's a jacket, and she's one year old. It doesn't matter if she doesn't match."

My mother huffs, and I can tell by that look on her face that Emmy is going to come home in a brand-new jacket this afternoon. I kiss Emmy on the cheek, and my mother heads for the door.

I hand Rob the diaper bag, and he hoists it over his shoulder. "Want me to carry her?" he asks my mother.

She squeezes Emmy tighter. "I've got her." She addresses me over her shoulder. "We'll be back in a few hours."

"About what time?" I ask her. I don't usually clarify a time with her, but I'm thinking about asking Atlas what he's doing right now. We can maybe grab lunch since we're both off today and I'm kid-free.

"I'll text you. Why? Are you going somewhere?" she asks. "I figured you'd just catch up on sleep."

I don't dare tell her I might sneak away to meet a guy. She'd ask me questions well past the botanical garden closing hours. "Yeah, I'll probably just sleep. I'll keep my phone on, though. Have fun."

My mother is out the door and down the hallway, but Rob pauses and looks at me. "Make sure you park your car in the same spot. She'll notice if you move it, and she'll ask questions." He winks, a clear indication that he can read me better than she can.

"Thanks for the heads-up," I whisper.

I close the door and go find my phone. I've been rushing to get Emmy dressed and out the door, so I haven't looked at my phone since I hung up with my mother. I have a missed call from Atlas from twenty minutes ago.

My stomach flips with anticipation. I hope he's off today. I use my phone camera to check my appearance, and then I call him back over video chat.

I hated when he called me over video chat the first time, but now it feels like the natural thing to do. I always want to see his face. I like seeing what he's wearing and where he's at and the faces he makes when he says the things he says.

I'm already smiling when I hear the sound that indicates he's answered the call. He lifts the phone, and when I finally make out what I'm looking at, I can see he's standing in an unfamiliar kitchen. It's white and bright and different from the kitchen I remember when I visited his house almost two years ago.

"Morning," he says. He's smiling, but he looks tired, like he either just woke up or is about to fall asleep.

"Hey."

"Sleep well?" he asks.

"I did. Finally." I squint my eyes trying to see past him. "Did you remodel your kitchen?"

Atlas glances over his shoulder, and then looks back at me. "I moved."

"What? When?"

"Earlier this year. Sold my house and got a place closer to the restaurant."

"Oh. That's nice." Closer to the restaurant means closer to me. I wonder how far apart we live now. "Are you cooking?"

Atlas aims his phone at his countertop. There's a pan of eggs, a pile of bacon, pancakes, and . . . *two plates. Two* glasses of juice. My heart drops. "That's a lot of food," I say, attempting to hide the immense jealousy running through me.

"I'm not alone," he says, panning the screen back to his face.

My disappointment must be clearly written all over me, because he immediately shakes his head.

"No, Lily. That's not . . ." He laughs and seems flustered. His reaction is adorable but not entirely reassuring yet. He holds the phone up a little higher until I can see a person standing behind him. I'm not sure who's with him, but it isn't another woman.

It's a kid.

A kid who looks just like Atlas, and he's staring right at me with eyes that look identical to Atlas's eyes. *Does he have a child I don't know about?*

What is going on?

"She thinks I'm your son," the kid says. "You're freaking her out."

Atlas immediately aims the phone back at his own face. "He's not my son. He's my brother."

Brother?

Atlas moves the phone so that I'm looking at his brother again. "Say hi to Lily."

"No."

Atlas rolls his eyes and shoots me an apologetic look. "He's kind of a jerk." He says that right in front of his little brother.

"Atlas!" I whisper, shocked at every part of this conversation.

"It's okay, he knows he's a jerk."

I see the kid laugh behind him, so I know he knows Atlas is kidding. But I am so confused. "I had no idea you had a brother."

"I didn't know, either. Found out last night after our date."

I think back on last night and how it was obvious something was bothering him about the text he received, but I had no idea it was a family issue. I guess this explains why his mother was trying to contact him. "Sounds like you have a lot to work through today."

"Wait, don't hang up yet," he says. He walks out of the kitchen and into another room for privacy. He closes a door and sits down on his bed. "Biscuits still have about ten minutes, I can chat."

"Wow. Pancakes *and* biscuits. He's a lucky kid. I had black coffee for breakfast."

Atlas smiles, but his smile doesn't reach his eyes. He seemed like he was in a good mood in front of his brother, but now that I have him alone, I can see the stress in the way he's holding himself. "Where's Emmy?" he asks.

"My mother has her for a few hours."

When it registers that we're both off work and I don't have Emmy, he sighs like he's bummed. "You mean you actually have a free day?"

"It's okay, we're taking it slow, remember? Besides, it's not every day you find out you have a little brother."

He dives a hand through his hair and sighs. "He's the one who has been vandalizing the restaurants."

I startle at that comment. I need to hear more of this story.

"That's why my mother tried calling me last week, to see if I'd heard from him. I feel like a dick for blocking her number now."

"You didn't know." I'm standing in my living room, but I want to sit down for this conversation. I walk to the couch and set my phone on the arm of it, propping it up with the PopSocket. "Did he know about you?"

Atlas nods. "Yeah, and he thought I knew about him, which is why he was taking out his anger on my restaurants. Other than the thousands of dollars he cost me, he seems like a good kid. Or he at least seems like he has the potential to be a good kid. I don't know, he's gone through a lot of the shit I went through with my mother, so there's no telling what that's done to him."

"Is your mother there, too?"

Atlas shakes his head. "I haven't told her I found him yet. I spoke to a friend of mine who's a lawyer, and he said the sooner I tell her the better, so she can't use it against me."

Use it against him? "Are you wanting to get custody of him?"

Atlas nods without hesitation. "I don't know if that's what Josh wants, but there isn't another option I could live with. I know what kind of mother she is. He mentioned wanting to find his father, but Tim is even worse than my mother."

"What kind of rights do you have as his brother? Any?"

Atlas shakes his head. "Not unless my mother agrees to let him live with me. Not looking forward to that conversation. She'll say no just to spite me, but . . ." Atlas releases a heavy sigh. "If he stays with her, he won't have a chance in hell. He's already harder than I was at that age. Angrier. I'm afraid of what that anger might turn into if he doesn't gain some stability in his life. But who's to say I'm capable of something like this? What if I fuck him up more than my mother has?"

"You won't, Atlas. You know you won't."

He accepts my reassurance with a quick flash of a smile. "That's easy for you to say; you're a natural at this whole raising-kids thing."

"I just fake it well," I say. "I have no idea what I'm doing. No parent does. We're all full of imposter syndrome, winging it every minute of the day."

"Why is that both comforting and terrifying?" he asks.

"You just summed up parenthood with those two words."

He exhales. "I should probably get back in there and make sure he isn't robbing me. I'll call you later today, okay?"

"Okay. Good luck."

The way Atlas silently mouths the word *goodbye* in return is sexy as hell.

When I end the call, I fall onto my bed and sigh. I love the way I feel after I talk to him. He makes me giddy and energized and happy, even when the call is as shocking and chaotic as that one was.

I wish I knew where he lived. I'd go give him a drive-by hug like the one he gave me last night. I hate that he's dealing with this, but at the same time I'm happy for him. I can't imagine how alone he's felt since I met him, not having a single family member in his life.

And that poor kid. It's like Atlas all over again, as if one kid feeling that unloved by their mother wasn't enough.

My phone chimes, indicating I have a text. I smile when I see it's from him. I smile even bigger when I see how long the text is.

Thank you for being the most comforting part of my life right now. Thank you for always being the beacon I need every time I feel lost. Whether you mean to shine on me or not. I am grateful for you. I've missed you. I absolutely should have kissed you.

I'm covering my mouth with my hand when I finish reading it. I'm filled with so much emotion, I don't know where to put it.

Josh is lucky to have you in his life now.

Within seconds, Atlas hearts my text. Then I send another one.

And you're right. You absolutely should have kissed me.

Atlas hearts that text, too.

Chapter Seventeen
Atlas

Josh doesn't trust me, but I'll wear him down. I'm willing to bet he doesn't trust anyone, so I'm not taking it personally. If his childhood is anything like mine was, I'm sure he's been toughened at the age of twelve in a way that no kid should be familiar with.

As much as he glares at me with distrustful eyes, I can also sense that he's curious about me. He doesn't ask many questions, but he watches me in a way that makes it obvious he has a million questions on the tip of his tongue. For whatever reason, he keeps swallowing them down. He's probably wondering why I went so easy on him last night after finding out he's the one who damaged my restaurants. He's also probably wondering why I didn't know about him, and how I turned out so vastly different from my mother and Tim.

Whatever he's wondering, he's attempting to keep a tight lid on his expressions. I don't want to make him feel uncomfortable, so I've been doing most of the talking while he eats breakfast. It's not that hard; I have just as many questions for him as he does for me. It's one of the reasons I couldn't sleep last night when we finally made it to my house. I kept listening for the sound of him trying to sneak out of the house. I was honestly shocked he was still here this morning.

As much as my questions are probably annoying him, I can remember what it was like to be twelve. All I wanted was for someone to be interested in who I was, even if they were faking interest. If his life is anything like mine was, he's gone twelve years being ignored, and I refuse to allow him to feel that way under my roof. But I've only been asking him safe questions. I'll ease into the more difficult stuff.

Josh eats one thing at a time. A biscuit first, then bacon. He's cutting into the pancakes for the first time when I say, "What are you interested in? Any hobbies?"

He takes a bite, and one of his eyebrows raises a bit, but I don't know if it's because of the food or my question. "Why?"

"Why am I asking you what you're interested in?"

His neck is stiff when he nods.

"I've missed twelve years of your life. I want to know who you are."

Josh breaks eye contact and forks more pancakes into his mouth. "Manga," he mutters.

That surprises me. But thanks to Theo, I actually know what manga is. "What's your favorite series?"

"*One Piece.*" He shakes his head, erasing that answer. "No, *Chainsaw Man* is probably my favorite."

That's about as far into that conversation as I can go without sounding ignorant. "We can go to a bookstore later today if you want."

He nods. "These are good pancakes."

"Thanks."

I watch him take a drink of his juice, and when he sets the glass down, he says, "What are you interested in?" He nods toward the plate. "Other than cooking."

I don't know how to answer that. Most of my time is given to my restaurants. Whatever time I have left over is spent on house repairs, laundry, sleep. "I like the Cooking Channel."

Josh chuckles. "That's sad."

"Why?"

"I said besides cooking."

It's a harder question than I thought, now that it's being thrown back at me. "I like museums," I say. "And going to the movies. And traveling. I just don't do any of those things."

"Because you're always working?"

"Yeah."

"Like I said. Sad." He leans over his plate to catch another bite of pancake.

The get-to-know-you questions are backfiring, so I cut right to the chase. "What was your fight about?"

He shrugs. "Half the time I don't even know what the hell I do wrong. She just gets mad for no reason."

I can relate to that. I let him eat for a while before I pose another question. "Where have you been staying?"

Josh doesn't look at me. He scoots food around on his plate for a moment, and then says, "Your restaurant." His eyes slowly journey back over to mine. "You have a really comfortable couch in your office."

"You've been sleeping *inside* the restaurant? For how long?"

"Two weeks."

I'm in shock. "How have you been getting in?"

"You don't have an alarm at that one restaurant, and I finally figured out how to pick the lock after a few tries. Your other restaurant was too hard to get into, though."

"You know how to pick . . ." I can't help but laugh. Brad and Darin are going to love saying *I told you so*. "Why'd you go from sleeping there to vandalizing it?"

Josh looks at me reluctantly. "I don't know. I guess I was mad." He pushes his plate away and leans back in his chair. "What now? Do I have to go back to her?"

"What do you want to happen?"

"I want to live with my dad." He scratches at his elbow. "Can you help me find him?"

I want to find Tim about as much as I wanted to find my mother, which is not at all. "Do you know anything about him?"

"I think he lives in Vermont now. I just don't know where."

"When's the last time you saw him?"

"A few years ago. But he doesn't know where to find me anymore."

Josh looks every bit his age right now. A fragile kid, abandoned by his father but refusing to lose hope. I don't want to be the one to rip that from him, so I just nod. "Yeah, I'll see what I can do. But for now, I need to let your mother know you're okay. I have to call her."

"Why?"

"If I don't, this could be considered kidnapping."

"Not if I'm here willingly," he says.

"Even if you're here willingly. You aren't old enough to decide where you want to live, and right now, your mother has legal custody of you."

He grows visibly irritated. He stabs at his breakfast with a scowl, but doesn't take another bite.

I step away to call Sutton. I unblocked her number after she left my restaurant last night in case she needed to get in touch with me. I dial her number and put the phone to my ear. After a few rings, she finally answers with a very groggy hello.

"Hey. I found him."

"Who is this?"

I briefly close my eyes while I wait for her to wake up and remember her son is missing. After a few quiet seconds, she goes, "Atlas?"

"Yeah. I found Josh."

I can hear rustling from her end like she's hopping out of bed. "Where has he been?"

I really don't want to answer that. I know she's his mother, but I feel like it's none of her business where he's been, which is an unusual opinion to have. "I'm not sure where he's been, but he's with me now. Listen . . . I was wondering if he could stay here for a while? Maybe give you a break?"

"You want him to stay there with *you*?" The way she puts the emphasis on that last word makes me wince. This is going to be harder than I thought. She's the type of person who fights for the sake of fighting, no matter what outcome she really wants.

I could enroll him in school and make sure he attends," I offer up. "Take the truancy heat off you." It's quiet on her end, like maybe she's contemplating that.

"Such a *martyr*," she mutters. "Bring him back. Now." She ends the call.

I attempt to call her back three times, but she sends the calls to voice mail.

"That didn't sound promising," Josh says. He's standing

in the doorway of the kitchen. I'm not sure how much he heard on my end, but at least he couldn't hear her end.

I slide my phone in my pocket. "She wants you back today. But I'll call a lawyer tomorrow. Hell, I'll call Child Protective Services if you want me to. There's just not much I can do on a Sunday."

Josh's shoulders drop when I say that. "Will you at least give me your phone number?" He asks that like he's scared I'm going to say no.

"Of course. I'm not going to abandon you now that I know you exist."

He picks at a hole in his sleeve, avoiding eye contact with me when he says, "I wouldn't blame you for being mad at me. I cost you a lot of money."

"You did do that," I say. "Those croutons were expensive."

Josh laughs for the first time this morning. "Dude, those croutons were fucking *delicious*."

I groan. "Don't use that word."

$\bullet \quad \bullet \quad \bullet$

The Risemore Inn is clear on the other side of Boston. It takes us forty-five minutes with traffic to get there, and it's not even a weekday. When we pull into the parking lot, Josh doesn't immediately get out of the car. He just sits quietly in the passenger seat, staring at the building like it's the last place he wants to be.

I wish I didn't have to return him to his mother, but I put in another call to my lawyer friend this morning after talking with Sutton. He said if I want to go about this the right way without her having ammunition against me, the only thing I can do is return him. And then, if I want to take her to court, he said I need to get a lawyer and go through the process.

Anything done *outside* the process could be a mark against me.

Apparently, you can't just kidnap your sibling, even if you know they're in danger.

I wanted to explain all of this to Josh in more detail—to let him know I'm not just abandoning him with her—but he's so hell-bent that he's going to live with his dad, I'm not sure he even wants to live with me. And I'm not sure I'm prepared to raise a little brother, but as long as I'm alive, there's no way I can willingly leave him in this woman's permanent custody without at least trying.

Until I can figure out what to do next, I don't want him to find himself in a situation where he has no food to eat, or no money to extend their hotel stay. I pull out my wallet and hand him a credit card.

"Can I trust you with this?"

Josh looks at the credit card in my hand, and his eyes grow a little wide. "I don't know why you would. I've spent the last two weeks trying to destroy your businesses."

I push the credit card toward him. "Use it for basic necessities. Food, minutes for your phone." We stopped on the way here and got him a prepaid phone so he could stay in touch with me. "Maybe some new clothes that fit."

Josh reluctantly takes the credit card out of my hand. "I don't even know how to use one of these."

"You just swipe it. But don't tell Sutton you have it." I

point at his phone. "Hide it between your case and your phone."

He pops the case off his phone and puts the credit card inside of it. Then he says, "Thank you." He puts his hand on the car door. "Are you coming to talk to her?"

I shake my head. "It's probably best if I don't. It'll probably just make her angrier."

Josh sighs, and then gets out of the car. We stare at each other for a few seconds before he finally closes the car door.

I feel like such a dick bringing him back here. But I have to do this the right way. If I don't return him, she could file charges on me. And knowing her, she probably would. It's best if I just leave him for today and then as soon as the week begins tomorrow, I can make phone calls and figure out what I can do to move him in with me.

I know if he stays here with her, he isn't going to have a chance in hell. I lucked out finding Lily. She saved my life. But I'm not sure there's enough luck in the world for *both* of us to be saved by a random stranger.

I'm all he has.

I remain in my car as Josh makes his way across the parking lot. He walks up the stairs and knocks on the second door from the end. He looks over his shoulder at me, so I wave right as the door swings open.

I can see the rage in Sutton's eyes all the way from my position in the parking lot. She immediately begins yelling at him. *And then she slaps him.*

My hand is on the door handle before Josh even has a chance to react to the slap. Sutton's hand is now gripping Josh's arm as she yanks him into the hotel room. I'm several feet away from my car when I see him trip over the threshold and disappear into the room.

I'm taking the stairs two at a time, my heart racing. I reach the door before she even closes it. Josh is still trying to scramble to his feet, but she's hovering over him, scolding him.

"I could have gone to *jail*, you little shit!"

She has no idea I'm behind her. I wrap my arm around her waist and pull her away from Josh by picking her up and dropping her onto the mattress behind me. It happens so fast, she's too shocked to react.

I help Josh to his feet. His phone is a few feet away on the floor, so I grab it and hand it to him, then urge him toward the door.

Sutton realizes what's happening, and she jumps off the bed. She's following us out the door. "Bring him back!" I feel her hands on me now. She's yanking at my shirt, trying to get me to stop or move aside so she can get to Josh.

I urge him forward. "Go to the car." He continues toward the stairs, and then I stop walking and spin around to face her. She sucks in a quick gasp after seeing the absolute fury in my eyes. Then she slaps her palms against my chest and shoves me.

"He's *my* son!" she yells. "I'll call the police!"

I release an exasperated laugh. I want to tell her to call the police. I want to scream at her. But most of all, I want to get Josh away from her. She's not going to ruin his life on my watch.

I don't even have the energy to say anything to her at all. This woman isn't worth my words. I just walk away, leaving her screaming at me like old times.

Josh is already sitting in the front seat of my car when I make it back. I slam my door and grip my steering wheel with both hands before starting the car. I need to calm myself down before I get back on the road.

Josh seems unusually calm for what just happened. It makes me wonder if that's an average interaction between them because he isn't even breathing heavily. He's not crying. He's not cussing. He's just watching me, and I realize how I react in this moment is quite possibly something he'll absorb for a lifetime.

I slide my hands down the steering wheel and calmly exhale.

Josh's cheek is red, and there's a small gash on his forehead that's bleeding. I retrieve a napkin from the glove box and hand it to him, then flip the visor down so he can see where to wipe.

"I saw her slap you, but where'd the cut come from?"

"I think I hit the TV stand."

Slow and steady, Atlas. I put my car in reverse and back out of the parking lot. "Maybe we should swing by the emergency room and have them check out your cut. Make sure you don't have a concussion."

"It's okay. I can usually tell when it's a concussion."

He can usually tell? I clench my jaw as soon as he says that. I realize I have absolutely no idea what kind of hell this kid has already been through, and I was about to send him right back into the fire. "Better to be safe," I say, but what I mean is, *Better to get this documented in case we need proof of her abuse at a later date.*

Chapter Eighteen
Lily

It's been five days since I've seen Atlas. I try not to stress over how busy we are because I know it'll get better once I'm comfortable enough to let him spend time around Emmy. But the responsible thing to do is to let Emmy's father know when I start seeing someone else before I bring anyone around her.

It's just frustrating that the responsible thing to do is also a terrifying thing to do. I plan to put it off for as long as possible. There's no shame in being patient.

The flower shop is understaffed this week with Lucy's upcoming wedding, and Atlas has been dealing with legal stuff regarding custody, running two businesses, and taking care of a kid. On top of all that, the fever my mother had last week turned into the full-fledged flu, so she hasn't been able to watch Emmy at all. I've brought her with me two out of the three days I've worked this week.

It's just been a week from hell. Too busy to even get a drive-by hug.

Ryle and Marshall took the girls to the zoo today. Emmy is more than likely too young to enjoy it, so it should make for an interesting day for Ryle.

The custody exchange was fine this morning, even though we haven't spoken since our conversation on the roof last week about her middle name. He was a little curt, but I prefer his curtness to the subtle passes he sometimes still makes at me.

Allysa is working with me today since she doesn't have Rylee. She just returned with coffee now that we're caught up on everything. We got all our orders out with the delivery truck an hour ago, so this is the first time we've actually had time to speak in private since my date with Atlas last week.

Allysa hands me my coffee and then taps the mouse on the computer to check for new online orders.

"What are you wearing to Lucy's wedding?" I ask her.

"We're not going."

"What?"

"We can't. It's my parents' fortieth wedding anniversary. Ryle and I are doing that surprise dinner."

She told me about that, but I had no idea it was the same day as Lucy's wedding.

"It's the only evening Ryle could get away," she says.

I deflate. I hate Ryle's schedule. I know it'll get better over time, when he's no longer one of the newest surgeons on staff, but even when his hours aren't making custody difficult, he's making my best friend choose between a wedding and her parents.

I know it's not Ryle's fault, but I like silently blaming stuff on him that he has no control over. It feels good.

"Does Lucy know you aren't going?"

Allysa nods. "She's fine with it. Two less mouths to feed." She takes a sip of her coffee. "Are you taking Atlas?"

"I didn't invite him. I thought you and Marshall were going, and I didn't want to ask you and Marshall to lie for me again." I felt bad that I asked Allysa to watch Emmy last week for my date because I knew she'd have to lie to Ryle if it came up. And she *did* end up having to lie to him.

"When are you planning to tell Ryle you're back on the dating scene?"

I groan. "Do I have to?"

"He'll find out eventually."

"I wish I could just pretend I was dating some guy named Greg. I don't know that he'd be as threatened by a Greg. Maybe I don't have to be specific about who I'm dating, and he won't be as angry. I'll ease him into the knowledge of it being Atlas after a decade or two."

Allysa laughs, but then she looks at me curiously. "Why does Ryle hate Atlas so much, anyway?"

"He didn't like that I kept mementos from back when Atlas and I dated."

Allysa is staring at me. Waiting. "What else?"

I shake my head. There's nothing else. "What do you mean?"

"Did you cheat on Ryle with Atlas?"

"*What?* No. *God*, no. I never would have done that to Ryle." I'm a little offended by her question, but then again I'm not. Ryle's reaction would naturally make anyone question what led to that kind of reaction.

Allysa's eyes are swimming in puzzlement. "I still don't get it. If you weren't actively cheating on him with the guy, why does Ryle hate him?"

I release an exaggerated sigh. "I've asked myself that a million times, Allysa."

She makes an annoyed face only siblings could reserve

for each other. "I never wanted to ask because I thought you were ashamed that you cheated on my brother and just didn't want to tell me."

"I haven't even kissed Atlas since I was sixteen. Ryle just couldn't handle that my past sometimes crept into my present, in an absolutely platonic way."

"Wait. You haven't kissed Atlas since you were sixteen?" She latched on to the absolute wrong point of this conversation. "Not even on your date last week?"

"We're taking it slow. And that's fine by me. The slower we take things, the more time it gives me before I have to break it to your brother."

"I think you should just rip off the Band-Aid." She points at my phone on the counter. "Text Ryle right now and tell him you're dating Atlas. He'll get over it; he doesn't have a choice."

"This is something I need to tell him in person."

"You're too considerate."

"You're too naïve. If you think Ryle is going to *get over it*, you don't know your brother very well."

"I've never claimed to." Allysa sighs and drops her chin into her hand. "Marshall told me he told you I cheated on him."

I am so glad she's changing the subject. "Yeah, that was a shock."

"Drunken mistake. I was nineteen; nothing counts before you turn twenty-one."

I laugh. "Is that right?"

"Yep." She hops on the counter and starts swinging her legs. "Tell me more about Atlas. Tell me like I'm your best friend and not your ex-husband's sister."

And we're back to this conversation. That was a quick break. "You sure this isn't awkward for you?"

"Why, because Ryle is my brother? No, not awkward at all. He should have been nicer to you, and then you wouldn't have to date Greek gods." She wiggles her eyebrows with a grin. "So, what's he like? He seems mysterious."

"He's not, really. Not to me." I can feel the smile wanting to spread across my face, so I let it. "He's so easy to talk to. And he's kind. He's *Marshall* kind, but not as outgoing. He's more reserved. He works a lot, and I have Emmy all the time, so it's been hard to make time for anything together. Plus, he just found out he has a little brother this week, so his life is kind of chaotic right now. Texts and phone calls are our primary source of communication, so that sucks."

"Is that why you keep checking your phone?"

I can feel my cheeks warm when she says that. I hate that she's noticed. I've tried my best to be inconspicuous with this. I don't want anyone to know how often Atlas and I text, or how often I *think* about texting him, or how often I think *about* him.

Maybe I'm scared to talk about it with Allysa because I don't want to allow myself to be happy about Atlas until I know Ryle isn't going to be furious over Atlas.

I receive a text right in the middle of that thought, and it takes everything in me to fight my smile when I look at my phone and read it.

"Is that him?" Allysa asks.

I nod.

"What's he saying?"

"He asked me if I want him to bring me lunch."

"*Yes*," Allysa says emphatically. "Tell him you're starving, and so is your friend."

I laugh and then reply to Atlas with, **Could you bring lunch for two today? My coworker gets jealous when you bring me food.**

He immediately replies with, **Be there in an hour.**

•   •   •

When Atlas finally shows up, both Allysa and I are busy with customers. He's carrying a brown paper bag. I motion for him to wait by the counter, so he stands patiently while we finish up. Allysa is finished first, and for at least five minutes, she and Atlas are having a conversation I can't hear from this side of the shop. I'm trying to give my attention to the customer in front of me, but knowing Allysa is speaking freely to Atlas has me more than nervous. I never know what's going to come out of her mouth.

Atlas looks pleased, though. Whatever she's telling him, he's enjoying it.

It feels like a decade later when I'm finally free to join them. Atlas leans in and greets me with a kiss on the cheek when I reach him. His fingers graze my elbow for several seconds after our greeting before he pulls his hand away. That simple physical gesture sends a current through me, making it hard to focus without being too obvious that I get giddy around him.

Allysa smiles at me knowingly. "Adam Brody, huh?"

I have no idea what she's referring to until I look at Atlas and he's grinning. I had a poster of Adam Brody on my bedroom wall the first time Atlas came to my house.

I shove Atlas's arm. "I was fifteen!"

He laughs, and I love that Allysa is being nice to him. I know she has every right to give complete loyalty to her brother, but it's not in her to be rude to people simply because other people don't like them.

She's not a ride-or-die friend, nor is she a ride-or-die sister. That's what I love the most about her, because I'm not ride-or-die, either. If you do something stupid, I'm going to be the friend who tells you you're doing something stupid. I'm not going to join you in your stupidity.

I want my friends to treat me the same way. I prefer honesty over loyalty any day, because with honesty *comes* loyalty.

"Thank you for lunch," I say. "Did you get Josh's school situation settled?"

Atlas has been working to enroll him in a school more local to where he lives, rather than the school Josh was in all the way across town.

"I did. Fingers crossed they don't look too hard into the enrollment forms I had to fill out. I lied a little."

"I'm sure it'll be fine," I say. "I can't wait to meet him."

"How old is he?" Allysa asks.

"He just turned twelve," Atlas says.

"Whoa," Allysa says. "Worst age ever. But at least you don't have to pay for day care. Silver lining." Allysa snaps her fingers. "Speaking of children, Lily won't have Emerson next Saturday because she's going to a wedding. A night out all by herself as a single adult."

I roll my head and look at her. "I was about to invite him. I didn't need your help."

Atlas perks up. "A wedding, huh?" A sly smile plays on his lips. "You plan on sleeping through it?"

I immediately blush, and that makes Allysa curious. Atlas turns to her and says, "She didn't tell you she slept through our first date?"

I'm not even looking at Allysa, but I can feel her staring. "I was tired," I say, excusing the inexcusable. "It was an accident."

"Oh, I absolutely need more of this story," Allysa says.

"She fell asleep on our drive there. Slept in a parking lot for over an hour. We never even made it into the restaurant."

Allysa starts laughing, and I kind of want to crawl under the counter and hide now.

"Who's getting married?" Atlas asks me.

"My friend Lucy. She works here."

"What time?"

"It's at seven. Nighttime wedding if you can swing it."

"I can." Atlas does this thing with his eyes where he briefly looks like he wishes we were alone. It's sending tingles of warmth crawling down my spine. "I need to get back. Enjoy your lunch." He nods at Allysa. "It was nice officially meeting you."

"You too," she says.

He gets halfway to the exit when he starts whistling. He walks away in a cheerful mood, and it makes my heart swell to see him so happy. I have no idea if his good mood has anything to do with me, but the teenage girl in me who was worried about him all those years ago is extremely pleased to see him doing so well in life.

"What's wrong with him?"

When I glance at Allysa, she's staring curiously at the door Atlas just disappeared out of. "What do you mean?"

"Why isn't he married? Why doesn't he have a girl-friend?"

"Hopefully he'll have a girlfriend soon." I can't say it without smiling.

"He's probably bad in bed. Maybe that's why he's single."

"He is definitely not bad in bed."

Her jaw drops. "You said you haven't even kissed him yet; how would you know?"

"As *adults*," I say. "You forget I have a history with him. He was my first, and he was very, very good. And I'm sure he's gotten even better."

Allysa stares at me for a beat, then says, "I'm happy for you, Lily." But she's frowning. "Marshall is going to like him, too. He's so *likable*." She says that like it's the worst possible outcome.

"And that's a bad thing?"

"I don't know if it's a *good* thing," she says. "This whole thing is muddled; you know that. I don't need to explain it to you. But I can absolutely see why you're hesitant to tell Ryle. Knowing his ex-wife is sharing a bed with that block of perfection has to be extremely emasculating."

I raise a brow. "Not as emasculating as beating your wife should feel." I'm a little shocked when the words come out of my mouth, but I can't take them back. I don't think I need to, though, because luckily, my best friend isn't a ride-or-die sister.

Rather than be offended, Allysa agrees with a nod. "Touché, Lily. Touché."

Chapter Nineteen
Atlas

I have no idea if twelve is too young to take an Uber, but I didn't want to leave Josh at my place alone after school again, so I had one drop him off here at the restaurant. We discussed earlier this week that he should probably help out up here to pay off the damages he accrued.

I've been watching the Uber on a map, so I meet him out front. When he gets out of the car, he looks like a completely different kid from the one I met several days ago. He's wearing clothes that fit him, I took him for a haircut yesterday, and he's carrying a backpack full of books rather than cans of spray paint.

I doubt Sutton would even recognize him if she saw him.

"How was school?" Today was his second day at the new school. Yesterday he said it was okay but didn't expand.

"It was okay."

I guess that's as much as I'll get from a twelve-year-old. I open the door to my restaurant, and Josh pauses before walking in. He looks up at the building and assesses it. "Funny how I slept here for two weeks but this is the first time ever I'm walking through the entrance."

I laugh and follow him into the restaurant. I'm excited for him to meet Theo, even though I haven't had a chance to tell Theo about Josh yet. Theo arrived a few minutes ago and came through the back right as I was heading toward the front to fetch Josh.

Theo hasn't been to the restaurant since last week, and I haven't brought Josh around because I had to take some time off in order to attempt to get his life straightened out. When we walk through the double doors that lead to the busy kitchen, Josh pauses in wonder. He stares wide-eyed at the commotion. I'm sure the place is a lot different during the day than it was when he'd sleep here at night.

The door to my office is open, which means Theo must be in there doing his homework. I lead Josh in that direction, and he follows me as we make our way into the office. Theo is seated at my desk, reading. He looks up at me, then looks at Josh. He leans back in the desk chair and pulls in his chin. "What are you doing here?"

"What are *you* doing here?" Josh asks Theo.

They're asking each other this like they know each other. I didn't think they would since the schools here are so big, and there are so many. I wasn't even sure which school Theo attended. "Do you two know each other?"

Theo says to me, "Yeah, he's a new kid at my school." Then to Josh, he says, "But how do you know Atlas?"

Josh drops his backpack and nudges his head toward me as he plops onto the sofa. "He's my brother."

Theo looks at me and then at Josh. Then at me. "Why didn't I know you had a brother?"

"Long story," I say.

"Don't you think that's something your therapist should know about?"

"You haven't been here all week," I say.

"I had math practice after school every day," he says.

"Math practice? How does one practice math?"

Josh pipes in. "Wait. Theo is your *therapist*?"

Theo answers him with, "Yeah, but he doesn't pay me. Hey, did you get Trent for math?"

"No, I got Sully," Josh says.

"Bummer." Theo looks over at me, and then back at Josh. Then back at me. "How have you never mentioned you have a brother?" Theo can't seem to get past that fact, but I don't have time to explain it to him right now. The kitchen is running behind.

"Josh can tell you. I have a kitchen to run." I leave them in the office and head back to help out with all the chits we're behind on.

I like that they know each other, but I like it even more that Theo seemed comfortable around him. I know Theo much better than I know my little brother, and I feel like Theo would have had some sort of reaction if he was displeased to see Josh.

·   ·   ·

About an hour later, the kitchen is fully staffed, and I have a few minutes to break free. When I walk into the office, Josh and Theo are having what looks like an intense discussion about a manga Theo is holding. "Sorry to interrupt." I motion for Josh to follow me. "You finish your homework?"

"Sure," he says.

"'Sure'?" I don't know him well enough to know what kind of answer *sure* is. "Is that a yes? A no? A mostly?"

"Yes." He sighs, following me out of the kitchen. "Mostly. I'll finish it tonight; my brain hurts."

I introduce him to a few people in the kitchen, finishing with Brad. "Josh, this is Brad. He's Theo's father." I gesture toward Josh. "This is Josh, my little brother." Brad wrinkles his forehead in confusion but says nothing. "Josh has a debt to pay off. You have any work for him?"

"I have debt?" Josh asks, befuddled.

"Crouton debt."

"Oh. That."

Brad immediately puts two and two together. He nods slowly, and then says to Josh, "You ever washed dishes?"

Josh rolls his eyes and follows Brad to the sink.

I feel bad making him work, but I'd feel even worse if there weren't any consequences to the thousands of dollars he cost me. I'll let him do dishes for an hour and then we'll call it even.

I mostly just wanted him out of my office so I could talk to Theo about him. I haven't had a chance to talk to him without Josh in the room.

Theo is at my desk, stuffing papers into his backpack. I sit on the couch, prepared to ask him about Josh, but Theo speaks first. "You kiss Lily yet?"

Always about me, never about him.

"Not yet."

"What the heck, Atlas? I swear, you are so lame sometimes."

"How well do you know Josh?" I ask, changing the subject.

"He's only been in school for two days, so not super well. We have a couple of classes together."

"How's he doing in that school?"

"No clue. I'm not his teacher."

"I don't mean his grades. I mean his interactions. Is he making friends? Is he nice?"

Theo tilts his head. "You're asking *me* if your brother is nice? Shouldn't you know?"

"I just met him."

"Yeah, me too," Theo says. "And you're asking me a loaded question. Kids are mean sometimes. You know that."

"Are you saying Josh is mean?"

"There are different kinds of mean. Josh is the better kind of mean."

I'm not following at all. Theo can see that, so he expands. "He's like a bully to the bullies, if that makes sense."

This conversation is making me uncomfortable. "So Josh is . . . *king* of the bullies? That sounds bad."

Theo rolls his eyes. "It's hard to explain. But I'm sure it's not surprising that I'm not the most popular kid in that school. I'm on the math team, and I'm . . ." He shrugs off the last word. "But I don't have to worry about kids like Josh. When you ask me if he's nice, I don't know how to answer that, because he isn't nice. But he isn't mean, either. Or at least he isn't mean to the nice people."

I don't speak up immediately because I'm trying to absorb all this information. I might be more confused than I was before this conversation. But it does make me feel good to know that Theo isn't scared of Josh.

"Anyway," Theo says, zipping his backpack. "You and Lily. Did it fizzle out already?"

"No, we're just busy. I'm going to a wedding with her tomorrow, though."

"You finally gonna kiss her?"

"If she wants me to."

Theo nods. "She probably will as long as you refrain from saying anything cheesy, like, *Look at the ships, let's lock lips!*"

I grab one of the couch pillows and throw it at him. "I'm getting a new therapist who doesn't bully me."

Chapter Twenty
Lily

It's challenging being the florist for a wedding *and* a guest. I've been running all day to make sure the flowers at the venue were set up the way Lucy wanted them. And on top of that, we're closing early for the wedding, so Serena needed help getting all the deliveries completed and onto the truck.

By the time Atlas makes it to my apartment to pick me up, I'm not even close to being ready. I just received a text from him asking if he should come up. I'm sure he's cautious because everything is so new with us, and he doesn't know who might be here if he were to knock on the door, and if I'd want them to know Atlas is my date to the wedding.

I was hesitant to invite him to the wedding for that very reason, but I'm confident no one at Lucy's wedding would even know Ryle. We run in different circles. And on the off chance they do know Ryle, and it might get back to him that I was with someone, the risk is worth the reward. I've been looking forward to this night since Atlas agreed to come with me.

Come up, I'm still getting ready.

Atlas knocks at my door moments later. When I open the door to let him in, my eyes feel like they might double in size like they do in the cartoons. "Wow." I'm staring at him all dressed up in his black designer suit. He stands in the hallway for longer than I'd normally make someone wait before inviting them in because I forget basic things like hospitality when I'm in his presence.

He's holding a bouquet, but it isn't flowers. It's *cookies*.

He hands them to me. "Figured you get enough flowers," he says. He leans in and kisses my cheek, and I want to tilt my face just enough so that his lips land on mine, but hopefully I won't have to be patient for much longer.

"These are perfect," I say, motioning for him to enter. "Come in. I need, like, fifteen minutes to get dressed."

I've been so busy today, I haven't even had a chance to eat. I open one of the cookies and bite into it. Then, with a mouthful, I say, "I'm sorry if this is tacky. I'm starving." I point toward my bedroom. "You can wait in my room with me while I get ready; it won't take me long."

Atlas is looking around, taking everything in as he follows me to my bedroom.

My dress is laid out on the bed, so I pick it up and walk to my bathroom. I leave the door cracked a bit so that I can talk to him while I change. "Where's Josh?"

"You remember Brad from that poker night?"

"I do, actually."

"His son, Theo, is at my house with Josh. They go to school together."

"How's he liking school?"

I can't see Atlas, but he's closer to the bathroom when he says, "Fine, I guess." It sounds like he's right next to the door. I slip the dress over my head and open the door farther. I chose a merlot-colored fitted dress with spaghetti straps. It has a matching shawl, but it's still hanging in the closet.

Atlas looks me over when I appear in the doorway. His eyes journey up the length of me, but I don't give him time to compliment me.

"Can you zip me up?" I give him my back and lift my hair, but I can feel him hesitate. Or maybe he's soaking in the moment.

A couple of seconds later, I feel his fingers press against my back as he raises the zipper. It sends chills rolling over my skin. When he's finished, I drop my hair and turn and face him. "I need to put on makeup." I start to back into the bathroom, but Atlas grips my waist.

"Come here," he says, pulling me until I smush against him. He admires my face for a couple of seconds, smiling appreciatively. Seductively. Like he's about to kiss me. "Thank you for inviting me."

I return the smile. "Thank you for coming. I know you've had a busy week."

Atlas's eyes look tired. The usual glimmer has dulled a little, like he's been stressed and could use a night of relaxation. I can't help but touch his cheek when I say, "We can Uber there if you want. You seem like you could use a drink."

Atlas touches my hand that's cupping his cheek. He tilts his face so that he can kiss the inside of my palm. Then he pulls my hand away and threads his fingers through it. He opens his mouth to say something else, but I see it the second his eyes get a glimpse of my tattoo.

Atlas has never seen the heart tattoo on my shoulder—the one I got because he always used to kiss me there. He touches it softly with his fingers, tracing the shape of it. His eyes flicker up to mine. "When did you get this?"

My voice catches, and I'm forced to clear my throat. "In college." I've thought about this moment a lot—what he would say if he ever saw it, how it would make him feel.

He quietly regards me and then looks at the tattoo again. He's so close, I can feel his breath trickling across my collarbone. "Why'd you get it?"

I got it for so many reasons, but I choose to say the most obvious one. "Because. I missed you."

I wait for him to lower his head and press a kiss there like he's done so many times before. I wait for him to kiss *me*. To press his mouth to mine in a silent thank-you.

Atlas doesn't do any of those things. He continues staring at the tattoo for a beat, but then he releases his hold on me and turns away. His voice is detached when he says, "You should probably finish getting ready or we'll be late." He takes a couple of steps toward my bedroom door, and then, without looking back, he says, "I'll wait in the living room."

I feel like I just got the breath knocked out of me.

His entire demeanor changed. It wasn't at all what I expected from him. I stand frozen in place for a few depressing seconds, but then I force myself to finish getting ready. Maybe I'm misreading his reaction and it wasn't a negative one. Maybe he liked it so much, he needed alone time to process.

Whatever the reason is for his unexpected reaction, I fight back the sting of tears the entire time I'm trying to do my makeup. I can't help it. I think my feelings might be hurt, and that's not something I expected to happen tonight at all.

I go to my closet and find my shoes and grab my shawl, and I half expect Atlas to be gone when I walk out of my bedroom, but he's still here. He's standing by the wall in the hallway looking at pictures of Emmy. When he hears me exit the bedroom, he looks in my direction, and then full-on turns to face me.

"Wow." He looks genuinely pleased when I'm back in his presence, so the whiplash is a little confusing. "You're beautiful, Lily."

I appreciate his compliment, but I can't move past what just happened. And if there's one thing I've learned from the relationship I was in before and the relationship I witnessed between my parents, it's that I refuse to be someone who brushes everything under a rug. I don't even want there to be a rug.

"Why did my tattoo upset you?"

My question catches him off guard. He fidgets with his tie, and seems to be looking for an excuse, but nothing comes to him, and the hallway remains silent, other than a ragged, slow breath he pulls in. "It wasn't the tattoo."

"What is it? Why are you mad at me?"

"I'm not mad at you, Lily." He says that convincingly, but he's not the same after seeing the tattoo, and I don't want us to start out with lies. Apparently, he doesn't, either, because I can see him working through what to say to me next. He looks uncomfortable, like he doesn't want to have this conversation, or at least he doesn't want to have it right now.

He shoves his hands in the pockets of his pants and sighs. "That night I took you to the emergency room . . . they bandaged up your shoulder while we were there." His voice sounds pained, but when he makes eye contact with me, that pained sound is nothing compared to the turmoil in his expression. "I heard you tell the nurse he bit you, but I wasn't close enough to see that . . ." Atlas pauses midsentence and swallows hard. "I wasn't close enough to see that you had the tattoo, and that he bit . . ." Atlas stops speaking again. He's so upset, he can't even finish his sentence. He just moves on to another one. "Is that why he did it? Because he read your journals and knew you got the tattoo for me?"

My knees feel shaky.

I can see why Atlas didn't want to have this conversation. It's too much for a casual chat while we're on our way out the door. I press a hand flat against my nervous stomach, prepared to answer him, but it's hard to talk about. Especially knowing how upset it's making Atlas on my behalf.

I don't want to hurt him, but I also don't want to lie to him, or protect Ryle in any way. Because Atlas is right. That's exactly why Ryle did what he did, and I hate that Atlas will now forever pair my tattoo with that awful memory.

My lack of response is enough confirmation for him. He winces and turns away from me. I can see the deep breath he forces himself to take in order to remain calm. He looks like he wants to explode, but Ryle isn't here for him to explode on.

Atlas is so angry, but this is an anger I'm not afraid of.

I realize the significance of this moment. I'm alone with an angry man in my apartment, but I'm not in fear for my life, because he isn't angry at me. He's angry at the person who *hurt* me. It's a protective anger, and there's a world of difference between my reactions to Ryle's anger versus my reaction to Atlas's anger.

When Atlas turns to me again, I can see the hard set of

his jaw and the veins in his neck when he says, "How am I supposed to be civil around him, Lily?" There's guilt in his voice when he whispers, "I should have been there for you. I should have done more."

I can understand the anger, but Atlas has absolutely nothing to feel guilty for. I wasn't at a point in my life where Atlas could have said or done anything to change my views of Ryle. I had to get to that point on my own.

I walk closer to Atlas and press my back into the wall across from him. He does the same on the opposite wall until we're facing each other. He's working through a lot of emotions right now, and I want to give him the space to do that. But I also have a lot to say about the guilt Atlas is holding on to.

"The first time Ryle hit me, it was because I laughed at him. I was tipsy, and I thought something was funny that wasn't funny, and he backhanded me."

Atlas has to break eye contact after hearing me say that. I don't know if he wants these details, but I've been wanting to say all this to him for a long time. He remains still against the wall, but it looks like it's taking everything in him not to run straight to wherever Ryle is right now. His eyes are sharp when he looks back at me, waiting for me to finish.

"The second time, he pushed me down the stairs. That argument started because he found your number hidden in my phone case. And when he bit me on my shoulder . . . You're right. It was because he read the journals and found out my tattoo was because of you, and that the magnet I kept on my refrigerator was from you." I look down briefly because it's hard seeing how much this is affecting him. "I used to think the things I did somehow warranted his reactions. Like maybe if I wouldn't have laughed, he wouldn't have hit me. Maybe if I didn't have your number in my phone, he wouldn't have gotten angry enough to push me down a flight of stairs."

Atlas isn't even looking at me anymore. His head is leaned back against the wall, and he's staring at the ceiling, taking everything in, frozen in his anger.

"Every time I would start to take on the guilt and justify Ryle's actions, I would think about you. I would ask myself what your reaction would have been compared to Ryle's. Because I know it would have been different. If I would have laughed at you under the same circumstances that I laughed at Ryle, you would have laughed *with* me. You never would have backhanded me. And if any man on this planet gave me their phone number as a way to protect me from someone they feared was dangerous, you would *appreciate* them for that. You wouldn't have pushed me down a flight of stairs. And if the journals I let you read were about another boy in high school besides you, you would have teased me. You probably would have highlighted lines you thought were cheesy and laughed about them with me."

I stop speaking until Atlas brings his focus back to mine, and then I finish. "Every time I would doubt myself and think that what Ryle did to me was in any way deserved, all I had to do was think about you, Atlas. I think about how differently each scenario would have been if it were you, and that helped me remember that none of it was my fault. You're a big part of the reason I got through it, even though you weren't there."

Atlas silently soaks up everything I've said for maybe five seconds, but then he closes the distance between us and kisses me. Finally. *Finally.*

His right hand curls around my waist as he tugs me against him, his tongue sliding gently and warmly against my lips, coaxing his way past them. His left hand snakes its way through my hair until he's molding his palm to the back of my head. A spool of yearning begins to unravel inside me.

He doesn't kiss me with any trepidation. His mouth meets mine with confidence, and mine responds to his with relief. I pull at him, wanting his warmth to sink into me. His mouth and his touch are familiar since we've done this dance before, but completely new at the same time because this kiss is made up of a whole new set of ingredients. Our first kiss was made of fear and youthful inexperience.

This kiss is hope. It's comfort and safety and stability. It's everything I've been missing in my adult life, and I am so happy Atlas and I have each other again, I could cry.

Chapter Twenty-One
Atlas

There have been a lot of things in my life that have made me angry, but nothing filled me with rage like seeing Lily's tattoo and the faded scars that circled it in the shape of a bite mark.

How any man can do that to a woman, I'll never understand. How any *human* can do that to a human they're supposed to love and want to protect, I will never understand.

But what I do understand is that Lily deserves better. And I get to be the one to *give* her better. Starting with this kiss that we can't seem to stop. Every time we pause to look at each other, we go right back to kissing like we have to make up for all the lost time in this one kiss.

I trail kisses down her jaw until I meet her collarbone. I've always loved kissing her there, but until I read her journal, I didn't know she was aware of how much I loved kissing her there. I press my lips to her tattoo, determined to make sure she remembers the good parts of us in all the future kisses I'm going to give her in this spot. If it takes a million kisses for her not to think about the scars that surround her heart tattoo, then I'll kiss her there a million and *one* times.

I press kisses up her neck, then her jaw. When I'm looking at her again, I slide the shoulder strap of her dress back in place because as much as I could stay right here for hours,

I'm supposed to be taking her to a wedding. "We should go," I whisper.

She nods, but I kiss her again. I can't help it. I've been waiting for this moment since I was a teenager.

•   •   •

I can't really say how the wedding went because I was more focused on Lily than anything else. I didn't know anyone there, and after finally kissing Lily tonight, it was hard to focus on anything other than wanting it to happen again. I could tell Lily craved to be alone with me as much as I wanted to be alone with her. Being forced to patiently sit next to her after what happened between us in her hallway was torture.

As soon as we got to the reception and Lily saw how crowded it was, she was relieved. She said Lucy would never know if we left early, and I don't even know Lucy, so I wasn't about to argue with her when, after less than an hour of mingling, she grabbed my hand and we slipped out.

We've just pulled back up to Lily's apartment complex, and while I'm almost positive she wants me to go upstairs with her, I'm not going to assume. I open her door and wait for her to put her shoes back on. She took them off in the car because they were hurting her feet, but they look difficult to fasten. There are strings, and Lily is struggling with them in the passenger seat. I doubt she wants to walk barefoot on the parking garage floor, though.

"I can carry you on my back."

She glances up at me and laughs like I'm joking. "You want to give me a piggyback ride?"

"Yeah, grab your shoes."

She stares at me for a moment, but then she grins like she's excited. I turn around and she's still laughing when she wraps her arms around my neck. I help her hoist herself onto my back and then I kick the car door shut.

When we make it to her apartment, I lean forward so she can use her key to unlock her door. Once we're inside, she's laughing when I lower her to her feet. I turn around just as she drops her shoes and starts to kiss me again.

Picking up right where we left off, I guess.

"What time do you need to be home?" she asks.

"I told Josh ten or eleven." I look at the clock and it's just after ten. "Should I call him and tell him I might be late?"

Lily nods. "You're definitely gonna be late. Call him and I'll make us drinks." She walks to the kitchen, so I take out my phone and call Josh. I video-chat him so I can make sure he's not throwing a party at my house. I doubt Theo would let him, but I'm not taking any chances with either of those two.

When Josh answers the video call, the phone is lying on the floor. I can see his chin and the light from the TV. He's holding a controller. "We're in the middle of a tournament," he says.

"Just checking in. Everything okay?"

"It's fine!" I hear Theo yell.

Josh starts shaking his remote, hitting buttons, but then he yells, "Shit!" He tosses the controller aside and picks up the phone, bringing it closer to his face. "We lost."

Theo appears behind him. "That doesn't look like a wedding. Where are you?"

I don't answer him. "I might be a little late tonight."

"Oh, are you at Lily's?" Theo says, moving closer to the phone screen. He's grinning. "Did you finally kiss her? Can she hear me? What line did you use to get her to invite you in? *Lily! We watched people wed, let's hop into—*"

I immediately end the call before he finishes that rhyme, but Lily heard that whole conversation. She's standing a few feet away from me, holding two glasses of wine. Her head is tilted in confusion. "Who was that?"

"Theo."

"How old is he?"

"Twelve."

"You talk to a twelve-year-old about us?"

She seems amused by this. I take a glass of wine from her, and right before I sip it, I say, "He's my therapist. We meet every Thursday at four."

She laughs. "Your therapist is in junior high?"

"Yeah, but he's about to get fired." I wrap my hand around Lily's waist and pull her to me. When I kiss her, she tastes like the red wine she poured. I kiss her deeper to get more of that taste. More of her.

When she pulls back, she says, "This is weird."

I don't know what she's referring to as weird. I hope she's not referring to us, because *weird* is the last word I'd use to describe this. "What's weird?"

"Having you here. Not having a kid here. I'm not used to free time, or . . . guy time." She takes another sip of her wine and then separates from me. She sets her wineglass on the counter and walks toward her bedroom. "Come on, let's take advantage of it."

I follow her lead entirely too quickly.

Chapter Twenty-Two
Lily

I'm trying to act confident about this, but as soon as I walk into my bedroom, I lose every bit of the confidence that got me in here.

It's just that it's been so long since I've been with anyone. Probably since right after getting pregnant with Emmy. I haven't had sex postbaby, and I haven't had sex with Atlas since I was sixteen, and both of these thoughts start swirling together to create this monstrous invasive-thought tornado in my mind.

I'm standing in the middle of my bedroom when Atlas appears in the doorway a few seconds later. I put my hands on my hips and just . . . stand here. He's staring at me. I feel like I'm supposed to make the next move since I'm the one who just invited him into my bedroom.

"I don't know what to do next," I admit. "It's been a while."

Atlas laughs. Then he saunters toward the bed because of course he can't just walk in an unattractive way. Every move he makes is sexy. Him removing his suit jacket right now is sexy. He tosses it onto my dresser and then kicks off his shoes. *God, even that was sexy.* Then he sits down on my bed.

"Let's talk." He leans against my headboard and then crosses his ankles. He looks very relaxed. *And sexy.*

I can't imagine lying down on that bed in this dress. It would be uncomfortable, and probably not very much fun to try to remove if we get to that point. "Let me change clothes first." I walk into my closet and close the door.

I turn on the light, but nothing happens. The bulb is out. *Shit.* I can't get dressed in the dark. I don't have my phone on me, so I can't use the flashlight app to help.

I do my best, but it takes a minute to get the zipper down. When I finally do, instead of stepping out of the dress, for some reason I pull the dress over my head, and of course it snags in my hair. I try to set my hair free, but the dress is heavy, and it's taking forever in the dark, and I can't walk out to find a mirror because Atlas is out there. I keep trying to untangle it. After a few defeating minutes, Atlas finally taps on the door.

"You okay in there?"

"No. I'm stuck."

"Can I open the door?"

I'm standing in my bra and panties with a dress halfway over my head, but this is what I deserve. This is closet karma. "Okay, but I'm not really dressed."

I hear Atlas laugh, but when he opens the door and sees my situation, he immediately springs into action by flicking the light switch. It does nothing, of course.

"The bulb is out."

He moves toward me to inspect my situation. "What happened?"

"My hair is stuck."

Atlas pulls out his phone and uses the light to help him see what I'm tangled on. He tugs my hair and my dress in opposite directions, and then, magically, my dress is on the floor.

I smooth out my hair. "Thank you." I fold my arms over myself. "This is embarrassing."

The light from Atlas's phone is still on, so he can see that I'm standing in my bra and panties. He turns off his phone light, but the closet door is open, and there's a lamp on in the bedroom, so I'm still very visible to him.

There's a moment of hesitation on both our parts. He can't tell if he should walk away and let me finish getting dressed, and I can't tell if I want him to.

And then suddenly we're kissing.

It just happened, as if we moved toward each other at the same time. One of his hands slips around to the back of my head, and the other goes directly to my lower back, so low that his fingers are skimming over my panties.

I wrap both my arms around his neck and pull him to me so hard, we stumble into a line of clothes. Atlas rights us again, but I can feel his smile in his kiss. He pulls far enough away from my mouth so that he can speak. "What is it with you and closets?" Then he kisses me again.

We make out in the closet for a few minutes, and it's everything I remember about all the times we used to sneak make-out sessions when we were younger. The desire, the thrill, the newness of doing things you've never done, or in this case, haven't done in a long time.

It reminds me of how much I loved being in a bed with him. Whether we were kissing or talking or doing other things, the memories I made with him in my bedroom are some of my absolute favorite memories. He's kissing my neck when I whisper, "Take me to my bed."

He doesn't hesitate. He slides his hands down my ass and grips my thighs, hoisting me up. He carries me out of the closet, across the bedroom, and then plants me onto my mattress where he proceeds to climb on top of me.

The feel of him against me only makes me more desperate for him, but he treats this like he used to treat our make-out sessions. With patience and appreciation—like making out is enough, and that it's a privilege just to be kissing me.

I don't know where he finds that patience, because I kind of want him to take off his clothes and treat me like this is his only chance to have me.

Maybe he would if he thought that—but we both know this is just the beginning. He's taking it slow because I asked him to. I'm sure if I asked him to go faster, he would do that, too.

Considerate Atlas.

We eventually come to a point where we have to make a decision. I have a condom in my drawer, and he probably has a little time before he needs to leave, but when we stop kissing long enough to look at each other, he shakes his head. We're both breathing heavily, and a little worn out from being so worked up for so long, so he rolls off me and falls onto his back.

He's still dressed. I'm still in my bra and underwear. We never got further than that.

"As much as I want to," he breathes, "I don't want to have to leave right after." He rolls onto his side and places a hand on my stomach. He's looking down at me with eyes that are unsatisfied, like he wants to say, *Never mind*, and ravish me.

I sigh and close my eyes. "Sometimes I hate responsibility."

Atlas laughs, and then I feel him move closer. He kisses the corner of my mouth and says, "I don't have to leave *yet*." When he says that, his index finger slips beneath the hem of my panties, right below my belly button. He drags it back and forth, waiting for a reaction.

I lift my hips, hoping that's enough of a conversation.

Every part of my body feels like it's on fire when he slips two more fingers into my underwear. Then, when his entire hand makes the move, I'm a goner. I release a trembling breath and grip the sheet at my sides, arching my back and my hips up and against his hand.

He brings his mouth to mine, but he doesn't kiss me. He remains close to my lips, using the movement of my hips and the sounds of my moans to guide him toward the finish.

He's extremely intuitive. It doesn't take me long at all before I'm tensing around his hand, pulling his neck down so that I can kiss him through the end of it.

When it's over, he slides his hand out of my panties but then cups me there, leaving his hand over me while I recover. My chest is heaving as I try to catch my breath.

Atlas is breathing heavily, too, but I need a minute to recover before I can do anything about it.

"Lily." Atlas kisses me gently on the cheek. "I think you . . ." He pauses, so I open my eyes and look at him. He shifts his eyes to my breasts, and then back at my face.

Then he pulls at his white shirt and looks down at it and I see there's some kind of stain on it.

Oh, shit.

I look down at my bra and it's soaking wet. *Oh my God.* Breast milk. Everywhere. I am such an idiot.

Atlas doesn't seem at all fazed by it. He rolls off the bed and says, "I'll give you some privacy."

I'm a little mortified that my bra is covered in breast milk, so I grab the sheet and cover my chest with it before meeting Atlas at the foot of my bed. It kind of killed the mood. "Are you leaving?"

"Of course not." He kisses me and then leaves the room as if it's completely normal for a man to make out with a woman who is breastfeeding a baby that isn't even his. It has to be at least a little awkward for him, but he covers it well.

I spend the next several minutes in the bathroom pumping, and then I take a quick ten-second shower. I throw on an oversized T-shirt and some pajama shorts before heading back into my living room.

Atlas is sitting on my couch, waiting patiently with his phone in his hand. When he hears me enter the living room, he glances up at me and looks me up and down. I'm still a little embarrassed, so when I sit next to him, I don't sit *right* next to him. I sit, like, two feet from him, and then I mutter, "Sorry about that."

"Lily." He can sense my embarrassment, so he reaches for me. "Come here." He settles against the couch and pulls my leg over his so that I'm straddling him. He slides his hands up my thighs, to my waist, and lets his head fall lazily against the couch. "Everything about tonight was perfect. Don't you dare apologize."

I roll my eyes. "You're being nice. I got breast milk on you."

Atlas slides a hand around the back of my neck and pulls me to him. "Yeah, while we were making out. Trust me, I don't mind one bit." He kisses me after that, which might be a mistake because *here we go again.*

It's going to be impossible for him to leave at this rate. I probably should have put on another bra, but I honestly thought I was going to the living room to tell him goodbye. I didn't know we were going to pick up where we left off on the couch, but I don't mind it at all.

We're situated so perfectly, we don't even have to adjust to get the most out of this position. He groans during our kiss, and that just urges me on even more.

One of Atlas's hands slides up the back of my shirt, and I can feel him hesitate when his hand never meets a bra. He pauses our kiss and looks me in the eye. I'm still moving against him, and the way he's looking at me is piercing my core. He starts to move his hand from my back around to my breast. When he cups it in his hand, that seems to flip a switch in him. In both of us.

Our kiss turns feverish as I start to unbutton his shirt. Nothing else is said. We just frantically remove every piece of clothing left between us, and we don't even bother moving to the bedroom. We barely pause the kissing when he reaches for his wallet and pulls out a condom and puts it on.

And then, as if it's the most natural thing in the world, Atlas kisses me while he pushes into me, and I feel every bit as loved as I did the first time this happened between us. There are so many feelings that come out in this moment, I'm not sure I've ever experienced anything so chaotically beautiful when we're finally connected.

He sighs against my neck, like the same feelings are running through him. He starts to move in and out, slowly, kissing me gently the whole time. But several minutes later, the kisses are frantic and we're both sweaty, and I am so completely and wholly in the moment, nothing else matters to me other than the fact that we're together again, and it's right. Everything about this is so right.

I'm exactly where I belong, being loved by Atlas Corrigan.

Chapter Twenty-Three
Atlas

I should definitely go home, but it is so hard to crawl out of this bed after the last couple of hours with her. Once the couch happened, then the shower happened. Now we're both too tired to do anything other than talk.

She's lying on her back, her arms folded beneath her head. She's staring at me, listening intently as I tell her about my meeting with a lawyer yesterday. "He says I did the right thing by taking him to the hospital. They were legally obligated to notify Child Protective Services. I'm not sure how I feel about that, though. It puts the power in the hands of the state, and what if they don't think I'm the best place for him?"

"Why wouldn't they?"

"I work a lot. I'm not married, so Josh will be alone some of the time. And I have no experience raising kids. They might think Tim is a better fit since he's the biological father. They could even give him back to my mother; I'm not even sure what she did is enough to have him removed from her custody."

Lily leans toward me and presses a kiss against my forearm. "I'm going to tell you what you told me the first time you FaceTimed me. You said, 'You're stressing over things that haven't even happened yet.'"

I fold my lips together momentarily. "I did say that."

"You did," she says. She tucks herself against me, wrapping a leg over my thigh. "It'll work out, Atlas. You're the best thing for him, and anyone who has vested interest will see that. I promise."

I fold myself around her, fitting her head under my chin. It's incredible how much we've both changed physically since we were teens, but we somehow still fit together just as perfectly as we did back then.

"I've been wanting to ask you something," she says, pulling back far enough to look at me. "Remember our first time? What happened after that night? After my father hurt you."

I'm not surprised she's thinking about that, because I've thought about it as well tonight. This is the first time we've been intimate since that night that ended so terribly, so it's hard not to compare them.

That was what her very last journal entry was about. It was painful to read, seeing how much she was hurting. I wish more than anything it could have ended better than it did.

"I don't remember a lot from that night," I admit. "I woke up in the hospital the next day, confused. I knew your father was the one who had hurt me, I remembered that much, but I had no idea if he did to you what he had done to me. I hit the call button several times, and when no one came to my room, I somehow hobbled into the hallway with a broken ankle. I was frantic, asking if you were okay, but the poor nurse had no idea what I was talking about."

Lily tightens her grip around me as I talk.

"She finally calmed me down enough to get your information from me, and then she came back to let me know that I was the only one brought in with injuries. She asked me if your father was Andrew Bloom. I told her yes, and I told her I wanted to press charges. When I asked her if she could have an officer come to the room, she looked at me sympathetically. I remember her exact words. She said, 'The law is on his side, honey. No one turns him in. Not even his wife.'"

Lily exhales against my chest, so I pause and press a kiss against the top of her head. "Then what?" she whispers.

"I did it anyway," I say. "I knew if I didn't report him, your mother would never get out of that situation. I made the nurse contact an officer, and when one finally arrived that afternoon, he wasn't there to listen to my statement. He was there to make it clear that if anyone was going to be arrested, it wouldn't be your father. He said your father could have me arrested for breaking into houses and forcing myself on his daughter. Those were the officer's exact words, like the relationship you and I had was something criminal. I felt guilty about that for years."

Lily looks up at me and places a hand on my cheek. "What? Atlas, we're only two and a half years apart. You did absolutely nothing wrong."

I appreciate that she says that, but it doesn't change the fact that I felt guilty for bringing stress into her life. But I also felt guilty for leaving her once I did bring stress into her life. "I don't know that any choice I made back then would have felt right. I didn't want to stay and put you in more danger by showing up at your house again. And I didn't want to be arrested because then I wouldn't have been able to go to the military. I thought the best thing would be to put space between us, and then someday I would contact you down the line and see if you ever still thought of me like I thought of you."

"Every day," she whispers. "I thought of you every single day."

I run my hand over her back for a while, and then I stroke my fingers through her hair, wondering how in the world she can make me feel so whole when I had no idea I was only half of myself without her.

Of course I've missed her all these years, and if I could have snapped my fingers and brought her back into my life, I would have in a heartbeat. But we had built lives without each other, her with Ryle and me with my career, and I assumed that was our fate. I had grown used to not living life with her. But now that she's back, I don't know that I could ever feel whole again without her. Especially after tonight.

"Lily," I whisper.

She doesn't respond. I pull back a little and can see that her eyes are closed, and her arm has gone limp around me. I'm scared if I move, I'll wake her up. But I told Josh I'd only be a couple of hours later than the time I initially gave him, and I'm at three hours now. I'm not even sure I'm allowed to leave twelve-year-olds by themselves.

Brad was okay with it when I asked if they were fine by themselves, and if he doesn't even allow Theo to have a phone, I doubt he'd let me leave them alone while I went on a date unless Brad has left Theo alone before.

Maybe I should google what the age limit is in Boston for a kid to stay by themselves.

I'm overthinking this. Of course, they're fine. Neither of

them has called or texted with any kind of emergency, and twelve-year-olds even babysit other kids sometimes.

I think I'm fine, but I still need to get home. I don't know Josh well enough yet to be convinced he isn't throwing a rager in my house right now. I slowly remove my arm from beneath Lily's head and ease out of her bed. I dress as quietly as I can, and then I go in search of a pen and paper. I don't want to wake her up, but I don't want to leave without saying anything. Especially after the night we had.

I find a notebook and a pen in her kitchen drawer, so I sit at the table to write her a letter. When I finish, I take it back to her bedroom and I set the note on the pillow next to her. Then I kiss her goodnight.

Chapter Twenty-Four
Lily

There's a pounding in my head.

And *outside* my head.

I lift my face off my pillow and feel drool on my chin. I wipe it away with the corner of my pillowcase. I sit up and see that Atlas left a note beside me. I grab for it, but then hear the knock again, so I tuck the note under my pillow for later and force myself to clear space in my foggy brain to make room for what's happening in this moment.

Emmy is at my mother's.

I just had the best night of sleep I've had in two years.

Someone is at my door.

I reach for my phone on my nightstand and try to focus on the screen. I have several missed calls from Ryle, which makes me concerned something is wrong. But the only thing I have from my mother is a picture of Emmy eating breakfast from half an hour ago.

Phew. Emmy is okay. I immediately relax, but knowing Ryle is probably the one knocking on my door doesn't allow for much relaxation.

"Hold on!" I yell.

I throw on something quick—a T-shirt and jeans—and then I open the door to let him in. He moves past me, into the apartment, without being invited in. "Is everything okay?" He looks panicked, but also relieved to see that I'm alive.

"I was asleep. Everything is fine." He can tell I'm annoyed. He glances around the room for Emmy. "She spent the night at my mother's."

"Oh." He's disappointed. "I tried calling because I wanted to pick her up for a few hours. You weren't answering your phone, and you're always awake by now . . ." Ryle's voice trails off when he sees the couch. I don't have to look at the couch to know what he's staring at. My T-shirt and panties are still tossed haphazardly over the back of it, I'm sure.

"Let me call my mother and let her know you're coming." I go get my phone from my room, hoping Ryle isn't about to question me. He's ruining the good mood Atlas left me in last night.

When I walk back into the living room, I pause while searching for my mother's contact on my phone. Ryle is holding a wineglass in his hand, inspecting it. It's the one Atlas drank from. Mine is on the counter next to it—a clear indication that someone was here *with* me drinking wine last night.

Before my underwear got removed and left on the couch.

I can see Ryle's jealousy bubbling over when he sets down the wineglass and looks straight at me. "Did someone stay the night?"

I don't bother denying it. I'm an adult. A single adult. *Well, possibly not single anymore, but that's another matter.* "We're divorced, Ryle. You can't ask me questions like that."

Maybe that was the wrong thing to say, because Ryle immediately responds by taking two quick steps toward me.

"I can't ask you if someone spent the night in the home my daughter *lives* in?"

I take a step back. "That's not what I meant. And I wouldn't bring anyone around her without your approval; that's why she's at my mother's."

Ryle's eyes are narrowed, accusing. He looks disgusted by me. "You won't leave her with me overnight, but you'll drop her off somewhere else when you want to get fucked?" He laughs. "Great parenting, Lily."

Now I'm getting angry. "This is only the second time I've ever left her overnight since she was born almost a year ago. Don't shame me for taking a night for myself. And when I do take a night for myself, what I do during that time is not your business."

Ryle has that look in his eye—the distant void that always took over right before he'd go too far.

My anger instantly turns to fear, and when Ryle can see that I'm backing away from him, he releases this sound of rage. A guttural, angry noise of frustration that reverberates in the room.

He leaves my apartment, slamming the front door shut behind him. I hear him yell the word *fuck* in the hallway.

I'm not sure which angle his rage is coming at me from. Is he mad I'm moving on? Is he mad my mother has Emmy? Or is it that I allow my mother overnights with her but I'm still not comfortable with Ryle having overnights? Maybe he's angry about all three things presenting at once.

I blow out a calming breath, relieved he's gone, but before I can think about what to do next, Ryle is opening my door again. He's looking at me from the hallway with a very flat affect when he says, "Is it him?"

I can feel my heart catch in my throat when he asks that. He doesn't say Atlas's name, but who else could he be referring to? I don't immediately deny it, which is enough of a confirmation for him.

Ryle looks up at the ceiling briefly, and then shakes his head. "So I had a right to be concerned about him the whole time?"

The entire past few minutes have been a roller coaster of emotions, but nothing has been as tumultuous as the question that just left his mouth. I take a few steps until I'm standing in my doorway, prepared to close the door on him as soon as I say my piece.

"If you truly believe that I would have been unfaithful to you, then go ahead and believe that. I don't have the energy to keep convincing you otherwise. I've explained this to you before, so I'm not saying it again. I never would have left you for Atlas. I didn't *leave* you for Atlas. I left you because I deserve to be treated better than the way I was treated by you."

I go to close the door, but before I can take a step back, Ryle moves forward and pushes me until my back is flat against the open living room door. His eyes are filled with fury when he slides his left hand to the base of my throat, applying pressure as if he wants to hold me in place. He slaps his right palm flat against the door by my head, and it scares me so much, I immediately squeeze my eyes shut, not wanting to see what's about to come next.

A huge wave of anxiety and fear rolls over me so intensely, I'm scared I might pass out. I can feel Ryle's breath crashing against my cheek as it moves through his clenched teeth because his face is so close to mine. My heart is pounding so hard, there's no way he can't feel that fear beating against his palm with the way his hand is pressed against me. I want to scream, but I'm terrified if I make a noise, it'll make him even angrier.

Several seconds pass between the moment Ryle pins me against the door and the moment he starts to realize what he's done. What more he was likely *about* to do.

My eyes are still shut, but I can feel the remorse in the way he leans forward and presses his forehead against the door, right next to my head. He still has me caged in, but he's released the pressure in the hand that was gripping my neck, and there's a struggling sound coming from him, as if he's trying not to cry.

It takes me back to the last night he hurt me. The apologies he was whispering as I drifted in and out of consciousness. *I'm sorry, I'm sorry, I'm sorry.*

My heart is shattered, because Ryle hasn't changed at all. As much as I hoped he had, and as much as I know he wanted to, he's still the same man he's always been. I somehow held on to a sliver of hope that he had become stronger for Emmy, but this is absolute confirmation that I'm making the right choices for her.

Ryle is clinging to me like I can make this better, and at one point in time I thought I could. He's a broken man, but he isn't broken because of me. He was broken before he met me. Sometimes people think if they love a broken person enough, they can be what finally repairs them, but the problem with that is the other person just ends up broken, too.

I can't afford to allow anyone to break me anymore. I have a daughter I need to be whole for.

I gently press my hands against his chest and urge him back into the hallway. When I'm finally in a position where there's enough space between us to shut the door, I close it and lock it, and then I immediately call my mother and tell her to put Emmy in the car and meet me at the park. I don't want them to be at her house if Ryle still plans on showing up there.

After I end the call, I move with purpose through my apartment. If I stop and allow myself to get lost in what just happened, I might cry. I don't have time to cry right now. I get dressed to go to the park because I need to be present for my daughter in every way that I can be.

Before I walk out the door, I grab the note Atlas wrote me and tuck it into my purse. I have a feeling his words are going to be the only bright spot to this day.

•   •   •

My premonition is coming true. I hear a loud clap of thunder as soon as I pull into the parking lot of the park. There's a storm brewing to the east, and it's heading this direction. *Fitting.*

It's not raining yet, though, so I scan the playground until I spot my mother. She's holding Emmy, and they're going down the slide together. She hasn't spotted me yet, so I take a moment to pull Atlas's letter out of my purse. I'm still reeling from my interaction with Ryle. I'd like to read something that can hopefully put me in a better mood before I greet my daughter.

Dear Lily,

I'm sorry I had to leave without saying goodbye, but you fall asleep so easily. I don't mind it—I like watching you sleep. Even when it's in a car in the middle of a date.

I used to watch you sleep sometimes when we were younger. I liked how peaceful you looked, because when you were awake, there was always a quiet fear in you. But when you slept, the fear was gone, and it always put me at ease.

I can't begin to tell you what tonight meant to me. I don't think I have to put it into words because you were here. You felt it, too.

I know I mentioned earlier that I carried a lot of guilt about what happened between us, but I don't want you to think I carry regret for loving you back then. If there's any-thing at all I regret, it's that I didn't fight harder for you. I think that's where the majority of my guilt stems from—knowing if I didn't leave you, you never would have met a man who would end up hurting you the way your father hurt your mother.

But no matter how we got here, we're here. I had to get to a point where I realized I was always worthy of being loved by you. I hate that we didn't get here sooner, because there are so many things in your life I wish you didn't have to go through, or that I could have prevented. But any other path wouldn't have given you Emerson, so I'm grate-ful this is where we ended up.

I love watching you talk about her. I can't wait to get to know her. But that'll come in time, along with all the other things I'm looking forward to. We'll continue to take this at whatever pace you're comfortable with. Whether I get to talk to you every day or see you once a month, anything is better than the years I had to go not knowing anything about you.

I'm so happy you're happy. That's all I've ever wanted for you.

But I will say, nothing beats knowing I'm the one you get to be happy with now.

Love,
Atlas

I flinch so hard, I almost rip the letter in two when someone bangs on my window. I gasp and glance up to see my mother standing next to my car. Emmy lights up when she sees me through the window, and that smile is all it takes to make me smile in return.

Well, her smile and the letter in my hand.

I fold it up and tuck it back into my purse. My mother opens my door. "Is everything okay?"

"Yeah, it's fine." I take Emmy from her, but my mother's eyes are squinting with suspicion.

"You sounded scared when you asked me to meet you at the park."

"It's fine," I say, wanting to brush it off. "I just didn't want Ryle to pick her up today. He's not in a very good mood, and he knew she was with you, so . . ."

I blow out a breath and walk over to the empty swing set. I take a seat in one of the swings and place Emmy on my lap, facing out. I kick the ground and give the swing a little push, watching as my mother takes a seat in the swing next to us.

"Lily." My mother is looking at me with concern. "Just tell me what happened."

I know Emerson is only one and can't understand me yet, but it still makes me uncomfortable to talk about her father in her presence. I'm convinced babies and toddlers can sense moods, even if they can't understand what you're saying.

I attempt to explain my situation without mentioning names. "I'm sort of seeing someone?" That confession comes out like a question because we haven't made it official, but I don't think Atlas and I have to put a label on it to know where this is headed.

"Really? Who?"

I shake my head. I'm not about to tell her it's Atlas, even though she probably wouldn't know who I was talking about. She saw him twice when I was younger, and we never once spoke about him. And if she does remember him, I'm sure she doesn't want to, considering her husband put him in the hospital.

There may come a day when I officially introduce Atlas to my mother, and I don't want her to know him from my past or she might feel mortified.

"Just someone I met. It's early. But . . ." I sigh and kick the ground again to give us another small push. "Ryle found out, and he isn't happy."

My mother winces, like she knows all too well what *he isn't happy* implies.

"He came by this morning, and his reaction was scary. I

panicked, thinking he was going to show up at your place to get her, so I didn't want you to be home."

"What did he do?"

I shake my head. "I'm not hurt. It's just been a while since I've seen that side of him, so I'm a little shaken, but I'm okay." I kiss Emmy on top of her head. I'm surprised to feel a tear skating down my cheek, so I quickly wipe it away. "I just don't know what to do about his visits now. I almost wish something *would* have happened so I could have reported him this time. But then I feel like an awful mother for thinking that way about her father."

My mother reaches over and squeezes my hand. It makes my swing come to a still, so I twist until we're facing her. "No matter what you decide to do, you are *not* an awful mother. Precisely the opposite." She releases my hand and grips the chains, staring at Emmy. "I admire the choices you've made for her. Sometimes I get sad that I couldn't be that strong for you."

I immediately shake my head. "You can't compare our situations, Mom. I had a lot of support that enabled me to make the choice I made. You had no one."

She gives me a sad, appreciative smile. Then she leans back and kicks at the ground to give herself a little shove. "Whoever he is, he's a lucky guy." She glances over at me. "Who is he?"

I laugh. "No, you don't. I'm not talking about him to you until he's a for-sure thing."

"He already is a for-sure thing," she says. "I can see it in your smile."

We both look up at the same time when it starts sprinkling. I tuck Emmy under my chin and we begin to head back toward the parking lot. My mother kisses Emmy before I put her in the car seat. "I love you. Gamma loves you, Emmy."

"Gamma?" I ask. "Last week it was Nannie."

"I still haven't settled on one yet." My mother kisses me on the cheek and then rushes to her car.

I climb into my car right when the bottom falls out of the sky. Huge drops of rain assault the windshield, the pavement, the hood of my car. They're so fat, they sound like acorns hitting my car.

I sit for a moment, waiting to figure out where I'm going before I start the car. I don't want to go home yet because Ryle might show back up. I definitely don't want to go to Allysa's because I'll absolutely run into him in the apartment building where he lives.

I feel very protective of Emmy right now because Ryle has every right on paper to show up and take her from me for the day, but I'm not allowing my daughter around him on a day I know his fuse is nonexistent.

I look in my rearview mirror, and Emmy is just sitting peacefully, looking out the window at the rain. She has no idea the kind of chaos that surrounds her existence, because to her, *I'm* her entire existence. Every ounce of her trust is in me. She depends on me for everything, and she's just sitting there happy and comfortable, as if I have it all under control.

I don't feel like I have it under control, but the fact that she assumes I do is good enough for me. "Where do we go today, Emmy?"

Chapter Twenty-Five
Atlas

"What time did you get home last night?" Josh asks. He's shuffling into the kitchen wearing two different socks: one of them a new one I bought him and one of them mine. Theo and Josh were asleep when I got home, but I still woke up three hours before they did. Brad just left with Theo about twenty minutes ago.

"That's none of your business." I point at the table, where Josh's homework sits unfinished. He promised he would do it yesterday if I let Theo spend the night, but I have a feeling the video games and manga and anime got in the way. "You didn't do your homework?"

Josh looks at the pile of papers and then back at me. "No."

"Get to it." I say that with confidence, but I have no idea how to do this. I've never had to tell a kid to do homework before. I don't even know how to ground him if he *doesn't* do his homework. I feel like I'm acting. I am. I'm an imposter.

"I'm not avoiding it," Josh says. "I just can't do it."

"Is it too hard? What is it, math?"

"No, I did the math. Math is easy. It's this stupid shit I have to do for computer class."

"Stupid *crap*," I say, correcting him. *I think.* Maybe "stupid crap" is just as bad. I sit down next to Josh to see what it is he's having trouble with. He slides the assignment in front of me, and I look over it.

It's a research assignment about ancestry. There are five things required for the term, and one of them is a family tree that was due on Friday. The other is a generational assignment using an ancestry website that's due next Friday.

"We're supposed to find our relatives using some website. I don't know any of their names or even where to start," he says. "Do you?"

I shake my head. "Not really. I met Sutton's father once, but he died when I was a kid. I don't even remember his name."

"What about my dad's parents?" Josh asks.

"I don't know anything about his family, either."

Josh takes the papers from me. "They really should stop having kids do these things; no one has normal families anymore."

"You're right, actually." I hear a text ping on my phone in the kitchen, so I stand up to go check it.

"Did you ever try to find my dad for me?" Josh asks.

I did try, but Tim never responded to the voice mail I left him. I just don't want to tell Josh that because I know it'll be disappointing. I pick up my phone but walk back to Josh before looking at my texts. "I haven't had a chance to really look into it yet. You sure you want me to?"

Josh nods. "He might want to hear from me. I'm sure Sutton has done everything she can to keep us apart."

I feel a stab of concern in the center of my chest. I was hoping Josh would be comfortable enough here to not want to find his dad, but that was a ridiculous hope. He's a twelve-year-old boy. Of course he wants to find his father.

"I'll help you try to find him." I point to the papers. "But do what you can with that for now. As long as you try, they can't give you a bad grade for not knowing your grandparents."

Josh leans over his work, and I finally look down at the text. It's from Lily.

Can I call you?

She should know she can call me any second of the day, and I would answer. I take my phone to my room and call her without texting her back. She picks up in the middle of the first ring.

"Hey," she says.

"Hi."

"What are you doing?"

"Helping Josh with his homework. Trying to pretend I'm not thinking about you." She's quiet after I say that, and I immediately sense something is off. "Are you okay?"

"Yeah, I just. I don't want to go home. I was wondering if I could come to your place?"

"Sure. Is Emmy still with your mom?"

She sighs. "That's the thing. I have her with me. I know that's weird, but I'll explain when I get there."

If she's bringing Emerson to my house, something is definitely off. She's been adamant she didn't want to bring her around me before Ryle knew about us. "I'll text you my address."

"Thank you. I'll be there in a little while." She ends the call, and I fall back onto my mattress wondering what in the hell happened in the time between slipping out of her bed last night and this phone call.

Did she get my letter? Did I say something wrong?

Is she about to break things off with me?

All those concerns swirl in my gut as I wait for her, but my biggest concern is one I don't even want to allow my mind to entertain. *Did Ryle hurt her?*

.   .   .

I'm watching for them when she pulls into my driveway, so I meet her outside. I can immediately tell something is wrong when she gets out of the car. But I don't think it's related to me because she seems relieved to see me. I pull her in for a hug because she looks like she needs one. "What happened?"

She places her hands on my chest and pulls back to look up at me. She seems hesitant to say anything. She glances into the back window to check on her daughter, who is asleep in the car seat.

Then Lily just starts to cry. She drops her face against my chest and sobs into my shirt, and it's the most heartbreaking thing. I press my lips into her hair and give her a moment.

She doesn't need long. She composes herself fairly quickly and then wipes at her eyes. "I'm sorry," she says. "I've been holding that in all morning since Ryle left."

The mention of his name makes my spine stiffen. I knew this had to do with him.

"He knows about us," she says.

"What happened?" It's taking everything in me to stand where I am and not run to find him. My bones feel as if they're crackling with anger. "Are you hurt?"

"No. But he's really upset, and I don't want to be home alone right now. I know I shouldn't be bringing Emmy around you yet, but I feel safer with her here than if Ryle tried to show up and take her today. I'm sorry, I just don't want to be anywhere he might find me."

I tilt her chin up until she's looking at me. "I'm happy you're here. *Both* of you. Stay the whole day if you want."

She exhales and presses her lips against mine. "Thank you." She moves to the back door to grab her daughter out of her car seat. Emerson doesn't even wake up. She's limp in Lily's arms, passed out. "She's been at the park for an hour; she's exhausted."

I stare at Emerson in wonder, still amazed by how much she looks like Lily. She's the spitting image of her mother, and I'm not at all upset that she looks nothing like her father. "Do you need me to grab anything?"

"Her diaper bag is in the passenger seat."

I grab it, and we make our way into the house. Josh looks over his shoulder when he hears me walk inside. Lily waves at him, and he nods his head, but then when he notices Emerson, he turns completely around in his chair.

"That's a baby," he says.

"It is," Lily replies. "Her name is Emerson."

Josh looks at me. "Is it yours?" He uses the Sharpie in his hand to point at Emerson. "Is that my niece?"

Lily laughs uncomfortably.

I probably should have warned Josh before they showed up. "No, I am not a dad, and you are not an uncle."

Josh stares at us for a minute, then shrugs and says, "Okay." He turns around and gives his attention back to his homework.

"Sorry about that," I say quietly. I set Emerson's diaper bag near the couch. "Want me to get a blanket for her?"

Lily nods, so I grab a thick quilt from the hallway closet and lay it on the floor next to the couch. I double it over to give it more cushion, and she places Emerson on it. Emerson sleeps through the entire transfer.

"Don't let her fool you—she's a very light sleeper." Lily kicks off her shoes and sits on the couch, pulling her feet beneath her. I sit down next to her, hoping she feels like talking about what happened, because I need to know why she's scared.

Josh can't see us from the dining room, so I give Lily a quick kiss. I doubt he can hear us from where he is, but I whisper anyway. "What happened?"

She sighs with her entire body and leans against the couch, facing me. "He showed up to get Emmy, and I wasn't expecting him. He saw our wineglasses. My clothes. He put two and two together, and he had the exact reaction I was afraid he would have."

"What reaction was that?"

"He got angry. But he left before it got too bad."

Too *bad*? *What does that even mean?* "Does he know it was me who was there?"

Lily nods. "That's practically the first thing he asked. He got angry, and I asked him to leave. And he did . . . but . . ."

She stops talking, and for the first time, I notice her hand is trembling. God, I hate him so much. I pull her to me so that her cheek is pressed against my chest and I hold her. "What did he do that scared you, Lily?"

Her palm is pressed right over my heart. She whispers, "He pushed me against the door, and he got close to my face, and I thought he was going to hit me or . . . I don't know. He didn't, though." She must feel my heart hammering twice as fast against my chest now, because she lifts her head and looks at me. "I'm fine, Atlas. I promise. Nothing happened after that; it's just been a long time since I've seen him that angry."

"He pushed you against the door. That's not nothing."

Her eyes flick away, and she lays her head back on my chest. "I know. I *know*. I just don't know what to do about it. I don't know what to do about Emmy. I was actually getting close to letting him have an overnight with her, and now I don't even want him to have unsupervised visits."

"He doesn't deserve unsupervised visits. You need to take him back to court."

Lily sighs, and I can tell this is probably the part of her life that causes her the most stress. I can't imagine what it must be like for her to watch him drive off with her little girl in his car, knowing what he's capable of. I'm glad she came here today. I know it's important to her that she waited to bring Emmy around me, but she made the right decision. Ryle might show back up to apologize and get Emmy, and he'll find her at all her usual places.

He won't find her here. Besides, Lily and I know this thing that's been brewing between us is absolutely a long-term situation. She doesn't have to worry about me forming an attachment to Emmy and then disappearing. As long as Lily wants me around, I'm not going anywhere.

She lifts her face to look at me again, and there's a smudge of mascara near her temple. I wipe it away. "This conflict with him," she says. "This is what I tried to warn you about. It could be a constant thing, especially now that he knows you're back in my life."

She's saying this like she's giving me the opportunity to bow out of this thing with her. I can't believe she assumes that's even crossing my mind. "You could have fifty ex-husbands who try to make our lives hell, but as long as I have you, I will be absolutely unaffected by anyone else's negativity. That's a promise."

That makes her smile for the first time since she showed up here. I don't want to do or say anything that could steal that smile, so I change the subject away from her weak-ass ex-husband.

"Are you thirsty?"

She pushes off my chest and grins even bigger. "Yes. I'm thirsty *and* I'm hungry. Why else would I show up at a chef's house?"

•   •   •

Lily and Emerson have been here for about four hours now. Once Josh did as much of his homework as he could, he started playing with Emerson. Lily said she's been taking steps for a few weeks now, and Josh finds it hilarious that she follows him everywhere. He moved around for an hour while she stumbled after him, but now she's asleep again. She fell asleep on the floor next to me with her head on my leg. Lily offered to move her, but I wouldn't let her.

I would be lying if I said this wasn't a little surreal. Deep down, I know that Lily and I are going to work out. She's my person, and I am hers, and that's something I've known since the first week we met. But looking at Emerson, knowing this child is likely going to end up becoming a huge part of my life—that's a lot to take in. I could be her stepfather someday. I'll likely be more of an influence in her life than her biological father, because Lily and I will eventually move in together. We'll likely marry someday.

I'd never admit any of this out loud because people like Theo would say I'm getting ahead of myself, but the truth is, I'm years behind where I want to be with Lily. Where I could have been with her.

This is a hugely significant day, even if I don't see Emerson again for months. This could be the first day I'm spending with someone who might one day end up becoming my daughter.

I brush thin strands of strawberry hair behind Emerson's ear and try to understand where some of Ryle's anger is coming from. He can't be clueless to what Lily moving on would mean for his relationship with Emerson. Lily has Emerson the majority of the time, so whoever Lily chooses to bring into her life will also be around Emerson that same amount of time.

I'm not excusing Ryle's behavior by any means. If I had my way, he'd get a job offer in Sudan, and we'd only have to deal with him once a year.

But that's not the reality here. Ryle lives in the same city as his daughter, and his ex-wife is moving on with someone else. That can't be easy on anyone. While I can understand how difficult it probably is for him, I'll never understand his failure to recognize that it's no one's fault but his own. If he would have been a more mature, more rational man, Lily never would have left him. He'd have his wife and his daughter, and me and Lily wouldn't even be in contact.

I'm worried for Lily. I'm worried Ryle is a little bit like

my mother, and that he's going to retaliate by fighting for the sake of fighting, and for no other reason.

"Have you ever made a report against Ryle?" I ask, looking at Lily. She's sitting on the floor next to me, watching Emerson sleep on my leg.

"No." There's a drop of shame in Lily's response.

"Do the two of you have a custody agreement?"

She nods. "I have full custody, but it comes with stipulations. Because of his schedule, I'm required to be flexible, but technically he gets her two days a week."

"He pays child support?"

She nods. "He does. He's never been late."

I'm relieved he at least provides her that, but knowing the answers to these questions is making Lily's situation seem even more precarious.

"Why?" she asks.

I shake my head. "It's not my business." *Is it?* I don't even know. I'm trying to take things slow and give Lily space, but that part of me is warring with the part of me that wants to protect her.

Lily lifts a hand and pulls my focus to hers. "It is your business, Atlas. We're together now."

Her response makes my heart stutter. Did she just make us official? "Are we? Together?" I smile and urge her closer to me, my pulse thrumming. "Are me and you a thing, Lily Bloom?"

Her lips grin against mine. She's nodding when she kisses me.

I think we both knew it was official long before last night, but if her daughter weren't asleep on my leg right now, I'd probably pick Lily up and spin her around. I am that happy.

And that much more invested.

My quick burst of adrenaline begins to slow again, bringing me back to my thoughts from before Lily declared us official.

Ryle. Custody. Immaturity.

Lily's head is on my shoulder and her hand is on my chest, so she feels it when I exhale all the air from my lungs. She lifts her head and looks at me anxiously. "Just say it."

"Say what?" I ask her.

"Your thoughts about my situation. Your eyebrows are all scrunched together like you're worrying about something." She lifts her hand and uses her thumb to smooth out my serious expression.

"Is it too late to tell the court he was a danger to you in the past? Maybe that would help prevent him from getting overnights with her."

"Once two people agree on a custody arrangement, you can't use past evidence to modify an arrangement. Unfortunately, I never reported him, so I can't use the abuse as a defense at this point."

That is unfortunate. But I can understand her attempting to keep things civil with him at the time. I'm just worried it might come back on her in a negative way.

"He's too busy to have her half the time, or even overnights, really. I doubt he would ever try to get joint custody of her."

I press my lips together and nod, hoping she's right. I don't know him like she does, but from what I do know of him, he seems to hold grudges. And people who hold grudges tend to need retaliation. Parents do this all the time.

They don't like what another parent is doing, or who they're seeing, so they use their child as a weapon. And that worries me. I could absolutely see Ryle making the decision to take her to court, simply to get back at her for being with me. And he would likely get what he wants. He's never hurt Emerson, he's never been reported for hurting Lily, he's never been late on child support. And he has a successful career. All these things are in his favor.

When I glance at Lily, it looks like she's about to sink into the floor. I didn't mean to upset her even more by talking about this.

"I'm sorry. I'm not trying to be a pessimist. We can change the subject."

"You aren't a pessimist, Atlas. You're a realist, and I need that from you." She lifts her head off my shoulder and peeks over at Emmy, who is still asleep on my leg. Then Lily settles against me again, releasing a quiet sigh. "You know, even if I had reported Ryle and fought for sole custody, my chances were slim. He has no criminal history, and he has money for the best lawyers. Almost every lawyer I spoke to encouraged me to work it out civilly with him because they've seen cases like ours, and the arrangement Ryle was agreeing to at the time was my best option."

I grab her hand and lace my fingers through hers. She wipes away a tear that skates down her cheek. I hate that I even brought it up, but these fears are already in her. I'm just glad to know she's thinking about it because she needs to stay a step ahead of Ryle. "Whatever happens, you aren't alone in this anymore."

Lily smiles appreciatively.

Emerson begins to stir awake on my leg. She opens her eyes and looks at me, and then immediately searches for Lily. She makes a beeline for her, right across my lap. When she's in Lily's arms, I lift my leg and stretch it. I haven't been able to move it for over half an hour and it's asleep.

"We should go," she says. "I feel guilty for even being here with her. I'd be livid if Ryle took her around a girlfriend without me knowing."

"I think your situations are a little different. Ryle isn't having to find a safe place to hide your daughter for the day because he's scared of your temper. Don't be so hard on yourself."

Lily shoots me a grateful look.

I help her gather their things and I walk her to the car. Once Emerson is in her car seat, Lily moves close to say goodbye. I burrow my fingers in her hips and tug her closer. I dip my head, grazing her nose, and then I catch her lips with mine. I kiss her deeply, wanting her to still feel it on her drive home.

I slide my hands into the back pockets of her jeans and squeeze her ass. It makes her laugh. Then she sighs wistfully. "I already miss you."

I nod in agreement. "There's been a lot of that on my end," I admit. "I'm kind of obsessed with you, Lily Bloom." I kiss her cheek and then force myself to release her.

This is the only negative aspect to finally being with the person you're meant to be with. You go years aching to be with them, and when they finally become a significant part of your life, it somehow hurts even *more*.

Chapter Twenty-Six
Lily

You disappoint me Lily.

I'm staring at my phone in shock.

Is this a joke?

You treat me like a monster im her goddamn father

It's five in the morning. I woke up to use the bathroom, and naturally, I glanced at my phone before attempting to get the last hour of sleep before my alarm goes off.

All the texts are from Ryle. I haven't heard from him since he showed up at my house on Sunday. It's been four days, and he never even bothered to reach out and apologize for losing his temper on me. He was silent for four days and then *this*?

I was happier before I met you.

I read through the barrage of text messages, knowing full well he was drunk when he sent them last night. The first one was sent at midnight, and the last one, from two in the morning, reads, **have fun fucking the homeless guy.**

I drop my phone onto my bed, my hands trembling. I can't believe he sent these. I was hoping the four days of silence was a stretch of remorse on his part, but it's obvious he's been stewing in his anger.

This is so much worse than I thought.

I try to go back to sleep, but I can't. I get up and make myself a cup of coffee, but my stomach is too upset to drink it. I spend the next half hour standing in my kitchen, staring at nothing, replaying those texts over and over in my mind.

When Emerson finally wakes up, I'm relieved. I am more than welcoming to the distraction of our chaotic morning routine.

.   .   .

By the time I drop her off with my mother and make it to work, it's eight o'clock sharp. I'm the first one at the flower shop, so I distract myself with as much as I can until Serena and Lucy show up. Lucy can tell something is wrong with me, she even asks me if I'm okay at one point, but I reassure her that I'm fine.

I pretend I *am* fine, but I'm watching the front door every chance I get, expecting Ryle to angrily burst through it. I wait for another mean text from him. I wait for the phone to ring.

Hours go by and there's nothing. Not even an apology.

I don't tell Atlas, I don't tell Allysa, I don't say anything to anyone throughout the day about what he's done. It's embarrassing. It's insulting to Atlas; it's insulting to me. I have no idea what to do about it, but I know that this isn't something I'm willing to tolerate. I refuse to go the next seventeen years of my daughter's life being abused in any way, even through text messages.

Serena has gone for the day, and it's just Lucy and me when the inevitable finally happens. It's after five, and we're just getting ready to close up shop so I can pick up

Emerson from my mother's when Ryle walks through the front door.

My anxiety shoots through me like an explosion of lava.

Lucy has never been Ryle's biggest fan, so she groans under her breath when she sees him and says, "I'll be in the back if you need me."

"Lucy, wait," I whisper. I look down at my phone like I'm busy with something so Ryle can't see my lips moving. "Stay." I glance at her so she can see the concern in my eyes. She just nods and finds something to make herself look busy.

My heart is hammering against my chest when Ryle approaches. I don't even try to hide behind a fake expression when I look him in the eye.

He holds my stare for a few seconds and then side-eyes Lucy. He nudges his head toward my office. "Can we talk?"

"I was just leaving." My words come out quick and firm. "I have to pick up our daughter."

I can see Ryle's left hand grip the edge of the counter. He squeezes it, and the muscles in his arm flex. "Please. It won't take long."

I look at Lucy. "Wait for me to lock up?" She gives me a reassuring nod, so I turn on my heels and walk to my office. I can hear him right behind me. I fold my arms over my chest and suck in a breath before I can face him.

I'm so sick of his remorse. I want to wipe that stupid frown off his face, I'm so angry.

"I'm sorry." He runs a hand through his hair and winces, coming closer. "I had too much to drink at an event last night and . . ."

I say nothing.

"I don't even remember sending those texts, Lily."

I still say nothing. He begins to fidget, growing uncomfortable in my silent anger. He slides his hands into his pockets and stares at his feet. "Did you tell Allysa?"

I don't answer that question. If anything, it infuriates me even more. He's worried what his sister will think of him more than what kind of damage he's doing to me? "No, but I told a lawyer." I'm lying, but it'll be the truth as soon as he leaves this building. From this point forward, I'm documenting everything he does to me. Atlas is right. Ryle looks perfect on paper, and if he's going to continue with abusive tactics, I need to protect myself and Emerson.

Ryle's eyes slowly journey to mine. "You *what?*"

"I sent them to my lawyer."

"Why would you do that?"

"Seriously? You pinned me against a door on Sunday, and then you sent me threatening texts in the middle of the night. I have done nothing to deserve this, Ryle!"

He pulls his hands from his pockets and squeezes the back of his neck as he spins to face the other direction. He stretches his back while he sucks in a breath. He seems to be holding that breath in while he silently counts in an attempt to subdue the anger building in him.

We both know how those techniques have worked in the past.

When he turns around, the remorse is gone. "You don't see the pattern, here? Are you really that blind?"

Oh, I definitely see a pattern, but I think we're looking at different ones.

"We've been fine for a *year*, Lily. We didn't have a single issue until he showed back up. Now we're fighting all the time, and you're getting lawyers involved?" He looks like he wants to punch the air.

"Stop blaming your behavior on other people, Ryle!"

"Stop ignoring the common fucking denominator for all of our problems, *Lily*!"

Lucy appears in the doorway of my office. She looks from me to Ryle, and then back to me. "Are you okay?"

Ryle lets out an exasperated laugh. "She's fine," he says, irritated. Ryle walks toward the door, and Lucy has to press herself against the doorframe to avoid being bumped into. "A fucking *lawyer*," I hear him mutter. "Let me take one guess as to whose idea that was." Ryle is walking toward the door like he's on a mission. Lucy and I both exit my office, most likely for the same reason. To lock him out once he exits the shop.

When Ryle reaches the front door of the building, he spins around and stabs me with a sharp glare. "I am a neurosurgeon. You work with *flowers*, Lily. Remember that before your lawyer does anything stupid to threaten my career. I pay for that fucking apartment you live in." His threat is punctuated by his hands slamming open the door.

Lucy is the one to lock it after he finally leaves because I'm frozen from the impact of that last insult. She walks back to me and pulls me in for a sympathetic hug.

I realize in this moment that the hardest part about ending an abusive relationship is that you aren't necessarily putting an end to the bad moments. The bad moments still rear their ugly heads every now and then. When you end an abusive relationship, it's the good moments you put an end to.

In our marriage, the few terrifying incidents were blanketed by so many good ones, but now that our marriage is over, the blanket has lifted and all I'm left with are the worst pieces of him. Where our marriage was once full of heart and flesh that cushioned the skeleton, all that's left is the skeleton now. Sharp, bony edges that slice right through me.

"You okay?" Lucy asks, smoothing her hands down my hair.

I nod. "Yeah, but . . . did it seem like he left here with a purpose? Like he was going somewhere else?"

Lucy's eyes scan the door again. "Yeah, he peeled out of the parking lot pretty fast. Maybe you should warn Atlas."

I immediately grab for my phone and call him.

Chapter Twenty-Seven
Atlas

It's only been half an hour since I checked my phone, so I'm alarmed when I see several missed calls and three texts from Lily.

> **Please call me.**
> **I'm okay but Ryle is angry.**
> **Did he show up there? Atlas, please call me.**

Shit.

"Darin, can you take over?"

Darin moves to finish plating for me, and I immediately walk to my office and call her. Her phone goes straight to voice mail. I try her again. Nothing.

I'm preparing to head out back to my car when my phone finally rings. I answer immediately with, "Are you okay?"

"I'm fine," she says.

I stop rushing toward the door and lean my shoulder into a wall. I release a breath, my heart rate plummeting back to normal.

It sounds like she's driving. "I'm going to pick up Emmy. I just wanted to warn you that he's angry. I was worried he might show up there."

"Thanks for the warning. You sure you're okay?"

"Yes. Call me when you get home. I don't care how late it is."

Ryle bursts through the kitchen doors in the middle of her sentence. He makes enough of a ruckus that everyone notices and pauses what they're doing. Derek, my head waiter, is right behind Ryle.

"I said I would *get* him," Derek is saying to Ryle. Derek looks at me and throws up his hands to let me know he tried to prevent the intrusion.

"I'll call you on my way home," I say. I fail to mention Ryle just showed up. I don't want her to be concerned. I end the call right as Ryle's eyes land on me.

I don't think he's here to congratulate me.

"Who is that?" Darin asks.

"My biggest fan." I nudge my head toward the back door, so Ryle starts walking in that direction.

The kitchen begins to buzz again, everyone ignoring Ryle's intrusion. Everyone but Darin. "You need me to do something?"

I shake my head. "I'll be fine."

Ryle pushes open the back door so hard, it slams against the outside wall.

What a piece of work. I head in that direction, but as soon as I open the back door and walk onto the back steps, Ryle comes at me from the left. He knocks me off the steps, and then, when I try to stand up, he punches me.

It's a good punch, too. I'll give him that.

Fuck.

I wipe my mouth and stand up, thankful he's at least giving me room to do that. It's not really a fair advantage when one person is on the ground when the punching begins. But Ryle doesn't seem like the type to play fair.

He's about to hit me again, but I back up and he ends up tripping. He pushes off the ground, and when he's back on his feet, he stares at me, fuming. He doesn't seem to be in attack mode in the moment.

"You done?" I ask him.

He doesn't respond, but I don't think he'll lunge for me again. Ryle straightens his shirt and smirks. "I liked it better when you fought back last time."

I struggle not to roll my eyes. "I have no desire to fight you."

He pops his neck and starts to pace. He has so much anger in him, I can't imagine what this must be like for Lily when she has to witness it. He's breathing heavily, his hands on his hips, his eyes piercing me like knives. I don't just see anger in his expression. I see a hell of a lot of pain.

I sometimes try to put myself in Ryle's shoes, but as much as I struggle to stand in them, they don't fit. They never will, because there isn't a single human in history with a past misfortunate enough to excuse beating the person you're supposed to protect.

"Just say whatever it is you came here to say."

Ryle wipes blood away from his knuckles with his shirt, and I notice his hand is swollen. It looks like he was punching things before he showed up and hit me. I'm glad I know Lily is okay, or he wouldn't be walking away in the same condition he showed up in.

"You think I don't know the lawyer was your idea?" he says.

I try to hide my surprise, but I have no idea what he's talking about. *Did she speak to a lawyer about her situation?* It makes me want to smile, but I'm sure a smile would antagonize Ryle, and I do enough of that simply by existing.

My lack of response is getting under his skin. Ryle's face twists in anger. "You might have her fooled right now, but you'll have your first fight with her. And your second. She'll see that marriage isn't fucking rainbows all the goddamn time."

"I could have a million arguments with her, but I can promise you they'll never end with her in the hospital."

Ryle laughs. He's trying to spin this to look like I'm the ridiculous one. I'm not the one who barged into his place of work because I couldn't control my emotions.

"You have no idea what Lily and I have been through," he says. "You have no idea what *I've* been through."

It's like he showed up wanting a fight, but I'm not giving him that, so he's using it as a venting session. Maybe I should give him Theo's number. I'm seriously at a loss here.

I don't want to come back to this moment tomorrow and see it as a lost opportunity. My only goal is to make Lily's life with this man more peaceful. The last thing I want to do is make things more difficult between us all, but until he gets it through his head that he's the only one in control of his reactions, I'm just as confused as Lily as to how to deal with him.

"You're right, Ryle." I nod slowly. "You're right. I have no idea what you've been through." I take a seat on the stairs to let him know he has no reason to feel threatened by me. And if he tries to attack me again while I'm sitting, I'm not going to respond to him with as much composure this time. I clasp my hands together and do my very best to speak in a way that might get through to him.

"Whatever happened in your past helped make you a great neurosurgeon, and the world needs that side of you. But your past also—for whatever reason—made you a shitty husband. The world doesn't need that side of you. Just because we get the opportunity to be something, that isn't a guarantee that we'll be good at it."

Ryle rolls his eyes. "That's dramatic."

"I watched them stitch her up, Ryle. Wake the fuck up, man. You were a horrible husband."

He stares at me for a beat, then says, "What has you convinced you'll be any better?"

"Treating Lily the way she deserves to be treated is the easiest part of my life. I think you should be relieved she's with someone like me."

He laughs. "Relieved? I should be *relieved*?" He takes several steps toward me, his anger ascending again. "*You're* the reason we aren't together!"

It takes everything in me to remain on these steps, and every ounce of patience I have not to return his shouts with my own. "*You're* the reason you aren't together. It was *your* anger and *your* fists that got you here. I was barely an acquaintance in Lily's life when she was with you, so do the mature thing and stop blaming me, and Lily, and everyone else for your actions." I stand up, but not to hit him. I just need to make room in my chest to exhale because if I don't, I'm not sure how much longer I can do this without raising my voice to his level. It's hard looking at him and remaining composed, knowing what he's done to Lily. "*Dammit*," I mutter. "This is ridiculous."

Ryle and I are both quiet for a moment. Maybe he can

tell I'm at my limit because I'm not keeping my frustration as under control anymore. I spin and face him, looking at him pleadingly. "This is our life now. Yours, mine, Lily's, *your daughter's*. We have to deal with this. Forever. Holidays, birthdays, graduations, Emerson's wedding. All these things are going to be difficult for you, but you're the only one who can make sure they aren't difficult for the rest of us, too. Because none of us owes you our happiness. *Especially* Lily."

Ryle shakes his head. He paces like he's trying to erase the asphalt and uncover earth. "You expect me to what—to cheer you two on? To wish you well? To encourage you to be a good father to *my* fucking daughter?" He laughs at the absurdity he finds in the idea of that, but I keep a very straight face.

"Yes. *Exactly* that."

I think my response throws him off. He pauses and threads his hands at the nape of his neck.

I take a step closer to him, but not in a threatening way. I don't want to yell. I want Ryle to hear the absolute sincerity in my voice. "As happy as I know I can make Lily, she'll never be fully happy until she has your acceptance and cooperation. And you're making it difficult, even though you know she deserves a good life. They both do. If you want your daughter to grow up with the best version of Lily, then please work with her. This is possible for all of us."

Ryle rolls his neck. "What are we, some kind of *team* now?"

I hate that he's trying to make any of this sound beyond the realm of possibility. "A team is the *only* thing people should be when kids are involved."

That hits him. I can see it in the way he flinches, and then subtly swallows. He turns around and faces away from me, taking a few steps while he contemplates everything I've said. When he turns back around and looks at me, there's a little less vitriol there.

"When things don't work out between the two of you and Lily needs somewhere to run, I'm not picking up the pieces this time." With that, Ryle walks away. He doesn't go through the restaurant this time. He heads down the alley, toward the street.

I can do nothing but stare at him with pity as he walks away. He truly doesn't know Lily at all.

At all.

Lily doesn't *run* to people. She didn't run after me when I left Maine. She didn't run *to* me when she left Ryle. She focused on being a mother. Yet that's what he expects her to do if things don't work out between us? *Run* to him like he's her home base?

Lily's home base is Emerson, and if he still can't see that, he's clueless.

If Lily had stayed with him, he would have spent the rest of their lives inventing issues in order to justify his excessive anger. Because I was never an issue in their marriage, and I never would have been.

I thought I pitied him before, but he's fighting for a woman he barely even knows, which means he's just fighting for the sake of fighting. He's got a very similar personality to my mother, and sometimes there's no fixing that. You just have to learn to live your life around it.

Maybe that's what Lily and I are going to have to do. Learn to live our lives the best we can while occasionally having to deal with the ridiculous wrath of Ryle.

That's fine. I'd go through this shit every day if it means I'm the one who gets to fall asleep next to her every night.

I walk up the steps and return to the hustle of the kitchen, and I get right back to work like he was never even here. I don't know if my response tonight made this situation better, but I definitely don't think I made it worse.

Darin hands me a wet rag. "You're bleeding." He points to the left side of my mouth, so I hold the rag there. "Was that her ex?"

"Yeah."

"Everything okay now?"

I shrug. "I don't know. He might get mad and come back. Hell, this could go on for years." I look at Darin and smile. "But she's worth it."

•　　•　　•

Three hours later, I'm knocking softly on Lily's apartment door. I texted her to let her know I was coming. I thought she might need another drive-by hug.

When she opens her door, it's clear that's exactly what she needs. And what *I* need. As soon as we're inside her living room, she slips her arms around my waist and I fold myself around her. We remain embraced for a couple of minutes.

When she lifts her face, her eyebrows draw apart when she sees the small cut on my lip. "He's such an immature asshole. Did you put ice on it?"

"I'll be fine. It didn't even swell."

Lily lifts up onto her toes and kisses my cut. "Tell me what happened."

We sit on the couch and I try to recall everything that

was said, but I'm sure I leave a few things out. When I'm finished speaking, she's leaning against the back of the couch with a leg draped over mine, concentrating. She's threading her fingers in and out of my hair.

She's quiet for a long time. Then she just looks at me with a sweetness that melts over me. "I'm convinced you're the only man on the planet who could get punched and then offer the aggressor *advice*." Before I can respond, she's sliding onto my lap, bringing her face close to mine. "Don't worry, I find it so much more appealing than if you would have fought him back."

I slide my hands up her back, surprised she's in such a good mood. I don't know why I thought this conversation would be a weight on her. But I guess this is the best possible outcome. Ryle knows we're a thing, I had a chance to say my piece, and we all came out of it relatively unharmed.

"I can't stay long, but I can probably stretch this hug out for another fifteen minutes before Josh notices I'm late."

She raises an eyebrow. "When you say 'hug,' do you mean . . ."

"I mean get naked—we're down to fourteen minutes." I push her onto her back and kiss her, and we don't stop for fourteen minutes. Then seventeen. Then twenty.

It's thirty minutes later before I finally walk out of her apartment.

Chapter Twenty-Eight
Lily

Allysa has the bright idea of just setting them on the floor on a layer of trash bags, so it'll be an easy cleanup. Emmy and her cousin, Rylee, are both covered in cake now.

Emmy has no idea what's going on, but she's enjoying herself. We ended up having a small party for her here at Allysa's. My mother is here, Ryle's parents, Marshall, and Allysa.

Ryle is also here, but he's about to leave. He snaps a couple of photos on his phone before giving both the girls a quick kiss goodbye.

I heard him telling Marshall it's been a busy day with work, but he made the party. I was happy he made it in time for presents, and he stayed until the cake was mostly demolished. I know it'll mean something to Emmy someday when she sees the pictures.

We haven't spoken the entire time he's been here. We've circled around each other, pretending everything is fine in front of everyone, but Ryle is anything but fine. I can feel the tension radiating from him while standing across the room. Being ignored by him is better than being blamed by him, though. I'd take the silent treatment over the alternative any day.

Unfortunately, I don't get the silent treatment for long.

Ryle is making eye contact with me for the first time today. I made the mistake of standing alone, so he takes this as an opportunity to walk over and stand beside me. I stiffen, not wanting to do this right now. We haven't spoken since he insulted me while walking out of my flower shop last week. I know we need to have a conversation, but our daughter's birthday party is not the time or place.

Ryle slips his hands into his pockets. He tucks his chin against his chest and stares at the floor. "What did your lawyer say?"

Anger climbs up my chest. I side-eye him and give my head a shake. "We aren't having this conversation right now."

"Then when?"

It's not really a matter of when, but *who with*? Because I'm not going to discuss anything while we're alone ever again. He's proven to me that I'm not safe when I'm alone with him, so that privilege is over.

"I'll text you," I say, and then I walk away, leaving Ryle standing alone. My mother is holding Emmy, wiping cake off her face and hands, so I head in their direction, but Allysa pulls me aside before I reach them.

"Let's chat," she says. I follow her to her bedroom, where she sits on her bed.

She only brings me to her bedroom when she wants to confront me about something, and her timing is always impeccably intuitive. I roll my eyes as soon as I walk into her room, and then I sit down on her bed. "What do you want to know?" It's been a couple of weeks since we've caught up alone. There's a lot she could be wondering about my life. It's been pretty eventful here lately.

Allysa falls back onto the bed. "Things between you and Ryle feel kind of off today."

"It's noticeable?"

"I notice everything. Are you okay?"

I think long and hard about that question. *Are you okay?* I used to hide from that question because I wasn't okay. Even months after Emerson's birth, when someone would ask me that, I would put on a smile while I shriveled up inside.

This is the first time I'm not lying when I say, "Yes. I'm okay."

Allysa regards me silently. There's a reassurance in her expression, like she might even believe me this time. She grabs my hand and pulls me until I'm lying on the bed next to her. She locks our arms at the elbows, and we just stare up at the ceiling, enjoying a moment of silence in a house full of people.

I'm glad I still have Allysa. That would have been the most heartbreaking thing of all to have to lose in my divorce. I'm grateful she's so full of forgiveness and positivity.

I wish I could say the same for her brother. Sometimes I feel like Ryle has a monster inside him that is on a constant search to be offended. His dark side feeds off drama, and if no one gives him any, he makes it up. But I can't be a player in his game anymore. I know my intentions were pure when I was married to Ryle, no matter how much Ryle wanted his delusions to be true so they could excuse his behavior.

"How are things with Adonis?"

I laugh. "You mean Atlas?"

"I said what I said. Adonis, the beautiful Greek god you're in love with."

I laugh again. "Wasn't Adonis a product of incest?"

Allysa shoves me. "Stop deflecting. How are things going?"

I roll onto my stomach and lift up on my elbow. "Good, if we'd ever get to spend time together. His restaurant doesn't open until my flower shop closes. We haven't even spent an entire night with each other yet."

"What's Atlas doing right now? Working?"

I nod.

"You should see if he can take off early and I'll keep Emerson tonight. We don't have plans tomorrow; you could come get her whenever."

My eyes widen at her offer. "For real?"

Allysa climbs off the bed. "Rylee loves it when she's here. Go spend the night with your Adonis."

•   •   •

I didn't text Atlas to let him know I was on my way to Corrigan's. He told me he'd be working there tonight, and I thought it might be fun to surprise him, but when I walk through the doors that lead to the kitchen, I'm amazed at how busy it is. No one even hears me enter, so I look around until I spot him.

Atlas is inspecting each plate as they're given to him to place on trays, then the waitstaff quickly disappear with the food through the double doors. This place is more upscale than Bib's, and I thought Bib's was upscale. All the waiters are dressed in formal attire. Atlas is in a white chef's coat that matches a couple of the others in the kitchen.

They've got such a groove going, I question whether I

should have shown up. I feel like I'll be in the way if I walk over to him, but I suddenly feel very awkward that I just showed up without letting him know.

I recognize Darin as soon as he spots me. He smiles and nods his head, then gets Atlas's attention. He motions toward me, and when Atlas turns around and sees me in his kitchen, his eyes light up. But only momentarily. The fact that I'm here instantly changes his excitement to concern. He makes a beeline for me, sidestepping around a waiter who is walking back into the kitchen with an empty tray.

"Hey. Everything okay?"

"It's fine. Allysa decided to keep Emmy for the night, so I thought I'd stop by."

Atlas smiles hopefully. "Is she keeping her for the whole night?" There's a flicker of flirtation in his eyes.

I nod.

"Hot behind!" someone yells from behind me. *Hot behind?* My eyes widen just as Atlas pulls us out of the way of a waiter carrying a tray of food.

"Kitchen slang," he says. "Means you're in the way of hot food."

"Oh."

Atlas laughs, and then looks over his shoulder at all the plates he's falling behind on. "Give me about twenty minutes to get us caught up?"

"Of course. I didn't come here to ask you to leave early. I thought I could watch you work for a while; it's kind of fun."

Atlas points to a metal counter. "Sit there. It's the best view, and you won't get knocked over. Gets pretty busy back here. Be done soon." He lifts my chin and bends to kiss me, then he backs away and returns to what he was doing before I walked in.

I take a seat on the counter and pull up my legs, crossing them so that I'm completely out of the way. I notice a few of the employees stealing glances at me, which makes me somewhat uncomfortable. Out of all the people back here right now, I've only met Darin, so I have no idea who any of them are. I do wonder what they're thinking of the random girl Atlas just kissed who is now watching them work.

I don't know if Atlas normally brings women around, but I get the feeling he doesn't. Everyone is looking at me like this is an anomaly.

Darin comes over to greet me as soon as he gets a chance. He gives me a quick hug and says, "Good to see you again, Lily. You still hustling unassuming poker players?"

I laugh. "Not for a while now. Do you guys still have your poker nights?"

He shakes his head. "Nah, we're too busy now that Atlas has both restaurants. It was difficult finding a night we could all meet up."

"That's a shame. Are you working here now?"

"Not officially. Atlas wanted to see how I work with the menu here; he's thinking of promoting me to head chef." He leans in and smiles. "He said he wants more time off. I guess now I know why." Darin tosses a rag over his shoulder. "It was good seeing you. Sounds like you'll be around more often." He winks before walking away.

Knowing Atlas is making an effort to spend less time at work makes my stomach swirl with happiness.

I spend the next fifteen minutes silently watching Atlas

work. Every now and then he'll glance at me and give me a warm smile, but the rest of the time, he's focused on his job. His intensity and confidence are mesmerizing.

No one seems intimidated by him, but everyone appears to want his opinion. He's constantly being asked questions, and he responds to each one of them with patience. In between those moments of teaching, there's a lot of yelling. Not the kind of yelling I'd expect to find in a kitchen, but people calling out food orders and cooks yelling their acknowledgments. It's loud and busy, but the vibe is a rush.

It's honestly not at all what I expected to find. I thought I'd see a whole new side to Atlas—one where he barked orders with anger and behaved like all the chefs I've seen on television. But, thankfully, that's not at all what is happening in this kitchen.

After a thrilling half an hour goes by, Atlas finally steps away from his station. He washes his hands before walking over to me. I get this knot of excitement in my stomach when he leans forward and presses his mouth to mine, like he doesn't care that all his staff can see us.

"Sorry that took so long," he says.

"I enjoyed it. It was different than I expected."

"How so?"

"I thought all chefs were assholes and screamed at their staff."

He laughs. "No assholes in this kitchen. Sorry to disappoint." He uncrosses my legs so he can stand between them. "Guess what?"

"What?"

"Josh is staying over at Theo's tonight."

I can't hold back my grin. "What a wonderful coincidence."

Atlas's eyes sweep over me, and then he leans his head against mine, pressing his lips lightly against my ear. "Your place or mine?"

"Yours. I want to be in a bed that smells like you."

He nips at my ear, sending chills down my neck. Then he takes my hands and helps me down from the counter. He gives his attention to someone passing by. "Hey, can you take over the pass?"

The guy says, "You bet."

Atlas looks back at me and says, "Meet you at my house."

·   ·   ·

I stopped by my apartment before going to his restaurant to pack a bag just in case this was a possibility, so I get to his place before he does. While I wait for Atlas, I use the time in my car to check in with Allysa.

Did she fall asleep okay?

Just fine. How's your night going?

Just fine. ;)

Have fun. I expect a full report.

Atlas's headlights shine through my car as he pulls into his driveway. I'm still gathering my things when he opens my car door. As soon as I climb out of the car, Atlas dips an impatient hand into my hair and kisses me. It's the kind of kiss that screams *I've missed kissing you.*

When he pulls back, he studies my face with a gentle smile. "I liked you watching me in the kitchen tonight."

A shiver passes over me. "I like watching you." I can't say

it without grinning. I grab my bag from the passenger seat, and Atlas takes it from me and hoists it over his shoulder. I follow him through the garage. He still has moving boxes piled up along one wall. There's a weight bench in pieces on the floor next to the unpacked boxes. There are two full baskets of laundry sitting in front of a washer and dryer.

Seeing a little bit of disarray in his garage is comforting. I was beginning to think he was too good to be true, but Atlas Corrigan is behind on life and behind on laundry like the rest of us.

He unlocks his house and holds the door open for me. It's smaller than his last one, but it's more him. And it's not a cut-and-paste brick building in a subdivision of similar-looking homes. The houses in this neighborhood have character. Each one is vastly different, from the pink two-story house on the corner to the modern boxy glass one at the other end of the street.

Atlas's house is a bungalow-style home nestled in between two larger homes. When I was here last time, I noted that he somehow got the biggest backyard of the three. *Plenty of room for a garden someday . . .*

Atlas enters his security code into his keypad. "It's nine five nine five," he says. "If you ever need in."

"Nine five nine five," I repeat, noting it's the same number combination as his phone. He's a man of commitment. I like it.

His security code isn't a key to his house, but it feels almost as significant. He places my bag on his couch and then flips on the living room light. My back is to the wall, and I'm standing out of the way, watching him. It's a good thing he informed me that he liked it when I was watching him at work, because watching Atlas is my favorite pastime. I could live my life as a fly on his wall and be content. "What's your routine when you get home at night?"

Atlas tilts his head. "What do you mean?"

I gesture at the room. "What do you do when you get home at night? Pretend I'm not here."

He regards me silently. Then he walks toward me, pausing right in front of me. He presses a hand onto the wall beside my head and leans in. "Well," he whispers. "First, I take off my shoes."

I hear one of his shoes being kicked off, then the other. He's suddenly an inch lower and even closer to my mouth. He feathers his lips lightly across mine, sending fireworks popping beneath my skin. "Then . . ." He kisses the corner of my mouth. "I take a shower." He pushes off the wall and backs away, his eyes locked on mine in a dare.

He disappears into his bedroom.

I'm inhaling a steadying breath when I hear his shower start running. I slip off my shoes and leave them next to his, then I follow the path he took down the hallway. I gently push open the half-closed door and take in his bedroom in person for the first time. I've seen it in our video chats, but I didn't come in here when I came to his house the first time. I recognize his black headboard and the denim-blue accent wall behind it, but the rest of his bedroom is new to me. I pass over everything in search of the bathroom door.

He left it open. His shirt is on the floor by the doorway.

I don't know why my heart is pounding like it'll be my first time seeing Atlas without clothes. It's not like I'm brand-new to this, or him, or even to showering with him. But every time I'm with him, it's like my heart gets amnesia.

I make it to the doorway of his bathroom, disappointed to see that his shower is hidden behind half of a stone wall. I can hear the breaks and splashes in the shower stream, and I feel a tightening in every curve of my body.

I don't leave my clothes with his. I stay dressed and slowly make my way over to the shower. I press my back flush against the long wall of his bathroom, and I inch closer to the shower opening, leaning my head in just enough to get a peek at him.

Atlas is standing under the stream of water, his eyes closed, the water coming down directly on his face as he runs his fingers through his hair. I stay quiet and still and continue leaning against the wall while I watch him.

He knows I'm here, but he ignores my presence and allows me to soak up the sight of him. I want to run my hands over the rise and fall of muscles across his shoulders, and I want to kiss the dimples in his lower back. He is absolutely beautiful.

Once he rinses all the soap out of his hair and off his face, he looks toward me. His eyes catch mine, and they narrow. Darken. Then he faces me, my gaze falling, falling . . .

"Lily."

My eyes move back up to his, and he's smirking. Then, so quickly, he strides across the wet tile and yanks me away from the wall until I'm wrapped in his arms. He pulls me into the shower with him, and I gasp from the rush of it all.

He catches my gasp in his mouth as he grips my thighs, pulling my wet-blue-jean-covered legs around him. My back meets the shower wall, taking some of my weight off Atlas so that he can free up a hand.

He uses that free hand to unbutton my shirt.

I use both of mine to help him. We stop kissing long enough for him to lower me to my feet so that he can slip the shirt down my arms. The shirt plops against the shower floor with a small splash just as Atlas's fingers meet the button on my jeans.

His mouth is hungry and back on mine as he slides his hands between my hips and my panties, tugging my clothes down one difficult inch at a time.

.He grips the waistband on the sides of my jeans and lowers himself down my body as he works to slide them off me. Once they're around my ankles, I help him by kicking them off, then he places his hands on the backs of my calves and slowly works his way back up me.

When he's fully standing again, his fingers gather behind my back at the clasp of my bra. My stomach clenches as he begins to unfasten it. His mouth finds mine again, but this kiss is gentle and slow, like the removal of this last piece of clothing deserves to be savored.

I feel his hands slide to my shoulders, and then he tucks his fingers beneath the straps and slips them down my arms. My bra begins to fall away from me, and Atlas pulls away from my mouth long enough to admire me. His hand curves over my hip, and then slides over my ass, squeezing me.

I wrap my arms around his neck and slide my lips across his jaw, settling my mouth over his ear. "Then what?"

I watch as chills break out over his arms. He groans, and then lifts me higher up the wall until we're aligned at the waist. I roll my hips into him, wanting to feel him hard against me, and he meets my movement with a quick thrust, forcing me to gasp. It's obvious we both want this, but he still looks at me for permission before he takes me right here in the shower. We've had the proper conversations about my being on birth control, and both of us having been tested, so I just nod and whisper a desperate "Yes."

I grip his shoulders tighter in an attempt to take more weight off his arms so that he can position himself to push into me. He uses his left arm to hold me up and his right hand to grip himself, and then he rolls his hips forward and up until I feel the pressure of him inside of me.

He sighs into my neck at the same time I release all the breath in my chest. It comes out like a moan, and that sound encourages Atlas to get that noise out of me again.

My legs are tight around his waist, but he thrusts against me hard enough for them to unlock at the ankles. I start to slip down him, but he hoists me back up and repositions himself until I'm filled with him all over again.

I release another moan, and he rolls into me a second time, and a third time, and it may not be as graceful against a water-soaked shower wall as it is in a bed, but I can't get enough of the unruly side of him.

He gives me that unruly side of him for several minutes before we're both too weak and breathless to continue this without the support of a bed. He doesn't say anything after he pulls out of me and lowers me to my feet. He just turns off the water and then grabs a towel. He starts at my hair, squeezing water out of it with both his hands, and then he slowly works his way down my body with the towel until I'm dry enough.

He does a quick swipe of himself with the towel before grabbing my hand and walking me out of the bathroom.

I don't know how something as simple as him holding my hand on our way to the bedroom can make my heart expand.

Atlas lifts the blanket and motions for me to climb into his bed. It's so comfortable, it feels like I'm nestling into a cloud. He scoots in next to me, stopping only when he can't come even a centimeter closer to me. He's on his side, but he rolls me so that I'm flat on my back, tucked against him.

I like this position. I like the way he's holding himself up on his elbow, hovering over me. I like the slight grin in his eyes, as if I'm a reward he's earned.

Atlas lowers himself and we're no longer easing into these kisses. It's an immediate deep and hungry kiss that starts with the dive of his tongue and ends with him impressively reaching for a condom and putting it on without interrupting the strength of his kiss. Atlas grips the inside of my thigh and pushes my leg aside to make room for himself.

Then he's above me, pushing into me, and he moves against me until I find myself in the middle of a beautiful falling apart.

•   •   •

Atlas is on his back on the bed, and I'm curled into him, my leg draped over his thigh. These are the moments I look forward to sharing with him the most. The quiet minutes we get to steal from the chaos of our lives, where it's just the two of us, satiated, content. My head is resting on his chest, his fingers are trailing back and forth over my arm.

He kisses the top of my head and says, "How long has it been since we ran into each other on the street?"

"Forty days," I say. *I've been counting.*

He makes a *huh* sound, like that surprises him.

"Why? Does it feel longer?"

"No, I just wanted to know if you've been counting like I have."

I laugh and press my lips against his skin, right over his heart.

"How were things at the party today?" he asks me. I know what he's asking without him having to say it. He wants to know how Ryle treated me.

"The party was good. I spoke to Ryle for maybe five seconds."

"Was he unkind?"

"No. We just stayed out of each other's way, mostly."

Atlas runs his fingers through my hair, pulling them through the strands and letting them fall over my back. He takes another handful and repeats the movement. "That's progress. Hopefully it'll just get easier from here."

"Hopefully." I do hope things between Ryle and I continue to get easier, but I'm no longer letting his reactions control my happiness. I'm all-in with Atlas, and I want to be present in that part of my life. If that makes Ryle upset or uncomfortable, Ryle is going to have to bear the burden of those feelings. "I might ask Allysa to have a sit-down with me and Ryle this week. I want to discuss what happened, and what to do going forward, but I don't want to discuss it with him alone."

"That's smart."

Ryle and I may never get to a point where we can be more than merely civil. But I'd be okay with civil. What I'm not okay with are the insults, the threatening texts, the outbursts. He's got a lot of work to do, and I'm finally willing to hold him to task.

I probably should have been firmer earlier on, but I've been trying to make it work in the least dramatic way possible. But I'm done bending my own life for Ryle's sake.

My loyalty is to the people who bring positivity into my life. My loyalty is to the people who want to build me up and see me happy. Those are the people I'm going to make decisions about my life for.

I'm going to continue doing the best I can, and that's all I can do. I may not have made all the right decisions in the right time frames, but the fact that I found the courage to make those decisions at all is what I'm going to keep focusing on.

Atlas slips a finger beneath my chin, tilting my head back so that I'm looking at him. He's got this look on his face like he's right where he wants to be. "I can't tell you how much I've enjoyed this," he says. He pulls me closer, sliding me up his chest so that I'm eye to eye with him. He caresses the side of my head. "I wish I could have you in my bed like this every night. I want to shower with you and cook with you and watch TV with you and go grocery shopping with you. I want *everything* with you. I hate that we have to pretend like we don't already know we're spending the rest of our lives together."

It's incredible how fast a heart rate can double. I slide my fingers over his lips. "We aren't pretending. We *are* going to spend the rest of our lives together."

"How long do we have to wait until we start?"

"From the looks of it, we've already started," I say.

"How long do I have to wait before I ask you to move in with me?"

Heat swirls in my stomach. "Six months, at least."

He nods as if he's taking mental notes. "And how long before I'm allowed to propose?"

A thickness forms in my throat, making it hard to swallow. "A year. Year and a half."

"A year from when we move *in* together or a year from *now?*"

"From now."

He grins, pulling me flat against him. "Good to know."

I can't help but laugh into his neck. "That was a surprising conversation."

"Yeah, my therapist is going to kill me when I tell him about it."

I'm smiling as I roll off him and lay on my side. I snuggle into the crook of his arm and run my fingers over Atlas's chest, and then trail them over the ridges of his stomach. His muscles clench and twitch beneath my fingernails. "Do you work out?"

"When I can."

"It shows."

Atlas laughs lightheartedly. "Are you trying to flirt with me, Lily?"

"Yes."

"I don't need compliments. You're naked and in my bed. Not much else you need to do; you won me over years ago."

I lift my head and smirk, like that's a challenge. "You don't think so?"

He shakes his head, smiling lazily. He runs his thumb over my bottom lip. "Pretty sure I am filled to capacity. I think I may have even reached enlightenment tonight."

I keep my eyes locked with his, but I readjust myself, and then I slowly start to slide down his body. "I think I can still impress you," I whisper. He releases a deep exhale when I press a kiss to his stomach. My gaze is still on his face, and I love that his expression begins to tighten while he watches me.

He swallows when I start to move the sheet aside, until he's no longer covered below the waist. His eyes darken. "*Fuck*, Lily."

He allows his head to fall back against his pillow as soon as my tongue slides up the length of him.

He groans when I take him in my mouth, and then I prove him *very* wrong.

Chapter Twenty-Nine
Atlas

I can't get enough of her, but I think it's okay because she can't seem to get enough of me. She woke me up this morning by sliding on top of me and kissing my neck.

She ended up on her back seconds later with my mouth between her thighs.

Maybe we're so hungry for each other because we know it's rare that we'll get days like this. Or maybe it's because we've missed each other for so many years.

Or maybe this is just what things are like when you're in love. I've been with women aside from Lily, but I'm convinced she's the only one I've ever truly loved.

My feelings for Lily are amplified unlike anything I've ever experienced. They're even more amplified than the feelings I had for her when we were younger. It's different now—stronger, deeper, more exciting. There's no way in hell I'd walk away from her now like I did back then.

I know I was in a different headspace entirely at the age of eighteen, and that had a lot to do with why I didn't feel like I should stick around for her. But I'm all-in now. I absolutely hate the idea of taking it slow. I get why we need to, but I don't have to like it. I want her near me every day, because I feel absolutely unfulfilled on the days I can't see her.

Now that we've stayed the night together, I have a feeling the ache is going to get worse. I'm going to grow irritable when I have to go too long without seeing her. She's standing right next to me while we brush our teeth, but I'm already dreading that she's about to leave.

Maybe if I offer to cook her breakfast, I'll get her for at least another hour.

"Why do you have a spare toothbrush?" Lily asks me. She spits her toothpaste into my sink and winks at me. "You have overnight guests a lot?"

I smile at her and rinse my mouth, but I don't answer that question. I have that toothbrush for her, but I don't want to admit it. I've made a lot of small moves over the years that were all excused with *just in case Lily* . . .

After she left my place a couple of years ago while she was hiding from Ryle, I went out and bought a lot of things just in case she needed to come back. An extra toothbrush, more comfortable pillows for my guest room, a change of clothes in case she showed up in an emergency.

I had a Lily emergency kit, if you will. I guess now it's more of a Lily *sleepover* kit. And yes, I brought it all to the new house with me when I moved. I've always had a little bit of hope that we'd end up together someday.

Hell, if I'm being honest with myself, I've had a great deal of hope. I've based a lot of my decisions on the possibility that Lily might come back into my life. I even chose this house over another one I was considering, simply because of the back-yard. It looked like a backyard Lily would fall in love with.

I wipe my mouth on a hand towel and then hand it to her to use. "Can I make you breakfast before you go?"

"Yeah, but kiss me first. I taste better than I did this morning." She stands on her tiptoes and I wrap my arms around her and lift her the rest of the way to my mouth. I kiss her while I walk her out of the bathroom and then drop her onto my mattress. I hover over her.

"You want pancakes? Crepes? An omelet? Biscuits and gravy?" Before she can answer me, my doorbell rings. "Josh is home." I give her a quick peck. "He likes pancakes. Will that work?"

"I love pancakes."

"Pancakes it is." I walk to the living room and unlock the door for Josh. I open it, and then I immediately freeze at the sight of my mother.

I sigh, frustrated I didn't use the peephole.

She looks at me flatly, her arms folded across her chest. "I got a visit from a caseworker yesterday." Her eyes are accusing, but at least she isn't yelling.

I am not about to do this with Lily here. I step outside and try to close the door, but my mother slaps it open. "Josh, get out here!" she yells into the house.

"He isn't here." I keep my voice low.

"Where is he?"

"At a friend's house." I pull my phone out of my pocket and check the time. Brad said he'd have Josh here by ten, and it's ten fifteen. *Please don't let him show up while Sutton is here.*

"Call him," she demands.

The door is wide open from when Sutton pushed it, so I can see out of the corner of my eye when Lily emerges from the hallway.

This is not how I wanted my morning with Lily to end. I can feel the regret slide all the way through me. I shoot her an apologetic look, and then give my attention back to Sutton.

"What did the caseworker say?" I ask her.

Her mouth screws into a tight twist, and then she looks to her left. "They're not even opening an investigation. If you don't return him to me today, I'll file charges."

I know the steps Child Protective Services has to take during an investigation, and they haven't even contacted Josh for an interview yet. "You're lying. I'd like you to leave."

"I'll leave when I have my son."

I exhale. "He doesn't want to live with you right now." *Or ever*, but I save that sting.

"He doesn't want to *live* with me," she repeats with a laugh. "What kid that age *wants* to live with their parents? And how many parents *haven't* slapped a kid that age? They don't end custody over that. *Jesus* Christ." She folds her arms over her chest again. "The only reason you're doing this is to get back at me."

If she knew me, she would know I'm not vengeful like she is. But of course, the conclusion she comes up with is something that only fits her own personality. "Do you miss him?" I ask her, my voice calm. "Honestly. Do you miss him? Because if you're doing this to prove something to someone, just let it go. *Please*."

Brad's car turns onto the street, and I wish there were a way I could ask him to keep driving. But he's pulling up to the curb before I can even reach my phone. Sutton follows my line of sight and sees Josh opening the back door of Brad's car.

She immediately walks toward the car, but Josh pauses when he sees her. More like *freezes*. He doesn't know what to do.

Sutton snaps her fingers and points at her car. "Let's go. We're leaving."

Josh immediately looks at me. I shake my head and motion for him to come inside. Brad can sense something is off, so he puts the car in park and opens his door.

Josh ducks his head and walks directly across the yard, past Sutton, and rushes toward me. Sutton is hot on his trail, so I try to get Josh inside quick enough to close the door on her, but she's too fast. I'm not about to injure her with the door, so I just let her inside.

I guess we're doing this now.

I wave to Brad to let him know he can go, and then I look at Lily, who is standing against a wall, watching everything unfold with a surprised look on her face.

I mouth, *I'm sorry.*

Josh tosses his backpack on the floor and sits down on the couch, firmly folding his arms. "I'm not going with you," he says to Sutton.

"This isn't up to you."

Josh looks directly at me, pleading. "You said I could stay here."

"You can."

Sutton shoots daggers at me like I'm out of line. Maybe I am. Maybe it's not my business to be getting in the way of a mother and her child, but she should have thought twice about that before she made me that child's brother. I can't turn the other way and just hope he makes it out okay.

"If you don't come with me, I'll have your brother arrested."

Josh slaps his hands on the couch and pushes himself up. "Why can't it be *my* choice?" he yells. "Why do I have to live with either one of you? I've told you both I want to live with my dad, but no one will help me *find* him!" Josh's voice cracks, and then he's marching down the hallway. The slam of his door makes me flinch . . . or maybe it was what he said before running to his room.

Either way, I feel punctured.

Sutton can see the sting because she's staring at me, assessing my reaction to that.

Then she starts to laugh. "Oh, *Atlas*. You thought you were doing something here? Forming a *bond* with him?" She shakes her head and throws up her hand in defeat. "Take him to his daddy. You'll be running back to me next week, just like you did the last time you needed my help."

She walks to the door and leaves, and I'm too dazed by everything that just happened to walk over and lock it.

Lily does it for me.

She starts to walk toward me with a face full of sympathy, but as soon as she pulls me in for a hug, I shake my head and separate myself from her. "I need a minute."

Chapter Thirty
Lily

Atlas closes his bedroom door behind him, and I find myself alone in his living room.

I feel awful for both of them. I can't believe that was his mother. *Or maybe I can.* After hearing stories of her, I imagined her to be that unhinged, but I guess I expected her to look different. Both Atlas and his brother look so much like her that it makes it difficult to see that kind of behavior come from someone Atlas is related to. They are polar opposites.

I take a seat on the edge of the couch, shocked that I just witnessed all of that. I've never seen Atlas that affected. I want to go hug him, but I can absolutely understand that he needs a moment alone.

Josh, too. The poor kid.

I don't want to leave before saying goodbye to Atlas, but I also don't want to disturb him until he's had a moment to recover. I walk to the kitchen and open the refrigerator. I look for the ingredients to make breakfast for them.

• • •

I kept it simple because that's all I really know how to do. I made scrambled eggs and bacon and put a pan of biscuits in the oven. When the biscuits are almost ready, I go tap on

Josh's bedroom door. I can at least offer him something to eat while I wait for Atlas to come out of his room.

Josh opens the door about two inches and looks at me.

"You want some breakfast?" I ask him.

"Is Sutton gone?"

I nod, so he opens the door and follows me down the hall. Josh gets himself something to drink while I pull the biscuits out and make us both a plate of breakfast. I sit across from him at the table, and he eyes me while he eats. I feel like I'm being sized up.

"Where's Emerson?" he asks.

"She's with her aunt."

Josh nods and takes a bite of his food. Then: "How long have you and my brother been together?"

I shrug. "That depends. I've known him since I was fifteen, but we started dating about a month and a half ago."

There's a flash of surprise on Josh's face. "Really? Were you, like, friends back then or something?"

"Or something." I take a sip of my coffee, and then set it down carefully. "Your brother didn't have anywhere to live when I met him, so I helped him for a while."

Josh leans back in his chair. "Really? I thought he lived with our mom."

"When she and your dad would allow it," I say. "But he spent a lot of time trying to survive without their help." I hope I'm not saying too much, but I feel like Josh needs a better understanding of Atlas. "Go easy on your brother, okay? He cares a lot about you."

Josh stares at me for a beat, then nods. He leans over his plate again, taking a bite of bacon. He drops the bacon back onto the plate and wipes his mouth with a napkin. "His cooking is normally better than this."

I laugh. "That's because I made it."

"Oh, shit," Josh says. "Sorry."

I don't take offense at all because I'm sure he's getting used to Atlas's cooking. "Do you think you want to be a chef like him? He told me you like helping out at the restaurants."

Josh shrugs. "I don't know. It's fun. Maybe. But I feel like I'll get tired of it. He works a lot of nights. I feel like I'll get tired of *any* career after a few years, though, so I don't know what I'll do."

"Sometimes I feel like I still don't know what I want to be when I grow up."

"I thought you owned a flower shop or something. That's what Atlas told me."

"I do. Before that, I used to work at a marketing firm." I push my plate aside and fold my arms on the table. "I still feel like you do, though. Worried about boredom. Why are we expected to pick one thing to try and be successful at? What if I want to do something completely different every five years?"

Josh nods like he's in complete agreement. "The teachers at school talk like we have to decide on one thing we love and stick with it, but I want to do a hundred things."

I love how animated he is right now. He reminds me so much of a younger Atlas. "Like what?"

"I want to be a professional fisherman. I don't know how to fish, but it sounds fun. And I want to be a chef. And sometimes I think it would be fun to make a movie."

"Sometimes I dream of selling my flower shop and opening a clothing boutique."

"I want to make pottery and sell it at fairs."

"I'd like to write a book someday."

"I want to be the captain of a ship," he says.

"I think it would be fun to be an art teacher."

"I think it would be fun to be a bouncer at a strip club."

I sputter laughter at that, but I'm not the only one laughing. Josh and I glance up at Atlas, who is leaning in the doorway, laughing at our conversation.

I'm relieved to see him in a better mood than the one his mother left him in. Atlas smiles at me warmly.

"Lily made us breakfast," Josh says to him.

"I see that." Atlas walks over and kisses me on the cheek, then picks up a piece of bacon and takes a bite.

"Kind of sucks," Josh mutters in warning.

"Don't insult my girlfriend or I'll stop cooking for you." Atlas steals the last slice of bacon off Josh's plate.

"These eggs are great, Lily," Josh says with fake enthusiasm.

I laugh while Atlas takes a seat next to me. As much as I want to spend the entire day here with him, I've already stayed longer than I intended.

It also feels like he and Josh have a lot to work out today.

"I have to go," I say regretfully. Atlas nods, and I scoot back from the table. "I'm gonna go grab my stuff." I walk to the bedroom, but I don't close Atlas's door, so I hear their conversation as I'm packing my bag.

Atlas says, "You feel like taking a road trip today?"

"Where to?" Josh asks.

"I found your dad's address."

I pause gathering my things and walk closer to the door so I can hear Josh's response.

"You did?" There's a new excitement in Josh's voice. "Does he know we're coming?"

"No, I only got his address. I don't know how to get in touch with him. But you were right: He's in Vermont." I can hear the dread Atlas is attempting to cover up in his voice all the way from his bedroom. *God, I hate this for him.*

I hear Josh running toward his room. "He is going to be so shocked!"

I finish packing with a heavier heart. When I walk back into the kitchen, Atlas is standing in front of the sink, staring out the window into his backyard. He doesn't hear me, so I put my hand on his shoulder.

He immediately pulls me in and kisses me on the side of my head. "I'll walk you to your car."

He carries my bag to the car and places it in the backseat. I open my door, but we hug again before I climb inside.

This is the kind of hug Atlas gave me when he showed up at my apartment needing a hug that night. It's long and sad, and I don't want to let go of him. "What do you think is going to happen when you get there?" I ask.

Atlas finally releases me, but keeps his hand on my hip while he leans against my car. He sighs, threading his finger through a belt loop on my jeans. "I don't know. Why do I feel so worried for him?"

"Because you love him."

Atlas's eyes scroll over my face. "Is that why I always feel worried for you? Because I love you?"

My breath hitches at his question. "I don't know. Do you?"

Atlas digs his fingers into my waist, and he pulls me to him. He lifts his hand and traces a finger down my neck, until it meets my tattoo. "I've loved you for years and years and years, Lily. You know that." He moves his finger and then kisses me there, and that move coupled with his words takes everything in me to keep my composure.

"I've loved you for just as long."

Atlas nods. "I know you have. No one on this earth loves me like you do." He cradles my head in both of his hands, and he tilts my face up to his and he kisses me. When he pulls back, he looks at me longingly, like I've already left and he's already sad about it. Or maybe that's just what I'm imagining he feels, since that's what *I* feel.

"I'll call you tonight. I love you."

"I love you, too. Good luck today."

I drive home with such conflicted feelings. Every moment with him over this last day was more than I could have hoped for, but knowing what he's about to face makes my heart feel like a piece of it broke off and stayed with him.

I'm going to be thinking about him all day. I'm hoping they don't find Tim, but if they do, I hope Josh makes the right decision.

Chapter Thirty-One
Atlas

It's a three-hour drive there. Josh hasn't said much. He's been reading, although if he's as nervous as I am about this, I'm not sure he's actually absorbing anything he's reading. He's been on the same page for five minutes. It's a drawing of what looks like a battle scene, but mostly all I see is cleavage.

"Is that manga appropriate for a twelve-year-old?" I ask him.

He shifts ever so slightly so that the cover of the book is all I can see. "Yes."

His voice dropped an entire octave on that lie. At least he's a horrible liar. If he ends up staying with me, detecting when he is or isn't telling me the truth should be easy.

If he ends up staying with me, maybe I should buy him a few self-help books for balance. I'll stock his bookshelves with whatever graphic novels he wants, and then secretly slip in a few of my own to supplement my lack of skills as a guardian. *Untamed, Man Enough, The Subtle Art of Not Giving a F*ck.* Heck, maybe even some sacred text from every major world religion. I'll take whatever help I can get.

Especially after today. As much as Josh may think this is a one-way trip, I know in my heart he's coming right back to Boston with me. I just hope he doesn't come back kicking and screaming.

When the GPS says we're turning onto the street, Josh's hand tightens around his manga. He doesn't look up from it, though, even though he still hasn't turned the page. When I spot Tim's address on the curb in front of a run-down frame house, I pull the car over. The house is across the street on the driver's side, but Josh pretends to be sunk into his story.

"We're here."

Josh drops his book and finally looks up. I point to the house, and Josh stares at it for a good ten seconds. Then he puts the book in his backpack.

He brought most of his things with him. The clothes I bought him, some of the books. They're all stuffed so tight in a backpack that barely zips, and he holds it in his lap with the hope that he has at least one parent that will take him.

"Can we wait a little bit?" he asks.

"Sure."

While he waits, he fidgets with everything. The air vents, his seat belt, the music on his Bluetooth. Ten minutes pass while I patiently give him the time to work up whatever courage he's in need of that will help him open the door.

I look at the house, taking my attention off Josh for a while. There's an old white Ford in the driveway, which is probably why Josh hasn't worked up the courage to walk across the street and knock on his door yet. It's an indicator that someone is probably home.

I haven't tried to talk him out of this because I know what it's like to want to know your father. He's going to live in this fantasy until he's able to confront his reality. As a kid, I had the highest hopes for family, too, but after years of being disappointed, I realized that just because you're born into a group of people, that doesn't make them your family.

"Should I just go knock?" Josh finally asks. He's scared, and to be honest, I'm not feeling the bravest right now, either. I went through a lot with Tim. I'm not looking forward to seeing him again, and I am absolutely dreading the potential outcome of this meeting.

I don't think this is the best place for Josh, and I'm in no position to tell him he can't reconnect with his father. But my biggest fear is that he's going to choose to stay here. That Tim is going to be like my mother and welcome Josh with open arms, simply because he knows it's the one thing I don't want to happen.

"I can go with you if you want," I say, even though it's the last thing I want to do. I'll have to stand in front of that man and pretend I don't want to punch him for the sake of my little brother.

Josh doesn't move for a while. I'm staring at my phone, attempting to appear patient as he works up courage, but I want to throw the car in drive and get him out of here.

I eventually feel Josh's finger briefly graze an old scar on my arm, so I look over at him. He's staring at my arm, taking in the faded scars that remain from the shit I endured living with Sutton and Tim. Josh has never asked me about the scars, though.

"Did Tim do that to you?"

I clench my arm and nod. "Yeah, but it was a long time ago. How he treats a son might be completely different from how he treated a stepson."

"That shouldn't matter, right? If he treated you like that, why should he get another chance with me?"

It's the first time Josh has come close to admitting his father isn't a hero.

I don't want to be the person he blames in the future for not having a relationship with his dad, but I want to tell him he's right. His father *shouldn't* get another chance. He left and never looked back. There's no excuse good enough to walk away from your son.

There's this toxic belief that family should stick together simply because they're family. But the best thing I ever did for myself was walk away from them. It scares me to think of where I might be had I not done that. It scares me to think of where Josh might end up if he *doesn't* do that.

Josh looks past me, toward the house. His eyes grow a little wider, prompting me to turn and look.

Tim is outside, making his way from the front door to his truck. Josh and I watch in mutually stunned silence.

He looks fragile—older and smaller. Or maybe that's because I'm no longer a kid.

He's swigging from the last of a beer can when he opens the front door to his truck. He tosses the empty can into the bed and then leans inside his cab in search of something.

"I don't know what to do," Josh whispers. He seems all of the twelve years old that he is right now. It kind of breaks my heart to see him so nervous. Josh's eyes are pleading for truth when he looks back at me, like he needs me to guide him in this moment.

I've never said a bad word about Tim to Josh, but knowing I'm not being completely honest with him about my feelings feels like I'm doing a disservice to him as a brother. Maybe my silence on the matter is more damaging than my truth would be.

I sigh and set my phone down, giving this moment my full attention. Not that it didn't have my full attention before, but I was trying to give Josh space. It doesn't seem like he wants it, though. He wants brutal honesty, and what else is an older brother good for if not for that?

"I don't know my dad," I admit. "I know his name, but that's about it. Sutton said he left when I was young, probably about the same age you were when Tim left. It used to bother me, not knowing my father. I used to worry about him. I imagined there was something awful that was keeping him away, like he was locked up in a prison somewhere on a wrongful conviction. I used to come up with these wild scenarios that would excuse how he could know I existed but not be in my life. Because what kind of man could have a son and *not* want to know him?"

Josh is still staring across the yard at Tim, but I can see that he's soaking up every word I'm saying.

"My father never sent a penny of child support. He never made an effort at all. My father never bothered to do a Google search, because if he had, he would have easily found me. Hell, *you* did that at the age of *twelve*. You found me, and you're a kid. He's a grown-ass adult."

I move so that I have Josh's full attention. "So is Tim. He is a capable, grown man, and if he cared about anything more than himself, he would have made an effort. He knows your name, he knows what city you live in, he knows how old you are."

Josh's eyes are starting to tear up.

"It blows my mind that this man has you for a son, and you *want* to be in his life, yet he still hasn't made an effort. You're a privilege, Josh. Believe me, if I'd known you existed, I would have knocked over buildings to find you."

As soon as I say that, a tear trickles out of his eye, so Josh quickly looks out his passenger window, away from Tim's house, away from me. I see him wipe at his eyes, and it breaks my heart.

It also makes me angry as hell that they kept him from me knowingly. My mother knew I would have been a good brother to him, which is why she chose not to let us be a part of each other's lives. She knew my love for him would outweigh the love she was capable of, so she selfishly kept us apart.

But I don't want my anger for my mother or Tim or even my father to bleed into Josh's decision. He's old enough to make up his own mind, so he can take my honesty and his hope, and I'll support him in whatever he decides to do with those things.

When Josh finally looks back at me, his eyes are still filled with tears and questions and indecision. He's looking at me like I need to be the one to make this decision for him.

I just shake my head. "They took twelve years from us, Josh. I don't think I can forgive them for that, but I won't be upset if you do want to forgive them. I only ever want to be honest with you, but you are your own person, and if you want to give your father a chance to get to know you, I'll put a smile on my face and walk you straight to his front door. You just let me know how to be here for you and I'll be here."

Josh nods and uses his shirt to wipe away another tear. He inhales, and on his exhale, he says, "He has a truck."

I don't know what he means by that, but I follow his line of sight back to Tim's truck.

"All this time I imagined him to be really poor, without a way back to Boston," he says. "I even thought maybe he never came because he wasn't physically able to drive, like maybe his vision was too bad or something. I don't know. But he has a truck and he never even tried."

I don't interfere with his thought process. I just want to be here for him when he finalizes it.

"He doesn't deserve me, does he." He says it like a statement rather than a question.

"Neither of them deserves you."

He doesn't move for an entire minute as he stares past me out the window. But then he looks at me firmly, sitting a little taller. "You know that homework I'm behind on? The family tree?" Josh pulls at his seat belt and begins to fasten it. "They never said how big the tree needed to be. I'll just draw a baby seedling. They don't have branches." He pats the dash. "Let's go."

I laugh hard at that. I wasn't expecting it. The way this kid weaves humor into the most depressing moments gives me hope for him. I think he's gonna be okay.

"A seedling, huh?" I start the car and pull on my own seat belt. "That might work."

"I can draw a seedling with two tiny branches. Yours and mine. We'll be on our own brand-new, tiny family tree—one that starts with us."

I feel heat behind my eyes, so I grab my sunglasses off

the dash and put them on. "A whole new family tree that starts with us. I like it."

He nods. "And we'll do a much better job of keeping it alive than our shitty parents did."

"That shouldn't be too hard." I am absolutely relieved by this decision. Josh may change his mind in the future, but I have a strong suspicion that even if he contacts his father going forward, he's never going to choose him over me. Josh reminds me a lot of myself, and devotion is a trait we have in spades.

"Atlas?" Josh says my name right as I put the car in drive.

"Yeah?"

"Can I flip him off?"

I stare back at Tim and his truck and his house. It's an immature request, but one I happily respond to with, "Please do."

Josh leans as far toward my window as his seat belt will allow. I roll down the window and honk the horn. Tim looks over at us right as I start to drive away.

Josh flips him off and yells, "Ass hole," out my window. Once we're out of Tim's eyesight, Josh falls back against his seat, laughing.

"It's *asshole*, Josh. *One* word."

"Asshole," he says, pronouncing it the correct way.

"Thank you. Now stop saying it. You're twelve."

Chapter Thirty-Two
Lily

Are you at home?

The text is from Atlas, so I respond to it with, **For a minute. Why?**

I pack baby food into Emmy's diaper bag and then rush around the room, grabbing her a change of clothes. I throw a can of formula in as well, since I'm no longer breastfeeding, and then I scoop her up. "You ready to go see Rylee?"

Emmy smiles when I say Rylee's name.

When I picked her up this morning from Allysa's, I had a talk with both her and Marshall about everything that's happened with Ryle. Allysa agreed that it was smart to show my lawyer the texts he sent me. She also agreed that it's time we have a serious sit-down with Ryle. I'm nervous, but knowing she and Marshall have my back is extremely reassuring.

As soon as we make it to my front door, there's a knock. I glance through the peephole, relieved to see Atlas standing there. But Josh isn't with him, so my heart immediately sinks. *Did he actually choose to stay with his father over Atlas?* I swing open the door.

"What happened? Where's Josh?"

Atlas smiles, and the assurance in his smile fills me with instant relief. "It's fine. He's at my house."

I blow out a breath. "Oh. Why are you here, then?"

"I'm on my way to my restaurant. I was driving by and thought I'd run up and steal a hug."

I smile, and he holds the door open for me. He can't give me a full-on hug since I have Emerson perched on my hip, so he gives me a quick kiss on the side of my head. "Liar. My apartment isn't on your way. And it's Sunday—your restaurant is closed."

"Details," he says, waving off my point. "Where are you headed?"

"Allysa's. We're having dinner with them tonight." I hoist the diaper bag onto my shoulder, but he takes it from me.

"I'll walk you out." He slings the diaper bag over his shoulder. Emmy reaches for him, and I think we're both a little surprised when she willingly transfers from my arms to his. She tucks her head against his chest, and the sight of it makes me pause for a second. It makes Atlas take a pause, too. But then he smiles at me and begins walking down to my car. He holds my hand the whole way.

I take Emmy from him and buckle her into her car seat. We're finally in a position where Atlas can give me an actual hug, so he pulls me to him. His hug feels like an entire conversation. He's holding me in a way that makes it feel like he's needing strength—like he wants to take a piece of me with him. "Where are you going again?" I ask him, pulling back.

"I really am going to my restaurant," he says. "I asked Sutton to meet me there. We need to have a serious discussion about Josh, and I'd like to do it when it's just me and her. She feeds off an audience, so I refuse to give her one."

"Wow. I'm actually on my way to Allysa's to have that

sit-down with Ryle I told you I wanted. What is this, problem-solving Sunday?"

Atlas laughs softly. "Hopefully."

I kiss him. "Good luck."

He smiles gently. "You too. Be safe, and call me as soon as you can." He presses his mouth to mine one last time, and then when he pulls away, he says, "Love you, babe."

He walks to his car, and I don't know why his words leave me so flustered, but I'm smiling as I get into my car. *Love you, babe.* I'm still smiling as I drive away. My good mood surprises me, considering what I'm on my way to do, and how it's more of a spontaneous intervention than a planned sit-down. I *am* going to Allysa and Marshall's for dinner, but Ryle has no idea I'm heading over there with a purpose.

•   •   •

"Lasagna?" I ask Marshall when he opens the front door. I could smell the garlic and tomatoes from the hallway.

"Allysa's favorite," he says, closing the door behind me. He reaches for Emmy. "Come to Uncle Marshall," he says, pulling her to him.

She's giggling as soon as he makes a face at her. Marshall is one of Emmy's favorite people, but I think we'd be hard-pressed to find a kid who doesn't love Marshall. "Is Allysa in the kitchen?"

Marshall nods. "Yeah. He's in there, too," he says, whispering. "We didn't mention you were coming."

"Okay." I set Emmy's diaper bag down and head for the kitchen. I see Ryle and Allysa's mother sitting with Rylee in the living room when I pass by. I wave at her, and she smiles, but I don't stop to chat. I go in search of Allysa.

When I walk through the kitchen door, I find Ryle leaning over the bar, chatting casually with Allysa, but as soon as he makes eye contact with me, his spine stiffens and he stands up straight.

I don't react at all. I don't want Ryle to think he holds any sort of control over me anymore.

Allysa has been expecting me. She acknowledges me with a nod and then she closes the lasagna in the oven. "Perfect timing." She drops the pot holders on the counter and points at the table. "We have forty-five minutes until it's ready," she says, guiding both Ryle and me toward the table.

"What is this?" Ryle asks, looking back and forth between the two of us.

"Just a conversation," Allysa says, urging him to take a seat. Ryle rolls his eyes but reluctantly takes a seat across from both Allysa and me. He leans back in his chair, folding his arms over his chest. Allysa looks over at me, giving me the floor.

I'm not sure why I'm not scared right now. Maybe Atlas already having had a conversation with Ryle has put most of my concerns to rest. Having Allysa and Marshall in the apartment with us also feels like a layer of protection. And Ryle's mother, even though she has no clue what's about to transpire. Ryle keeps his behavior in check when his mother is around, so I'm grateful for her presence.

Whatever is giving me strength right now, I don't sit and question it. I take advantage of it. "You asked yesterday if I spoke to my lawyer," I say to Ryle. "I did. She had some suggestions."

Ryle chews on his bottom lip for a few seconds. Then he lifts a brow, indicating he's listening.

"I want you to undergo anger management."

As soon as the words come out of my mouth, Ryle laughs. He stands up, prepared to push in his chair and end this conversation, but as soon as he does, Allysa says, "Sit down, please."

Ryle looks at her, and then me, and then back at her. Several seconds pass as he takes in what's happening. It's apparent he feels deceived right now, but I'm not here to give him empathy, and neither is his sister.

Ryle loves and respects Allysa, so he eventually returns to his seat, despite his current anger.

"While you're undergoing anger management, I would prefer for your visits with Emerson to take place here, or somewhere Marshall or Allysa are present."

Ryle swings his eyes to Allysa, and the look of betrayal he shoots her would have given me chills at one point in our past, but right now that look does nothing to me.

I continue. "Depending on your interactions with me going forward, we'll decide as a family when we feel comfortable with you having unsupervised visits with the girls."

"The *girls*?" Ryle repeats incredulously, looking at Allysa. "Did she convince you I'm not safe around my own niece?" His voice is louder now.

The kitchen door swings open, and Marshall walks in. He takes a seat at the head of the table and looks from Ryle to Allysa. "Your mom has the girls in the living room," he says to Allysa. "What'd I miss?"

"Are you aware of this?" Ryle asks Marshall.

Marshall stares at him for a beat, and then leans forward. "Am I aware you lost your temper with Lily last week and pinned her against a door? Or am I aware of the texts you sent her? Or the threats you made when she said she was talking to her lawyer?"

Ryle stares blankly at Marshall. His face reddens, but he doesn't immediately react. He's trapped in a corner, and he knows it. "A goddamn intervention," Ryle mutters, shaking his head. He's annoyed, irritated, a little bit betrayed. Understandable. But he can either agree to cooperate, or he can fracture the few remaining relationships left in his life.

Ryle pegs me with a jaded stare. "What else?" he asks, somewhat smugly.

"I've given you more than enough grace, Ryle. You know I have. But from this point forward, please know that Emerson is what matters to me. If you do anything threatening or harmful to me or our daughter, I will sell everything I own to fight you in court."

"And I'll help her," Allysa says. "I love you, but I'll help her."

Ryle's jaw is twitching. His expression is blank otherwise. He looks at Allysa and then at Marshall. The tension in the room is palpable, but so is the support. I could cry, I'm so grateful for them.

I could cry for all the victims who don't *have* people like them.

Ryle stews over everything for a long beat. It's so quiet, but I've made the point I wanted to make, and I've made it obvious that there's no room for negotiation.

He eventually scoots back from the table and stands. He

brings his hands to his hips and stares down at the floor. Then he drags in a long inhale before he heads for the kitchen door. Before he leaves, he looks back toward us, but makes eye contact with none of us. "I'm off this Thursday. I'll be here around ten if you want to make sure Emerson is here."

He leaves, and as soon as he does, my shield of armor collapses, and I shatter. Allysa puts her arms around me, but I'm not crying because I'm upset. I'm crying because I am so, so relieved. It actually feels like we accomplished something significant. "I don't know what I'd do without you two," I say through my tears, hugging Allysa.

She runs her hand over my hair and says, "You'd be so miserable, Lily."

We both start to laugh. Somehow.

Chapter Thirty-Three
Atlas

I called Sutton after I dropped Josh off at my house and asked her to meet me at Bib's. I got here an hour before we agreed to meet. I've never cooked for her, so I'm hoping my making her a meal does something to her. Pleases her, puts her in a decent mood. Anything to make her less combative.

My phone pings, so I step away from the stove and look at the screen. I told her to text me when she arrived so I could let her in. She's five minutes early.

I walk through the dark restaurant and flip on some lights on my way through. She's standing near the front, smoking a cigarette. When she sees the door open, she flicks the cigarette into the street and then follows me inside.

"Is Josh here?" she asks.

"No. It's just me and you." I gesture toward a table. "Have a seat. What do you want to drink?"

She regards me silently for a moment, then says, "Red wine. Whatever you have open." She takes a seat in a booth, and I head back to plate our food. I made coconut shrimp because I know it's her favorite. I saw her fall in love with it when I was nine years old.

It was on the one and only road trip she took me on. We went to Cape Cod, which isn't all that far from Boston, but it's the only time I remember my mother ever doing something with me on a day off. She usually slept or drank her way through her days off, so the day trip to Cape Cod where we tried coconut shrimp for the first time is not something that went unappreciated by me.

I place our plates and drinks on a tray and walk it out to the table she's seated at. I set the food and wine in front of her, then take a seat across from her. I slide silverware to her side of the table.

She stares at her plate for a beat. "You cooked this?"

"I did. It's coconut shrimp."

"What's the occasion?" she asks, opening her napkin. "Is this an apology for assuming you could actually parent a kid like him?" She laughs like she told a joke, but the lack of noise in the restaurant makes her laugh fall flat. She shakes her head and picks up her glass of wine, sipping from it.

I know she has twelve years on me with Josh, but I'm willing to bet I already know him better than she does. Josh probably knows *me* better than she knows me, and I lived with her for seventeen years. "What was my favorite food growing up?" I ask her.

She stares back at me blankly.

Maybe that was a tough one. "Okay. What about my favorite movie?" Nothing. "Color? Music?" I give her a few more, hoping she can answer at least one of them.

She can't. She shrugs, setting down her wineglass.

"What kind of books does Josh like to read?"

"Is that a trick question?" she asks.

I settle back against the booth, attempting to hide my agitation, but it's living and breathing in every part of me.

"You don't know anything about the people you brought into this world."

"I was a single mother to both of you, Atlas. I didn't have time to worry about what you liked to read when I was busy trying to survive." She drops the fork she was about to use. "Jesus Christ."

"I didn't ask you to come here so I could make you feel bad," I say. I take a sip of my water, and then run my finger around the rim of my glass. "I don't even need an apology. Neither does he." I look at her pointedly, shocked that I'm about to say what I'm about to say. It's not what I came here to say to her at all, but the things I selfishly came here for aren't what's nagging at me. "I want to give you an opportunity to be a better mother to him."

"Maybe the issue is that he should be a better son."

"He's twelve. He's as good as he needs to be. Besides, the relationship you have with him isn't his responsibility."

She scratches her cheek and then flicks a hand in the air. "What is this? Why am I here? Do you want me to take him back because he's too much for you to handle?"

"Not even close," I say. "I want you to sign your rights over to me. If you don't, I'll take you to court, and it'll cost us both a ridiculous amount of money that neither of us wants to pay. But I'll pay it. If that's what it takes, I will drag this in front of a judge, who will take one look at your history and force you to undergo a year of parenting classes that we both know you have no interesting in completing." I lean forward, folding my arms together. "I want legal custody of him, but I'm not asking you to disappear. I don't want you to. The last thing I want is for that boy to grow up feeling as unloved by you as I felt."

She sits frozen in my words, so I pick up my fork and take a casual bite of my dinner.

She stares at me while I chew, and she's still staring at me as I wash down the food with a sip of water. I'm sure her brain is running a mile a minute, searching for an insult or a threat of her own, but she's got nothing.

"Every Tuesday night we're going to have dinner here, as a family. You are more than welcome to come. I'm sure he would enjoy that. I'll never ask you for a penny. All I ask is that you show up one night a week and be interested in who he is, even if you have to fake it."

I notice Sutton's fingers are shaking as she reaches for her wineglass. She must notice, too, because she makes a fist before grabbing it and pulls her hand back to her lap. "You must not remember Cape Cod if you think I was such a horrible mother to you."

"I remember Cape Cod," I say. "It's the one memory I try to hold on to so that I don't completely resent you. But while you feel like you did this wonderful thing by giving me that one memory of us that one time, I'm offering to give that to Josh every day of his life."

Sutton looks down at her lap when I say that. For the first time, she looks like she might be experiencing an emotion other than anger or irritation.

Maybe I am, too. When I decided to have this conversation with her on the drive home from Tim's house today, I fully planned on cutting her out of our lives forever. But even monsters can't survive without a heart beating inside their chest.

There's a heart in there somewhere. Maybe no one in

her life has ever let her know they're appreciative that it still beats.

"Thank you," I say.

Her eyes flicker up to mine. She thinks I'm testing her with that comment.

I shake my head, conflicted by what I'm about to say. "You were a single mother, and I know neither of our fathers helped you in any way. That must have been really difficult for you. Maybe you're lonely. Maybe you're depressed. I don't know why you can't look at motherhood like the gift that it is, but you're here. You showed up tonight, and that effort is worth a thank-you."

She looks down at the table, and it's a completely unexpected reaction when her shoulders begin to shake, but she fights back the tears with all that she is. She brings her hands up to the table and fidgets with her napkin, but never has to use it because she doesn't allow a single tear to fall.

I don't know what she went through that made her so hard. So unwilling to be vulnerable. Maybe one of these days she'll share that with me, but she has a lot to prove as a mother to Josh before she and I will ever get to that point.

She pulls her shoulders back, sitting up straighter. "What time will the dinner be on Tuesdays?"

"Seven."

She nods and looks like she's about to scoot out of the booth.

"I can get you a to-go box if you want to take it with you."

She nods quickly. "I'd like that. It's always been my favorite dish."

"I know. I remember Cape Cod." I take her plate to the kitchen and prepare it to go.

•   •   •

Josh is asleep on the couch when I finally make it back home. Anime is playing on the television, so I hit pause and set the remote on the coffee table.

I watch him sleep for a little while, overcome with relief after the day I've had. Things could have gone a lot differently. I press my lips together, choking back the emotional exhaustion as I watch him sleep in peace. I realize as I'm staring at him that I'm looking at him the same way Lily looks at Emerson, like she's so full of pride.

I pull the blanket off the back of the couch and drape it over him, then I walk to the table where Josh's homework is laid out. Everything is completed, even the family tree assignment.

He drew a tiny seedling sprouting from the ground with two small branches. One says *Josh* and one says *Atlas*.

Chapter Thirty-Four
Lily

I almost missed the note, I was in such a rush this morning. It was shoved under my front door and was caught on the entry rug.

I had Emmy on my hip, a purse and a diaper bag on my shoulder, and coffee in my free hand. I managed to bend and pick up the note without spilling any of it. *Supermom.*

I had to wait until I got a quiet moment at work to open it. When I unfold the note and see Atlas's handwriting, I feel a shiver of relief run through me. Not because I thought the note would be from anyone other than Atlas. We've been together several months now, and he leaves me notes all the time. But this is one of the first notes he's left that a small part of me hasn't dreaded opening, in the off chance the note *was* from Ryle.

I make a mental note of the significance of this moment.

I do that a lot. Mentally note significant things that are clues my life is finally getting back to normal. I don't do it as often as I used to, but that's a good thing. Ryle is such a small part of my life now, I sometimes forget how eternally complicated I used to believe it would be.

He's still a part of Emmy's life, but I've been demanding more structure from him. He sometimes tries to push back on how strict I am with her visits, but I'm never going to be comfortable until she can tell me in her own words what her visits with Ryle are like. I'm hoping anger management is helping, but only time will tell.

The contact Ryle and I do have is still sometimes terse, but all I've ever wanted out of our divorce was my freedom from fear, and I truly feel like I have that.

I'm hiding in my office storage closet, sitting cross-legged on the floor because I wanted to read this letter uninterrupted. It's been months since I forced Atlas to hide out in here, but it still smells like him.

I unfold the note and trace the little open heart he drew at the top left-hand corner of the first page. I'm already smiling as I begin to read.

Dear Lily,

> *I don't know if you're aware of the date, but we have officially been dating for half of an entire year. Do people celebrate half-year anniversaries? I would have gotten you flowers, but I don't like to make the florist work too hard.*
>
> *I decided to give you this note, instead.*
>
> *They say there are two sides to every story, and I've read a couple of stories of yours that, even though they happened the way you said they did, I had an entirely different experience.*
>
> *You kind of brushed over this moment in your journals, even though I know it meant enough for you to get a tattoo. But I'm not sure you're aware of how much that moment meant to me.*

You say our first kiss happened on your bed, but that's not the one I count as our first kiss. Our first kiss happened on a Monday in the middle of the day.

It was that time I got sick and you took care of me. You noticed I was ill as soon as I crawled through your window. I remember you taking immediate action. You gave me medicine, water, and blankets, and forced me to sleep on your bed.

I don't remember ever being sicker than that in my entire life. I do believe you witnessed the most awful day I've ever lived through. And I've lived through some awful days. But when you're in it, there seems to be nothing worse in the moment than a horrible stomach bug.

I don't remember a lot of that night. I remember your hands, though. Your hands were always near me, either checking my temperature or wiping my face with a rag or holding my shoulders steady while I repeatedly had to fold over the side of your bed throughout the night.

That's what I remember: your hands. You had a light pink polish on, I even remember the name of the color because I had been with you when you painted your nails. It was called Surprise Lily and you told me you picked it because of the name.

I could barely open my eyes, but every time I did, there they were, your slender helping hands with your Surprise Lily fingernails, holding up my water bottle, feeding me medicine, tracing my jaw.

Yes, Lily. I remember that moment, even though you didn't write about it.

After hours of being ill, I remember waking up, or at

least becoming more aware of my surroundings. My head was pounding and my mouth was parched and my eyelids were too heavy to open, but I felt you.

I felt your breath on my cheek. Your fingertips were on my jaw and you traced them all the way down to my chin.

You thought I was asleep—that I couldn't feel you touching me, watching me, but I had never felt more than I did in that moment.

It was the exact moment I realized that I loved you. I kind of hated realizing something that monumental in the middle of such a shitty day, but it hit me so hard I thought I was going to cry for the first time in years and I didn't know what to do with that feeling.

But, man, Lily, I had gone my whole life not knowing what love felt like. I didn't have the love a mother and son should have, or a father and son, or a sibling. And until you, I had never spent that kind of time with anyone unrelated to me, especially a girl. Not long enough to truly get to know a girl, or for them to get to know me, or for us to connect and deepen that connection, and then for that girl to prove to be caring and helpful and kind and worried and everything that you were to me.

I'm not even saying it was the moment I realized I was IN love with you. It was just the first moment I realized I loved something, anything, anyone, ever. It was the first time my heart had ever reacted. At least in a positive way. People had done things to me in the past that made my heart shrink, but never expand like that. When your fingers were trickling over my chin like soft drops of rain, I thought my heart was going to swell so big it might pop.

I pretended to slowly wake up in that moment. I put my arm over my eyes, and you quickly pulled your hand back. I remember craning my neck and looking at your window to see if it was light outside. It almost was, so I started to pull myself out of your bed, pretending not to know you were awake. You sat up and asked me if I was leaving, and I had to swallow before I could get my voice to work. It barely did. I said something like, "Your parents will be up soon."

You told me you were going to skip school and come back for me in a couple of hours. I nodded without speaking, because I was still sick, but I had to get out of your bedroom before I said something or did something to embarrass myself. I didn't trust the feeling that was buzzing beneath my skin. It was creating this burning need to look at you and say, I love you, Lily! *It's funny how, as soon as you feel love for the first time, you suddenly have this huge desire to profess it. The words felt like they were forming right in the center of my chest, and even though I was weaker than I'd probably ever been, I had never lifted your window and crawled out of it that fast before.*

I shut it and flattened my back against the cold wall of your house, and I exhaled. My breath turned to fog, and I closed my eyes, and after the absolute worst eight hours of my life, I somehow cracked a smile.

I thought about love the rest of the morning. Even after you'd come back to get me once your parents were gone and I spent several more hours being sick at your house, I was thinking about love. When your Surprise Lily fingernails would flash across my line of sight every time you checked my temperature, I'd think about love. Every time you'd walk into your room and adjust the covers, tucking them under my chin, I'd think about love.

And then when I finally started to feel a little better around lunchtime, I stood in the shower, weak and dehydrated from being sick, yet I somehow felt like I was standing taller than I ever had before.

That whole morning and into the rest of the day, I knew something significant had happened. For the first time, I had felt a flicker of what I knew life could be. Before that moment, I never gave much thought to falling in love, or having a family someday, or even the idea of cultivating a successful career. Life to me had always felt like a burden I had to bear. Something heavy and murky that made waking up difficult and falling asleep a little bit scary. But that's because I had gone eighteen years not knowing what it felt like to care about someone so much, you want them to be the first thing you see when you open your eyes. I even felt a desire to make something of myself because you were the first person I ever wanted to become something better for.

That was the day we laid on your couch together and you told me you wanted me to watch your favorite cartoon with you. It was the first time you had ever snuggled up to me, your back to my chest as we lay under the blanket with my arm wrapped over you. It was hard to focus on the television because the words I love you *were still tickling their way up my throat, and I didn't want to say it,* couldn't *say it, because I didn't want you to think it was too fast, or that those words held no weight for me. They were the heaviest damn thing I'd ever carried.*

But I think about that day so much, Lily, and I have no idea if that's what love feels like for everyone, like it's an airplane that just fell from the sky and crashed right through you. Because most people, they have love seeping in and out their whole lives. They're born being wrapped in it and they go their whole childhood being protected by it, and they have people in their lives that welcome their love in return, so I'm not sure it hits people like it hit me—in one small moment, in such a colossal way.

You were wearing this shirt I loved. It was too big for you, and the sleeve was always falling off your shoulder. I should have been watching the cartoon, but I couldn't stop staring at that stretch of exposed skin between your neck and your shoulder. As I was looking at it, I once again felt that incredible pull to say I love you, *and the words were there, right on the tip of my tongue, so I leaned forward and pressed them against your skin.*

And that's where they stayed, hidden and quiet, until I worked up the courage to speak them out loud to you six months later.

I had no idea you remembered that kiss, or all the times I kissed you in that spot after that day. Even when I read it in your journal, you rushed past it in a hurry to get to what you considered our actual first kiss, so I had no idea that it even meant anything to you until the moment I saw your tattoo. I can't tell you what that means to me, knowing that you have our heart placed in the very spot where I once secretly buried the words I love you.

I want you to promise me something, Lily. When you look at that tattoo, I don't want you to think about anything other than the words I've written in this letter. And every time I kiss you there, I want you to remember why I kissed you there the first time. Love. *Discovering it, giving it, receiving it, falling in it, living in it,* leaving *for it.*

I'm writing this letter while sitting on the floor of Josh's bedroom. My experience with Josh tonight is kind of what sparked my memory. He's sick with a stomach bug. Maybe not as sick as I was the day I first realized I loved you, but very, very sick nonetheless. He caught it from Theo, who had it a few days ago.

I've never taken care of a sick person before, so I have no medicine at all. I think I'm about to make a pharmacy run. I might slip this letter under your apartment door on my way there.

It isn't fun taking care of a sick person. The sounds, the smell, the lack of sleep—it's actually almost as bad for the person doing the caring. Every time I check his temperature or force him to drink water, I think about you and how you cared for me with such a gentle parental instinct. I'm trying to replicate that in my care for Josh, but I don't think I'm as good at this as you were.

You were so young, just a few years older than Josh is now. But I'm sure you felt much older than you were. I know I did. We had been through things no kid should have to experience. It makes me wonder if Josh feels his age, or if he feels older than he should because of all he's been through.

I want him to feel young for as long as he can. I want him to enjoy his time with me. I want him to know what *love is long before I did. And I hope that love has been seeping slowly into him so that it doesn't hit him all at once like it did me. I want him to grow up with it, wrapped in it, surrounded by it. I want him to* witness *it.*

I want to be an example for him. I want us *to be an example for him, and for Emerson. Me and you, Lily.*

It's been six months.

Move in with me.

Love,
Atlas

As soon as I finish reading the letter, I set it down and wipe my eyes. If this is how much I cry when he asks me to move in with him, I have no idea how I'll survive a proposal.

Or wedding vows, for that matter.

I pick up my phone and call Atlas over video chat. It rings for ten long seconds, and when Atlas finally answers it, he's lying on his living room couch. He's smiling through his obvious exhaustion from being up all night with Josh.

"Hey, beautiful." His voice is barely awake.

"Hi." My hand is curled into a fist, and I'm resting my cheek on it, pushing down my huge smile. "How's Josh feeling?"

"He's okay," Atlas says. "He's sleeping, but I think I stayed up so long, my brain is too overwhelmed to shut off now." He puts a fist to his mouth and stifles a yawn.

"Atlas." I say his name sympathetically because he does look absolutely drained. "Do you need me to come over and give you a hug?"

"You mean do I need you to come *home* and give me a hug?"

I smile when he says that. "Yes. That's exactly what I meant. Do you need me to come *home* and give you a hug?"

He nods. "I do, Lily. Come home."

Chapter Thirty-Five
Atlas

"Aren't you rich?" Brad asks. "Couldn't you hire people to do this for you?"

"I own two restaurants. I'm not even close to rich. And why would I hire someone when I have you guys?"

"At least we're going *down*stairs," Theo says.

"Take notes from your son, Brad. Silver lining."

We don't have much left to move. Lily didn't need a lot of her stuff since my house is already furnished, so she donated most of it to a local domestic violence shelter. We should have her apartment completely cleared out by this afternoon.

Brad is the only person I know with a truck, so he and Theo have been helping us load the things we can't fit into our cars. Emerson's crib, Lily's living room television, some of the artwork hanging on her walls.

Josh lucked out. He's at baseball practice, so he didn't have to help with the move.

I was surprised when he came home a few months ago and told me he had signed up for tryouts. He made the team and has been giving it everything he has. Between Lily and I, we haven't missed a single game.

I texted our mother his schedule, but so far she hasn't shown up to a game. She's only shown up once to the dinners we started having every Tuesday night. I was hoping she would want to be more involved, but I'm not surprised she isn't. I doubt Josh is surprised, either. We don't focus too much on what isn't working out in our lives. We focus on what *is*, and there's a lot to be grateful for. The two main things being that I was able to get custody of Josh, and Lily and Emerson are moving in with us. Funny how drastically life can change on a dime.

The Atlas of last year wouldn't know what to think of the Atlas of this year.

Lily is heading up the stairs right as I reach the bottom of them. She grins and gives me a kiss in passing, then runs up the rest of the steps.

Theo shakes his head. "Still can't believe you made it this far with her." He hoists his box up with his knee and then presses his back against the exit door to push it open. He holds it open for me and Brad, but I pause once we're in the parking garage.

There's a car that resembles Ryle's pulling into a parking spot a few spaces away from Brad's truck.

A sense of dread washes over me. I haven't had a single interaction with him since that day he attempted to fight me at my restaurant, but that was months ago. I have no idea how much he's warmed up to the idea of me and Lily, but from the look he's shooting in my direction, it doesn't seem like he's warmed up much.

Someone else is with him. A man gets out of the passenger seat, and from what Lily has told me, it looks like he could be Ryle's brother-in-law. I've met Lily's mother, and I've met Allysa and Rylee, but I've never met Marshall.

I walk over to Brad's truck and load up the box I'm carrying, but I'm watching Ryle's car the whole time. Theo and Brad head back inside, unaware of Ryle's presence. Marshall lifts Emerson out of the backseat and closes the door. Ryle remains in the car as Marshall walks Emerson in my direction.

He holds out a hand. "Hey. Atlas, right? I'm Marshall."

I return his handshake. "Yeah, good to meet you."

He nods, but when Emerson sees me, Marshall has to clasp a tighter hand around her because she lunges for me. I step forward and take her from him.

"Hey, Emmy. Did you have fun today?"

Marshall watches me with her for a moment, then says, "Be careful. She puked on Ryle twice today."

"Is she not feeling well?"

"She's fine, but she's been with the two of us all day. Both the girls had sugar for breakfast. And snack. *And* lunch *and* second snack and . . ." He waves a dismissive hand. "Lily and Issa are used to it."

Emerson reaches up and pulls the sunglasses off my head. She tries to put them on her own face, but they're crooked, so I help her adjust them until she's wearing them right. She grins at me, and I smile back at her.

Marshall glances over at the car that Ryle's sitting in, and then back to me. "Sorry he's not getting out. This is all still a little weird for him. Her moving in with you."

When Marshall says "her," he doesn't mean Lily. He's looking at Emerson. I nod in understanding, because I do understand. "It's fine. I can't imagine this is easy for him."

Marshall ruffles Emmy's hair and then says, "I'll get out

of here so you guys can finish up. It was good finally meeting you."

"You too," I say. And I mean that. Marshall seems like someone I could be friends with if the circumstances were different.

He turns to head back to Ryle's car, but he pauses and faces me again before he gets very far. "Thank you," he says. "Lily means a lot to my wife, so . . . yeah. Thanks for making Lily happy. She deserves it." As soon as Marshall says that, he shakes his head and holds up his hands, taking a step back. "I'll go now before it gets too awkward." He makes a beeline for Ryle's car, but I kind of wish he wouldn't have run off so fast. I would have thanked him, too. I know his support has meant a lot to Lily.

Marshall shuts the passenger door, and Ryle puts his car in drive and heads out.

I glance at Emmy, who is now chewing on my sunglasses. "You want to go say hi to Mommy?" I start to walk in the direction of the building, but I pause when I see Lily standing in the doorway to the stairwell.

As soon as she sees me, she spins around and wipes quickly at her eyes. I'm not sure why she's crying, but I walk a little bit slower so she can erase the tears before she greets her daughter. Sure enough, several seconds later, she spins around with a big grin and takes Emmy from me.

"Did you have fun with your daddy today?" she asks, right before she smothers Emmy with several kisses.

When she looks at me, I shoot her a curious look, wondering why she was crying. She gestures to the parking lot, where Ryle's car was moments before.

"That was a big thing," she says. "I mean, I know Marshall was with him, but the fact that he felt okay enough to leave her with you . . ." She's starting to tear up again, which makes her sigh and roll her eyes at her own reaction. "It feels good knowing the men in her life can at least *pretend* to get along for her sake."

It honestly makes me feel good, too. I'm glad she was upstairs when they showed up. I know Ryle sat in the car while Marshall handed her over, but it was a step in the right direction. Maybe Ryle and I needed an exchange like that just as much as Lily did.

We just proved cooperation is possible, even if it stings.

I wipe at Lily's wet cheek, and then I give her a quick kiss. "I love you." I put my hand on Lily's lower back and guide her toward the stairs. "One more trip before you're stuck with me forever."

Lily laughs. "I can't wait to be stuck with you forever."

Chapter Thirty-Six
Lily

I'm curled up on Atlas's couch, exhausted from moving.

Our couch.

This is going to take some getting used to.

I had Theo and Josh help me unpack the rest of Emerson's and my things because Atlas has a late night at work. I wake up early, he gets home late, but it's exciting that we'll now get more pieces of each other, even when it's in passing. And we have Sundays together.

But tonight is a Friday, and tomorrow is a Saturday, Atlas's busiest days, so I'm entertaining Josh and Theo until my mother returns with Emerson. The three of us have been watching *Finding Nemo*, but it's almost over.

I honestly didn't think they would sit through it because they're at the age when preteens tend to want to separate themselves from Disney cartoons. But I'm learning that Gen Z is a different breed. The more time I spend with these two, the more I think they're unlike any generation that came before them. They're less prone to peer pressure and more supportive of individuality. I'm a little bit jealous of them.

Josh stands when the credits begin to roll.

"Did you like it?"

He shrugs. "It was pretty funny, considering it started

with the brutal slaughter of all that caviar." He takes his empty bag of popcorn toward the kitchen, but Theo is still staring at the television. He's shaking his head slowly.

I'm still stuck on Josh's description of the beginning of the movie . . .

"I don't get it," Theo says.

"The caviar comment?"

Theo looks between me and the television. "No. I don't get why Atlas said that to you about finally reaching the shore. It wasn't even a quote in the movie. He told me he said it because of *Finding Nemo*. I waited for someone to say it through the entire movie."

I'm sure I'll have to get used to a lot of things now that I live with Atlas, but knowing he talks to this kid about our relationship is probably not one of the things I'll ever get used to.

The confusion in Theo's eyes flips like a light switch. "Oh. *Oh.* Because when life gets them down, they keep swimming, so Atlas was saying life will no longer . . . *okay.*" His mind is still going a mile a minute behind those eyes. He starts to shake his head as he pushes himself off the floor. "I still think it's cheesy," he mutters. Theo's phone buzzes right as he stands. "I gotta go—my dad's here."

Josh is back in the living room. "You aren't staying over?"

"I can't tonight; my parents are taking me to a thing in the morning."

"I want to go to a thing," Josh says.

Theo is pulling on his shoes when he hesitates. "Yeah, I don't know."

"Where are you going?"

Theo's eyes flash briefly to mine, and then back to Josh. "It's a parade." He says it quietly, but also like it's a warning.

"A parade?" Josh tilts his head. "Why are you being weird? What kind of parade is it? A pride parade?"

Theo swallows like maybe him and Josh haven't had this conversation, so I'm nervous on Theo's behalf. But I've been around Josh enough over the last several months to know that he values his friendship with Theo.

Josh grabs his shoes and sits next to me on the couch and starts putting them on. "What are you saying? I'm not allowed to go to a pride thing because I like girls?"

Theo shifts from one foot to the other. "You can go. I just . . . I didn't know if you knew."

Josh rolls his eyes. "You can tell a lot about a person by their taste in manga, Theo. I'm not a dumbass."

"*Josh*," I say.

"Sorry." He grabs a jacket from the closet. "Can I stay over at Theo's tonight?"

Josh's casual attitude about this monumental moment between the two of them reminds me so much of Atlas.

Considerate Josh.

But his question about leaving with Theo kind of stumps me. My eyes widen slightly. I've only lived here four days. Josh hasn't asked me permission for anything before, and Atlas and I haven't really laid ground rules. "Yeah, sure. But let your brother know where you are."

I really don't think Atlas will mind. Now that we live together, we're going to have to tackle things like this when it comes to Josh and Emerson. Who parents who, when, how. It's kind of exciting. I like figuring out life with Atlas.

My mother still hasn't returned with Emerson yet, so once Josh and Theo have left, the house is quiet and empty for the first time since we moved in. I've never been here alone before. I spend my alone time walking through rooms, looking in cabinets, familiarizing myself with my new house.

My new house. That's fun to say.

I go out back and sit in a chair on the deck, staring over the backyard. It's the perfect backyard for a garden. Almost unheard-of for a place this far into the city. It's like Atlas searched for a house specifically for the perfect garden space just in case I ever came back into his life. I know that's not at all why he chose this house, but it's fun imagining he did it for that reason.

My phone rings, startling me. It's Atlas returning an earlier call with a video chat.

"Hi."

"What are you doing?" he asks.

"Picking out a spot for my garden. Josh wanted to stay over with Theo, so I let him go. I hope that's okay."

"Of course it is. Did they help you at all?"

"Yeah, we got most of it done."

Atlas looks relieved by that. He runs a hand down the side of his face like he's releasing stress. It looks like it's been a busy day, but Atlas tucks it away beneath a smile. "Where's Emerson?"

"My mom is on her way back with her."

He sighs like he's sad he couldn't get a glimpse of her. "I'm starting to miss her," he says. The words come out soft and fast, like he's a little bit scared to admit he's starting to love my daughter. But I caught his words, and I'm keeping them next to all the other sweet things he's ever said to me. "I'll be home in about three hours. Will you be awake?"

"If I'm not, you know what to do."

Atlas gives his head a little shake, and his mouth ticks up in the corner. "I love you. Be home soon."

"I love you, too."

As soon as we end our call, I hear Emerson's sweet voice, so I immediately turn around. My mother is standing in the doorway holding her. She's smiling like she caught some of that conversation.

I stand up to grab Emerson from her, and she clings to me. Should be an easy night. When she gets cuddly like this, it means she's ready to fall asleep. I motion for my mother to have a seat next to me.

"This is cute," she says.

It's her first time here. I would show her around, but Emerson is already rubbing her face into my chest, trying to fight her tiredness. I want to give her a chance to fall asleep before I stand up.

"What a magnificent place for a garden," my mother says. "You think he chose this place on purpose, hoping you'd come back into his life?"

I shrug. "I was actually wondering that myself, but I didn't want to assume." I pause, then turn and look at her after her question actually registers. *Back into his life?* I never told her Atlas was a friend from back in Maine. I just assumed she didn't remember him.

I assumed she had no idea that the Atlas in my life now was anyone from my past.

She can see the surprise on my face, so she says, "It's a unique name, Lily. I remember him."

I smile, but I'm also confused as to why she never brought it up before now. I've been dating him for over six months, and she's been around him a handful of times.

I guess I shouldn't be surprised, though. My mother has always been a little hard to get to open up. I can't blame her. She spent years with a man who left her no voice, so I'm sure it's been hard for her to learn how to use it again.

"Why didn't you ever say anything?" I ask her.

She shrugs. "I figured you would bring it up to me if you wanted me to know."

"I wanted to, but I didn't want it to feel awkward for you being around him. Not after what Dad did to him."

She looks away from me, her eyes scanning the backyard. She's quiet for a beat. "I never told you this, but I spoke to Atlas once. Kind of. I came home from work early and the two of you were asleep on the couch. Talk about a shock," she says, laughing. "I thought you were so sweet and innocent, but there you were on my living room sofa asleep with a random boy. I was about to yell at you, but when he woke up, he looked so scared. Not scared of me, really, now that I think about it. He looked more scared of the possibility of losing you. Anyway, he left in a quiet hurry, so I followed him outside because I was going to threaten him and tell him never to come back. But he just . . . he did the weirdest thing, Lily."

"What did he do?" My heart is in my throat.

"He hugged me," she says, her voice tinted with a drop of laughter.

My jaw drops. "He *hugged* you? You caught him with your daughter red-handed and he hugged you?"

She nods. "He did. And it was a knowing hug, too. It was like he carried this genuine sorrow for me, and I felt that in his hug. Like he was encouraging me, or comforting me. And then he just . . . walked away. I never even got the chance to yell at him for being in my house with you unsupervised. Maybe that was his plan—it could have been a manipulation tactic, I don't know."

I shake my head. "It wasn't a tactic." *Considerate Atlas.*

"I knew you were seeing him. And I knew you were hiding him from your father rather than me, so I didn't take it personally. I never interfered because I liked that you had someone, Lily." She gestures toward the house behind us. "And now look. You have him forever."

That story makes me squeeze Emerson a little tighter.

"It makes me happy to know there's a man in your life that gives meaningful hugs like that," my mother says.

"He gives more than great hugs," I deadpan.

My mother scoffs. "Lily!" She stands up, shaking her head. "I'm going home now."

I'm laughing to myself as she leaves. Then I use my free hand to text Atlas.

I love you so much, you idiot.

Chapter Thirty-Seven
Atlas

"Are you seriously about to do this?" Theo asks.

I'm standing in front of a mirror, adjusting my tie. Theo is sitting on the couch, attempting to convince me to let him read my vows before the wedding. "I'm not reading them to you."

"You're going to embarrass yourself," he says.

"I'm not. They're good."

"Atlas. Come on. I'm trying to help you. For all I know, you probably end them with something like, *It is my wish for you to be my fish*."

I laugh. I don't know how he still comes up with these lines after two years of this. "Do you practice your insults when you lie awake at night?"

"No, they come naturally."

Someone knocks on the door and opens it a crack. "Five minutes."

I give myself one more glance in the mirror before turning to Theo. "Where's Josh? I need to make sure he's ready."

"I'm not supposed to tell you."

I tilt my head. "Where is he, Theo?"

"Last time I saw him, he was in the gazebo with his tongue down some girl's throat. He's gonna make you a grandad soon."

"I'm his brother. I'd be an uncle, not a grandad." I look out the window, but the gazebo is empty. "Go find him, please."

Josh and I are a lot alike, but he's a little bit more confident with girls than I was at that age. He just turned fifteen, and so far, this is my least-favorite age. I'm sure when he's old enough to drive next year, it's going to age me an entire decade.

I need to think about something else. I'm already nervous. Maybe Theo is right, and I should look over my vows again to make sure there's nothing I want to change or add.

I pull the page out of my pocket and unfold it, and then grab a pen in case I want to make any very last-minute changes.

Dear Lily,

I'm used to writing you letters that no one else will ever read, which may be why I had a difficult time when I first attempted to write these vows. The idea that they were going to be read out loud to you in front of other people was a little bit terrifying.

But vows aren't meant to be something you make in private. The purpose of a vow is to make an intentional promise that is witnessed, whether it's witnessed by God, or friends and family.

It has to make you wonder, though, or at least it made me wonder what the purpose is behind the need for a public vow. I couldn't stop my mind from questioning what must have happened in the past to create the necessity for love to be witnessed.

Does it mean that somewhere along the way, a promise was broken? A heart was shattered?

It's disappointing if you really sit and think about why vows even exist. If we trusted everyone to keep their word, vows wouldn't be necessary. People would fall in love, and they'd stay in love, faithfully, forever, the end.

But that's the issue, I guess. We're people. We're human. And humans can sometimes be disappointing.

That realization led me down another path in my thought process while writing these vows. I began to wonder, if humans are so often disappointing and so rarely successful at love, what can we do to ensure ours is a love that will stand the test of time? If half of all marriages end in divorce, that would mean half of every set of vows ever made have ended up broken. How do we ensure we're not one of the couples who becomes a statistic?

Unfortunately, Lily, we can't. We can only hope, but we can't guarantee that the words we stand here and promise one another today won't end up in the file of a divorce lawyer a few years down the road.

I apologize. I realize these vows are making marriage sound like an extremely depressing cycle that only ends happily half the time.

But for someone like me, that's actually kind of exciting.

Half the time?

Fifty-fifty?

One out of two?

If someone would have told me when I was a teenager that I would have a fifty-fifty chance of living my entire life with you, I would have felt like the luckiest human on the planet.

If someone would have told me that I had a 50 percent chance of being loved by you, I would have wondered what the hell I did to get so lucky.

If someone would have told me that we'd get married one day, and I'd get to give you your dream honeymoon in Europe, and that our marriage would have a 50 percent chance of being successful, I would have immediately asked what size your ring finger was so that we could get started.

Maybe the idea of love ending being a negative thing is simply a matter of perspective. Because to me, the idea that a love came to an end means that, at some point, there was love that existed. And there was a time in my life, before you, when I was completely untouched by it.

The teenage version of me wouldn't have seen potential heartbreak as a bad thing. I was jealous of anyone who had ever loved something enough to experience losing it. Before you, I had never met love at all.

But then you came along, and you changed that. Not only did I get the opportunity to be the first person to ever fall in love with you, but I also got to experience a shared heartbreak with you. And then, like a miracle, I was given the opportunity to fall in love with you all over again.

Two times in one life.

How can one man be so lucky?

All things considered, the fact that I made it here, that we made it here, to our wedding day, is quite frankly more than I ever dreamed I would get out of life. One breath, one kiss, one day, one year, one lifetime. I'll take whatever you'll give me, and I vow that I will cherish every second I'm lucky enough to spend with you from this moment on, just as I've cherished every second I've ever spent with you before this moment.

Optimistically speaking, we could live our entire lives together, happily, until we're old and frail and it takes an entire day for me just to reach your lips to kiss you good-night. If that happens, I vow that I will be immensely grateful for the love that carried us through our life together.

Pessimistically speaking, we could break each other's hearts again tomorrow—I know we won't, but even if we did, I vow that I will be immensely grateful for the love that led to that heartbreak until the day that I die. If it's my destiny to end up a statistic, there's no one else I'd rather become a statistic with than you.

But you once told me I was a realist, so I want to end my vows realistically. In my heart, I believe we're going to leave here today and face a journey together that's full of hills, valleys, peaks, and canyons. Sometimes you're going to need me to hold your hand down the hills, and sometimes I'll need you to lead me up the mountain, but everything, from this point forward, we're going to face together. It's you and me, Lily. In good times and bad, for richer or poorer, in sickness and in health, in the past and for forever, you are my favorite person. Always have been. Always will be. I love you. Everything that you are.

Atlas

I exhale, the page trembling in my hand. They're exactly how I want them, so I start to fold the paper when Josh walks into the room. He's joined by Darin, Brad, Theo, and Marshall.

Marshall is holding open the door. "You ready? It's time."

I nod, more than ready, but before I stuff my vows back into my pocket, I decide to make one small change. I don't touch anything already written, but I do add a line to the very end.

P.S. It is my wish for you to be my fish.

Acknowledgments

It Ends with Us is the one book I have been adamant that I would never write a sequel for. I felt like it ended where it needed to end, and I didn't want to put Lily through more stress.

But then #BookTok happened, and the online petition, and the messages and videos, and I realized most of you weren't asking for me to put them through more pain. You simply wanted to see Lily and Atlas happy. When I started playing around with an outline, I quickly realized how much I needed to see Lily and Atlas happy as well. For everyone who asked for more, thank you. This book wouldn't exist without you.

I have so many people to thank, and not necessarily for the existence of *It Starts with Us*, but more for the continued support over the years that resulted in me writing a book I never thought I'd have the courage to complete. From family to friends to bloggers to readers to publishers and agents, in no particular order, I just want to say THANK YOU for your continued support, and for ensuring I continue to love writing.

Levi Hoover, Cale Hoover, Beckham Hoover, and Heath Hoover. My four favorite men on the whole planet. I couldn't do any of this if it weren't for your encouragement and support.

Lin Reynolds, Murphy Fennell, and Vannoy Fite. My three favorite women on the planet.

To the entire Bookworm Box and Book Bonanza team and board members. Thank y'all for everything you do!

To my agents, Jane Dystel and Lauren Abramo, and the entire Dystel, Goderich & Bourret team.

Thank you to my editor, Melanie Iglesias Pérez; my publicist, Ariele Fredman Stewart; and my publisher, Libby McGuire; and the entire Atria team.

To Stephanie Cohen and Erica Ramirez. Thank you for helping make my dreams come true and always having my best interest at heart. I love you both more than words can say, and every time I walk into our office, it feels like coming home.

Thank you to Pamela Carrion and Laurie Darter for everything you do and for keeping me entertained daily.

Thank you to the team at Simon & Schuster Audio for bringing my books to life.

Thank you to author Susan Stoker for being such a champion for other authors and always keeping us in the know with your weekly messages of congratulations.

And a huge thank-you to the following for always being there: Tarryn Fisher, Anna Todd, Lauren Levine, Shanora Williams, Chelle Lagoski Northcutt, Tasara Vega, Vilma Gonzalez, Anjanette Guerrero, Maria Blalock, Talon Smith, Johanna Castillo, Jenn Benando, Kristin Phillips, Amy Fite, Kim Holden, Caroline Kepnes, Melinda Knight, Karen Lawson, Marion Archer, Kay Miles, Lindsey Domokur, and so many others.

Thank you to CoHorts, BookTok, Weblich, bloggers, librarians, and everyone who puts their hearts into spreading your love for reading.

Most of all, thank you to every single person who has ever taken the time to message or email an author to let them know what their books mean to you. You are a huge part of the reason we write.

It Ends
with Us

Also by Colleen Hoover

Slammed
Point of Retreat
This Girl
Hopeless
Losing Hope
Finding Cinderella
Maybe Someday
Ugly Love
Maybe Not
Confess
November 9
Without Merit
All Your Perfects

It Ends with Us

Colleen Hoover

ATRIA PAPERBACK

NEW YORK LONDON TORONTO SYDNEY NEW DELHI

For my father, who tried his very best not to be his worst.

And for my mother, who made sure we never saw him at his worst.

Part One

Chapter One

As I sit here with one foot on either side of the ledge, looking down from twelve stories above the streets of Boston, I can't help but think about suicide.

Not my *own*. I like my life enough to want to see it through.

I'm more focused on other people, and how they ultimately come to the decision to just end their own lives. *Do they ever regret it?* In the moment after letting go and the second before they make impact, there has to be a little bit of remorse in that brief free fall. Do they look at the ground as it rushes toward them and think, *"Well, crap. This was a bad idea."*

Somehow, I think not.

I think about death a lot. Particularly today, considering I just—twelve hours earlier—gave one of the most epic eulogies the people of Plethora, Maine, have ever witnessed. Okay, maybe it wasn't the most epic. It very well could be considered the most disastrous. I guess that would depend on whether you were asking my mother or me. *My mother, who probably won't speak to me for a solid year after today.*

Don't get me wrong; the eulogy I delivered wasn't profound enough to make history, like the one Brooke Shields delivered at Michael Jackson's funeral. Or the one delivered by Steve Jobs's sister. Or Pat Tillman's brother. But it was epic in its own way.

I was nervous at first. It was the funeral of the prodigious Andrew Bloom, after all. Adored mayor of my hometown of Plethora, Maine. Owner of the most successful real-estate agency within city limits. Husband of the highly adored Jenny Bloom, the most revered teaching assistant in all of Plethora. And father of Lily Bloom—that strange girl with the erratic red hair who once fell in love with a homeless guy and brought great shame upon her entire family.

That would be me. I'm Lily Bloom, and Andrew was my father.

As soon as I finished delivering his eulogy today, I caught a flight straight back to Boston and hijacked the first roof I could find. *Again, not because I'm suicidal.* I have no plans to scale off this roof. I just really needed fresh air and silence, and dammit if I can't get that from my third floor apartment with absolutely no rooftop access and a roommate who likes to hear herself sing.

I didn't account for how cold it would be up here, though. It's not unbearable, but it's not comfortable, either. At least I can see the stars. Dead fathers and exasperating roommates and questionable eulogies don't feel so awful when the night sky is clear enough to literally feel the grandeur of the universe.

I love it when the sky makes me feel insignificant.

I like tonight.

Well . . . let me rephrase this so that it more appropriately reflects my feelings in past tense.

I *liked* tonight.

But unfortunately for me, the door was just shoved open so hard, I expect the stairwell to spit a human out onto the

4 | Colleen Hoover

rooftop. The door slams shut again and footsteps move swiftly across the deck. I don't even bother looking up. Whoever it is more than likely won't even notice me back here straddling the ledge to the left of the door. They came out here in such a hurry, it isn't my fault if they assume they're alone.

I sigh quietly, close my eyes and lean my head against the stucco wall behind me, cursing the universe for ripping this peaceful, introspective moment out from under me. The least the universe could do for me today is ensure that it's a woman and not a man. If I'm going to have company, I'd rather it be a female. I'm tough for my size and can probably hold my own in most cases, but I'm too comfortable right now to be on a rooftop alone with a strange man in the middle of the night. I might fear for my safety and feel the need to leave, and I really don't want to leave. As I said before . . . I'm comfortable.

I finally allow my eyes to make the journey to the silhouette leaning over the ledge. As luck would have it, he's definitely male. Even leaning over the rail, I can tell he's tall. Broad shoulders create a strong contrast to the fragile way he's holding his head in his hands. I can barely make out the heavy rise and fall of his back as he drags in deep breaths and forces them back out when he's done with them.

He appears to be on the verge of a breakdown. I contemplate speaking up to let him know he has company, or clearing my throat, but between thinking it and actually doing it, he spins around and kicks one of the patio chairs behind him.

I flinch as it screeches across the deck, but being as though he isn't even aware he has an audience, the guy doesn't stop with just one kick. He kicks the chair repeatedly, over and over. Rather than give way beneath the blunt force of his foot, all the chair does is scoot farther and farther away from him.

That chair must be made from marine-grade polymer.

I once watched my father back over an outdoor patio table made of marine-grade polymer, and it practically laughed at him. Dented his bumper, but didn't even put a scratch on the table.

This guy must realize he's no match for such a high-quality material, because he finally stops kicking the chair. He's now standing over it, his hands clenched in fists at his sides. To be honest, I'm a little envious. Here this guy is, taking his aggression out on patio furniture like a champ. He's obviously had a shitty day, as have I, but whereas I keep my aggression pent up until it manifests in the form of passive-aggressiveness, this guy actually has an outlet.

My outlet used to be gardening. Any time I was stressed, I'd just go out to the backyard and pull every single weed I could find. But since the day I moved to Boston two years ago, I haven't had a backyard. Or a patio. I don't even have weeds.

Maybe I need to invest in a marine-grade polymer patio chair.

I stare at the guy a moment longer, wondering if he's ever going to move. He's just standing there, staring down at the chair. His hands aren't in fists anymore. They're resting on his hips, and I notice for the first time how his shirt doesn't fit him very well around his biceps. It fits him everywhere else, but his arms are huge. He begins fishing around in his pockets until he finds what he's looking for and—in what I'm sure is probably an effort to release even more of his aggression—he lights up a joint.

I'm twenty-three, I've been through college and have done this very same recreational drug a time or two. I'm not going to judge this guy for feeling the need to toke up in private. But that's the thing—he's *not* in private. He just doesn't know that yet.

He takes in a long drag of his joint and starts to turn back toward the ledge. He notices me on the exhale. He stops walking the second our eyes meet. His expression holds no shock, nor does it hold amusement when he sees me. He's about ten feet away, but there's enough light from the stars that I can see his eyes as they slowly drag over my body without revealing a single thought. This guy holds his cards well. His gaze is narrow and his mouth is drawn tight, like a male version of the *Mona Lisa*.

"What's your name?" he asks.

I feel his voice in my stomach. That's not good. Voices should stop at the ears, but sometimes—not very often at all, actually—a voice will penetrate past my ears and reverberate straight down through my body. He has one of those voices. Deep, confident, and a little bit like butter.

When I don't answer him, he brings the joint back to his mouth and takes another hit.

"Lily," I finally say. *I hate my voice.* It sounds too weak to even reach his ears from here, much less reverberate inside *his* body.

He lifts his chin a little and nudges his head toward me. "Will you please get down from there, Lily?"

It isn't until he says this that I notice his posture. He's

standing straight up now, rigid even. Almost as if he's nervous I'm going to fall. *I'm not.* This ledge is at least a foot wide, and I'm mostly on the roof side. I could easily catch myself before I fell, not to mention I've got the wind in my favor.

I glance down at my legs and then back up at him. "No, thanks. I'm quite comfortable where I am."

He turns a little, like he can't look straight at me. "Please get down." It's more of a demand now, despite his use of the word *please.* "There are seven empty chairs up here."

"Almost six," I correct, reminding him that he just tried to murder one of them. He doesn't find the humor in my response. When I fail to follow his orders, he takes a couple of steps closer.

"You are a mere three inches from falling to your death. I've been around enough of that for one day." He motions for me to get down again. "You're making me nervous. Not to mention ruining my high."

I roll my eyes and swing my legs over. "Heaven forbid a joint go to waste." I hop down and wipe my hands across my jeans. "Better?" I say as I walk toward him.

He lets out a rush of air, as if seeing me on the ledge actually had him holding his breath. I pass him to head for the side of the roof with the better view, and as I do, I can't help but notice how unfortunately cute he is.

No. Cute is an insult.

This guy is *beautiful.* Well-manicured, smells like money, looks to be several years older than me. His eyes crinkle in the corners as they follow me, and his lips seem to frown, even when they aren't. When I reach the side of the building that overlooks the street, I lean forward and stare down at the cars below, trying not to appear impressed by him. I can tell by his haircut alone that he's the kind of man people are easily impressed by, and I refuse to feed into his ego. Not that he's done anything to make me think he even *has* one. But he is wearing a casual Burberry shirt, and I'm not sure I've ever been on the radar of someone who could casually afford one.

I hear footsteps approaching from behind, and then he leans against the railing next to me. Out of the corner of my eye, I watch as he takes another hit of his joint. When he's finished, he offers it to me, but I wave it off. The last thing I need is to be under the influence around this guy. His voice is a drug in itself. I kind of want to hear it again, so I throw a question in his direction.

"So what did that chair do to make you so angry?"

He looks at me. Like *really* looks at me. His eyes meet mine and he just stares, hard, like all my secrets are right there on my face. I've never seen eyes as dark as his. Maybe I have, but they seem darker when they're attached to such an intimidating presence. He doesn't answer my question, but my curiosity isn't easily put to rest. If he's going to force me down from a very peaceful, comfortable ledge, then I expect him to entertain me with answers to my nosy questions.

"Was it a woman?" I inquire. "Did she break your heart?"

He laughs a little with that question. "If only my issues were as trivial as matters of the heart." He leans into the wall so that he can face me. "What floor do you live on?" He licks his fingers and pinches the end of his joint, then puts it back in his pocket. "I've never noticed you before."

"That's because I don't live here." I point in the direction of my apartment. "See that insurance building?"

He squints as he looks in the direction I'm pointing. "Yeah."

"I live in the building next to it. It's too short to see from here. It's only three stories tall."

He's facing me again, resting his elbow on the ledge. "If you live over there, why are you here? Your boyfriend live here or something?"

His comment somehow makes me feel cheap. It was too easy—an amateurish pickup line. From the looks of this guy, I know he has better skills than that. It makes me think he saves the more difficult pickup lines for the women he deems worthy.

"You have a nice roof," I tell him.

He lifts an eyebrow, waiting for more of an explanation.

"I wanted fresh air. Somewhere to think. I pulled up Google Earth and found the closest apartment complex with a decent rooftop patio."

He regards me with a smile. "At least you're economical," he says. "That's a good quality to have."

At least?

I nod, because I *am* economical. And it *is* a good quality to have.

"Why did you need fresh air?" he asks.

Because I buried my father today and gave an epically disastrous eulogy and now I feel like I can't breathe.

I face forward again and slowly exhale. "Can we just not talk for a little while?"

He seems a bit relieved that I asked for silence. He leans

over the ledge and lets an arm dangle as he stares down at the street. He stays like this for a while, and I stare at him the entire time. He probably knows I'm staring, but he doesn't seem to care.

"A guy fell off this roof last month," he says.

I would be annoyed at his lack of respect for my request for silence, but I'm kind of intrigued.

"Was it an accident?"

He shrugs. "No one knows. It happened late in the evening. His wife said she was cooking dinner and he told her he was coming up here to take some pictures of the sunset. He was a photographer. They think he was leaning over the ledge to get a shot of the skyline, and he slipped."

I look over the ledge, wondering how someone could possibly put themselves in a situation where they could fall by accident. But then I remember I was just straddling the ledge on the other side of the roof a few minutes ago.

"When my sister told me what happened, the only thing I could think about was whether or not he got the shot. I was hoping his camera didn't fall with him, because that would have been a real waste, you know? To die because of your love of photography, but you didn't even get the final shot that cost you your life?"

His thought makes me laugh. Although I'm not sure I should have laughed at that. "Do you always say exactly what's on your mind?"

He shrugs. "Not to most people."

This makes me smile. I like that he doesn't even know me, but for whatever reason, I'm not considered *most people* to him.

He rests his back against the ledge and folds his arms over his chest. "Were you born here?"

I shake my head. "No. Moved here from Maine after I graduated college."

He scrunches up his nose, and it's kind of hot. Watching this guy—dressed in his Burberry shirt with his two-hundred-dollar haircut—making silly faces.

"So you're in Boston purgatory, huh? That's gotta suck."

"What do you mean?" I ask him.

The corner of his mouth curls up. "The tourists treat you like a local; the locals treat you like a tourist."

I laugh. "Wow. That's a very accurate description."

"I've been here two months. I'm not even in purgatory yet, so you're doing better than I am."

"What brought you to Boston?"

"My residency. And my sister lives here." He taps his foot and says, "Right beneath us, actually. Married a tech-savvy Bostonian and they bought the entire top floor."

I look down. "The *entire* top floor?"

He nods. "Lucky bastard works from home. Doesn't even have to change out of his pajamas and makes seven figures a year."

Lucky bastard, indeed.

"What kind of residency? Are you a doctor?"

He nods. "Neurosurgeon. Less than a year left of my residency and then it's official."

Stylish, well spoken, *and* smart. *And smokes pot.* If this were an SAT question, I would ask which one didn't belong. "Should doctors be smoking weed?"

He smirks. "Probably not. But if we didn't indulge on

occasion, there would be a lot more of us taking the leap over these ledges, I can promise you that." He's facing forward again with his chin resting on his arms. His eyes are closed now, like he's enjoying the wind against his face. He doesn't look as intimidating like this.

"You want to know something that only the locals know?"

"Of course," he says, bringing his attention back to me.

I point to the east. "See that building? The one with the green roof?"

He nods.

"There's a building behind it on Melcher. There's a house on top of the building. Like a legit house, built right on the rooftop. You can't see it from the street, and the building is so tall that not many people even know about it."

He looks impressed. "Really?"

I nod. "I saw it when I was searching Google Earth, so I looked it up. Apparently a permit was granted for the construction in 1982. How cool would that be? To live in a house on top of a building?"

"You'd get the whole roof to yourself," he says.

I hadn't thought of that. If I owned it I could plant gardens up there. I'd have an outlet.

"Who lives there?" he asks.

"No one really knows. It's one of the great mysteries of Boston."

He laughs and then looks at me inquisitively. "What's another great mystery of Boston?"

"Your name." As soon as I say it, I slap my hand against my forehead. It sounded so much like a cheesy pickup line; the only thing I can do is laugh at myself.

He smiles. "It's Ryle," he says. "Ryle Kincaid."

I sigh, sinking into myself. "That's a really great name."

"Why do you sound sad about it?"

"Because, I'd give anything for a great name."

"You don't like the name Lily?"

I tilt my head and cock an eyebrow. "My last name . . . is Bloom."

He's quiet. I can feel him trying to hold back his pity.

"I know. It's awful. It's the name of a two-year-old little girl, not a twenty-three-year-old woman."

"A two-year-old girl will have the same name no matter how old she gets. Names aren't something we eventually grow out of, Lily Bloom."

"Unfortunately for me," I say. "But what makes it even worse is that I absolutely love gardening. I love flowers. Plants. Growing things. It's my passion. It's always been my dream to open a florist shop, but I'm afraid if I did, people wouldn't think my desire was authentic. They would think I was trying to capitalize off my name and that being a florist isn't really my dream job."

"Maybe so," he says. "But what's that matter?"

"It doesn't, I suppose." I catch myself whispering, "*Lily Bloom's*" quietly. I can see him smiling a little bit. "It really is a great name for a florist. But I have a master's degree in business. I'd be downgrading, don't you think? I work for the biggest marketing firm in Boston."

"Owning your own business isn't downgrading," he says.

I raise an eyebrow. "Unless it flops."

He nods in agreement. "Unless it flops," he says. "So what's your middle name, Lily Bloom?"

I groan, which makes him perk up.

"You mean it gets worse?"

I drop my head in my hands and nod.

"Rose?"

I shake my head. "Worse."

"Violet?"

"I wish." I cringe and then mutter, *"Blossom."*

There's a moment of silence. "Goddamn," he says softly.

"Yeah. Blossom is my mother's maiden name and my parents thought it was fate that their last names were synonyms. So of course when they had me, a flower was their first choice."

"Your parents must be real assholes."

One of them is. *Was.* "My father died this week."

He glances at me. "Nice try. I'm not falling for that."

"I'm serious. That's why I came up here tonight. I think I just needed a good cry."

He stares at me suspiciously for a moment to make sure I'm not pulling his leg. He doesn't apologize for the blunder. Instead, his eyes grow a little more curious, like his intrigue is actually authentic. "Were you close?"

That's a hard question. I rest my chin on my arms and look down at the street again. "I don't know," I say with a shrug. "As his daughter, I loved him. But as a human, I hated him."

I can feel him watching me for a moment, and then he says, "I like that. Your honesty."

He likes my honesty. I think I might be blushing.

We're both quiet again for a while, and then he says, "Do you ever wish people were more transparent?"

"How so?"

He picks at a piece of chipped stucco with his thumb until it breaks loose. He flicks it over the ledge. "I feel like everyone fakes who they really are, when deep down we're all equal amounts of screwed up. Some of us are just better at hiding it than others."

Either his high is setting in, or he's just very introspective. Either way, I'm okay with it. My favorite conversations are the ones with no real answers.

"I don't think being a little guarded is a negative thing," I say. "Naked truths aren't always pretty."

He stares at me for a moment. "*Naked truths*," he repeats. "I like that." He turns around and walks to the middle of the rooftop. He adjusts the back on one of the patio loungers behind me and lowers himself onto it. It's the kind you lie on, so he pulls his hands behind his head and looks up at the sky. I claim the one next to him and adjust it until I'm in the same position as him.

"Tell me a naked truth, Lily."

"Pertaining to what?"

He shrugs. "I don't know. Something you aren't proud of. Something that will make me feel a little less screwed up on the inside."

He's staring up at the sky, waiting on me to answer. My eyes follow the line of his jaw, the curve of his cheeks, the outline of his lips. His eyebrows are drawn together in contemplation. I don't understand why, but he seems to need conversation right now. I think about his question and try to find an honest answer. When I come up with one, I look away from him and back up to the sky.

"My father was abusive. Not to me—to my mother. He

would get so angry when they fought that sometimes he would hit her. When that happened, he would spend the next week or two making up for it. He would do things like buy her flowers or take us out to a nice dinner. Sometimes he would buy me stuff because he knew I hated it when they fought. When I was a kid, I found myself looking forward to the nights they would fight. Because I knew if he hit her, the two weeks that followed would be great." I pause. I'm not sure I've ever admitted that to myself. "Of course if I could, I would have made it to where he never touched her. But the abuse was inevitable with their marriage, and it became our norm. When I got older, I realized that not doing something about it made me just as guilty. I spent most of my life hating him for being such a bad person, but I'm not so sure I'm much better. Maybe we're both bad people."

Ryle looks over at me with a thoughtful expression. "Lily," he says pointedly. "There is no such thing as *bad people*. We're all just people who sometimes do bad things."

I open my mouth to respond, but his words strike me silent. *We're all just people who sometimes do bad things.* I guess that's true in a way. No one is exclusively bad, nor is anyone exclusively good. Some are just forced to work harder at suppressing the bad.

"Your turn," I tell him.

Based on his reaction, I think he might not want to play his own game. He sighs heavily and runs a hand through his hair. He opens his mouth to speak, but then clamps it shut again. He thinks for a bit, and then finally speaks. "I watched a little boy die tonight." His voice is despondent. "He was only five years old. He and his little brother found a gun in his parents' bedroom. The younger brother was holding it and it went off by accident."

My stomach flips. I think this may be a little too much truth for me.

"There was nothing that could be done by the time he made it to the operating table. Everyone around—nurses, other doctors—they all felt so sorry for the family. *Those poor parents,*' they said. But when I had to walk into the waiting room and tell those parents that their child didn't make it, I didn't feel an ounce of sorrow for them. I wanted them to suffer. I wanted them to feel the weight of their ignorance for keeping a loaded gun within access of two innocent children. I wanted them to know that not only did they just lose a child, they just ruined the entire life of the one who accidentally pulled the trigger."

Jesus Christ. I wasn't prepared for something so heavy.

I can't even conceive how a family moves past that. "That poor boy's brother," I say. "I can't imagine what that's going to do to him—seeing something like that."

Ryle flicks something off the knee of his jeans. "It'll destroy him for life, that's what it'll do."

I turn on my side to face him, lifting my head up onto my hand. "Is it hard? Seeing things like that every day?"

He gives his head a slight shake. "It should be a lot harder, but the more I'm around death, the more it just becomes a part of life. I'm not sure how I feel about that." He makes eye contact with me again. "Give me another one," he says. "I feel like mine was a little more twisted than yours."

I disagree, but I tell him about the twisted thing I did a mere twelve hours ago.

"My mother asked me two days ago if I would deliver the eulogy at my father's funeral today. I told her I didn't feel comfortable—that I might be crying too hard to speak in front of a crowd—but that was a lie. I just didn't want to do it because I feel like eulogies should be delivered by those who respected the deceased. And I didn't much respect my father."

"Did you do it?"

I nod. "Yeah. This morning." I sit up and pull my legs beneath me as I face him. "You want to hear it?"

He smiles. "Absolutely."

I fold my hands in my lap and inhale a breath. "I had no idea what to say. About an hour before the funeral, I told my mother I didn't want to do it. She said it was simple and that my father would have wanted me to do it. She said all I had to do was walk up to the podium and say five great things about my father. So . . . that's exactly what I did."

Ryle lifts up onto his elbow, appearing even more interested. He can tell by the look on my face that it gets worse. "Oh, no, Lily. What did you do?"

"Here. Let me just reenact it for you." I stand up and walk around to the other side of my chair. I stand tall and act like I'm looking out over the same crowded room I was met with this morning. I clear my throat.

"Hello. My name is Lily Bloom, daughter of the late Andrew Bloom. Thank you all for joining us today as we mourn his loss. I wanted to take a moment to honor his life by sharing with you five great things about my father. The first thing . . ."

I look down at Ryle and shrug. "That's it."

He sits up. "What do you mean?"

I take a seat on my lounge chair and lie back down. "I stood up there for two solid minutes without saying another word. There wasn't one great thing I could say about that man—so I just stared silently at the crowd until my mother realized what I was doing and had my uncle remove me from the podium."

Ryle tilts his head. "Are you kidding me? You gave the anti-eulogy at your own father's funeral?"

I nod. "I'm not proud of it. I don't *think*. I mean, if I had my way, he would have been a much better person and I would have stood up there and talked for an hour."

Ryle lies back down. "Wow," he says, shaking his head. "You're kind of my hero. You just roasted a dead guy."

"That's tacky."

"Yeah, well. Naked truth hurts."

I laugh. "Your turn."

"I can't top that," he says.

"I'm sure you can come close."

"I'm not sure I can."

I roll my eyes. "Yes you can. Don't make me feel like the worst person out of the two of us. Tell me the most recent thought you've had that most people wouldn't say out loud."

He pulls his hands up behind his head and looks me straight in the eye. "I want to fuck you."

My mouth falls open. Then I clamp it shut again.

I think I might be speechless.

He shoots me a look of innocence. "You asked for the most recent thought, so I gave it to you. You're beautiful. I'm a guy. If you were into one-night stands, I would take you downstairs to my bedroom and I would fuck you."

I can't even look at him. His statement makes me feel a multitude of things all at once.

"Well, I'm not into one-night stands."

"I figured as much," he says. "Your turn."

He's so nonchalant; he acts as if he didn't just stun me into silence.

"I need a minute to regroup after that one," I say with a laugh. I try to think of something with a little shock value, but I can't get over the fact that he just said that. *Out loud.* Maybe because he's a neurosurgeon and I never pictured someone so educated throwing around the word *fuck* so casually.

I gather myself . . . somewhat . . . and then say, "Okay. Since we're on the subject . . . the first guy I ever had sex with was homeless."

He perks up and faces me. "Oh, I'm gonna need more of this story."

I stretch my arm out and rest my head on it. "I grew up in Maine. We lived in a fairly decent neighborhood, but the street behind our house wasn't in the best condition. Our backyard butted up to a condemned house adjacent to two abandoned lots. I became friends with a guy named Atlas who stayed in the condemned house. No one knew he was living there other than me. I used to take him food and clothes and stuff. Until my father found out."

"What'd he do?"

My jaw tightens. I don't know why I brought this up when I still force myself not to think about it on a daily basis.

"He beat him up." That's as naked as I want to get about that subject. "Your turn."

He regards me silently for a moment, as if he knows there's more to that story. But then he breaks eye contact. "The thought of marriage repulses me," he says. "I'm almost thirty years old and I have no desire for a wife. I *especially* don't want children. The only thing I want out of life is success. Lots of it. But if I admit that out loud to anyone, it makes me sound arrogant."

"Professional success? Or social status?"

He says, "Both. Anyone can have children. Anyone can get married. But not everyone can be a neurosurgeon. I get a lot of pride out of that. And I don't just want to be a great neurosurgeon. I want to be the best in my field."

"You're right. It does make you sound arrogant."

He smiles. "My mother fears I'm wasting my life away because all I do is work."

"You're a neurosurgeon and your mother is *disappointed* in you?" I laugh. "Good lord, that's insane. Are parents ever really happy with their children? Will they ever be good enough?"

He shakes his head. "My children wouldn't be. Not many people have the drive I do, so I'd only be setting them up for failure. That's why I'll never have any."

"I actually think that's respectable, Ryle. A lot of people refuse to admit they might be too selfish to have children."

He shakes his head. "Oh, I'm *way* too selfish to have children. And I'm definitely way too selfish to be in a relationship."

"So how do you avoid it? You just don't date?"

He cuts his eyes to me, and there's a slight grin affixed to his face. "When I have time, there are girls who satisfy those needs. I don't lack for anything in that department, if that's what you're asking. But love has never appealed to me. It's always been more of a burden than anything."

I wish I looked at love like that. It would make my life a hell of a lot easier. "I envy you. I have this idea that there's a perfect man out there for me. I tend to become jaded easily, because no one ever meets my standards. I feel like I'm on an infinite search for the Holy Grail."

"You should try my method," he says.

"Which is?"

"One-night stands." He raises an eyebrow, like it's an invitation.

I'm glad it's dark, because my face is on fire. "I could never sleep with someone if I didn't see it going anywhere." I say this out loud, but my words lack conviction when I say it to him.

He drags in a long, slow breath, and then rolls onto his back. "Not that kind of girl, huh?" He says this with a trace of disappointment in his voice.

I match his disappointment. I'm not sure I'd even want to turn him down if he made a move, but I might have just thwarted that possibility.

"If you wouldn't *sleep* with someone you just met . . ." His eyes meet mine again. "Exactly how far would you go?"

I don't have an answer for that. I roll onto my back because the way he's looking at me makes me want to rethink one-night stands. I'm not necessarily against them, I suppose. I've just never been propositioned for one by someone I would consider it with.

Until now. I *think*. Is he even propositioning me? I've always been terrible at flirting.

He reaches out and grabs the edge of my lounge chair. In one swift movement and with very minimal effort, he drags my chair closer to him until it bumps his.

My whole body stiffens. He's so close now, I can feel the warmth of his breath cutting through the cold air. If I were to look at him, his face would be mere inches from mine. I refuse to look at him, because he'd probably kiss me and I know absolutely nothing about this guy, other than a couple of naked truths. But that doesn't weigh on my conscience at all when he rests a heavy hand on my stomach.

"How far would you go, Lily?" His voice is decadent. Smooth. It travels straight to my toes.

"I don't know," I whisper.

His fingers begin to crawl toward the hem of my shirt. He begins to slowly inch it upward until a slither of my stomach is showing. "*Oh, Jesus*," I whisper, feeling the warmth from his hand as he slides it up my stomach.

Against my better judgment, I face him again and the look in his eyes completely captivates me. He looks hopeful and hungry and completely confident. He sinks his teeth into his bottom lip as his hand begins to tease its way up my shirt. I know he can feel my heart thrashing around in my chest. Hell, he can probably *hear* it.

"Is this too far?" he asks.

I don't know where this side of me is coming from, but I shake my head and say, "Not even close."

With a grin, his fingers brush the underneath of my bra, lightly trickling over my skin that is now covered in chills.

As soon as my eyelids fall shut, the piercing of a ring rips through the air. His hand stiffens when we both realize it's a phone. *His* phone.

He drops his forehead to my shoulder. "Dammit."

I frown when his hand slips out from beneath my shirt. He fumbles in his pocket for his phone, standing up and walking several feet away from me to take the call.

"Dr. Kincaid," he says. He listens intently, his hand gripping the back of his neck. "What about Roberts? I'm not even supposed to be on call right now." More silence is followed with, "Yeah, give me ten minutes. On my way."

He ends the call and slides his phone back in his pocket. When he turns to face me, he looks a little disappointed. He points to the door that leads to the stairwell. "I have to . . ."

I nod. "It's fine."

He considers me for a moment, and then holds up a finger. "Don't move," he says, reaching for his phone again. He walks closer and holds it up as if he's about to snap a picture of me. I almost object, but I don't even know why. I'm fully clothed. It just doesn't feel that way for some reason.

He snaps a picture of me lying in the lounge chair, my arms relaxed above my head. I have no idea what he plans to do with that picture, but I like that he took it. I like that he had the urge to remember what I look like, even though he knows he'll never see me again.

He stares at the photo on his screen for a few seconds and smiles. I'm half-tempted to take a picture of him in return, but I'm not sure I want a reminder of someone I'll never see again. The thought of that is a little depressing.

"It was nice meeting you, Lily Bloom. I hope you defy the odds of most dreams and actually accomplish yours."

I smile, equally saddened and confused by this guy. I'm not sure that I've ever spent time with someone like him before—someone of a completely different lifestyle and tax bracket. I probably never will again. But I'm pleasantly surprised to see that we aren't all that different.

Misconception confirmed.

He looks down at his feet for a moment as he stands in somewhat of an unsure pose. It's as if he's suspended between the desire to say something else to me and the need to leave. He glances at me one last time—this time without so much of a poker face. I can see the disappointment in the set of his mouth before he turns and walks in the other direction. He opens the door and I can hear his footsteps fade as he rushes down the stairwell. I'm alone on the rooftop once again, but to my surprise, I'm a little saddened by that now.

Chapter Two

Lucy—*the roommate who loves to hear herself sing*—is rushing around the living room, gathering keys, shoes, a pair of sunglasses. I'm seated on the couch, opening up shoeboxes stuffed with some of my old things from when I lived at home. I grabbed them when I was home for my father's funeral this week.

"You work today?" Lucy asks.

"Nope. I have bereavement leave until Monday."

She stops in her tracks. "Monday?" She scoffs. "Lucky bitch."

"Yes, Lucy. I'm *so* lucky my father died." I say it sarcastically, of course, but I cringe when I realize it's not actually very sarcastic.

"You know what I mean," she mutters. She grabs her purse as she balances on one foot while sliding her shoe onto the other. "I'm not coming home tonight. Staying over at Alex's house." The door slams behind her.

We have a lot in common on the surface, but beyond wearing the same size clothes, being the same age, and both having four-letter names that start with an *L* and end with a *Y*, there's not much else there that makes us more than just roommates. I'm okay with that, though. Other than the incessant singing, she's pretty tolerable. She's clean and she's gone a lot. Two of the most important qualities in a roommate.

I'm pulling the lid off the top of one of the shoeboxes when my cell phone rings. I reach across the couch and grab it. When I see that it's my mother, I press my face into the couch and fake-cry into a throw pillow.

I bring the phone to my ear. "Hello?"

There's three seconds of silence, and then—"Hello, Lily."

I sigh and sit back up on the couch. "Hey, Mom." I'm really surprised she's speaking to me. It's only been one day since the funeral. That's 364 days sooner than I expected to hear from her.

"How are you?" I ask.

She sighs dramatically. "Fine," she says. "Your aunt and uncle went back to Nebraska this morning. It'll be my first night alone since . . ."

"You'll be fine, Mom," I say, trying to sound confident.

She's quiet for too long, and then she says, "Lily. I just want you to know that you shouldn't be embarrassed about what happened yesterday."

I pause. *I wasn't. Not even the slightest bit.*

"Everyone freezes up once in a while. I shouldn't have put that kind of pressure on you, knowing how hard the day was on you already. I should have just had your uncle do it."

I close my eyes. *Here she goes again.* Covering up what she doesn't want to see. Taking blame that isn't even hers to take. *Of course* she convinced herself that I froze up yesterday, and that's why I refused to speak. *Of course she did.* I have half a mind to tell her it wasn't a mistake. I didn't freeze up. I just had nothing great to say about the unremarkable man she chose to be my father.

But part of me does feel guilty for what I did—specifically

because it's not something I should have done in the presence of my mother—so I just accept what she's doing and go along with it.

"Thanks, Mom. Sorry I choked."

"It's fine, Lily. I need to go, I have to run to the insurance office. We have a meeting about your father's policies. Call me tomorrow, okay?"

"I will," I tell her. "Love you, Mom."

I end the call and toss the phone across the couch. I open the shoebox on my lap and pull out the contents. On the very top is a small wooden, hollow heart. I run my fingers over it and remember the night I was given this heart. As soon as the memory begins to sink in, I set it aside. Nostalgia is a funny thing.

I move a few old letters and newspaper clippings aside. Beneath all of it, I find what I was hoping was inside these boxes. And also sort of hoping *wasn't*.

My Ellen Diaries.

I run my hands over them. There are three of them in this box, but I'd say there are probably eight or nine total. I haven't read any of these since the last time I wrote in them.

I refused to admit that I kept a diary when I was younger because that was so cliché. Instead, I convinced myself that what I was doing was cool, because it wasn't technically a diary. I addressed each of my entries to Ellen DeGeneres, because I began watching her show the first day it aired in 2003 when I was just a little girl. I watched it every day after school and was convinced Ellen would love me if she got to know me. I wrote letters to her regularly until I turned sixteen, but I wrote them like one would write entries in a diary.

Of course I knew the last thing Ellen DeGeneres probably wanted was a random girl's journal entries. Luckily, I never actually sent any in. But I still liked addressing all the entries to her, so I continued to do that until I stopped writing in them altogether.

I open another shoebox and find more of them. I sort through them until I grab the one from when I was fifteen years old. I flip it open, searching for the day I met Atlas. There wasn't much that happened in my life worth writing about before he entered it, but somehow I filled six journals full before he ever came into the picture.

I swore I'd never read these again, but with the passing of my father, I've been thinking about my childhood a lot. Maybe if I read through these journals I'll somehow find a little strength for forgiveness. Although I fear I'm running the risk of building up even more resentment.

I lie back on the couch and I begin reading.

Dear Ellen,

Before I tell you what happened today, I have a really good idea for a new segment on your show. It's called, "Ellen at home."

I think lots of people would like to see you outside of work. I always wonder what you're like at your home when it's just you and Portia and the cameras aren't around. Maybe the producers can give her a camera and sometimes she can just sneak up on you and film you doing normal things, like watching TV or cooking or gardening. She could film you for a few seconds without you knowing and then she could scream, "Ellen at home!" and scare you. It's only fair, since you love pranks.

Okay, now that I told you that (I keep meaning to and have been forgetting) I'll tell you about my day yesterday. It was interesting. Probably my most interesting day to write about yet, if you don't count the day Abigail Ivory slapped Mr. Carson for looking at her cleavage.

You remember a while back when I told you about Mrs. Burleson who lived behind us? She died the night of that big snowstorm? My dad said she owed so much in taxes that her daughter wasn't able to take ownership of the house. Which is fine by her, I'm sure, because the house was starting to fall apart anyway. It probably would have been more of a burden than anything.

The house has been empty since Mrs. Burleson died, which has been about two years. I know it's been empty because my bedroom window looks out over the backyard, and there hasn't been a single soul that goes in or out of that house since I can remember.

Until last night.

I was in bed shuffling cards. I know that sounds weird, but it's just something I do. I don't even know how to play cards. But when my parents get into fights, shuffling cards just calms me down sometimes and gives me something to focus on.

Anyway, it was dark outside, so I noticed the light right away. It wasn't bright, but it was coming from that old house. It looked more like candlelight than anything, so I went to the back porch and found Dad's binoculars. I tried to see what was going on over there, but I couldn't see anything. It was way too dark. Then after a little while, the light went out.

This morning, when I was getting ready for school, I saw something moving behind that house. I crouched down at my bedroom window and saw someone sneaking out the back door. It was a guy and he had a backpack. He looked around like he was making sure no one saw him, and then he walked between our house and the neighbor's house and went and stood at the bus stop.

I'd never seen him before. It was the first time he rode my bus. He sat in the back and I sat in the middle, so I didn't talk to him. But when he got off the bus at school, I saw him walk into the school, so he must go there.

I have no idea why he was sleeping in that house. There's probably no electricity or running water. I thought maybe he did it as a dare, but today he got off the bus at the same stop as me. He walked down the street like he was going somewhere else, but I ran straight to my room and watched out the window. Sure enough, a few minutes later, I saw him sneaking back inside that empty house.

I don't know if I should say something to my mother. I hate to be nosy, because it's none of my business. But if that guy doesn't have anywhere to go, I feel like my mother would know how to help him since she works at a school.

I don't know. I might wait a couple days before I say something and see if he goes back home. He might just need a break from his parents. Same as I wish I could have sometimes.

That's all. I'll let you know what happens tomorrow.

—Lily

Dear Ellen,

I fast-forward through all your dancing when I watch your show. I used to watch the beginning when you danced through the audience, but I get a little bored with it now and would rather just hear you talk. I hope that doesn't make you mad.

Okay, so I found out who the guy is, and yes, he's still going over there. It's been two days now and I still haven't told anyone.

His name is Atlas Corrigan and he's a senior, but that's all I *know. I asked Katie who he was when she sat next to me on the bus. She rolled her eyes and told me his name. But then she said, "I don't know anything else about him, but he smells." She scrunched up her nose like it grossed her out. I wanted to yell at her and tell her he can't help it, that he doesn't have any running water. But instead, I just looked back at him. I might have stared a little too much, because he caught me looking at him.*

When I got home I went to the backyard to do some gardening. My radishes were ready to be pulled, so I was out there pulling them. The radishes are the only thing left in my garden. It's starting to get cold so there's not much else I can plant right now. I probably could have waited a few more days to pull them, but I was also outside because I was being nosy.

I noticed as I was pulling them that some were missing. It looked like they had just been dug up. I know I didn't pull them and my parents never mess with my garden.

That's when I thought about Atlas, and how it was more than likely him. I hadn't thought about how—if he doesn't have access to a shower—he probably doesn't have food, either.

I went inside my house and made a couple of sandwiches. I grabbed two sodas out of the fridge and a bag of chips. I put them in a lunch bag and I ran it over to the abandoned house and set it on the back porch by the door. I wasn't sure if he saw me, so I knocked real hard and then ran back to my house and went straight to my room. By the time I got to the window to see if he was going to come outside, the bag was already gone.

That's when I knew he'd been watching me. I'm kind of nervous now that he knows I know he's staying there. I don't know what I'll say to him if he tries to talk to me tomorrow.

—Lily

Dear Ellen,

I saw your interview with the presidential candidate Barack Obama today. Does that make you nervous? Interviewing people who could potentially run the country? I don't know a lot about politics, but I don't think I could be funny under that kind of pressure.

Man. So much has happened to both of us. You just interviewed someone who might be our next president and I'm feeding a homeless boy.

This morning when I got to the bus stop, Atlas was already there. It was just the two of us at first, and I'm not gonna lie, it was awkward. I could see the bus coming around the corner and I was wishing it would drive a little faster. Right when it pulled up, he took a step closer to me and, without looking up, he said, "Thank you."

The doors opened on the bus and he let me walk on first. I didn't say You're welcome *because I was kind of shocked by my reaction. His voice gave me chills, Ellen.*

Has a boy's voice ever done that to you?

Oh, wait. Sorry. Has a girl's *voice ever done that to you?*

He didn't sit by me or anything on the way there, but on the way back from school, he was the last one getting on. There weren't any empty seats, but I could tell by the way he scanned all the people on the bus that he wasn't looking for an empty seat. He was looking for me.

When his eyes met mine, I looked down at my lap real quick. I hate that I'm not very confident around guys. Maybe that's something I'll grow into when I finally turn sixteen.

He sat down next to me and dropped his backpack between his legs. That's when I noticed what Katie was talking about. He did kind of smell, but I didn't judge him for that.

He didn't say anything at first, but he was fidgeting with a hole in his jeans. It wasn't the kind of hole that was there to make jeans look stylish. I could tell it was there because it was a genuine hole, due to his pants being old. They actually looked a little too small for him, because his ankles were showing. But he was skinny enough that they fit him just fine everywhere else.

"Did you tell anyone?" he asked me.

I looked at him when he spoke, and he was looking right back at me like he was worried. It was the first time I had actually gotten a good look at him. His hair was dark brown, but I thought maybe if he washed it, it wouldn't be as dark as it looked right then. His eyes were bright, unlike the rest of him. Real blue eyes, like the kind you see on a Siberian husky. I shouldn't compare his eyes to a dog, but that's the first thing I thought when I saw them.

I shook my head and looked back out the window. I thought he might get up and find another seat at that point, since I said I didn't tell anyone, but he didn't. The bus made a few stops, and the fact that he was still sitting by me gave me a little courage, so I made my voice a whisper. "Why don't you live at home with your parents?"

He stared at me for a few seconds, like he was trying to decide if he wanted to trust me or not. Then he said, "Because they don't want me to."

That's when he got up. I thought I'd made him mad, but then I realized he got up because we were at our stop. I grabbed my stuff and followed him off the bus. He didn't try to hide where he was heading today like he usually does. Normally, he walks down the street and goes around the block so I don't see him cut through my backyard. But today he started to walk toward my yard with me.

When we got to where I would normally turn to go inside and

he would keep walking, we both stopped. He kicked at the dirt with his foot and looked behind me at my house.

"What time do your parents get home?"

"Around five," I said. It was 3:45.

He nodded and looked like he was about to say something else, but he didn't. He just nodded again and started walking toward that house with no food or electricity or water.

Now, Ellen, I know what I did next was stupid, so you don't have to tell me. I called out his name, and when he stopped and turned around I said, "If you hurry, you can take a shower before they get home."

My heart was beating so fast, because I knew how much trouble I could get into if my parents came home and found a homeless guy in our shower. I'd probably very well die. But I just couldn't watch him walk back to his house without offering him something.

He looked down at the ground again, and I felt his embarrassment in my own stomach. He didn't even nod. He just followed me inside my house and never said a word.

The whole time he was in the shower, I was panicking. I kept looking out the window and checking for either of my parents' cars, even though I knew it would be a good hour before they got home. I was nervous one of the neighbors might have seen him come inside, but they didn't really know me well enough to think having a visitor would be abnormal.

I had given Atlas a change of clothes, and knew he not only needed to be out of the house when my parents got home, but he needed to be far away from our house. I'm sure my father would recognize his own clothes on some random teenager in the neighborhood.

In between looking out the window and checking the clock, I was filling up one of my old backpacks with stuff. Food that didn't need refrigerating, a couple of my father's T-shirts, a pair of jeans that were probably going to be two sizes too big for him, and a change of socks.

I was zipping up the backpack when he emerged from the hallway.

I was right. Even wet, I could tell his hair was lighter than it looked earlier. It made his eyes look even bluer.

He must have shaved while he was in there because he looked younger than he did before he got in the shower. I swallowed and looked back down at the backpack, because I was shocked at how different he looked. I was scared he might see my thoughts written across my face.

I looked out the window one more time and handed him the backpack. "You might want to go out the back door so no one sees you."

He took the backpack from me and stared at my face for a minute. "What's your name?" he said as he slung the pack over his shoulder.

"Lily."

He smiled. It was the first time he'd smiled at me and I had an awful, shallow thought in that moment. I wondered how someone with such a great smile could have such shitty parents. I immediately hated myself for thinking it, because of course parents should love their kids no matter how cute or ugly or skinny or fat or smart or stupid they are. But sometimes you can't control where your mind goes. You just have to train it not to go there anymore.

He held out his hand and said, "I'm Atlas."

"I know," I said, without shaking his hand. I don't know why I didn't shake his hand. It wasn't because I was scared to touch him.

I mean, I was scared to touch him. But not because I thought I was better than him. He just made me so nervous.

He put his hand down and nodded once, then said, "I guess I better go."

I stepped aside so he could walk around me. He pointed past the kitchen, silently asking if that was the way to the back door. I nodded and walked behind him as he made his way down the hall. When he reached the back door, I saw him pause for a second when he saw my bedroom.

I was suddenly embarrassed that he was seeing my bedroom. No one ever sees my bedroom, so I've never felt the need to give it a more mature look. I still have the same pink bedspread and curtains I've had since I was twelve. For the first time ever I felt like ripping down my poster of Adam Brody.

Atlas didn't seem to care how my room was decorated. He looked straight at my window—the one that looks out over the backyard— then he glanced back at me. Right before he walked out the back door he said, "Thank you for not being disparaging, Lily."

And then he was gone.

Of course I've heard the term disparaging *before, but it was weird hearing a teenage guy use it. What's even weirder is how everything about Atlas seems so contradictory. How does a guy who is obviously humble, well-mannered, and uses words like* disparaging *end up homeless? How does any teenager end up homeless?*

I need to find out, Ellen.

I'm going to find out what happened to him. You just wait and see.

—Lily

• • •

I'm about to open another entry when my phone rings. I crawl across the couch for it and I'm not the least bit surprised to see it's my mother again. Now that my father has passed and she's alone, she'll probably call me twice as much as she did before.

"Hello?"

"What do you think about my moving to Boston?" she blurts out.

I grab the throw pillow next to me and shove my face into it, muffling a scream. "Um. *Wow*," I say. "Really?"

She's quiet, and then, "It was just a thought. We can discuss it tomorrow. I'm almost to my meeting."

"Okay. Bye."

And just like that, I want to move out of Massachusetts. *She can't move here*. She doesn't know anyone here. She'd expect me to entertain her every day. I love my mother, don't get me wrong, but I moved to Boston to be on my own, and having her in the same city would make me feel less independent.

My father was diagnosed with cancer three years ago while I was still in college. If Ryle Kincaid were here right now, I'd tell him the naked truth that I was a little bit relieved when my father became too ill to physically hurt my mother. It completely changed the dynamic of their relationship and I no longer felt obligated to stay in Plethora to make sure she was okay.

Now that my father is gone and I never have to worry about my mother again, I was looking forward to spreading my wings, so to speak.

But now she's moving to Boston?

It feels like my wings were just clipped.

Where is a marine-grade polymer chair when I need one?!

I'm seriously stressing out and I have no idea what I'd do if my mother moves to Boston. I don't have a garden, or a yard, or a patio, or weeds.

I have to find another outlet.

I decide to clean. I place all of my old shoeboxes full of journals and notes in my bedroom closet. Then I organize my entire closet. My jewelry, my shoes, my clothes . . .

She cannot move to Boston.

Chapter Three

Six months later

"Oh."

That's all she says.

My mother turns and assesses the building, running a finger over the windowsill next to her. She picks up a layer of dust and wipes it between her fingers. "It's . . ."

"It needs a lot of work, I know," I interrupt. I point at the windows behind her. "But look at the storefront. It has potential."

She scrolls over the windows, nodding. There's this sound she makes in the back of her throat sometimes, where she agrees with a little hum but her lips remain tight. It means she doesn't *actually* agree. And she makes that sound. *Twice.*

I drop my arms in defeat. "You think this was stupid?"

She gives her head a slight shake. "That all depends on how it turns out, Lily," she says. The building used to house a restaurant and it's still full of old tables and chairs. My mother walks over to a nearby table and pulls out one of the chairs, taking a seat. "If things work out, and your floral shop is successful, then people will say it was a brave, bold, *smart* business decision. But if it fails and you lose your entire inheritance . . ."

"Then people will say it was a *stupid* business decision."

She shrugs. "That's just how it works. You majored in business, you know that." She glances around the room, slowly, as if she's seeing it the way it will look a month from now. "Just make sure it's brave and bold, Lily."

I smile. *I can accept that.* "I can't believe I bought it without asking you first," I say, taking a seat at the table.

"You're an adult. It's your right," she says, but I can hear a trace of disappointment. I think she feels even lonelier now that I need her less and less. It's been six months since my father died, and even though he wasn't good company, it has to be weird for her, being alone. She got a job at one of the elementary schools, so she did end up moving here. She chose a small suburb on the outskirts of Boston. She bought a cute two-bedroom house on a cul-de-sac, with a huge backyard. I dream of planting a garden there, but that would require daily care. My limit is once-a-week visits. Sometimes twice.

"What are you going to do with all this junk?" she asks.

She's right. There's so much junk. It'll take forever to clear this place out. "I have no idea. I guess I'll be busting my ass for a while before I can even think about decorating."

"When's your last day at the marketing firm?"

I smile. "Yesterday."

She releases a sigh, and then shakes her head. "Oh, Lily. I certainly hope this works out in your favor."

We both begin to stand when the front door opens. There are shelves in the way of the door, so I careen my head around them and see a woman walk in. Her eyes briefly scan the room until she sees me.

"Hi," she says with a wave. She's cute. She's dressed well,

but she's wearing white capris. A disaster waiting to happen in this dust bowl.

"Can I help you?"

She tucks her purse beneath her arm and walks toward me, holding out her hand. "I'm Allysa," she says. I shake her hand.

"Lily."

She tosses a thumb over her shoulder. "There's a help wanted sign out front?"

I look over her shoulder and raise an eyebrow. "There is?" *I didn't put up a help wanted sign.*

She nods, and then shrugs. "It looks old, though," she says. "It's probably been there a while. I was just out for a walk and saw the sign. Was curious, is all."

I like her almost immediately. Her voice is pleasant and her smile seems genuine.

My mother's hand falls down on my shoulder and she leans in and kisses me on the cheek. "I have to go," she says. "Open house tonight." I tell her goodbye and watch her walk outside, then turn my attention back to Allysa.

"I'm not really hiring yet," I say. I wave my hand around the room. "I'm opening up a floral shop, but it'll be a couple of months, at least." I should know better than to hold preconceived judgments, but she doesn't look like she'd be satisfied with a minimum wage job. Her purse probably cost more than this building.

Her eyes light up. "Really? I love flowers!" She spins around in a circle and says, "This place has a ton of potential. What color are you painting it?"

I cross my arm over my chest and grab my elbow. Rocking

back on my heels, I say, "I'm not sure. I just got the keys to the building an hour ago, so I haven't really come up with a design plan yet."

"Lily, right?"

I nod.

"I'm not going to pretend I have a degree in design, but it's my absolute favorite thing. If you need any help, I'd do it for free."

I tilt my head. "You'd work for free?"

She nods. "I don't really need a job, I just saw the sign and thought, '*What the heck*?' But I do get bored sometimes. I'd be happy to help you with whatever you need. Cleaning, decorating, picking out paint colors. I'm a Pinterest whore." Something behind me catches her eye and she points. "I could take that broken door and make it magnificent. *All* this stuff, really. There's a use for almost everything, you know."

I look around at the room, knowing full well I'm not going to be able to tackle this by myself. I probably can't even lift half this stuff alone. I'll eventually have to hire someone anyway. "I'm not going to let you work for free. But I could do $10 an hour if you're really serious."

She starts clapping, and if she weren't in heels, she might have jumped up and down. "When can I start?"

I glance down at her white capris. "Will tomorrow work? You'll probably want to show up in disposable clothes."

She waves me off and drops her Hermès bag on a dusty table next to her. "Nonsense," she says. "My husband is watching the Bruins play at a bar down the street. If it's okay, I'll just hang with you and get started right now."

• • •

Two hours later, I'm convinced I've met my new best friend. And she really is a Pinterest whore.

We write "Keep" and "Toss" on sticky notes, and slap them on everything in the room. She's a fellow believer in upcycling, so we come up with ideas for at least 75 percent of the stuff left in the building. The rest she says her husband can throw out when he has free time. Once we know what we're going to do with all the stuff, I grab a notebook and a pen and we sit at one of the tables to write down design ideas.

"Okay," she says, leaning back in her chair. I want to laugh, because her white capris are covered in dirt now, but she doesn't seem to care. "Do you have a goal for this place?" she asks, glancing around.

"I have *one*," I say. "Succeed."

She laughs. "I have no doubt you'll succeed. But you do need a vision."

I think about what my mother said. *"Just make sure it's brave and bold, Lily."* I smile and sit up straighter in my chair. "Brave and bold," I say. "I want this place to be different. I want to take risks."

She narrows her eyes as she chews on the tip of the pen. "But you're just selling flowers," she says. "How can you be brave and bold with flowers?"

I look around the room and try to envision what I'm thinking. I'm not even sure what I'm thinking. I'm just getting itchy and restless, like I'm on the verge of a brilliant idea. "What are some words that come to mind when you think of flowers?" I ask her.

She shrugs. "I don't know. They're sweet, I guess? They're alive, so they make me think of life. And maybe the color pink. And spring."

"Sweet, life, pink, spring," I repeat. And then, "Allysa, you're brilliant!" I stand up and begin pacing the floor. "We'll take everything everyone loves about flowers, and we'll do the complete opposite!"

She makes a face to let me know she isn't following.

"Okay," I say. "What if, instead of showcasing the *sweet* side of flowers, we showcased the *villainous* side? Instead of pink accents, we use darker colors, like a deep purple or even black. And instead of just spring and life, we also celebrate winter and death."

Allysa's eyes are wide. "But . . . what if someone wants *pink* flowers, though?"

"Well, we'll still give them what they want, of course. But we'll also give them what they don't *know* they want."

She scratches her cheek. "So you're thinking *black* flowers?" She looks concerned, and I don't blame her. She's only seeing the darkest side of my vision. I take a seat at the table again and try to get her on board.

"Someone once told me that there is no such thing as bad people. We're all just people who sometimes do bad things. That stuck with me, because it's so true. We've all got a little bit of good and evil in us. I want to make that our theme. Instead of painting the walls a putrid sweet color, we paint them dark purple with black accents. And instead of only putting out the usual pastel displays of flowers in boring crystal vases that make people think of life, we go edgy. Brave and bold. We put out displays of darker flowers wrapped in things like leather or silver chains. And rather than put them in crystal vases, we'll stick them in black onyx or . . . I don't know . . . purple velvet vases lined with silver studs. The ideas are endless." I stand up again. "There are floral shops on every corner for people who love flowers. But what floral shop caters to all the people who *hate* flowers?"

Allysa shakes her head. "None of them," she whispers.

"Exactly. None of them."

We stare at each other for a moment, and then I can't take it another second. I'm bursting with excitement and I just start laughing like a giddy child. Allysa starts laughing, too, and she jumps up and hugs me. "Lily, it's so twisted, it's brilliant!"

"I know!" I'm full of renewed energy. "I need a desk so I can sit down and make a business plan! But my future office is full of old vegetable crates!"

She walks toward the back of the store. "Well, let's get them out of there and go buy you a desk!"

We squeeze into the office and begin moving crates out one by one and into a back room. I stand on the chair to make the piles taller so we'll have more room to move around.

"These are perfect for the window displays I have in mind." She hands me two more crates and walks away, and as I'm reaching on my tiptoes to stack them at the very top, the pile begins to tumble. I try to find something to grab hold of for balance, but the crates knock me off the chair. When I land on the floor, I can feel my foot bend in the wrong direction. It's followed by a rush of pain straight up my leg and down to my toes.

Allysa comes rushing back into the room and has to move

two of the crates from on top of me. "Lily!" she says. "Oh my God, are you okay?"

I pull myself up to a sitting position, but don't even try to put weight on my ankle. I shake my head. "My ankle."

She immediately removes my shoe and then pulls her phone out of her pocket. She begins dialing a number and then looks up at me. "I know this is a stupid question, but do you happen to have a refrigerator here with ice in it?"

I shake my head.

"I figured," she says. She puts the phone on speaker and sets it on the floor as she begins to roll up my pant leg. I wince, but not so much from the pain. I just can't believe I did something so stupid. If I broke it, I'm screwed. I just spent my entire inheritance on a building that I won't even be able to renovate for months.

"*Heeey*, Issa," a voice croons through her phone. "Where you at? The game's over."

Allysa picks up her phone and brings it closer to her mouth. "At work. Listen, I need . . ."

The guy cuts her off and says, "At *work*? Babe, you don't even have a job."

Allysa shakes her head and says, "Marshall, listen. It's an emergency. I think my boss broke her ankle. I need you to bring some ice to . . ."

He cuts her off with a laugh. "Your *boss*? Babe, you don't even have a job," he repeats.

Allysa rolls her eyes. "Marshall, are you drunk?"

"It's *onesie* day," he slurs into the phone. "You knew that when you dropped us off, Issa. Free beer until . . ."

She groans. "Put my brother on the phone."

"Fine, fine," Marshall mumbles. There's a rustling sound that comes from the phone, and then, "Yeah?"

Allysa spits out our location into the phone. "Get here right now. Please. And bring a bag of ice."

"Yes *ma'am*," he says. The brother sounds like he may be a little drunk, too. There's laughter, and then one of the guys says, "*She's in a bad mood*," and then the line goes dead.

Allysa puts her phone back in her pocket. "I'll go wait outside for them, they're just down the street. Will you be okay here?"

I nod and reach for the chair. "Maybe I should just try to walk on it."

Allysa pushes my shoulders back until I'm leaning against the wall again. "No, don't move. Wait until they get here, okay?"

I have no idea what two drunken guys are going to be able to do for me, but I nod. My new employee feels more like my boss right now and I'm kind of scared of her at the moment.

I wait in the back for about ten minutes when I finally hear the front door to the building open. "What in the *world*?" a man's voice says. "Why are you all alone in this creepy building?"

I hear Allysa say, "She's back here." She walks in, followed by a guy wearing a onesie. He's tall, a little bit on the thin side, but boyishly handsome with big, honest eyes and a head full of dark, messy, way-past-due-for-a-haircut hair. He's holding a bag of ice.

Did I mention he was wearing a onesie?

I'm talking a legit, full-grown man in a SpongeBob onesie.

"This is your husband?" I ask her, cocking an eyebrow.

Allysa rolls her eyes. "Unfortunately," she says, glancing back at him. Another guy (also in a onesie) walks in behind them, but my attention is on Allysa as she explains why they're wearing pajamas on a random Wednesday afternoon. "There's a bar down the street that gives out free beer to anyone who shows up in a onesie during a Bruins game." She makes her way over to me and motions for the guys to follow her. "She fell off the chair and hurt her ankle," she says to the other guy. He steps around Marshall and the first thing I notice are his arms.

Holy shit. I know those arms.

Those are the arms of a neurosurgeon.

Allysa is his sister? The sister that owns the entire top floor, with the husband who works in pajamas and brings in seven figures a year?

As soon as my eyes lock with Ryle's, his whole face morphs into a smile. I haven't seen him in—*God, how long ago was that*—six months? I can't say I haven't thought about him during the past six months, because I've thought about him quite a few times. But I never actually thought I'd see him again.

"Ryle, this is Lily. Lily, my brother, Ryle," she says, motioning toward him. "And that's my husband, Marshall."

Ryle walks over to me and kneels down. "Lily," he says, regarding me with a smile. "Nice to meet you."

It's obvious he remembers me—I can see it in his knowing smile. But like me, he's pretending this is the first time we've met. I'm not sure I'm in the mood to explain how we already know each other.

Ryle touches my ankle and inspects it. "Can you move it?"

I try to move it, but a sharp pain shoots all the way up my leg. I suck in air through my teeth and shake my head. "Not yet. It hurts."

Ryle motions to Marshall. "Find something to put the ice in."

Allysa follows Marshall out of the room. When they're both gone, Ryle looks at me and his mouth turns up into a grin. "I won't charge you for this, but only because I'm slightly inebriated," he says with a wink.

I tilt my head. "The first time I met you, you were high. Now you're drunk. I'm beginning to worry you aren't going to make a very qualified neurosurgeon."

He laughs. "It would appear that way," he says. "But I promise you, I rarely ever get high and this is my first day off in over a month, so I really needed a beer. Or five."

Marshall comes back with an old rag wrapped around some ice. He hands it to Ryle, who presses it against my ankle. "I'll need that first aid kit out of your trunk," Ryle says to Allysa. She nods and grabs Marshall's hand, pulling him out of the room again.

Ryle presses his palm against the bottom of my foot. "Push against my hand," he says.

I push down with my ankle. It hurts, but I'm able to move his hand. "Is it broken?"

He moves my foot from side to side, and then says, "I don't think so. Let's give it a couple of minutes and I'll see if you can put any weight on it."

I nod and watch as he adjusts himself across from me. He sits cross-legged and pulls my foot onto his lap. He looks around the room and then directs his attention back at me. "So what is this place?"

I smile a little too big. "Lily Bloom's. It'll be a floral shop in about two months' time."

I swear, his whole face lights up with pride. "No way," he says. "You did it? You're actually opening up your own business?"

I nod. "Yep. I figured I might as well try it while I'm still young enough to bounce back from failure."

One of his hands is holding the ice against my ankle, but the other one is wrapped around my bare foot. He's brushing his thumb back and forth, like it's no big deal that he's touching me. But his hand on my foot is way more noticeable than the pain in my ankle.

"I look ridiculous, huh?" he asks, staring down at his solid red onesie.

I shrug. "At least you went with a non-character choice. It gives it a bit more maturity than the SpongeBob option."

He laughs, and then his smile disappears as he leans his head into the door beside him. He stares at me appreciatively. "You're even prettier in the daytime."

Moments like these are why I absolutely hate having red hair and fair skin. The embarrassment doesn't only show up in my cheeks—my whole face, arms, and neck grow flushed.

I rest my head against the wall behind me and stare at him just like he's staring at me. "You want to hear a naked truth?"

He nods.

"I've wanted to go back to your roof on more than one occasion since that night. But I was too scared you'd be there. You make me kind of nervous."

His fingers pause their strokes against my foot. "My turn?"

I nod.

His eyes narrow as his hand moves to the underneath of my foot. He slowly traces his fingers from the tops of my toes, down to my heel. "I still very much want to fuck you."

Someone gasps, and it isn't me.

Ryle and I both look at the doorway and Allysa is standing there, wide-eyed. Her mouth is open as she points down at Ryle. "Did you just . . ." She looks at me and says, "I am *so* sorry about him, Lily." And then she looks back at Ryle with venom in her eyes. "Did you just tell my boss you want to *fuck* her?"

Oh, dear.

Ryle pulls his bottom lip in and chews on it for a second. Marshall walks in behind Allysa and says, "What's going on?"

Allysa looks at Marshall and points at Ryle again. "He just told Lily he wants to *fuck* her!"

Marshall looks from Ryle to me. I don't know whether to laugh or crawl under the table and hide. "You did?" he says, looking back at Ryle.

Ryle shrugs. "It appears that way," he says.

Allysa puts her head in her hands, "Jesus Christ," she says, looking at me. "He's drunk. They're both drunk. Please don't judge me because my brother is an asshole."

I smile at her and wave it off. "It's fine, Allysa. Lots of people want to fuck me." I glance back at Ryle and he's still casually stroking my foot. "At least your brother speaks his mind. Not a lot of people have the courage to say what they're actually thinking."

Ryle winks at me and then carefully moves my ankle off his lap. "Let's see if you can put any weight on it," he says.

He and Marshall help me to my feet. Ryle points to a table a few feet away that's pushed up against a wall. "Let's try to make it to the table so I can wrap it."

His arm is secured around my waist, and he's gripping my arm tightly to make sure I don't fall. Marshall is more or less just standing next to me for support. I put a little weight on my ankle and it hurts, but it's not excruciating. I'm able to hop all the way to the table with a lot of assistance from Ryle. He helps me pull myself up until I'm seated on top of it, leaning against the wall with my leg stretched out in front of me.

"Well, the good news is that it isn't broken."

"What's the bad news?" I ask him.

He opens the first aid kit and says, "You'll need to stay off of it for a few days. Maybe even a week or more, depending on how it heals."

I close my eyes and lean my head against the wall behind me. "But I have so much to do," I whine.

He carefully begins to wrap my ankle. Allysa is standing behind him, watching him wrap it.

"I'm thirsty," Marshall says. "Anybody want something to drink? There's a CVS across the street."

"I'm good," Ryle says.

"I'll take a water," I say.

"Sprite," Allysa says.

Marshall grabs her hand. "You're coming with."

Allysa pulls her hand from his and crosses her arms over her chest. "I'm not going anywhere," she says. "My brother can't be trusted."

"Allysa, it's fine," I tell her. "He was making a joke."

She stares at me silently for a moment, and then says, "Okay. But you can't fire me if he pulls more stupid shit."

"I promise I won't fire you."

With that, she grabs Marshall's hand again and leaves the room. Ryle is still wrapping my foot when he says, "My sister works for you?"

"Yep. Hired her a couple of hours ago."

He reaches into the first aid kit and pulls out tape. "You do realize she's never had a job in her entire life?"

"She already warned me," I say. His jaw is tight and he doesn't look as relaxed as he did earlier. Then it hits me that he might think I hired her as a way to get closer to him. "I had no idea she was your sister until you walked in. I swear."

He glances at me, and then back down at my foot. "I wasn't suggesting you knew." He begins to tape over the ACE bandage.

"I know you weren't. I just didn't want you to think I was trying to trap you somehow. We want two different things from life, remember?"

He nods, and carefully sets my foot back on the table. "That is correct," he says. "I specialize in one-night stands and you're on the quest for your Holy Grail."

I laugh. "You have a good memory."

"I do," he says. A languid smile stretches across his mouth. "But you're also hard to forget."

Jesus. He *has* to stop saying things like that. I press my palms into the table and pull my leg down. "Naked truth coming."

He leans against the table next to me and says, "All ears."

I hold nothing back. "I'm very attracted to you," I say. "There's not much about you I don't like. And being as though you and I both want different things, if we're ever around each other again, I'd appreciate it if you could stop saying things that make me dizzy. It's not really fair to me."

He nods once, and then says, "My turn." He places his hand on the table next to me and leans in a little. "I'm very attracted to you, too. There's not much about *you* I don't like. But I kind of hope we're never around each other again, because I don't like how much I think about you. Which isn't all that much—but it's more than I'd like. So if you still aren't going to agree to a one-night stand, then I think it's best if we do what we can to avoid each other. Because it won't do either of us any favors."

I don't know how he ended up this close to me, but he's only about a foot away. His proximity makes it hard to pay attention to words that come out of his mouth. His gaze drops briefly to my mouth, but as soon as we hear the front door open, he's halfway across the room. By the time Allysa and Marshall make it to us, Ryle is busy restacking all the crates that fell. Allysa looks down at my ankle.

"What's the verdict?" she asks.

I push my bottom lip out. "Your doctor brother says I have to stay off of it for a few days."

She hands me my water. "Good thing you have me. I can work and do what I can to clean up while you rest."

I take a drink of the water and then wipe my mouth. "Allysa, I'm declaring you employee of the month."

She grins and then turns to Marshall. "Did you hear that? I'm the best employee she has!"

He puts his arm around her and kisses the top of her head. "I'm proud of you, Issa."

I like that he calls her *Issa*, which I'm assuming is short for Allysa. I think about my own name and if I'll ever find a guy who could shorten it into a sickeningly cute nickname. *Illy.*

Nope. Not the same.

"Do you need help getting home?" she asks.

I hop down and test my foot. "Maybe just to my car. It's my left foot, so I can probably drive just fine."

She walks over and puts her arm around me. "If you want to leave the keys with me, I'll lock up and come back tomorrow and start cleaning."

The three of them walk me to my car, but Ryle allows Allysa to do most of the work. He seems almost scared to touch me now for some reason. When I'm in the driver's seat, Allysa puts my purse and other things in the floorboard and sits in the passenger seat. She takes my phone out and begins programming her number into it.

Ryle leans into the window. "Make sure to keep ice on it as much as you can for the next few days. Baths help, too."

I nod. "Thanks for your help."

Allysa leans over and says, "Ryle? Maybe you should drive her home and take a cab back to the apartment, just to be safe."

Ryle looks down at me and then shakes his head. "I don't think that's a good idea," he says. "She'll be fine. I've had a few beers, probably shouldn't be driving."

"You could at least help her home," Allysa suggests.

Ryle shakes his head and then pats the roof of the car as he turns and walks away.

I'm still watching him when Allysa hands me back my phone and says, "Seriously. I'm really sorry about him. First he hits on you, then he's a selfish asshole." She climbs out of the car and closes the door, then leans through the window. "That's why he'll be single for the rest of his life." She points to my phone. "Text me when you get home. And call me if you need anything. I won't count favors as work-time."

"Thank you, Allysa."

She smiles. "No, thank *you*. I haven't been this excited about my life since that Paolo Nutini concert I went to last year." She waves goodbye and walks toward where Marshall and Ryle are standing.

They begin walking down the street and I watch them in my rearview mirror. As they turn the corner, I see Ryle glance over his shoulder and look back in my direction.

I close my eyes and exhale.

The two times I've spent with Ryle were on days I'd probably rather forget. My father's funeral and spraining my ankle. But somehow, him being present made them feel like less of the disasters they were.

I hate that he's Allysa's brother. I have a feeling this isn't the last time I'll be seeing him.

Chapter Four

It takes me half an hour to make it from my car to my apartment. I called Lucy twice to see if she could help me, but she didn't answer her phone. When I make it inside my apartment, I'm a little irritated to see her lying on the couch with the phone to her ear.

I slam our front door behind me and she glances up. "What happened to you?" she asks.

I use the wall for support as I hop toward the hallway. "Sprained my ankle."

When I make it to my bedroom door, she yells, "Sorry I didn't answer the phone! I'm talking to Alex! I was gonna call you back!"

"It's fine!" I holler back at her, and then slam my bedroom door shut. I go to the bathroom and find some old pain pills I had stuffed into a cabinet. I swallow two of them and then fall onto my bed and stare up at the ceiling.

I can't believe I'll be stuck in this apartment for an entire week. I grab my phone and text my mother.

Sprained my ankle. I'm fine, but can I send you a list of things to grab for me at the store?

I drop my phone onto my bed, and for the first time since she moved here, I'm thankful my mother lives fairly close to me. It actually hasn't been that bad. I think I like her more now that my father has passed away. I know it's because

I held a lot of resentment toward her for never leaving him. Even though a lot of that resentment has faded when it comes to my mother, I still have the same feelings when I think of my father.

It can't be good, still holding on to so much bitterness toward my father. But dammit, he was awful. To my mother, to me, to Atlas.

Atlas.

I've been so busy with my mother's move and secretly searching for a new building between work hours, I haven't had time to finish reading the journals I started reading all those months ago.

I hop pathetically to my closet, only tripping once. Luckily, I catch myself on my dresser. Once I have the journal in hand, I hop back to the bed and get comfortable.

I have nothing better to do for the next week now that I can't work. I might as well commiserate over my past while I'm forced to commiserate in the present.

Dear Ellen,

You hosting the Oscars was the greatest thing to happen to TV last year. I don't think I ever told you that. The vacuuming skit made me piss my pants.

Oh, and I recruited a new Ellen follower today in Atlas. Before you start judging me for allowing him inside my house again, let me explain how that came about.

After I let him take a shower here yesterday, I didn't see him again last night. But this morning, he sat by me on the bus again. He seemed a little happier than the day before, because he slid into the seat and actually smiled at me.

I'm not gonna lie, it was a little weird seeing him in my dad's clothes. But the pants fit him a lot better than I thought they were going to.

"Guess what?" he said. He leaned forward and unzipped his backpack.

"What?"

He pulled out a bag and handed it to me. "I found these in the garage. I tried to clean them up for you because they were covered in old dirt, but I can't do much without water."

I held the bag and stared at him suspiciously. It's the most I'd ever heard him say at once. I finally looked down at the bag and opened it. It looked like a bunch of old gardening tools.

"I saw you digging with that shovel the other day. I wasn't sure if you had any actual gardening tools, and no one was using these, so . . ."

"Thank you," I said. I was kind of in shock. I used to have a trowel, but the plastic broke off the handle and it started giving me blisters. I asked my mother for gardening tools for my birthday last year and when she bought me a full-sized shovel and a hoe, I didn't have the heart to tell her it's not what I needed.

Atlas cleared his throat and then, in a much quieter voice, he said, "I know it's not like a real gift. I didn't buy it or anything. But . . . I wanted to give you something. You know . . . for . . ."

He didn't finish his sentence, so I nodded and tied the bag back up. "Do you think you can hold them for me until after school? I don't have any room in my backpack."

He grabbed the bag from me and then brought his backpack up to his lap and put the bag inside of it. He wrapped his arms around his backpack. "How old are you?" he asked.

"Fifteen."

The look in his eyes made him seem a little bit sad about my age, but I don't know why.

"You're in tenth grade?"

I nodded, but honestly couldn't think of anything to say to him. I haven't really had much interaction with a lot of guys. Especially seniors. When I'm nervous, I kind of just clam up.

"I don't know how long I'll be staying at that place," he said, bringing his voice down again. "But if you ever need help with gardening or anything after school, it's not like I have much going on there. Being as though I have no electricity."

I laughed, and then wondered if I should have laughed at his self-deprecating comment.

We spent the rest of the bus ride talking about you, Ellen. When he made that comment about being bored, I asked him if he ever watched your show. He said he'd like to because he thinks you're funny, but a TV would require electricity. Another comment I wasn't sure if I should have laughed at.

I told him he could watch your show with me after school. I always record it on the DVR and watch it while I do my chores. I figured I could just keep the front door dead bolted, and if my parents got home early, I'd just have Atlas run out the back door.

I didn't see him again until the ride home today. He didn't sit by me this time because Katie got on the bus before him and sat next to me. I wanted to ask her to move, but then she'd think I had a crush on Atlas. Katie would have a field day with that one, so I just let her stay in my seat.

Atlas was at the front of the bus, so he got off before I did. He just kind of awkwardly stood there at the bus stop and waited for me to get off. When I did, he opened his backpack and handed me the bag of tools. He didn't say anything about my invitation to watch

TV from earlier this morning, so I just acted like it was a given.

"Come on," I told him. He followed me inside and I locked the dead bolt. "If my parents come home early, run out the back door and don't let them see you."

He nodded. "Don't worry. I will," he said, with kind of a laugh.

I asked him if he wanted anything to drink and he said sure. I made us a snack and brought our drinks to the living room. I sat down on the couch and he sat down in my dad's chair. I turned on your show and that's about all that happened. We didn't talk much, because I fast-forwarded through all the commercials. But I did notice he laughed at all the right times. I think good comedic timing is one of the most important things about a person's personality. Every time he laughed at your jokes, it made me feel better about sneaking him into my house. I don't know why. Maybe because if he's actually someone I could be friends with, it'd make me feel less guilty.

He left right after your show was over. I wanted to ask him if he needed to use our shower again, but that would have cut it real close to time for my parents getting home. The last thing I wanted was for him to have to run out of the shower and across my backyard naked.

Then again, that'd be kind of hilarious and awesome.

—Lily

Dear Ellen,

Come on, woman. Reruns? A full week of reruns? I get that you need time off, but let me make a suggestion. Instead of recording one show a day, you should record two. That way you'll get twice as much done in half the time, and we'd never have to sit through reruns.

I say "we" because I'm referring to Atlas and me. He's become my regular Ellen-*watching partner. I think he might love you as* much as I do, but I'll never tell him I write to you on a daily basis. That might seem a little too fan-girl.

He's been living in that house for two weeks now. He's taken a few more showers at my house and I give him food every time he visits. I even wash his clothes for him while he's here after school. He keeps apologizing to me, like he's a burden. But honestly, I love it. He keeps my mind off things and I actually look forward to spending time with him after school every day.

Dad got home late tonight, which means he went to the bar after work. Which means he's probably going to instigate a fight with my mother. Which means he'll probably do something stupid again.

I swear, sometimes I get so mad at her for staying with him. I know I'm only fifteen and probably don't understand all the reasons she chooses to stay, but I refuse to let her use me as her excuse. I don't care if she's too poor to leave him and we'd have to move into a crappy apartment and eat ramen noodles until I graduate. That would be better than this.

I can hear him yelling at her right now. Sometimes when he gets like this, I walk into the living room, hoping it'll calm him down. He doesn't like to hit her when I'm in the room. Maybe I should go try that.

—Lily

Dear Ellen,

If I had access to a gun or knife right now, I'd kill him.

As soon as I walked into the living room, I saw him push her down. They were standing in the kitchen and she'd grabbed his arm, trying to calm him down, and he backhanded her and knocked her straight to the floor. I'm pretty sure he was about to kick her, but he saw me walk into the living room and he stopped. He muttered *something under his breath to her and then walked to their bedroom and slammed the door.*

I rushed to the kitchen and tried to help her, but she never wants me to see her like this. She waved me away and said, "I'm fine, Lily. I'm fine, we just got into a stupid fight."

She was crying and I could already see the redness on her cheek from where he hit her. When I walked closer to her, wanting to make sure she was okay, she turned her back to me and gripped the counter. "I said I'm fine, Lily. Go back to your room."

I ran back down the hallway, but I didn't go back to my room. I ran straight out the back door and across the backyard. I was so mad at her for being short with me. I didn't even want to be in the same house as either of them, and even thought it was dark already, I went over to the house Atlas was staying in and I knocked on the door.

I could hear him moving inside, like he accidentally knocked something over. "It's me. Lily," I whispered. A few seconds later the back door opened and he looked behind me, then to the left and right of me. It wasn't until he looked at my face that he saw I was crying.

"You okay?" he asked, stepping outside. I used my shirt to wipe away my tears, and noticed he came outside instead of inviting me in. I sat down on the porch step and he sat down next to me.

"I'm fine," I said. "I'm just mad. Sometimes I cry when I get mad."

He reached over and tucked my hair behind my ear. I liked it when he did that and I suddenly wasn't nearly as mad anymore. Then he put his arm around me and pulled me to him so that my head was resting on his shoulder. I don't know how he calmed me down without even talking, but he did. Some people just have a calming presence about them and he's one of those people. Completely opposite of my father.

We sat like that for a while, until I saw my bedroom light turn on.

"You should go," he whispered. We could both see my mom standing in my bedroom looking for me. It wasn't until that moment that I realized what a perfect view he has of my bedroom.

As I walked back home, I tried to think about the entire time Atlas has been in that house. I tried to recall if I'd walked around after dark with the light on at night, because all I normally wear in my room at night is a T-shirt.

Here's what's crazy about that, Ellen: I was kind of hoping I had.

—Lily

I close the journal when the pain pills start to kick in. I'll read more tomorrow. *Maybe.* Reading about the things my dad used to do to my mom kind of puts me in a bad mood.

Reading about Atlas kind of puts me in a *sad* mood.

I try to fall asleep and think about Ryle, but the whole situation with him kind of makes me mad *and* sad.

Maybe I'll just think about Allysa, and how happy I am that she showed up today. I could use a friend—not to mention help—during these next few months. I have a feeling it's going to be more stressful than I bargained for.

Chapter Five

Ryle was correct. It only took a few days for my ankle to feel good enough that I could walk on it again. I waited a full week before attempting to leave my apartment, though. The last thing I need is to reinjure it.

Of course the first place I went was to my floral shop. Allysa was there when I arrived today, and to say I was shocked when I walked through the front doors is an understatement. It looked like a totally different building than the one I bought. There's still a ton of work that needs to be done, but she and Marshall had gotten rid of all the stuff we marked as trash. Everything else had been organized into piles. The windows had been washed, the floors had been mopped. She even had the area where I plan to put an office cleaned out.

I helped her for a few hours today, but she wouldn't let me do much that required walking at first, so I mostly drew out plans for the store. We picked out paint colors and set a goal date to open the store that's approximately fifty-four days from now. After she left, I spent the next few hours doing all the stuff she wouldn't let me do while she was there. It felt good to be back. But *Jesus Christ*, I'm tired.

Which is why I'm debating on whether or not to get up from the couch and answer the knock at my front door. Lucy is at Alex's again tonight and I just spoke to my mother five minutes ago on the phone, so I know it isn't either of them.

I walk to the door and check the peephole before opening it. I don't recognize him at first, because his head is down, but then he looks up and to the right and my heart freaks the hell out!

What is he doing here?

Ryle knocks again, and I try to brush my hair out of my face and smooth it down with my hands, but it's a lost cause. I worked my ass off today and I look like shit, so unless I have half an hour to take a shower, put on makeup, and throw on clothes before I open the door, he'll pretty much have to deal with me as is.

I open the door and his immediate reaction confuses me.

"Jesus Christ," he says, dropping his head against my door frame. He's panting like he's been working out, and that's when I notice that he doesn't look to be any more rested or clean than I am. He's got a couple of days' worth of stubble on his face—something I've never seen on him before—and his hair isn't styled like it usually is. It's a little erratic, like the look in his eye. "Do you have any idea how many doors I've knocked on to find you?"

I shake my head, because I don't. But now that he mentions it—*how in the hell does he know where I live?*

"Twenty-nine," he says. Then he holds up his hands and repeats the numbers with his fingers while he whispers, *"Two . . . nine."*

I let my gaze drop down to his clothes. He's in scrubs, and I absolutely *hate* that he's in scrubs right now. *Holy hell. So* much better than the onesie and *way* better than the Burberry.

"Why did you knock on twenty-nine doors?" I ask with a tilt of my head.

"You never told me which apartment was yours," he says, matter-of-factly. "You said you lived in this building, but I couldn't remember if you even said which floor. And for the record, I almost started with the third floor. I would have been here an hour ago if I went with my gut instinct."

"Why *are* you here?"

He runs his hands down his face and then points over my shoulder. "Can I come in?"

I glance over my shoulder and then open the door farther. "I guess. If you tell me what you want."

He walks inside and I close the door behind us. He glances around, wearing his stupid hot scrubs, and puts his hands on his hips as he faces me. He looks a little disappointed, but I'm not sure if it's in me or himself.

"There's a really big naked truth coming, okay?" he says. "Brace yourself."

I fold my arms over my chest and watch as he inhales a breath, preparing to speak.

"These next couple of months are the most important months in my entire career. I have to be focused. I'm closing in on the end of my residency, and then I'll have to sit for my exams." He's pacing my living room, talking frantically with his hands. "But for the past week, I haven't been able to get you out of my head. I don't know why. At work, at home. All I can think about is how crazy it feels when I'm near you, and I need you to make it stop, Lily." He stops pacing and faces me. "*Please* make it stop. Just once—that's all it'll take. I swear."

My fingers are digging into the skin of my arms as I watch him. He's still panting a little, and his eyes are still frantic, but he's looking at me pleadingly.

"When is the last time you've had sleep?" I ask him.

He rolls his eyes like he's frustrated that I'm not getting it. "I just got off a forty-eight-hour shift," he says dismissively. "*Focus*, Lily."

I nod and replay his words in my head. If I didn't know better . . . I'd almost think he was . . .

I inhale a calming breath. "Ryle," I say carefully. "Did you seriously just knock on twenty-nine doors so you could tell me that the thought of me is making your life hell and I should have sex with you so that you'll never have to think of me again? Are you *kidding* me right now?"

He folds his lips together and, after about five seconds of thought, he slowly nods his head. "Well . . . yeah, but . . . it sounds way worse when you say it."

I release an exasperated laugh. "That's because it's ridiculous, Ryle."

He bites his bottom lip and looks around the room, like he suddenly wants to escape. I open the door and motion for him to walk out. He doesn't. His eyes fall to my foot. "Your ankle looks good," he says. "How does it feel?"

I roll my eyes. "Better. I was able to help Allysa at the store for the first time today."

He nods and then makes like he's walking toward the door to leave. But as soon as he reaches me, he spins toward me and slaps his palms against the door on either side of my head. I gasp at both his proximity and his persistence. "Please?" he says.

I shake my head, even though my body is starting to trade sides and beg my mind to cave to him.

"I'm really good at it, Lily," he says with a grin. "You'll barely even have to do any work."

I try not to laugh, but his determination is as endearing as it is annoying. "Goodnight, Ryle."

His head drops between his shoulders and he shakes it back and forth. He pushes off the door and stands up straight. He half-turns, heading for the hallway, but then suddenly drops to his knees in front of me. He wraps his arms around my waist. "Please, Lily," he says through self-deprecating laughter. "*Please* have sex with me." He's looking up at me with puppy dog eyes and a pathetic, hopeful grin. "I want you so, so bad and I swear, once you have sex with me you'll never hear from me again. I promise."

There's something about a neurosurgeon *literally* on his knees begging for sex that does me in. *That's pretty pathetic.*

"Get *up*," I say, pushing his arms away from me. "You're embarrassing yourself."

He slowly stands up, dragging his hands up the door on either side of me until he has me caged in between his arms. "Is that a yes?" His chest is barely touching mine and I hate how good it feels to be wanted this much. I should be turned off by it, but I can hardly breathe when I look at him. Especially when he has this suggestive smile on his face.

"I don't feel sexy right now, Ryle. I worked all day, I'm exhausted, I smell like sweat and probably taste like dust. If you give me a little while to shower first, I might feel sexy enough to have sex with you."

He's nodding feverishly before I'm even finished speaking. "Shower. Take all the time you need. I'll wait."

I push him away from me and close the front door. He follows me to the bedroom and I tell him to wait on the bed for me.

Luckily, I cleaned my bedroom last night. Normally I have clothes lying around everywhere, books piled up on my nightstand, shoes and bras that don't quite make it to my closet. But tonight it's clean. My bed is even made up, complete with the ugly, quilted throw pillows my grandmother passed down to every person in our family.

I make a quick glance around the room, just to make sure nothing embarrassing will catch his eye. He takes a seat on my bed and I watch as he scans the room. I stand in the doorway to my bathroom and try to give him one last out.

"You say this will make it stop, but I'm warning you right now, Ryle. I'm like a drug. If you have sex with me tonight, it's only going to make things worse for you. But once is all you're getting. I refuse to become one of the many girls you use to—how did you word it that night? *Satisfy* your *needs*?"

He leans back on his elbows. "You aren't that kind of girl, Lily. And I'm not the kind of guy who needs someone more than once. We have nothing to worry about."

I close the door behind me, wondering how in the hell this guy talked me into this.

It's the scrubs. The scrubs are my weakness. It has nothing to do with him.

I wonder if there's a way he could leave them on during the sex?

• • •

I've never taken more than half an hour to get ready, but it's almost an hour before I'm finished in the bathroom. I shaved more parts of me than was probably necessary, and then spent a good twenty minutes having a freak-out, and had to talk myself out of opening the door and telling him to leave. But now that my hair is dry and I'm cleaner than I've ever been, I think I might be able to do this. I can totally have a one-night stand. I'm twenty-three years old.

I open the door and he's still there on my bed. I'm a little disappointed to see that his scrub top is on the floor, but I don't see his pants, so he must still be wearing them. He's under the covers, though, so I can't tell.

I close the door behind me and wait for him to roll over and look at me, but he doesn't. I take a few steps closer, and that's when I notice he's snoring.

Not just a light—*oh I just fell asleep*—snore. It's a middle of REM sleep kind of snore.

"Ryle?" I whisper. He doesn't even budge when I shake him. *You've got to be kidding me.*

I drop down onto the bed, not even caring if I wake him. I just spent an entire hour getting ready for him after busting my ass today, and this is how he treats this night?

I can't be mad at him, though, especially seeing how peaceful he looks. I can't imagine working a forty-eight-hour shift. Plus, my bed is really comfortable. It's so comfortable, it could make a person fall right back to sleep after a full night of rest. *I should have warned him about that.*

I check the time on my phone and it's almost 10:30 p.m. I put the phone on silent and then lie down next to him. His phone is on the pillow next to his head, so I grab it and swipe up the camera option. I hold his phone above us and make sure my cleavage looks good and pushed together. I snap a picture so he'll at least see what he missed out on.

I turn off the light and laugh to myself, because I'm falling asleep next to a half-naked man that I've never even kissed.

• • •

I can feel his fingers trailing up my arm before I even open my eyes. I force back a tired smile and pretend I'm still sleeping. His fingers trail over my shoulder and stop at my collarbone, just before they reach my neck. I have a small tattoo there that I got in college. It's a simple outline of a heart that's slightly open at the top. I can feel his fingers circle around the tattoo, and then he leans forward and presses his lips against it. I squeeze my eyes shut even tighter.

"Lily," he whispers, wrapping an arm around my waist. I moan a little, trying to wake up, and then roll onto my back so that I can look up at him. When I open my eyes, he's staring down at me. I can tell by the way the sunlight shines through my windows and across his face that it's not even seven a.m. yet.

"I am the most despicable man you've ever met. Am I right?"

I laugh, and nod a little. "Pretty damn close."

He smiles and then brushes my hair off my face. He leans forward and presses his lips to my forehead, and I hate that he just did that. Now *I'll* be the one plagued with sleepless nights, because I want to put this memory on repeat.

"I have to go," he says. "I'm really late. But one—I'm sorry. Two—I'll never do this again. This is the last you'll hear from me, I promise. And three—I'm *really* sorry. You have no idea."

I force a smile, but I want to frown because I absolutely hated his number two. I actually don't mind if he tries this again, but then I remind myself that we want two different things from life. And it's good that he fell asleep and we never even kissed, because if I would have had sex with him while he was wearing scrubs, I would have been the one showing up at his door on my knees, begging for more.

This is good. Rip the Band-Aid off and let him leave.

"Have a nice life, Ryle. I wish you all the success in the world."

He doesn't respond to my goodbye. He silently stares down at me with somewhat of a frown, and then says, "Yeah. You too, Lily."

Then he rolls away from me and stands up. I can't even look at him right now, so I roll onto my side so that my back is to him. I listen as he puts his shoes on and then reaches for his phone. There's a long pause before he moves again, and I know it's because he was staring at me. I squeeze my eyes shut until I hear the slam of the front door.

My face immediately grows warm, and I refuse to allow myself to mope. I force myself off the bed. I have work to do. I can't be upset that I'm not enough to make a guy want to remap all of his life goals.

Besides, I have my *own* life goals to worry about now. And I'm really excited about them. So much so, that I really don't have time for a guy in my life, anyway.

No time.

Nope.

Busy girl, here.

I am a brave and bold businesswoman with zero fucks to give for men in scrubs.

Chapter Six

It's been fifty-three days since Ryle walked out of my apartment that morning. Which means it's been fifty-three days since I've heard from him.

But that's okay, because for the last fifty-three days, I've been too busy to really give him much thought as I prepared for this moment.

"Ready?" Allysa says.

I nod, and she flips the sign to *Open* and we both hug and squeal like little kids.

We rush around the counter and wait for our first customer. It's a soft opening, so I haven't really done a marketing push yet, but we just want to make sure there aren't any kinks before our grand opening.

"It's really pretty in here," Allysa says, admiring our hard work. I look around us, bursting with pride. Of course I want to succeed, but at this point I'm not even sure if that matters. I had a dream and I busted my ass to make it come true. Whatever happens after today is just icing on the cake.

"It smells so good in here," I say. "I *love* this smell."

I don't know if we'll get any customers today, but we're both acting like this is the best thing that's ever happened to us, so I don't think that matters. Besides, Marshall will come in at some point today and my mother will come in after she gets off work. That's two customers for sure. That's plenty.

Allysa squeezes my arm when the front door begins to open. I suddenly grow a little panicked, because what if something goes wrong?

And then I do panic, because something just went wrong. *Terribly* wrong. My very first customer is none other than Ryle Kincaid.

He stops when the door closes behind him and he looks around in awe. "What?" he says, turning in a circle. "How in the . . . ?" He looks over at me and Allysa. "This is incredible. It doesn't even look like the same building!"

Okay, maybe I'm fine with him being the first customer.

It takes him a few minutes to actually make it to the counter because he can't stop touching things and looking at things. When he finally does reach us, Allysa runs around the counter and hugs him. "Isn't it beautiful?" she says. She waves her hand in my direction. "It was all her idea. All of it. I just helped with the dirty work."

Ryle laughs. "I find it hard to believe that your Pinterest skills didn't play a little part."

I nod. "She's being modest. Her skills were half of what brought this vision to life."

Ryle smiles at me and it might as well have been a knife to the chest, because *ouch.*

He slaps his hands on the counter and says, "Am I the first official customer?"

Allysa hands him one of our flyers. "You have to actually buy something to be considered a customer."

Ryle glances over the flyer and then sets it back down on

the counter. He walks to one of the displays and grabs a vase full of purple lilies. "I want these," he says, setting them on the counter.

I smile, wondering if he realizes he just picked lilies. *Kind of ironic.*

"Do you want us to deliver them somewhere?" Allysa says.

"You guys deliver?"

"Allysa and I don't," I reply. "We have a delivery driver on standby. We weren't sure if we'd actually need him today."

"Are you actually buying these for a girl?" Allysa asks. She's just prying into her brother's love life like a sister would naturally do, but I catch myself stepping closer to her so I can hear his answer better.

"I am," he says. His eyes meet mine and he adds, "I don't think about her very much, though. Hardly ever."

Allysa grabs a card and slides it to him. "Poor girl," she says. "You are such a dick." She taps her finger on the card. "Write your message to her on the front and the address you want them delivered to on the back."

I watch him as he bends over the card and writes on both sides. I know I don't have a right, but I'm brimming with jealousy.

"Are you bringing this girl to my birthday party Friday?" Allysa asks him.

I watch his reaction closely. He just shakes his head and without looking up he says, "No. Are you going, Lily?"

I can't tell by his voice alone if he's hoping I'll be there or hoping I won't. Considering the stress I seem to cause him, I'm guessing it's the latter.

"I haven't decided yet."

"She'll be there," Allysa says, answering for me. She looks at me and narrows her eyes. "You're coming to my party whether you like it or not. If you don't show up, I'll quit."

When Ryle is finished writing, he tucks the card into the envelope attached to the flowers. Allysa rings up his total and he pays in cash. He looks at me while he's counting out his money. "Lily, do you know that it's custom for a new business to frame the first dollar they make?"

I nod. *Of course* I know that. He *knows* I know that. He's just rubbing it in my face that his dollar will be the one framed on my wall for the life of this store. I almost encourage Allysa to give him a refund, but this is business. I have to leave my wounded pride out of it.

Once he has his receipt in hand, he taps his fist on the counter to get my attention. He dips his head a little and, with a genuine smile, he says, "Congratulations, Lily."

He turns and walks out of the store. As soon as the door closes behind him, Allysa is grabbing for the envelope. "Who in the hell is he sending flowers to?" she says as she pulls the card out. "Ryle doesn't *send* flowers."

She reads the front of the card out loud. "Make it stop."
Holy shit.

She stares at it for a moment, repeating the phrase. "*Make it stop?* What in the hell does that even *mean*?" she asks.

I can't take it another second. I grab the card from her and flip it over. She leans over and reads the back of it with me.

"He is such an idiot," she says with a laugh. "He wrote the address to our floral shop on the back." She takes the card out of my hands.

Wow.

Ryle just bought me flowers. Not just *any* flower. He bought me a bouquet of lilies.

Allysa picks up her phone. "I'll text him and tell him he screwed up." She shoots him a text and then laughs as she stares at the flowers. "How can a neurosurgeon be such an *idiot*?"

I can't stop grinning. I'm relieved she's staring at the flowers and not at me or she may put two and two together. "I'll keep them in my office until we figure out where he intended for them to go." I scoop up the vase and whisk away my flowers.

Chapter Seven

"Stop fidgeting," Devin says.

"I'm not fidgeting."

He loops his arm through mine as he walks me toward the elevator. "Yes, you are. And if you pull that top up over your cleavage one more time, it'll defeat the whole purpose of your little black dress." He grabs my top and yanks it back down, and then proceeds to reach inside to adjust my bra.

"Devin!" I slap his hand away and he laughs.

"Relax, Lily. I've touched way better boobs than yours and I'm still gay."

"Yeah, but I bet those boobs were attached to people you probably hang out with more than once every six months."

Devin laughs. "True, but that's half your fault. You're the one who left us high and dry to play with flowers."

Devin was one of my favorite people at the marketing firm I worked at, but we weren't close enough to where we actively became friends outside of work. He stopped by the floral shop this afternoon and Allysa took to him almost immediately. She begged him to come to the party with me and since I didn't really want to show up alone, I ended up begging him to come, too.

I smooth my hands over my hair and try to catch a glimpse of my reflection in the elevator walls.

"Why are you so nervous?" he asks.

"I'm not nervous. I just hate showing up to places where I don't know anyone."

Devin smirks knowingly and then says, "What's his name?"

I release a pent-up breath. *Am I that transparent?* "Ryle. He's a neurosurgeon. And he wants to have sex with me really, really bad."

"How do you know he wants to have sex with you?"

"Because he literally got down on his knees and said, '*Please, Lily. Please have sex with me.*'"

Devin raises an eyebrow. "He begged?"

I nod. "It wasn't as pathetic as it sounds. He's usually more composed."

The elevator dings and the doors begin to open. I can hear music pouring from down the hallway. Devin takes both of my hands in his and says, "So what's the plan? Do I need to make this guy jealous?"

"No," I say, shaking my head. "That wouldn't be right." But . . . Ryle does make it a point every time he sees me to tell me he hopes he never sees me again. "Maybe just a little?" I say, scrunching up my nose. "A smidge?"

Devin pops his jaw and says, "Consider it done." He puts his hand on my lower back as he walks me out of the elevator. There's only one visible door in the hallway, so we make our way over and ring the doorbell.

"Why is there only one door?" he says.

"She owns the whole top floor."

He chuckles. "And she works for *you*? Damn, your life just keeps getting more and more interesting."

The door begins to open, and I'm extremely relieved to

see Allysa standing in front of me. There's music and laughter pouring out of the apartment behind her. She's holding a champagne glass in one hand and a riding crop in the other. She sees me staring at the riding crop with a confused look on my face, so she tosses it over her shoulder and grabs my hand. "It's a long story," she says, laughing. "Come in, come in!"

She pulls me in and I squeeze Devin's hand and drag him behind me. She continues pulling us through a crowd of people until we reach the other side of the living room. "Hey!" she says, tugging on Marshall's arm. He turns around and smiles at me, then pulls me in for a hug. I glance behind him, and around us, but there's no sign of Ryle. *Maybe I got lucky and he got called in to work tonight.*

Marshall reaches out for Devin's hand and shakes it. "Hey, man! Good to meet you!"

Devin wraps an arm around my waist. "I'm Devin!" he yells over the music. "I'm Lily's sexual partner!"

I laugh and elbow him, then lean in to his ear. "That's Marshall. Wrong guy, but nice effort."

Allysa grabs my arm and starts to pull me away from Devin. Marshall begins speaking to him, and my hand is reaching out behind me as I'm being pulled in the opposite direction.

"You'll be fine!" Devin yells.

I follow Allysa into the kitchen, where she shoves a glass of champagne in my hand. "Drink," she says. "You deserve it!"

I take a sip of the champagne, but I can't even appreciate it now that I'm getting a look at her industrial-sized kitchen with two full stovetops and a fridge bigger than my apartment. "Holy shit," I whisper. "You actually *live* here?"

She giggles. "I know," she says. "And to think, I didn't even have to marry him for money. Marshall had seven bucks and drove a Ford Pinto when I fell in love with him."

"Doesn't he still drive a Ford Pinto?"

She sighs. "Yeah, but we have a lot of good memories in that car."

"Gross."

She wiggles her eyebrows. "So . . . Devin is cute."

"And probably more into Marshall than me."

"Ah, man," she says. "That's a bummer. I thought I was playing matchmaker when I invited him to the party tonight."

The kitchen door opens and Devin walks in. "Your husband is looking for you," he says to Allysa. She twirls her way out of the kitchen, giggling the whole time. "I really like her," Devin says.

"She's great, huh?"

He leans against the island and says, "So. I think I just met The Beggar."

My heart flutters down my chest. I think *The Neurosurgeon* has a better ring to it. I take another sip of my champagne. "How do you know it was him? Did he introduce himself?"

He shakes his head. "Nah, but he overheard Marshall introducing me to someone as '*Lily's date.*' I thought the look he gave me was going to set me on fire. That's why I came in here. I like you, but I'm not willing to die for you."

I laugh. "Don't worry, I'm sure that death glare he gave you was really his smile. They're superimposed most of the time."

The door swings open again and I immediately stiffen, but it's only a caterer. I sigh with relief. Devin says, *"Lily,"* like my name is a disappointment.

"What?"

"You look like you're about to puke," he says, accusingly. "You really like him."

I roll my eyes. But then I let my shoulders drop and I fake cry. "I do, Devin. I do, I just don't *want* to."

He takes my glass of champagne and downs the remainder of it, then locks his arm in mine again. "Let's go mingle," he says, pulling me out of the kitchen against my will.

The room is even more crowded now. There have to be more than a hundred people here. I'm not even sure I know that many people.

We walk around and work the room. I stand back while Devin does most of the talking. He knows someone in common with every person he's met so far, and after about half an hour of following him around, I'm convinced he's made it a personal game to find someone in common with everyone here. The whole time I mingle with him, my attention is half on him and half on the room, searching for traces of Ryle. I don't see him anywhere and I begin to wonder if the guy Devin saw was even Ryle to begin with.

"Well, that's odd," a woman says. "What do you suppose it is?"

I look up and see that she's staring at a piece of art on the wall. It looks like a photograph blown up on canvas. I tilt my head to inspect it. The woman turns her nose up and says, "I don't know why anyone would bother turning that photograph into wall art. It's awful. It's so blurry, you can't even tell what it is." She walks away in a huff, and I'm relieved. I mean . . . it's a bit weird, but who am I to judge Allysa's taste?

"What do you think?"

His voice is low, deep, and *right* behind me. I close my eyes briefly and inhale a steadying breath before quietly exhaling, hoping he doesn't notice his voice has any effect on me whatsoever. "I like it. I'm not quite sure what it is, but it's interesting. Your sister has good taste."

He steps around me so that he's at my side, facing me. He takes a step closer until he's so close, he brushes my arm. "You brought a date?"

He's asking it like it's a casual question, but I know it isn't. When I fail to respond, he leans in until he's whispering in my ear. He repeats himself, but this time it isn't a question. "You brought a *date*."

I find the courage to look over at him and instantly wish I hadn't. He's in a black suit that makes the scrubs look like child's play. First I swallow the unexpected lump in my throat and then I say, "Is it a problem that I brought a date?" I look away from him and back at the photograph hanging on the wall. "I was trying to make things easier on you. You know. Just trying to *make it stop*."

He smirks and then downs the rest of his wine. "How *thoughtful* of you, Lily." He tosses his empty wineglass toward a trash can in the corner of the room. He makes the shot, but the glass shatters when it hits the bottom of the empty container. I glance around me, but no one saw what just happened. When I look back at Ryle, he's halfway down a hallway. He disappears into a room and I stand here, looking at the picture again.

That's when I see it.

The picture is blurred, so it was hard to make out at first. But I can recognize that hair from anywhere. That's *my* hair. It's hard to miss, along with the marine-grade polymer lounge chair I'm lying on. *This is the picture he took on the rooftop the first night we met.* He must have had it blown up and distorted so no one would notice what it was. I bring my hand to my neck, because my blood feels like it's bubbling. *It's really warm in here.*

Allysa appears at my side. "It's weird, huh?" she says, looking at the picture.

I scratch at my chest. "It's really hot in here," I say. "Don't you think?"

She glances around the room. "Is it? I hadn't noticed, but I'm a little drunk. I'll tell Marshall to turn on the air."

She disappears again, and the more I stare at the picture, the angrier I get. The man has a picture of me hanging in the apartment. He bought me flowers. He's giving me attitude because I brought a date to his sister's party. He's acting like there's actually something between us, and we've never even kissed!

It all hits me at once. The anger . . . the irritation . . . the half glass of champagne I had in the kitchen. I'm so mad, I can't even think straight. If the guy wants to have sex with me so bad . . . he shouldn't have fallen asleep! If he doesn't want me to swoon, he shouldn't buy me flowers! He shouldn't hang cryptic pictures of me where he lives!

All I want is fresh air. I need fresh air. Luckily, I know just where to find it.

Moments later, I burst through the door to the rooftop.

There are stragglers from the party up here. Three of them, seated on the patio furniture. I ignore them and walk to the ledge with the good view and lean over it. I suck in several deep breaths and try to calm myself down. I want to go downstairs and tell him to make up his damn mind, but I know I need to have a clear head before I do that.

The air is cold, and for some reason, I blame that on Ryle. Everything is his fault tonight. *All of it.* Wars, famine, gun violence—it all somehow links back to Ryle.

"Can we have a few minutes alone?"

I spin around, and Ryle is standing near the other guests. Immediately, all three of them nod and begin to stand up to give us privacy. I hold up my hands and say, "Wait," but none of them look at me. "It's not necessary. Really, you don't have to leave."

Ryle stands stoically with his hands in his pockets while one of the guests mutters, "It's fine, we don't mind." They begin to file back down the stairwell. I roll my eyes and spin back toward the ledge once I'm alone with him.

"Does everyone always do what you say?" I ask, irritated.

He doesn't respond. His footsteps are slow and deliberate as he closes in on me. My heart begins to beat like it's on a speed-date, and I start scratching at my chest again.

"Lily," he says from behind me.

I turn around and grip the ledge behind me with both hands. His eyes journey down to my cleavage. As soon as they do, I yank at the top of my dress so he can't see it, and then I grip the ledge again. He laughs and takes another step closer. We're almost touching now, and my brain is mush. It's pathetic. I'm pathetic.

"I feel like you have a lot to say," he says. "So I'd like to give you the opportunity to speak your naked truth."

"Hah!" I say with a laugh. "Are you sure about that?"

He nods, so I prepare to let him have it. I push against his chest and make my way around him so that he's the one leaning against the ledge now.

"I can't tell what you *want*, Ryle! And every time I get to the point where I start to not give a shit, you show up again out of the blue! You show up at my work, you show up at my apartment door, you show up at parties, you . . ."

"I live here," he says, excusing the last one. That pisses me off even more. I clench my fists.

"Ugh! You're driving me crazy! Do you want me or do you *not*?"

He stands up straight and takes a step toward me. "Oh, I want you, Lily. Make no mistake about that. I just don't *want* to want you."

My whole body sighs at that comment. Partly out of frustration and partly because everything he says makes me shiver and I hate that I allow him to make me feel like this.

I shake my head. "You don't get it, do you?" I say, softening my voice. I feel too defeated right now to keep yelling at him. "I like you, Ryle. And knowing that you only want me for one night makes me really, *really* sad. And maybe if this were a few months ago, we could have had sex and it would have been fine. You would have walked away and I could have easily moved on with my life. But it's not a few months ago. You waited too long, and too many pieces of me are invested in you now, so please. Stop flirting with me. Stop hanging pictures of me in your apartment. And stop sending me flowers. Because when you do those things, it doesn't feel *good*, Ryle. It actually kind of hurts."

I feel deflated and exhausted and I'm ready to leave. He regards me silently, and I respectfully give him time to make his rebuttal. But he doesn't. He just turns around, leans over the ledge, and stares down at the street like he didn't hear a single word I said.

I walk across the roof and open the door, half expecting him to call out my name or ask me not to leave. I get all the way back to the apartment before I finally lose all hope of that happening. I push through the crowd and make it through three different rooms before I spot Devin. When he sees the look on my face, he just nods and begins to make his way across the room toward me.

"Ready to go?" he asks, looping his arm through mine.

I nod. "Yes. *So* ready."

We find Allysa in the main living room. I tell her and Marshall goodnight, using the excuse that I'm just exhausted from opening week and I'd like to get some sleep before work tomorrow. Allysa gives me a hug and walks us to the front door.

"I'll be back on Monday," she says to me, kissing me on the cheek.

"Happy birthday," I say to her. Devin opens the door, but right before we step into the hallway, I hear someone yell my name.

I turn around and Ryle is pushing through the crowd on the other side of the room. "Lily, wait!" he yells, still trying to make his way over to me. My heart is erratic. He's walking quickly, stepping around people, growing more frustrated with every person in his way. He finally reaches a break in the crowd and makes eye contact with me again. He holds my gaze as he marches toward me. He doesn't slow down. Allysa has to step out of his way as he walks straight up to me. At first, I think he might kiss me, or at least give a rebuttal to everything I said to him upstairs. But instead, he does something I'm not at all prepared for. He scoops me up into his arms.

"Ryle!" I yell, gripping him around the neck, afraid he might drop me. "Put me down!" He has an arm wrapped under my legs and one under my back.

"I need to borrow Lily for the night," he says to Devin. "That okay?"

I look at Devin and shake my head, wide-eyed. Devin just smirks and says, "Be my guest."

Traitor!

Ryle starts to turn and walk back toward the living room. I look at Allysa as I pass her. Her eyes are wide with confusion. "I'm going to kill your brother!" I yell at her.

Everyone in the entire room is staring now. I'm so embarrassed, I just press my face against Ryle's chest as he walks me down the hallway and into his bedroom. Once the door is shut behind us, he slowly lowers my feet back to the floor. I immediately start to yell at him and try to push him out of the way of the bedroom door, but he spins me and shoves me against the door, grabbing both of my wrists. He presses them against the wall above my head and says, "Lily?"

He's looking at me so intently, I stop trying to fight him off of me and I hold my breath. His chest is pressing against mine, my back is pressed to the door. And then his mouth is on mine. Warm pressure against my lips.

Despite the strength behind them, his lips are like silk. I'm shocked at the moan that rushes through me, and even more shocked when I part my lips and want more. His tongue slides against mine and he releases my wrists to grab my face. His kiss grows deeper and I grasp at his hair, pulling him closer, feeling the kiss in my entire body.

Both of us become a medley of moans and gasps as the kiss brings us over the edge, our bodies wanting more than our mouths can deliver. I feel his hands as he reaches down and grabs my legs, lifting me up and hooking them around his waist.

My God, this man can kiss. It's as if he takes kissing as seriously as he takes his profession. He begins to pull me away from the door when I'm hit with the realization that yes, his mouth is capable of a lot. But what his mouth has failed to do is respond to everything I told him upstairs.

For all I know, I've just given in. I'm giving him what he wants: a one-night stand. And that's the last thing he deserves right now.

I pull my mouth from his and push on his shoulders. "Put me down."

He keeps walking toward his bed, so I say it again. "Ryle, put me down right now."

He stops walking and lowers me to the floor. I have to back away and face the other direction to gather my thoughts. Looking at him while I still feel his lips on mine is more than I can deal with right now.

I feel his arms go around my waist, and he rests his

head on my shoulder. "I'm sorry," he whispers. He turns me around and brings a hand up to my face and brushes his thumb across my cheek. "It's my turn now, okay?"

I don't respond to his touch. I keep my arms folded across my chest and wait to hear what he has to say before I allow myself to respond to his touch.

"I had that picture made the day after I took it," he says. "It's been in my apartment for months now, because you were the most beautiful thing I'd ever seen and I wanted to look at it every single day."

Oh.

"And that night I showed up at your door? I went searching for you because no one in the history of my life has ever crawled under my skin and refused to leave like you did. I didn't know how to handle it. And the reason I sent you flowers this week is because I am really, really proud of you for following your dream. But if I sent you flowers every time I've had the urge to send you flowers, you wouldn't even be able to fit inside your apartment. Because that's how much I think about you. And yes, Lily. You're right. I'm hurting you, but *I'm* hurting, too. And until tonight . . . I didn't know why."

I have no idea how I even possibly find the strength to speak after that. "Why are you hurting?"

He drops his forehead to mine and says, "Because. I have no idea what I'm doing. You make me want to be a different person, but what if I don't know how to be what you need? This is all new to me and I want to prove to you that I want you for so much more than just one night."

He looks so vulnerable right now. I want to believe the

genuine look in his eye, but he's been so adamant since the day that I met him that he wants the exact opposite of what I want. And it terrifies me that I'll give in to him and he'll walk away.

"How do I prove myself to you, Lily? Tell me and I'll do it."

I don't know. I barely know the guy. I know him enough to know that sex with him won't be enough for me, though. But how do I know sex won't be the only thing he wants?

My eyes instantly lock with his. "Don't have sex with me."

He stares at me for a moment, completely unreadable. But then he starts to nod his head like he's finally getting it. "Okay," he says, still nodding. "Okay. I will not have sex with you, Lily Bloom."

He walks around me to his bedroom door and he locks it. He flips off the light, leaving only a lamp on, and then takes off his shirt as he walks toward me.

"What are you doing?"

He tosses his shirt on a chair and then slips off his shoes. "We're going to sleep."

I glance at his bed. Then at him. "Right now?"

He nods and walks over to me. In one swift movement, he lifts my dress up and over my head, until I'm standing in the middle of his bedroom floor in my bra and panties. I cover myself, but he doesn't even look twice. He pulls me toward the bed and lifts the covers for me to crawl in. As he's walking over to his side of the bed he says, "It's not like we haven't slept together before without having sex. Piece of cake."

I laugh. He reaches his dresser and plugs his phone in to a charger. I take a moment to skim his bedroom. This certainly isn't the type of spare bedroom I'm used to. Three of my bedrooms could fit in here. There's a couch against the other wall, a chair facing a television and a full office off the bedroom that looks complete with a floor-to-ceiling library. I'm still trying to see everything around me when the lamp goes off.

"Your sister is *really rich*," I say as I feel him pull the covers over both of us. "What the hell does she do with the ten bucks an hour I pay her? Wipe her ass with it?"

He laughs and grabs my hand, sliding his fingers through mine. "She probably doesn't even cash the checks," he says. "Have you ever checked?"

I haven't. Now I'm curious.

"Goodnight, Lily," he says.

I can't stop smiling, because this is kind of ridiculous. And so great.

"Goodnight, Ryle."

．　　　．　　　．

I think I might be lost.

Everything is so white and so clean, it's blinding. I shuffle through one of the living rooms and try to find my way to the kitchen. I have no idea where my dress ended up last night, so I pulled on one of Ryle's shirts. It falls past my knees, and I wonder if he has to buy shirts that are too big for him just so they'll fit his arms.

There are too many windows and way too much sun, so I'm forced to shield my eyes as I go in search of coffee.

I push through the kitchen doors and find a coffeemaker. *Thank you, Jesus.*

I set it to brew and then go in search for a mug when

the kitchen door opens behind me. I spin around and I'm relieved to see that Allysa isn't always a perfect concoction of makeup and jewelry. Her hair is in a messy topknot and mascara is smeared down her cheeks. She points at the coffeemaker. "I'm gonna need me some of that," she says. She pulls herself up on the island and then slouches forward.

"Can I ask you a question?" I say.

She barely has the energy to nod.

I wave my hand around the kitchen. "How did this happen? How in the hell did your entire house become spotless between the party last night and me waking up just now? Did you stay up and clean?"

She laughs. "We have people for that," she says.

"People?"

She nods. "Yep. There are people for *everything*," she says. "You'd be surprised. Think of something. Anything. We probably have people for it."

"Groceries?"

"People," she says.

"Christmas décor?"

She nods. "People for that, too."

"What about birthday gifts? Like for family members?"

She grins. "Yep. *People.* Everyone in my family receives a gift and a card for every occasion and I never have to lift a finger."

I shake my head. "Wow. How long have you been this rich?"

"Three years," she says. "Marshall sold a few apps he developed to Apple for a lot of money. Every six months, he creates updates and sells those, too."

The coffee transitions into a slow drip, so I grab a mug and fill it up. "You want anything in yours?" I ask. "Or do you have people for that?"

She laughs. "Yes. I have you, and I'd like sugar, please."

I stir some sugar into her cup and walk it over to her, then pour myself a cup. It grows quiet for a while as I mix in creamer, waiting for her to say something about me and Ryle. The conversation is inevitable.

"Can we just get the awkwardness out of the way?" she says.

I sigh, relieved. "Please. I hate this." I face her and take a sip of my coffee. She sets hers down beside her and then grips the countertop.

"How did that even *happen*?"

I shake my head, trying my best not to smile like I'm love-struck. I don't want her to think I'm weak, or a fool for giving in to him. "We met before I knew you."

She tilts her head. "Wait," she says. "Before we got to know each other *better* or before we knew each other at *all*?"

"At all," I say. "We had a moment one night, about six months before I met you."

"A moment?" she says. "As in . . . a one-night stand?"

"No," I say. "No, we never even kissed until last night. I don't know, I can't explain it. We just had this sort of flirtation thing going on for a really long time and it finally came to a head last night. That's all."

She picks up her coffee again and takes a slow drink from it. She stares down at the floor for a while and I can't help but notice she looks a little sad.

"Allysa? You're not mad at me, are you?"

She immediately shakes her head. "No, Lily. I just . . ." She sets down her coffee cup again. "I just know my brother. And I love him. I really do. But . . ."

"But what?"

Allysa and I both look in the direction of the voice. Ryle is standing in the doorway with his arms folded across his chest. He's wearing a pair of gray jogging pants that are barely hanging on to his hips. No shirt. *I'll be adding this outfit to all the other ones I've catalogued in my head.*

Ryle pushes off the door and makes his way into the kitchen. He walks over to me and takes my cup of coffee out of my hands. He leans in and kisses me on the forehead, then takes a drink as he leans against the counter.

"I didn't mean to interrupt," he says to Allysa. "By all means, continue your conversation."

Allysa rolls her eyes and says, "Stop."

He hands me back my cup of coffee and turns around to grab his own mug. He begins to pour from the pot. "It sounded to me like you were about to give Lily a warning. I'm just curious as to what you have to say."

Allysa hops off the counter and carries her mug to the sink. "She's my friend, Ryle. You don't have the best track record when it comes to relationships." She washes out the mug and then leans her hip into the sink, facing us. "As her *friend*, I have the right to give her my opinion when it comes to the guys she dates. That's what friends *do*."

I'm suddenly feeling uncomfortable as the tension grows thicker between the two of them. Ryle doesn't even take a drink of his coffee. He walks toward Allysa and pours it out in the sink. He's standing right in front of her, but she won't even look at him. "Well, as your *brother*, I would hope you had a little more faith in me than you do. That's what *siblings* do."

He walks out of the kitchen, shoving the door open. When he's gone, Allysa takes a deep breath. She shakes her head and pulls her hands up to her face. "Sorry about that," she says, forcing a smile. "I need to shower."

"You don't have people for that?"

She laughs as she exits the kitchen. I wash my mug in the sink and head back to Ryle's bedroom. When I open the door, he's sitting on the couch, scrolling through his phone. He doesn't look up at me when I walk in and for a second, I think he might be mad at me, too. But then he tosses his phone aside and leans back into the couch.

"Come here," he says.

He grabs my hand and pulls me down on top of him so that I'm straddling him. He brings my mouth to his and kisses me so hard, it makes me wonder if he's trying to prove his sister wrong.

Ryle pulls away from my mouth and slowly rakes his eyes down my body. "I like you in my clothes."

I smile. "Well I have to get to work, so unfortunately, I can't keep them on."

He brushes the hair from my face and says, "I have a really important surgery coming up that I need to prepare for. Which means I probably won't see you for a few days."

I try to hide my disappointment, but I have to get used to it if he really wants to try and make something work between us. He's already warned me that he works too much. "I'm busy, too. Grand opening is on Friday."

He says, "Oh, I'll see you before Friday. Promise."

I don't hide my grin this time. "Okay."

He kisses me again, this time for a solid minute. He starts to lower me to the couch, but then he shoves away from me and says. "Nope. I like you too much to make out with you."

I lie down on the couch and watch him get dressed for work.

To my enjoyment, he puts on scrubs.

Chapter Eight

"We need to talk," Lucy says.

She's sitting on the couch, mascara streaked down her cheeks.

Oh, shit.

I drop my purse and rush over to her. As soon as I sit down next to her, she starts crying.

"What's wrong? Did Alex break up with you?"

She starts shaking her head and then I really start freaking out. *Please don't say cancer.* I grab her hand, and that's when I see it. "Lucy! You're engaged?"

She nods. "I'm sorry. I know we still have six months left on the lease, but he wants me to move in with him."

I stare at her for a minute. *Is that why she's crying? Because she wants out of her lease?* She reaches for a tissue and starts dabbing at her eyes. "I feel awful, Lily. You're going to be all alone. I'm moving and you won't have *anyone*."

What the . . .

"Lucy? Um . . . I'll be fine. I promise."

She looks up at me with hope in her expression. "Really?"

Why in the world does she have this impression of me? I nod again. "Yes. I'm not mad, I'm happy for you."

She throws her arms around me and hugs me. "Oh, thank you, Lily!" She starts giggling in between bouts of tears. When she releases me, she jumps up and says, "I have to go tell Alex!

He was so worried you wouldn't let me out of my lease!" She grabs her purse and shoes and disappears out the front door.

I lie back on the couch and stare up at the ceiling. *Did she just play me?*

I start laughing, because until this moment, I had no idea how much I've been waiting for this to happen. *The whole place to myself!*

What's even better, is when I do decide to have sex with Ryle, we can have it over here all the time and not have to worry about being quiet.

The last time I spoke to Ryle was when I left his apartment on Saturday. We agreed on a trial run. No commitments yet. Just a relationship feeler to see if it's something we both want. It's now Monday night and I'm a little disappointed I haven't heard from him. I gave him my phone number before we parted Saturday, but I don't really know texting etiquette, especially for *trial runs.*

Regardless, I'm not texting him first.

I decide to occupy my time with teenage angst and Ellen DeGeneres, instead. I'm not about to wait around to be beckoned by a guy I'm not even having sex with. But I don't know why I assume that reading about the *first* guy I had sex with will somehow get my mind off the guy I'm *not* having sex with.

Dear Ellen,

My great-grandfather's name is Ellis. My entire life, I thought that was a really cool name for such an old guy. After he died, I was reading the obituary. Would you believe that Ellis wasn't even his real name? His real name was Levi Sampson and I had no idea.

I asked my grandmother where the name Ellis came from. She said his initials were L.S. and everyone called him by his initials for so long, they just started sounding them out over the years.

Which is why they referred to him as Ellis.

I was looking at your name just now and it made me think of that. Ellen. Is that even your real name? You could be just like my great-grandfather and using your initials as a disguise.

L.N.

I'm onto you, "Ellen."

Speaking of names, do you think Atlas is a weird name? It is, isn't it?

Yesterday while I was watching your show with him, I asked him where he got his name from. He said he didn't know. Without even thinking, I told him he should ask his mother why she named him that. He just looked over at me for a second and said, "It's a little too late for that."

I don't know what he meant by that. I don't know if his mom died, or if she gave him up for adoption. We've been friends for a few weeks now and I still don't really know anything about him or why he doesn't have a place to live. I would just ask him, but I'm not sure if he really trusts me yet. He seems to have trust issues and I guess I can't blame him.

I'm worried about him. It started getting really cold this week and it's supposed to be even colder next week. If he doesn't have electricity, that means he doesn't have a heater. I hope he at least has blankets. Do you know how awful I would feel if he froze to death? Pretty freaking awful, Ellen.

I'll find some blankets this week and give them to him.

—Lily

Dear Ellen,

It's going to start snowing soon so I decided to harvest my garden today. I had already pulled the radishes so I just wanted to put some mulch and compost down, which wouldn't have taken me long, but Atlas insisted on helping.

He asked me a lot of questions about gardening and I liked that he seemed interested in my interests. I showed him how to lay the compost and mulch to cover the ground so that the snow wouldn't do too much damage. My garden is small compared to most gardens. Maybe ten feet by twelve feet. But it's all my dad will let me use of the backyard.

Atlas covered the whole thing while I sat cross-legged in the grass and watched him. I wasn't being lazy, he just took over and wanted to do it so I let him. I can tell he's a hard worker. I wonder if maybe keeping himself busy takes his mind off of things and that's why he always wants to help me so much.

When he was finished, he walked over and dropped down next to me on the grass.

"What made you want to grow things?" he asked.

I glanced over at him and he was sitting cross-legged, looking at me curiously. I realized in that moment that he's probably the best friend I've ever had, and we barely know anything about each other. I have friends at school, but they're never allowed to come over to my house for obvious reasons. My mother is always worried something might happen with my father and word might get out about his temper. I also never really get to go to other people's houses but I'm not sure why. Maybe my father doesn't want me staying over at friends' houses because I might witness how a good husband is supposed to treat his wife. He probably wants me to believe the way he treats my mother is normal.

Atlas is the first friend I've ever had that's ever been inside my house. He's also the first friend to know how much I like to garden. And now he's the first friend to ever ask me why I garden.

I reached down and pulled at a weed and started tearing it into little pieces while I thought about his question.

"When I was ten, my mother got me a subscription to a website called Seeds Anonymous," I said. "Every month I would get an unmarked package of seeds in the mail with instructions on how to plant them and care for them. I wouldn't know what I was growing until it came up out of the ground. Every day after school I'd run straight to the backyard to see the progress. It gave me something to look forward to. Growing things felt like a reward."

I could feel Atlas staring at me when he asked, "A reward for what?"

I shrugged. "For loving my plants the right way. Plants reward you based on the amount of love you show them. If you're cruel to them or neglect them, they give you nothing. But if you care for them and love them the right way, they reward you with gifts in the form of vegetables or fruits or flowers." I looked down at the weed I was tearing apart in my hands and there was barely an inch left of it. I wadded it up between my fingers and flicked it.

I didn't want to look over at Atlas because I could still feel him staring, so instead, I just stared out over my mulch-covered garden.

"We're just alike," he said.

My eyes flicked to his. "Me and you?"

He shook his head. "No. Plants and humans. Plants need to be loved the right way in order to survive. So do humans. We rely on our parents from birth to love us enough to keep us alive. And if our parents show us the right kind of love, we turn out as better humans overall. But if we're neglected . . ."

His voice grew quiet. Almost sad. He wiped his hands on his

knees, trying to get some of the dirt off. "If we're neglected, we end up homeless and incapable of anything meaningful."

His words made my heart feel like the mulch he had just laid out. I didn't even know what to say to that. Does he really think that about himself?

He acted like he was about to get up, but before he did I said his name.

He sat back down in the grass. I pointed at the row of trees that lined the fence to the left of the yard. "You see that tree over there?" In the middle of the row of trees was an oak tree that stood taller than all the rest of the trees.

Atlas glanced over at it and dragged his eyes all the way up to the top of the tree.

"It grew on its own," I said. "Most plants do need a lot of care to survive. But some things, like trees, are strong enough to do it by just relying on themselves and nobody else."

I had no idea if he knew what I was trying to say without me coming out and saying it. But I just wanted him to know that I thought he was strong enough to survive whatever was going on in his life. I didn't know him well, but I could tell he was resilient. Way more than I would ever be if I were in his situation.

His eyes were glued to the tree. It was a long time before he even blinked. When he finally did, he just nodded a little and looked down at the grass. I thought with the way his mouth twitched that he was about to frown, but instead he actually smiled a little.

Seeing that smile made my heart feel like I had just startled it right out of a dead sleep.

"We're just alike," he said, repeating himself from earlier.

"Plants and humans?" I asked.

He shook his head. "No. Me and you."

I gasped, Ellen. I hope he didn't notice, but I definitely sucked in a rush of air. Because what the heck was I supposed to say to that?

I just sat there, really awkward and quiet until he stood up. He turned like he was about to walk home.

"Atlas, wait."

He glanced back down at me. I pointed at his hands and said, "You might want to take a quick shower before you go back. Compost is made from cow manure."

He lifted his hands and looked down at them and then he looked down at his compost-covered clothes.

"Cow manure? Seriously?"

I grinned and nodded. He laughed a little and then before I knew it, he was on the ground next to me, wiping his hands all over me. We were both laughing as he reached to the bag next to us and stuck his hand inside, then smeared it down my arms.

Ellen, I am confident that the next sentence I am about to write has never been written or spoken aloud before.

When he was wiping that cow shit on me, it was quite possibly the most turned-on I have ever been.

After a few minutes, we were both lying on the ground, breathing hard, still laughing. He finally stood up and pulled me to my feet, knowing he couldn't waste minutes if he wanted a shower before my parents came home.

Once he was in the shower, I washed my hands in the sink and just stood there, wondering what he meant earlier when he said we were just alike.

Was it a compliment? It sure felt like one. Was he saying that he thought I was strong, too? Because I certainly didn't feel strong most of the time. In that moment, just thinking about him made me feel weak. I wondered what I was going to do about the way I was starting to feel when I was around him.

I also wondered how long I can keep hiding him from my parents. And how long he'll be staying at that house. Winters in Maine are unbearably cold and he won't survive without a heater.

Or blankets.

I gathered myself and went in search of all the spare blankets I could find. I was going to give them to him when he got out of the shower, but it was already five and he left in a hurry.

I'll give them to him tomorrow.

—Lily

Dear Ellen,

Harry Connick Jr. is freaking hilarious. I'm not sure if you've ever had him on your show, because I hate to admit I've probably missed an episode or two since you've been on the air, but if you've never had him, you should. Actually, have you ever watched **Late Night with Conan O'Brien?** *He has this guy named Andy who sits on the couch for every episode. I wish Harry could sit on your couch for every episode. He just has the best one-liners, and the two of you together would be epic.*

I just want to say thank you. I know that you don't have a show on TV for the sole purpose of making me laugh, but sometimes it feels that way. Sometimes my life just makes me feel like I've lost the ability to laugh or smile, but then I turn on your show and no matter what mood I'm in when I turn on the TV, I always feel better by the time your show is over.

So yeah. Thanks for that.

I know you probably want an update on Atlas, and I'll give you one in a second. But first I need to tell you about what happened yesterday.

My mother is a teaching assistant over at Brimer Elementary. It's a bit of a drive and that's why she never gets home until around five o'clock. My dad works two miles from here, so he's always home right after five.

We have a garage, but only one car can fit in it because of all my dad's stuff. My dad keeps his car in the garage and my mom keeps her car in the driveway.

Well, yesterday my mom got home a little bit early. Atlas was still at the house and we were almost finished watching your show when I heard the garage door start to open. He ran out the back door and I rushed around the living room cleaning up our soda cans and snacks.

It had started snowing really hard around lunchtime yesterday and my mother had a lot of stuff to carry in, so she pulled up in the garage so she could bring it all in through the kitchen door. It was work stuff and a few groceries. I was helping her bring everything inside when my dad pulled up in the driveway. He started honking his horn because he was mad that my mom was parked in the garage. I guess he didn't want to have to get out of his car in the snow. That's the only thing I can think of that would make him want her to move her car right then and there, instead of just waiting until she was finished unloading it. Come to think of it, why does my father always get the garage? You would think a man wouldn't want the woman he loves to get the shittier parking spot.

Anyway, my mother got that real scared look in her eye when he started honking and she told me to take all her stuff to the table while she moved her car out.

I'm not sure what happened when she went back outside. I heard a crash, and then I heard her scream, so I ran to the garage thinking maybe she had slipped on ice.

Ellen . . . I don't even want to describe what happened next. I'm still a little shocked by the whole thing.

I opened the garage door and didn't see my mom. I just saw my dad behind the car doing something. I took a step closer and realized why I couldn't see my mom. He had her pushed down on the hood with his hands around her throat.

He was choking her, Ellen!

I might cry just thinking about it. He was yelling at her, staring down at her with so much hatred. Something about not having respect for how hard he works. I don't know why he was mad, really, because all I could hear was her silence while she struggled to breathe. The next few minutes are a blur, but I know I started screaming at him. I jumped on his back and I was hitting him on the side of his head.

Then I wasn't.

I don't really know what happened, but I'm guessing he threw me off of him. I just remembered one second I was on his back and the next second I was on the ground and my forehead hurt like you wouldn't believe. My mom was sitting next to me, holding my head and telling me she was sorry. I looked around for my dad, but he wasn't there. He'd gotten into his car and drove off after I hit my head.

My mom gave me a rag and told me to hold it to my head because it was bleeding and then she helped me to her car and drove me to the hospital. On the way there she only said one thing to me.

"When they ask you what happened, tell them you slipped on the ice."

When she said that, I just looked out my window and started crying. Because I thought for sure this was the final straw. That she would leave him now that he had hurt me. That was the moment I realized that she'd never leave him. I felt so defeated, but I was too scared to say anything to her about it.

I had to get nine stitches in my forehead. I'm still not sure what I hit my head on, but it doesn't really matter. The fact is, my father was the reason I was hurt and he didn't even stay and check on me. He just left us both there on the floor of the garage and left.

I got home really late last night and fell right to sleep because they had given me some kind of pain pill.

This morning when I walked to the bus, I tried not to look directly at Atlas so he wouldn't see my forehead. I had fixed my hair so that you couldn't really see it and he didn't notice right away. When we sat down next to each other on the bus, our hands touched when we were putting our stuff on the floor.

His hands were like ice, Ellen. Ice.

That's when I realized that I forgot to give him the blankets I had pulled out for him yesterday because my mother got home sooner than I expected. The incident in the garage sort of took over all my thoughts and I completely forgot about him. It had snowed and iced all night and he had been over there at that house in the dark all by himself. And now he was so cold, I didn't know how he was even functioning.

I grabbed both of his hands in mine and said, "Atlas. You're freezing."

He didn't say anything. I just started rubbing his hands in mine to warm them up. I laid my head on his shoulder and then I did the most embarrassing thing. I just started to cry. I don't cry very much, but I was still so upset by what happened yesterday and then I was feeling so guilty that I forgot to take him blankets and it all hit me right there on the ride to school. He didn't say anything. He just pulled his hands from mine so I'd stop rubbing them and then he laid his hands on top of mine. We just sat there like that the whole ride to school with our heads leaned together and his hands on top of mine.

I might have thought it was sweet if it wasn't so sad.

On the ride home from school is when he finally noticed my head.

Honestly, I had forgotten about it. No one at school even asked me about it and when he sat down next to me on the bus, I wasn't even trying to hide it with my hair. He looked right at me and said, "What happened to your head?"

I didn't know what to say to him. I just touched it with my fingers and then looked out the window. I've been trying to get him to trust me more in hopes he would tell me why he doesn't have a place to live, so I didn't want to lie to him. I just didn't want to tell him the truth, either.

When the bus started moving, he said, "Yesterday after I left your house, I heard something going on over there. I heard yelling. I heard you scream, and then I saw your father leave. I was going to come check on you to make sure everything was okay, but as I was walking over I saw you leaving in the car with your mother."

He must have heard the fight in the garage and saw her leaving to take me to get the stitches. I couldn't believe he came over to our house. Do you know what my dad would do to him if he saw him wearing his clothes? I got so worried for him because I don't think he knows what my father is capable of.

I looked at him and said, "Atlas, you can't do that! You can't come to my house when my parents are home!"

Atlas got real quiet and then said, "I heard you scream, Lily." He said it like me being in danger trumped anything else.

I felt bad because I know he was just trying to help, but that would have made things so much worse.

"I fell," I said to him. As soon as I said it, I felt bad for lying. And to be honest, he looked a little disappointed in me, because I think we both knew in that moment that it wasn't as simple as a fall.

Then he pulled up the sleeve of his shirt and held out his arm.

Ellen, my stomach dropped. It was so bad. All over his arm he had these small scars. Some of the scars looked just like someone had stuck a cigarette to his arm and held it there.

He twisted his arm around so I could see that it was on the other side, too. "I used to fall a lot, too, Lily." Then he pulled his shirtsleeve down and didn't say anything else.

For a second I wanted to tell him it wasn't like that—that my dad never hurts me and that he was just trying to get me off of him. But then I realized I'd be using the same excuses my mom uses.

I felt a little embarrassed that he knows what goes on at my house. I spent the whole rest of the bus ride looking out the window because I didn't know what to say to him.

When we got home, my mom's car was there. In the driveway, of course. Not the garage.

That meant Atlas couldn't come over and watch your show with me. I was gonna tell him I would bring him blankets later, but when he got off the bus he didn't even tell me bye. He just started walking down the street like he was mad.

It's dark now and I'm waiting on my parents to go to sleep. But in a little while I'm gonna take him some blankets.

—Lily

Dear Ellen,

I'm in way over my head.

Do you ever do things you know are wrong, but are somehow also right? I don't know how to put it in simpler terms than that.

I mean, I'm only fifteen and I certainly shouldn't have boys spending the night in my bedroom. But if a person knows someone needs a place to stay, isn't it that person's responsibility as a human to help them?

Last night after my parents went to sleep, I snuck out the back *door to take Atlas those blankets. I took a flashlight with me because it was dark. It was still snowing really hard, so by the time I made it to that house, I was freezing. I beat on the back door and as soon as he opened it, I pushed past him to get out of the cold.*

Only . . . I didn't get out of the cold. Somehow, it felt even colder inside that old house. I still had my flashlight on and I shined it around the living room and kitchen. There wasn't anything in there, Ellen!

No couch, no chair, no mattress. I handed the blankets off to him and kept looking around me. There was a big hole in the roof over the kitchen and wind and snow were just pouring in. When I shined my light around the living room, I saw his stuff in one of the corners. His backpack, plus the backpack I'd given him. There was a little pile of other stuff I'd given him, like some of my dad's clothes. And then there were two towels on the floor. One I guess he laid on and one he covered up with.

I put my hand over my mouth because I was so horrified. He'd been there living like that for weeks!

Atlas put his hand on my back and tried to walk me back out the door. "You shouldn't be over here, Lily," he said. "You could get in trouble."

That's when I grabbed his hand and said, "You shouldn't be here, either." I started to pull him out the front door with me, but he yanked his hand back. That's when I said, "You can sleep on my floor tonight. I'll keep my bedroom door locked. You can't sleep here, Atlas. It's too cold and you'll get pneumonia and die."

He looked like he didn't know what to do. I'm sure the thought of being caught in my bedroom was just as scary as getting pneumonia and dying. He looked back at his spot in the living room and then he just nodded his head once and said, "Okay."

So you tell me, Ellen. Was I wrong letting him sleep in my room last night? It doesn't feel wrong. It felt like the right thing to do. But I sure would get in a lot of trouble if we had been caught. He slept on the floor, so it's not like it was anything more than me just giving him somewhere warm to sleep.

I did learn a little more about him last night. After I snuck him in the back door and to my room, I locked my door and made a pallet for him on the floor next to my bed. I set the alarm for 6 a.m. and told him he'd have to get up and leave before my parents woke up, since sometimes my mom wakes me up in the mornings.

I crawled in my bed and scooted over to the edge of it so I could look down at him while we talked for a little while. I asked him how long he thought he might stay there and he said he didn't know. That's when I asked him how he ended up there. My lamp was still on, and we were whispering, but he got real quiet when I said that. He just stared up at me with his hands behind his head for a moment. Then he said, "I don't know my real dad. He never had anything to do with me. It's always just been me and my mom, but she got remarried about five years ago to a guy who never really liked me much. We fought a lot. When I turned eighteen a few months ago, we got in a big fight and he kicked me out of the house."

He took a deep breath like he didn't want to tell me any more. But then he started talking again. "I've been staying with a friend of mine and his family since then, but his dad got a transfer to Colorado and they moved. They couldn't take me with them, of course. His parents were just being nice by letting me stay with them and I knew that, so I told them I talked to my mom and that I was moving back home. The day they left, I didn't have anywhere to go. So I went back home and told my mom I'd like to move back in until I graduated. She wouldn't let me. Said it would upset my stepfather."

He turned his head and looked at the wall. "So I just wandered around for a few days until I saw that house. Figured I would just stay there until something better came along or until I graduated. I'm signed up to go to the Marines come May, so I'm just trying to hang on until then."

May is six months away, Ellen. Six.

I had tears in my eyes when he finished telling me all that. I asked him why he didn't just ask someone if they could help him. He said he tried, but it's harder for an adult than a kid, and he's already eighteen. He said someone gave him a number for some shelters who might help him. There were three shelters in a twenty-mile radius of our town, but two of them were for battered women. The other one was a homeless shelter, but they only had a few beds and it was too far away for him to walk there if he wanted to go to school every day. Plus, you have to wait in a long line to try and get a bed. He said he tried it once, but he feels safer in that old house than he did at the shelter.

Like the naïve girl I am when it comes to situations like his, I said, "But aren't there other options? Can't you just tell the school counselor what your mom did?"

He shook his head and said he's too old for foster care. He's eighteen, so his mother can't get in trouble for not allowing him to go back home. He said he called about getting food stamps last week, but he didn't have a ride or money to get to his appointment. Not to mention he doesn't have a car, so he can't very well find a job. He said he's been looking, though. After he leaves my house in the afternoons he goes and applies at places, but he doesn't have an address or a phone number to put down on the applications so that makes it harder for him.

I swear, Ellen, every question I threw at him, he had an answer for. It's like he's tried everything not to be stuck in the situation he's in, but there isn't enough help out there for people like him. I got so mad at his whole situation, I told him he was crazy for wanting to go into the military. I wasn't so much whispering when I said, "Why in the heck would you want to serve a country that has allowed you to end up in this kind of situation?"

You know what he said next, Ellen? His eyes grew sad and he said, "It's not this country's fault my mother doesn't give a shit about me." Then he reached up and turned off my lamp. "Goodnight, Lily," he said.

I didn't sleep much after that. I was too mad. I'm not even sure who I'm mad at. I just kept thinking about our country and the whole world and how screwed up it is that people don't do more for each other. I don't know when humans started only looking out for themselves. Maybe it's always been this way. It made me wonder how many people out there were just like Atlas. It made me wonder if there were other kids at our school who might be homeless.

I go to school every day and internally complain about it most of the time, but I've never once thought that school might be the only home some kids have. It's the only place Atlas can go and know he'll have food.

I'll never be able to respect rich people now, knowing they willingly choose to spend their money on materialistic things rather than using it to help other people.

No offense, Ellen. I know you're rich, but I guess I'm not referring to people like you. I've seen all the stuff you've done for others on your show and all the charities you support. But I know there are a lot of rich people out there who are selfish. Hell, there are even selfish poor people. And selfish middle-class people. Look at my parents. We aren't rich, but we certainly aren't too poor to help other people. Yet, I don't think my dad has ever done anything for a charity.

I remember one time we were walking into a grocery store and

*an old man was ringing a bell for the Salvation Army. I asked
my dad if we could give him some money and he told me no, that
he works hard for his money and he wasn't about to let me give it
away. He said it isn't his fault that other people don't want to work.
He spent the whole time we were in the grocery store telling me
about how people take advantage of the government and until the
government stops helping those people by giving them handouts, the
problem won't ever go away.*

*Ellen, I believed him. That was three years ago and all this time
I thought homeless people were homeless because they were lazy or
drug addicts or just didn't want to work like other people. But now
I know that's not true. Sure, some of what he said was true to an
extent, but he was using the worst-case scenarios. Not everyone is
homeless because they choose to be. They're homeless because there
isn't enough help to go around.*

*And people like my father are the problem. Instead of helping
others, people use the worst-case scenarios to excuse their own
selfishness and greed.*

*I'll never be like that. I swear to you, when I grow up, I'm
going to do everything I can to help other people. I'll be like you,
Ellen. Just probably not as rich.*

—Lily

Chapter Nine

I drop the journal on my chest. I'm surprised to feel tears running down my cheeks. Every time I pick up this journal I think I'll be fine—that it all happened so long ago and I won't still feel what I felt back then.

I'm such a sap. It gives me this longing to hug so many people from my past. Especially my mother because for the past year, I haven't really thought about everything she had to go through before my father died. I know it probably still hurts her.

I grab my phone to call her and look at the screen. There are four missed texts from Ryle. My heart immediately skips. *I can't believe I had it on silent!* Then I roll my eyes, annoyed with myself, because I should *not* be this excited.

Ryle: Are you asleep?

Ryle: I guess so.

Ryle: Lily . . .

Ryle. : (

The sad face was sent ten minutes ago. I hit Reply and type, "Nope. Not asleep." About ten seconds later, I get another text.

Ryle: Good. I'm walking up your stairs right now. Be there in twenty seconds.

I grin and jump out of bed. I go to the bathroom and check my face. *Good enough.* I run to the front door and open it as soon as Ryle makes it up the stairwell. He practically drags himself up the top step, and then stops to rest when he finally reaches my door. He looks so tired. His eyes are red and there are dark circles under them. His arms slip around my waist and he pulls me to him, burying his face in my neck.

"You smell so good," he says.

I pull him inside the apartment. "Are you hungry? I can make you something to eat."

He shakes his head as he wrestles out of his jacket, so I skip the kitchen and head for the bedroom. He follows me, and then throws his jacket over the back of the chair. He kicks off his shoes and pushes them against the wall.

He's wearing scrubs.

"You look exhausted," I say.

He smiles and puts his hands on my hips. "I am. I just assisted in an eighteen-hour surgery." He bends down and kisses the heart tattoo on my collarbone.

No wonder he's exhausted. "How is that even possible?" I say. "Eighteen *hours?*"

He nods and then walks me to the side of the bed where he pulls me down next to him. We adjust ourselves until we're facing each other, sharing a pillow. "Yeah, but it was amazing. Groundbreaking. They'll write about it in medical journals, and I got to be there, so I'm not complaining. I'm just really tired."

I lean in and give him a peck on the mouth. He brings his hand to the side of my head and pulls back. "I know you're probably ready to have hot, sweaty sex, but I don't have the energy tonight. I'm sorry. But I've missed you and for some reason I sleep better when I sleep next to you. Is it okay that I'm here?"

I smile. "It's more than okay."

He leans in and kisses my forehead. He grabs my hand and then holds it between us on the pillow. His eyes close, but I keep mine open and stare at him. He has the type of face that people shy away from, because you could get lost in it. And to think, I get to look at this face all the time. I don't have to be modest and look away, because he's mine.

Maybe.

This is a trial run. I have to remember that.

After a minute, he releases my hand and begins to flex his fingers. I look down at his hand and wonder what that must be like . . . to have to stand for so long and use your fine motor skills for eighteen hours straight. I can't think of much else that would match that level of exhaustion.

I slide out of the bed and retrieve some lotion out of my bathroom. I go back to the bed and sit cross-legged next to him. I squirt some lotion on my hand and then pull his arm to my lap. He opens his eyes and looks up at me.

"What are you doing?" he mumbles.

"Shh. Go back to sleep," I say. I press my thumbs into the palm of his hand and rotate them upward and then out. His eyes fall shut and he groans into the pillow. I continue massaging his hand for about five minutes before switching to his other hand. He keeps his eyes closed the whole time. When I'm finished with his hands, I roll him onto his stomach and straddle his back. He assists me in pulling off his shirt, but his arms are like noodles.

I massage his shoulders and his neck and his back and his arms. When I'm finished, I roll off of him and lie down beside him.

I'm running my fingers through his hair and massaging his scalp when he opens his eyes. "Lily?" he whispers, looking at me sincerely. "You just might be the best thing that's ever happened to me."

Those words wrap around me like a warm blanket. I don't know what to say in response. He lifts a hand and gently cups my cheek, and I feel his stare deep in my stomach. Slowly, he leans forward and presses his lips to mine. I expect a peck, but he doesn't pull back. The tip of his tongue slides across my lips, parting them softly. His mouth is so warm, I moan as his kiss grows deeper.

He rolls me onto my back and then drags his hand down my body, straight to my hip. He moves closer, sliding his hand down my thigh. He pushes against me and a surge of heat shoots inside me. I grab a fistful of his hair and whisper against his mouth. "I think we've waited long enough. I would very much like for you to fuck me now."

He practically growls with a renewed sense of energy and begins to pull my shirt off. It becomes an interlude of hands and moans and tongues and sweat. I feel like this is the first time I've ever been touched by a man. The few who came before him were all boys—nervous hands and timid mouths. But Ryle is all confidence. He knows exactly where to touch me and exactly how to kiss me.

The only time he's not giving my body his undivided attention is when he reaches to the floor and fishes a condom out of his wallet. Once he's back under the covers and the condom is in place, he doesn't even hesitate. He takes me brazenly in one swift thrust and I gasp into his mouth, every muscle in me tensing.

His mouth is fierce and needy, kissing me everywhere he can reach. I grow so dizzy, I can do nothing but succumb to him. He's unapologetic in the way he fucks me. His hand comes between my headboard and the top of my head as he pushes harder and harder, the bed crashing against the wall with every push.

My fingernails dig into the skin of his back as he buries his face against my neck.

"Ryle," I whisper.

"Oh, *God*," I say.

"Ryle!" I scream.

And then I bite down on his shoulder to muffle every sound that comes after it. My whole body feels it—from my head to my toes and back up again.

I'm afraid I might literally pass out for a moment, so I tighten my legs around him and he tenses. "*Jesus*, Lily." His body ripples with tremors, and he shoves against me one last time. He groans, stilling himself on top of me. His body jerks with his release and my head falls back against the pillow.

It's a full minute before either of us is able to move. And even then, we choose not to. He presses his face into the pillow and lets out a deep sigh. "I can't . . ." He pulls back and looks down at me. His eyes are full of something . . . I don't know what. He presses his lips to mine and then says, "You were so right."

"About what?"

He slowly pulls out of me, coming down on his forearms. "You warned me. You said one time with you wouldn't be enough. You said you were like a drug. But you failed to tell me you were the most addictive kind."

Chapter Ten

"Can I ask you a personal question?"

Allysa nods as she perfects a bouquet of flowers about to go out for delivery. We're three days away from our grand opening, and it just keeps getting busier by the day.

"What is it?" Allysa asks, facing me. She leans into the counter and starts picking at her fingernails.

"You don't have to answer it if you don't want to," I warn.

"Well I can't answer it if you don't ask it."

That's a good point. "Do you and Marshall donate to charity?"

Confusion crosses her face and she says, "Yeah. Why?"

I shrug. "I was just curious. I wouldn't judge you or anything. I've just been thinking lately about how I might like to start a charity."

"What kind of charity?" she asks. "We donate to a few different ones now that we have money, but my favorite is this one we got involved with last year. They build schools in other countries. We've funded three new constructions in the past year alone."

I knew I liked her for a reason.

"I don't have that kind of money, obviously, but I'd like to do *something.* I just don't know what yet."

"Let's get through this grand opening first and then you can start thinking about philanthropy. One dream at a time,

Lily." She walks around the counter and grabs the trash can. I watch as she pulls the full bag out of it and ties it in a knot. It makes me wonder why—if she has people for everything— she would even want a job where she had to take out the trash and get her hands dirty.

"Why do you work here?" I ask her.

She glances up at me and smiles. "Because I like you," she says. But then I notice the smile completely leave her eyes right before she turns and walks toward the back to throw out the trash. When she comes back, I'm still watching her curiously. I say it again.

"Allysa? Why do you work here?"

She stops what she's doing and takes in a slow breath like maybe she's contemplating being honest with me. She walks back to the counter and leans against it, crossing her feet at her ankles.

"Because," she says, looking down at her feet. "I can't get pregnant. We've been trying for two years but nothing has worked. I was tired of sitting at home crying all the time, so I decided I should find something to keep my mind busy." She stands up straight and wipes her hands across her jeans. "And you, Lily Bloom, are keeping me *very* busy." She turns and starts messing with the same bouquet of flowers again. She's been perfecting them for half an hour. She picks up a card and stuffs it in the flowers, and then turns around and hands me the vase. "These are for you, by the way."

It's obvious Allysa wants to change the subject, so I take the flowers from her. "What do you mean?"

She rolls her eyes and waves me off to my office. "It's on the card. Go read it."

I can tell by her annoyed reaction that they're from Ryle.
I grin and run to my office. I take a seat at my desk and pull
out the card.

Lily,

I'm having serious withdrawals.
—Ryle

I smile and put the card back in the envelope. I grab my
phone and snap a picture of me holding the flowers with my
tongue sticking out. I text it to Ryle.

Me: I tried to warn you.

He immediately starts texting me back. I watch anxiously as the dots on my phone move back and forth.

**Ryle: I need my next fix. I'll be finished here in about thirty
minutes. Can I take you to dinner?**

**Me: Can't. Mom wants me to try a new restaurant with her
tonight. She's an obnoxious foodie. : (**

Ryle: I like food. I eat food. Where are you taking her?

Me: A place called Bib's on Marketson.

Ryle: Is there room for one more?

I stare at his text for a moment. *He wants to meet my mother?*
We aren't even officially dating. I mean . . . I don't *care* if he
meets my mother. She would love him. But he went from not
wanting anything to do with relationships, to possibly agreeing to test-drive one, to meeting the parents, all within five
days? *Good God.* I really *am* a drug.

Me: Sure. Meet us there in half an hour.

I walk out of my office and straight up to Allysa. I hold
my phone in front of her face. "He wants to meet my mother."

"Who?"

"Ryle."

"My brother?" she says, looking as shocked as I feel.

I nod. "Your brother. *My mother.*"

She grabs my phone and looks at the texts. "Huh. That's so weird."

I take my phone from her hands. "Thanks for the vote of confidence."

She laughs and says, "You know what I mean. It's Ryle we're talking about here. He's never, in the history of being Ryle Kincaid, met a girl's parents."

Of course hearing her say that makes me smile, but then I wonder if maybe he's doing this just to please me. If maybe he's doing things he doesn't really want to do just because he knows I want a relationship.

And then I smile even bigger, because isn't that what it's all about? Sacrificing for the person you like so that you can see them happy?

"Your brother must *really* like me," I say teasingly. I look back up at Allysa, expecting her to laugh, but there's a solemn look on her face.

She nods and says, "Yeah. I'm afraid he does." She grabs her purse from beneath the counter and says, "I'm gonna head out now. Let me know how it goes, okay?" She moves past me and I watch her as she makes her way out the door, and then I just stare at the door for a long time.

It bothers me that she doesn't seem excited about the prospect of me dating Ryle. It makes me wonder if that has more to do with her feelings toward me or her feelings toward him.

Twenty minutes later, I flip the sign to closed. *Just a few more days.* I lock the door and walk to my car, but stop short when I see someone leaning against it. It takes me a moment to recognize him. He's facing the other direction, talking on his cell phone.

I thought he was meeting me at the restaurant, but okay.

The horn beeps on my car when I hit the Unlock button, and Ryle spins around. He grins when he sees me. "Yes, I agree," he says into the phone. He wraps an arm around my shoulder and pulls me against him, pressing a kiss to the top of my head. "We'll talk about it tomorrow," he says. "Something really important just came up."

He hangs up the phone and slides it into his pocket, then he kisses me. It's not a hello kiss. It's an I've-been-thinking-about-you-nonstop kiss. He wraps both arms around me and spins me until I'm backed up against my car, where he continues to kiss me until I start to feel dizzy again. When he pulls back, he's looking down at me appreciatively.

"You know which part of you drives me the craziest?" He brings his fingers to my mouth and traces my smile. "These," he says. "Your lips. I love how they're as red as your hair and you don't even have to wear lipstick."

I grin and kiss his fingers. "I better watch you around my mom, then, because everyone says we have the same mouth."

He pauses his fingers against my lips and he stops smiling. "Lily. Just . . . *no.*"

I laugh and open my door. "Are we taking separate cars?"

He pulls the door open for me the rest of the way and says, "I took an Uber here from work. We'll ride together."

•   •   •

My mother is already seated at a table when we arrive. Her back is to the door as I lead the way.

I'm instantly impressed by the restaurant. My eyes are drawn to the warm, neutral colors painted on the walls and the almost full-sized tree in the middle of the restaurant. It looks like it's growing straight out of the floor, almost as if the entire restaurant was designed around the tree. Ryle follows closely behind me with his hand on my lower back. Once we reach the table, I begin to pull off my jacket. "Hey, Mom."

She looks up from her phone and says, "Oh, hey, honey." She drops her phone in her purse and waves her hand around the restaurant. "I already love it. Look at the lighting," she says, pointing up. "The fixtures look like something you'd grow in one of your gardens." That's when she notices Ryle, who is standing patiently next to me as I slide into the booth. My mother smiles at him and says, "We'll take two waters for now, please."

My eyes dart to Ryle and then back to my mother. "*Mom.* He's with me. He's not the waiter."

She looks up at Ryle again with confusion. He just smiles and reaches out his hand. "Honest mistake, ma'am. I'm Ryle Kincaid."

She returns the handshake, looking back and forth between us. He releases her hand and slides into the booth. She looks a little flustered when she finally says, "Jenny Bloom.

Nice to meet you." She places her attention back on me and raises an eyebrow. "A friend of yours, Lily?"

I can't believe I'm not better prepared for this moment. What in the heck do I introduce him as? My trial run? I can't say *boyfriend*, but I can't very well say *friend*. *Prospect* seems a little dated.

Ryle notices my pause, so he puts his hand on my knee and squeezes reassuringly. "My sister works for Lily," he says. "Have you met her? Allysa?"

My mother leans forward in her booth and says, "Oh! Yes! Of course. You two look so much alike now that you mention it," she says. "It's the eyes, I think. And the mouth."

He nods. "We both favor our mother."

My mother smiles at me. "People always say they think Lily favors me."

"Yes," he says. "Identical mouths. Uncanny." Ryle squeezes my knee under the table again while I try and suppress my laughter. "Ladies, if you'll excuse me, I need to head to the gentlemen's room." He leans in and kisses me on the side of the head before standing. "If the waiter comes, I'll just take water."

My mother's eyes follow Ryle as he walks away, and then she slowly turns back to me. She points at me and then to his empty seat. "How come I haven't heard about this guy?"

I smile a little. "Things are kind of . . . it's not really . . ." I have no idea how to explain our situation to my mother. "He works a lot, so we haven't really spent that much time together. At all. This is actually the first time we've been to dinner together."

My mother raises an eyebrow. "Really?" she says, leaning back in her seat. "He sure doesn't treat it like that. I mean—

he seems comfortably affectionate with you. Not normal behavior with someone you've just met."

"We didn't just meet," I say. "It's been almost a year since the first time I met him. And we've spent time together, just not on a date. He works a lot."

"Where does he work?"

"Massachusetts General Hospital."

My mother leans forward and her eyes practically bulge from her head. "Lily!" she hisses. "He's a *doctor*?"

I nod, suppressing my grin. "A neurosurgeon."

"Can I get you ladies something to drink?" a waiter asks.

"Yeah," I say. "We'll take three . . ."

And then I clamp my mouth shut.

I stare at the waiter and the waiter stares back at me. My heart is in my throat. I can't remember how to speak.

"Lily?" my mother says. She flicks her hand toward the waiter. "He's waiting for your drink order."

I shake my head and begin to stutter. "I'll . . . um . . ."

"Three waters," my mother says, interrupting my fumbled words. The waiter snaps out of his trance long enough to tap his pencil on his pad of paper.

"Three waters," he says. "Got it." He turns and walks away, but I watch as he glances back at me before pushing through the doors to the kitchen.

My mother leans forward and says, "What in the world is wrong with you?"

I point over my shoulder. "The waiter," I say, shaking my head. "He looked exactly like . . ."

I'm about to say, "*Atlas Corrigan*," when Ryle walks up and slides back into the seat.

He glances back and forth between us. "What'd I miss?"

I swallow hard, shaking my head. *Surely that wasn't really Atlas.* But those eyes—his mouth. I know it's been years since I saw him, but I'll never forget what he looked like. It *had* to be him. I know it was and I know he recognized me, too, because the second our eyes met . . . it looked like he'd seen a ghost.

"Lily?" Ryle says, squeezing my hand. "You okay?"

I nod and force a smile, then clear my throat. "Yep. We were just talking about you," I say, glancing back at my mother. "Ryle assisted in an eighteen-hour surgery this week."

My mother leans forward with interest. Ryle begins to tell her all about the surgery. Our water arrives, but it's a different waiter this time. He asks if we've had a chance to go over the menu and then tells us the chef's specials. The three of us order our food and I'm doing everything I can to focus, but my attention is all over the restaurant looking for Atlas. *I need to regroup.* After a few minutes, I lean over to Ryle. "I need to run to the restroom."

He stands up to let me out and my eyes are scanning the face of every waiter as I make my way across the room. I push through the door to the hallway that leads to the restrooms. As soon as I'm alone, my back meets the wall of the hallway. I lean forward and release a huge breath. I decide to take a moment and regain my composure before heading back out there. I bring my hands up to my forehead and close my eyes.

For nine years I've wondered what happened to him. *Years.*

"Lily?"

I glance up and suck in a breath. He's standing at the end of the hallway like a ghost straight out of the past. My eyes travel to his feet to make sure he's not suspended in the air.

He isn't. He's real, and he's standing right in front of me.

I stay pressed against the wall, not sure what to say to him. "Atlas?"

As soon as I say his name, he blows out a quick breath of relief and then takes three huge steps forward. I catch myself doing the same. We meet in the middle and throw our arms around each other. "Holy shit," he says, holding me in a tight embrace.

I nod. "Yeah. Holy shit."

He puts his hands on my shoulders and takes a step back to look at me. "You haven't changed at all."

I cover my mouth with my hand, still in shock, and give him the once-over. His face looks the same, but he's no longer the scrawny teenager I remember. "I can't say the same for you."

He looks down at himself and laughs. "Yeah," he says. "Eight years in the military will do that to ya."

We're both in shock, so nothing is said right after that. We just keep shaking our heads in disbelief. He laughs and then I laugh. Finally, he releases my shoulders and folds his arms over his chest. "What brings you to Boston?" he asks.

He says it so casually, and I'm thankful for that. Maybe he doesn't remember our conversation all those years ago about Boston, which would save me a lot of embarrassment.

"I live here," I say, forcing my answer to sound as casual as his question. "I own a flower shop over on Park Plaza."

He smiles knowingly, like it doesn't at all surprise him. I glance toward the door, knowing I should get back out there. He notices and then takes another step back. He holds my gaze for a moment and it gets really quiet. Way too quiet. There's so much to say but neither of us even knows where to start. The smile leaves his eyes for a moment and then he motions toward the door. "You should probably get back to your company," he says. "I'll look you up sometime. You said Park Plaza, right?"

I nod.

He nods.

The door swings open and a woman walks in holding a toddler. She moves between us, which puts even more distance between us. I take a step toward the door, but he remains in the same spot. Before I walk out, I turn back to him and smile. "It was really good to see you, Atlas."

He smiles a little, but it doesn't touch his eyes. "Yeah. You too, Lily."

•   •   •

I'm mostly quiet for the rest of the meal. I'm not sure Ryle or my mother even notice, though, because she's having no issue firing question after question at him. He takes it like a champ. He's very charming with my mother in all the right ways.

Unexpectedly running into Atlas tonight put such a wrinkle in my emotions, but by the end of dinner, Ryle has smoothed them back out again.

My mother takes her napkin and wipes her mouth, then points at me. "New favorite restaurant," she says. "Incredible."

Ryle nods. "I agree. I need to bring Allysa here. She loves trying new restaurants."

The food really is good, but the last thing I need is for either of these two to want to come back here. "It was okay," I say.

He pays for our meals, of course, and then insists we walk my mother to her car. I can already tell she'll be calling me about him tonight, simply by the prideful look on her face.

Once she's gone, Ryle walks me to my car.

"I requested an Uber so you wouldn't have to go out of your way to take me home. We have approximately . . ." He looks down at his phone. "One and a half minutes to make out."

I laugh. He wraps his arms around me and kisses my neck first, and then my cheek. "I would invite myself over, but I have an early surgery tomorrow and I'm sure my patient would appreciate it if I didn't spend the majority of the night inside you."

I kiss him back, both disappointed and relieved he's not coming over. "I have a grand opening in a few days. I should probably sleep, too."

"When's your next day off?" he says.

"Never. When's yours?"

"Never."

I shake my head. "We're doomed. There's just too much drive and success between the two of us."

"That means the honeymoon phase will last until we're eighty," he says. "I'll come to your grand opening Friday and then the four of us will go out and celebrate." A car pulls up beside us and he wraps his hand in my hair and kisses me goodbye. "Your mother is wonderful, by the way. Thank you for letting me come to dinner."

He backs away and climbs inside the car. I watch as it pulls out of the parking lot.

I have a really good feeling about that man.

I smile and turn toward my car, but throw a hand up to my chest and gasp when I see him.

Atlas is standing at the rear of my car.

"Sorry. Wasn't trying to scare you."

I blow out a breath. "Well, you did." I lean against the car and Atlas stays where he is, three feet away from me. He looks out at the street. "So? Who's the lucky guy?"

"He's . . ." My voice falters. This is all so weird. My chest is still constricted and my stomach is flipping, and I can't tell if it's leftover nerves from kissing Ryle or if it's the presence of Atlas. "His name is Ryle. We met about a year ago."

I instantly regret saying we met that long ago. It makes it sound like Ryle and I have been dating that long and we aren't even officially dating. "What about you? Married? Have a girlfriend?"

I'm not sure if I'm asking to extend the conversation he started, or if I'm genuinely curious.

"I do, actually. Her name is Cassie. We've been together almost a year now."

Heartburn. I think I have heartburn. *A year?* I place my hand on my chest and nod. "That's good. You seem happy."

Does he seem happy? I have no idea.

"Yeah. Well . . . I'm really glad I got to see you, Lily." He turns around to walk away, but then spins and faces me again, his hands shoved in his back pockets. "I will say . . . I kind of wish this could have happened a year ago."

I wince at his words, trying not to let them penetrate. He turns and walks back toward the restaurant.

I fumble with my keys and hit the button to unlock the car. I slide in and pull the door shut, gripping the steering wheel. For whatever reason, a huge tear falls down my cheek. A huge, pathetic, what-the-hell-is-this-wetness tear. I swipe at it and push the button to start my car.

I didn't expect to feel this much hurt after seeing him.

But it's good. This happened for a reason. My heart needed closure so I can give it to Ryle, but maybe I couldn't do that until this happened.

This is good.

Yes, I'm crying.

But it'll feel better. This is just human nature, healing an old wound to prepare for a fresh new layer.

That's all.

Chapter Eleven

I curl up in my bed and stare at it.

I'm almost finished with it. There aren't very many more entries.

I pick up the journal and place it on the pillow beside me. "I'm not going to read you," I whisper.

Although, if I read what's left, I'll be finished. Having seen Atlas tonight and knowing he has a girlfriend and a job and more than likely a home is enough closure I need on that chapter. And if I just finish the damn journal, I can put it back in the shoebox and never have to open it again.

I finally pick it up and roll onto my back. "Ellen DeGeneres, you are *such* a bitch."

Dear Ellen,

"Just keep swimming."

Recognize that quote, Ellen? It's what Dory says to Marlin in Finding Nemo.

"Just keep swimming, swimming, swimming."

I'm not a huge fan of cartoons, but I'll give you props for that one. I like cartoons that can make you laugh, but also make you feel something. After today, I think that's my favorite cartoon. Because I've been feeling like drowning lately, and sometimes people need a reminder that they just need to keep swimming.

Atlas got sick. Like really sick.

He's been crawling through my window and sleeping on the floor for a few nights in a row now, but last night, I knew something was wrong as soon as I looked at him. It was a Sunday, so I hadn't seen him since the night before, but he looked awful. His eyes were bloodshot, his skin was pale, and even though it was cold, his hair was sweaty. I didn't even ask if he was feeling okay, I already knew he wasn't. I put my hand on his forehead and he was so hot, I almost yelled for my mother.

He said, "I'll be fine, Lily," and then he started to make his pallet on the floor. I told him to wait there and then I went to the kitchen and poured him a glass of water. I found some medicine in the cabinet. It was flu medicine and I wasn't even sure if that's what was wrong with him, but I made him take some anyway.

He laid there on the floor, curled up into a ball, when, about half an hour later he said, "Lily? I think I'm gonna need a trash can."

I jumped up and grabbed the trash can from under my desk and knelt down in front of him. As soon as I set it down, he hunched over it and started throwing up.

God, I felt bad for him. Being so sick and not having a bathroom or a bed or a house or a mother. All he had was me and I didn't even know what to do for him.

When he was finished, I made him drink some water and then I told him to get on the bed. He refused, but I wasn't having it. I put the trash can on the floor next to the bed and made him move to the bed.

He was so hot and shaking so bad I was just scared to leave him on the floor. I laid down next to him and every hour for the next six hours he continued getting sick. I kept having to take the trash can to the bathroom to empty it out. I'm not gonna lie, it was gross. The grossest night I've ever had, but what else could I do? He needed me to help him and I was all he had.

When it came time for him to leave my room this morning, I told him to go back to his house and I'd be over to check on him before school. I'm surprised he even had the energy to crawl out of my window. I left the trash can next to my bed and waited for my mom to come wake me up. When she did, she saw the trash can and immediately held her hand to my forehead. "Lily, are you okay?"

I groaned and shook my head. "No. I was up all night sick. I think it's over now, but I haven't slept."

She picked up the trash can and told me to stay in bed, that she'd call the school and let them know I wasn't coming. After she left for work, I went and got Atlas and told him he could stay with me at the house all day. He was still getting sick, so I let him use my room to sleep. I'd check on him every half hour or so and finally around lunch he stopped throwing up. He went and took a shower and then I made him some soup.

He was too tired to even eat it. I got a blanket and we both sat down on the couch and covered up together. I don't know when I started feeling comfortable enough to snuggle up to him, but it just felt right. A few minutes later, he leaned over a little and pressed his lips against my collarbone, right between my shoulder and my neck. It was a quick kiss and I don't think he meant for it to be romantic. It was more like a thank-you gesture, without using actual words. But it made me feel all kinds of things. It's been a few hours now and I keep touching that spot with my fingers because I can still feel it.

I know it was probably the worst day of his life, Ellen. But it was one of my favorites.

I feel really bad about that.

We watched Finding Nemo *and when that part came up where Marlin was looking for Nemo and he was feeling really defeated, Dory said to him, "When life gets you down do you wanna know what you've gotta do? . . . Just keep swimming. Just keep swimming. Just keep swimming, swimming, swimming."*

Atlas grabbed my hand when Dory said that. He didn't hold it like a boyfriend holds his girlfriend's hand. He squeezed it, like he was saying that was us. He was Marlin and I was Dory, and I was helping him swim.

"Just keep swimming," I whispered to him.

—Lily

Dear Ellen,

I'm scared. So scared.

I like him a lot. He's all I think about when we're together and I feel worried sick about him when we're not. My life is beginning to revolve around him and that's not good, I know. But I can't help it and I don't know what to do about it, and now he might leave.

He left after we finished watching Finding Nemo *yesterday and then when my parents went to bed, he crawled in my window last night. He had slept in my bed the night before because he was sick, and I know I shouldn't have done it, but I put his blankets in the washing machine right before I went to bed. He asked where his pallet was and I told him he'd have to sleep on the bed again because I wanted to wash his blankets and make sure they were clean so he wouldn't get sick again.*

For a minute, it looked like he was going to go back out the window. But then he shut it and took off his shoes and crawled in the bed with me.

He wasn't sick anymore, but when he laid down I thought maybe

I had gotten sick because my stomach felt queasy. But I wasn't sick. I just always feel queasy when he's that close to me.

We were facing each other on the bed when he said, "When do you turn sixteen?"

"Two more months," I whispered. We just kept staring at each other, and my heart was beating faster and faster. "When do you turn nineteen?" I asked, just trying to make conversation so he couldn't hear how hard I was breathing.

"Not until October," he said.

I nodded. I wondered why he was curious about my age and it made me wonder what he thought about fifteen-year-olds. Did he look at me like I was just a little kid? Like a little sister? I was almost sixteen, and two and a half years apart in age isn't that bad. Maybe when two people are fifteen and eighteen, it might seem a little too far apart. But once I turn sixteen, I bet no one would even think twice about a two-and-a-half-year age difference.

"I need to tell you something," he said.

I held my breath, not knowing what he was going to say.

"I got in touch with my uncle today. My mom and I used to live with him in Boston. He told me once he gets back from his work trip I can stay with him."

I should have been so happy for him in that moment. I should have smiled and told him congratulations. But I felt all of the immaturity of my age when I closed my eyes and felt sorry for myself.

"Are you going?" I asked.

He shrugged. "I don't know. I wanted to talk to you about it first."

He was so close to me on the bed, I could feel the warmth of his breath. I also noticed he smelled like mint, and it made me wonder if he uses bottled water to brush his teeth before he comes over here. I always send him home every day with lots of water.

I brought my hand up to the pillow and started pulling at a feather sticking out of it. When I got it all the way out, I twisted it between my fingers. "I don't know what to say, Atlas. I'm happy you have a place to stay. But what about school?"

"I could finish down there," he said.

I nodded. It sounded like he already made up his mind. "When are you leaving?"

I wondered how far away Boston is. It's probably a few hours, but that's a whole world away when you don't own a car.

"I don't know for sure that I am."

I dropped the feather back onto the pillow and brought my hand to my side. "What's stopping you? Your uncle is offering you a place to stay. That's good, right?"

He tightened his lips together and nodded. Then he picked up the feather I'd been playing with and he started twisting it between his fingers. He laid it back down on the pillow and then he did something I wasn't expecting. He moved his fingers to my lips and he touched them.

God, Ellen. I thought I was gonna die right then and there. It was the most I'd ever felt inside my body at one time. He kept his fingers there for a few seconds, and he said, "Thank you, Lily. For everything." He moved his fingers up and through my hair, and then he leaned forward and planted a kiss on my forehead. I was breathing so hard, I had to open my mouth to catch more air. I could see his chest moving just as hard as mine was. He looked down at me and I watched as his eyes went right to my mouth. "Have you ever been kissed, Lily?"

I shook my head no and tilted my face up to his because I needed him to change that right then and there or I wasn't gonna be able to breathe.

Then—almost as if I were made of eggshells—he lowered his

mouth to mine and just rested it there. I didn't know what to do next, but I didn't care. I didn't care if we just stayed like that all night and never even moved our mouths, it was everything.

His lips closed over mine and I could kind of feel his hand shaking. I did what he was doing and started to move my lips like he was. I felt the tip of his tongue brush across my lips once and I thought my eyes were about to roll back in my head. He did it again, and then a third time, so I finally did it, too. When our tongues touched for the first time, I kind of smiled a little, because I'd thought about my first kiss a lot. Where it would be, who it would be with. Never in a million years did I imagine it would feel like this.

He pushed me on my back and pressed his hand against my cheek and kept kissing me. It just got better and better as I grew more comfortable. My favorite moment was when he pulled back for a second and looked down at me, then came back even harder.

I don't know how long we kissed. A long time. So long, my mouth started to hurt and my eyes couldn't stay open. When we fell asleep, I'm pretty sure his mouth was still touching mine.

We didn't talk about Boston again.

I still don't know if he's leaving.

—Lily

•   •   •

Dear Ellen,

I need to apologize to you.

It's been a week since I've written to you and a week since I've watched your show. Don't worry, I still record it so you'll get the ratings, but every day we get off the bus, Atlas takes a quick shower and then we make out.

Every day.

It's awesome.

I don't know what it is about him, but I feel so comfortable with him. He's so sweet and thoughtful. He never does anything I don't feel comfortable with, but so far he hasn't tried anything I don't feel comfortable with.

I'm not sure how much I should divulge here, since you and I have never met in person. But let me just say that if he's ever wondered what my boobs feel like . . .

Now he knows.

I can't for the life of me figure out how people function from day to day when they like someone this much. If it were up to me, we would kiss all day and all night and do nothing in between except maybe talk a little. He tells funny stories. I love it when he's in a talkative mood because it doesn't happen very often, but he uses his hands a lot. He smiles a lot, too, and I love his smile even more than I love his kiss. And sometimes I just tell him to shut up and stop smiling or kissing or talking so I can stare at him. I like looking at his eyes. They're so blue that he could be standing across a room and a person could tell how blue his eyes were. The only thing I don't like about kissing him sometimes is when he closes his eyes.

And no. We still haven't talked about Boston.

—Lily

Dear Ellen,

Yesterday afternoon when we were riding the bus, Atlas kissed me. It wasn't anything new to us because we had kissed a lot by this point, but it's the first time he ever did it in public. When we're together everything else just seems to fade away, so I don't think he even thought about other people noticing. But Katie noticed. She was sitting in the seat behind us and I heard her say, "Gross," as soon as he leaned over and kissed me.

She was talking to the girl next to her when she said, "I can't believe Lily lets him touch her. He wears the same clothes almost every day."

Ellen, I was so mad. I also felt awful for Atlas. He pulled away from me and I could tell what she said bothered him. I started to turn around to yell at her for judging someone she doesn't even know, but he grabbed my hand and shook his head no.

"Don't, Lily," he said.

So I didn't.

But for the rest of the bus ride, I was so angry. I was angry that Katie would say something so ignorant just to hurt someone she thought was beneath her. I was also hurt that Atlas appeared to be used to comments like that.

I didn't want him to think I was embarrassed that anyone saw him kiss me. I know Atlas better than any of them do, and I know what a good person he is, no matter what his clothes look like or that he used to smell before he started using my shower.

I leaned over and kissed him on the cheek and then rested my head on his shoulder.

"You know what?" I said to him.

He slid his fingers through mine and squeezed my hand. "What?"

"You're my favorite person."

I felt him laugh a little and it made me smile.

"Out of how many people?" he asked.

"All of them."

He kissed the top of my head and said, "You're my favorite person, too, Lily. By a long shot."

When the bus came to a stop on my street, he didn't let go of my hand when we started to walk off. He was in front of me in the aisle and I was walking behind him, so he didn't see it when I turned around and flipped off Katie.

I probably shouldn't have done it, but the look on her face made it worth it.

When we got to my house, he took the house key out of my hand and unlocked my front door. It was weird, seeing how comfortable he is at my house now. He walked in and locked the door behind us. That's when we noticed the electricity in the house wasn't working. I looked out the window and saw a utility truck down the street working on the power lines, so that meant we couldn't watch your show. I wasn't too upset because it meant we would probably just make out for an hour and a half.

"Does your oven run off gas or electricity?" he asked.

"Gas," I said, a little confused that he was asking about our oven.

He kicked off his shoes (which were really just a pair of my father's old shoes) and he started walking toward the kitchen. "I'm going to make you something," he said.

"You know how to cook?"

He opened the refrigerator and started moving things around. "Yep. I probably love to cook as much as you love to grow things." He took a few things out of the refrigerator and preheated the oven. I leaned against the counter and watched him. He wasn't even looking at a recipe. He was just pouring things into bowls and mixing them without even using a measuring cup.

I had never seen my father lift a finger in the kitchen. I'm pretty sure he wouldn't even know how to preheat our oven. I kind of thought most men were like that, but watching Atlas work his way around my kitchen proved me wrong.

"What are you making?" I asked him. I pushed my hands on the island and hoisted myself onto it.

"Cookies," he said. He walked the bowl over to me and stuck a spoon in the mixture. He brought the spoon up to my mouth and I tasted it. One of my weaknesses is cookie dough, and this was the best I'd ever tasted.

"Oh, wow," I said, licking my lips.

He set the bowl down beside me and then leaned in and kissed me. Cookie dough and Atlas's mouth mixed together is like heaven, in case you're wondering. I made a noise deep in my throat that let him know how much I liked the combination, and it made him laugh. But he didn't stop kissing me. He just laughed through the kiss and it completely melted my heart. A happy Atlas was near mind-blowing. It made me want to uncover every single thing about this world that he likes and give it all to him.

When he was kissing me, I wondered if I loved him. I've never had a boyfriend before and have nothing to compare my feelings to. In fact, I've never really wanted a boyfriend or a relationship until Atlas. I'm not growing up in a household with a great example of how a man should treat someone he loves, so I've always held on to an unhealthy amount of distrust when it comes to relationships and other people.

There have been times I've wondered if I could ever allow myself to trust a guy. For the most part, I hate men because the only example I have is my father. But spending all this time with Atlas is changing me. Not in a huge way, I don't think. I still distrust most people. But Atlas is changing me enough to believe that maybe he's an exception to the norm.

He stopped kissing me and picked up the bowl again. He walked it over to the opposite counter and started spooning dough onto two cookie sheets.

"You want to know a trick to cooking with a gas oven?" he asked.

I'm not sure I really ever cared about cooking before, but he somehow made me want to know everything he knew. It might have been how happy he looked when he talked about it.

"Gas ovens have hot spots," he said as he opened the oven door and put the cookie sheets inside. "You have to be sure and rotate the pans so they'll cook evenly." He closed the door and pulled the oven mitt off his hand. He tossed it on the counter. "A pizza stone helps, too. If you just keep it in the oven, even when you aren't baking pizza, it helps eliminate the hot spots."

He walked over to me and placed his hands on either side of me. The electricity kicked on right as he was pulling down the collar of my shirt. He kissed the spot on my shoulder he always loves kissing and slowly slid his hands up my back. I swear, sometimes when he's not even here I can still feel his lips on my collarbone.

He was about to kiss me on the mouth when we heard a car pull into the driveway and the garage door start to open. I jumped off the island, looking around the kitchen frantically. His hands went up to my cheeks and he made me look at him.

"Keep an eye on the cookies. They'll be finished in about twenty minutes." He pressed his lips to mine and then released me, rushing to the living room to grab his backpack. He made it out the back door right when I heard the engine to my father's car shut off.

I started gathering all the ingredients together when my father walked into the kitchen from the garage. He looked around and then saw the light on in the oven.

"Are you cooking?" he asked.

I nodded because my heart was beating so fast, I was scared he'd hear the trembling in my voice if I responded out loud. I scrubbed *for a moment at a spot on the counter that was perfectly clean. I cleared my throat and said, "Cookies. I'm baking cookies."*

He set his briefcase down on the kitchen table and then walked to the refrigerator and pulled out a beer.

"The electricity has been out," I said. "I was bored so I decided to bake while I waited for it to come back on."

My father sat down at the table and spent the next ten minutes asking me questions about school and if I'd thought about going to college. Occasionally when it was just the two of us, I saw glimpses of a how a normal relationship with a father could be. Sitting at the kitchen table with him discussing colleges and career choices and high school. As much as I hated him most of the time, I still longed for more of these moments with him. If he could just always be the guy he was capable of being in these moments, things would be so much different. For all of us.

I rotated the cookies like Atlas had said to do and when they were finished, I pulled them out of the oven. I took one off the cookie sheet and handed it to my father. I hated that I was being nice to him. It almost felt like I was wasting one of Atlas's cookies.

"Wow," my father said. "These are great, Lily."

I forced a thank-you, even though I didn't make them. I couldn't very well tell him that, though.

"They're for school so you can only have one," I lied. I waited until the rest of them cooled and then I put them in a Tupperware container and took them to my room. I didn't even want to try one without Atlas, so I waited until later last night when he came over.

"You should have tried one when they were hot," he said. "That's when they're the best."

"I didn't want to eat them without you," I said. We sat on the bed with our backs against the wall and proceeded to eat half the

bowl of cookies. I told him they were delicious, but failed to tell him they were by far the greatest cookies I'd ever eaten. I didn't want to inflate his ego. I kind of liked how humble he was.

I tried to grab at another one, but he pulled the bowl away and put the lid back on it. "If you eat too many you'll make yourself sick and you won't like my cookies anymore."

I laughed. "Impossible."

He took a drink of water and then stood up, facing the bed. "I made you something," he said, reaching into his pocket.

"More cookies?" I asked.

He smiled and shook his head, then held out a fist. I lifted my hand and he dropped something hard in the palm of my hand. It was a small, flat outline of a heart, about two inches long, carved out of wood.

I rubbed my thumb over it, trying not to smile too big. It wasn't an anatomically correct heart, but it also didn't look like the hand-drawn hearts. It was uneven and hollow in the middle.

"You made this?" I asked, looking up at him.

He nodded. "I carved it with an old whittling knife I found at the house."

The ends of the heart weren't connected. They just curved in a little, leaving a little space at the top of the heart. I didn't even know what to say. I felt him sit back down on the bed but I couldn't stop looking at it long enough to even thank him.

"I carved it out of a branch," he said, whispering. "From the oak tree in your backyard."

I swear, Ellen. I never thought I could love something so much. Or maybe what I was feeling wasn't for the gift, but for him. I closed my fist around the heart and then leaned over and kissed him so hard, he fell back onto the bed. I threw my leg over him and straddled him and he grabbed my waist and grinned against my mouth.

"I'm gonna carve you a damn house out of that oak tree if this is the reward I get," he whispered.

I laughed. "You have to stop being so perfect," I told him. "You're already my favorite person but now you're making it really unfair to all the other humans because no one will ever be able to catch up to you."

He brought his hand to the back of my head and rolled me until I was on my back and he was the one on top. "Then my plan is working," he said, right before kissing me again.

I held on to the heart while we kissed, wanting to believe it was a gift for no reason at all. But part of me was scared it was a gift to remember him by when he leaves for Boston.

I didn't want to remember him. If I had to remember him, it would mean he wasn't a part of my life anymore.

I don't want him to move to Boston, Ellen. I know that's selfish of me because he can't keep living in that house. I don't know what I'm more afraid might happen. Watching him leave or selfishly begging him not to go.

I know we need to talk about it. I'll ask him about Boston tonight when he comes over. I just didn't want to ask him last night because it was a really perfect day.

—Lily

Dear Ellen,

Just keep swimming. Just keep swimming.

He's moving to Boston.

I don't really feel like talking about it.

—Lily

Dear Ellen,

This is going to be a big one for my mother to hide.

My father is usually pretty cognizant of hitting her where it won't leave a visible bruise. The last thing he probably wants is for people in the town to know what he does to her. I've seen him kick her a few times, choke her, hit her on the back and the stomach, pull her hair. The few times he's hit her on the face, it's always just been a slap, so the marks wouldn't stay for long.

But never have I seen him do what he did last night.

It was really late when they got home. It was a weekend, so he and my mom went to some community function. My father has a real estate company and he's also the town mayor, so they have to do things in the public a lot like go to charity dinners. Which is ironic, since my father hates charities. But I guess he has to save face.

Atlas was already in my room when they got home. I could hear them fighting as soon as they walked through the front door. A lot of the conversation was muffled, but for the most part, it sounded like my father was accusing her of flirting with some man.

Now I know my mother, Ellen. She would never do something like that. If anything, a guy probably looked at her and it made my father jealous. My mother is really beautiful.

I heard him call her a whore and then I heard the first blow. I started to climb out of my bed but Atlas pulled me back and told me not to go in there, that I might get hurt. I told him it actually helps sometimes. That when I go in there, my father backs off.

Atlas tried to talk me out of it, but finally I got up and went out into the living room.

Ellen.

I just . . .

He was on top of her.

They were on the couch and he had his hand around her throat, but his other hand was pulling up her dress. She was trying to fight him off and I just stood there, frozen. She kept begging him to get off her and then he hit her right across the face and told her to shut up. I'll never forget his words when he said, "You want attention? I'll give you some fucking attention." And that's when she got real still and stopped fighting him. I heard her crying, and then she said, "Please be quiet. Lily is here."

She said, "Please be quiet."

Please be quiet while you rape me, dear.

Ellen, I didn't know one human was capable of feeling so much hate inside one heart. And I'm not even talking about my father. I'm talking about me.

I walked straight to the kitchen and I opened a drawer. I grabbed the biggest knife I could find and . . . I don't know how to explain it. It was like I wasn't even in my own body. I could see myself walking across the kitchen with the knife in my hand, and I knew I wasn't going to use it. I just wanted something bigger than myself that could scare him away from her. But right before I made it out of the kitchen, two arms went around my waist and picked me up from behind. I dropped the knife, and my father didn't hear it but my mother did. We locked eyes as Atlas carried me back to my bedroom. When we were back inside my room, I just started hitting him in the chest, trying to get back out there to her. I was crying and doing everything I could to get him out of my way, but he wouldn't move.

He just wrapped his arms around me and said, "Lily, calm down." He kept saying it over and over, and he held me there for a long time until I accepted that he wasn't gonna let me go back out there. He wasn't gonna let me have that knife.

He walked over to the bed and grabbed his jacket and started putting on his shoes. "We'll go next door," he said. "We'll call the police."

The police.

My mother had warned me not to call the police in the past. She said it could jeopardize my father's career. But in all honesty, I didn't care at that point. I didn't care that he was the mayor or that everyone who loved him didn't know the awful side of him. The only thing I cared about was helping my mother, so I pulled on my jacket and went to the closet for a pair of shoes. When I stepped out of my closet, Atlas was staring at my bedroom door.

It was opening.

My mother stepped inside and quickly shut it, locking it behind her. I'll never forget what she looked like. She had blood coming down from her lip. Her eye was already starting to swell, and she had a clump of hair just resting on her shoulder. She looked at Atlas and then me.

I didn't even take a moment to feel scared that she caught me in my room with a boy. I didn't care about that. I was just worried about her. I walked over to her and grabbed her hands and walked her to my bed. I brushed the hair off her shoulder and then from her forehead.

"He's gonna go call the police, Mom. Okay?"

Her eyes grew real wide and she started shaking her head. "No," she said. She looked over at Atlas and said, "You can't. No."

He was already at the window about to leave, so he stopped and looked at me.

"He's drunk, Lily," she said. "He heard your door shut, so he went to our bedroom. He stopped. If you call the police, it'll just make it worse, believe me. Just let him sleep it off, it'll be better tomorrow."

I shook my head and could feel the tears stinging my eyes. "Mom, he was trying to rape you!"

She ducked her head and winced when I said that. She shook her head again and said, "It's not like that, Lily. We're married, and sometimes marriage is just . . . you're too young to understand it."

It got really quiet for a minute, and then I said. "I hope to hell I never do."

That's when she started to cry. She just held her head in her hands and she started to sob and all I could do was wrap my arms around her and cry with her. I'd never seen her this upset. Or this hurt. Or this scared. It broke my heart, Ellen.

It broke me.

When she was finished crying, I looked around the room and Atlas had left. We went to the kitchen and I helped her clean up her lip and her eye. She never did say anything about him being there. Not one thing. I waited for her to tell me I was grounded, but she never did. I realized that maybe she didn't acknowledge it because that's what she does. Things that hurt her just get swept under the rug, never to be brought up again.

—Lily

Dear Ellen,

I think I'm ready to talk about Boston now.

He left today.

I've shuffled my deck of cards so many times, my hands hurt. I'm scared if I don't get out how I feel on paper, I'll go crazy holding it all in.

Our last night didn't go over so well. We kissed a lot at first, but we were both too sad to really care about it. For the second time in two days, he told me he changed his mind and that he wasn't *leaving. He didn't want to leave me alone in this house. But I've lived with these parents for almost sixteen years. It was silly of him to turn down a home in favor of being homeless, just because of me. We both knew that, but it still hurt.*

I tried to not be so sad about it, so when we were lying there, I asked him to tell me about Boston. I told him maybe one day when I got out of school, I could go there.

He got this look in his eye when he started talking about it. A look I'd never seen. Sort of like he was talking about heaven. He told me about how everyone has the greatest accents there. Instead of car, they say cah. He must not realize that he sometimes says his r's like that, too. He said he lived there from the ages of nine until he was fourteen, so I guess maybe he picked up a little bit of the accent.

He told me about how his uncle lives in an apartment building with the coolest rooftop deck.

"A lot of apartments have them," he said. "Some even have pools."

Plethora, Maine, probably didn't even have a building that was tall enough for a rooftop deck. I wondered what it would feel like to be that high up. I asked him if he ever went up there and he said yes. That when he was younger, sometimes he would go to the roof and just sit up there and think while he looked out over the city.

He told me about the food. I already knew he liked to cook but I had no idea how much passion he had for it. I guess because he doesn't have a stove or a kitchen, so other than the cookies he baked me, he's never really talked about cooking before.

He told me about the harbor and how, before his mother remarried, she used to take him fishing out there. "I mean, Boston isn't any different from any other big city, I guess," he said. "There's not a lot that makes it stand out. It's just . . . I don't know. There's a vibe. A really good energy. When people say they live in Boston, they're proud of it. I miss that sometimes."

I ran my fingers through his hair and said, "Well, you make it sound like the best place in the world. Like everything is better in Boston."

He looked at me and his eyes were sad when he said. "Everything is almost better in Boston. Except the girls. Boston doesn't have you."

That made me blush. He kissed me real sweet and then I said to him, "Boston doesn't have me yet. Someday I'll move there and I'll find you."

He made me promise. Said if I moved to Boston, everything really would be better there and it would be the best city in the world.

We kissed some more. And did other things that I won't bore you with. Although, that's not to say they were boring.

They were not.

But then this morning I had to tell him goodbye. And he held me and kissed me so much, I thought I might die if he let go.

But I didn't die. Because he let go and here I am. Still living. Still breathing.

Just barely.

—Lily

I flip to the next page, but then slam the book shut. There's only one more entry and I don't know that I really feel like reading it right now. Or ever. I put the journal back in my closet, knowing that my chapter with Atlas is over. He's happy now.

I'm happy now.

Time can definitely heal all wounds.

Or at least most of them.

I turn off my lamp and then pick up my phone to plug it in. I have two missed text messages from Ryle and one from my mother.

Ryle: Hey. Naked Truth commencing in 3 . . . 2 . . .

Ryle: I was worried that being in a relationship would add to my responsibilities. That's why I've avoided them my whole life. I already have enough on my plate, and seeing the stress my parents' marriage seemed to cause them, and the failed marriages of some of my friends, I wanted no part in something like that. But after tonight, I realized that maybe a lot of people are just doing it wrong. Because what's happening between us doesn't feel like a responsibility. It feels like a reward. And I'll fall asleep wondering what I did to deserve it.

I pull my phone to my chest and smile. Then I screen-shot the text because I'm keeping it forever. I open up the third text message.

Mom: A doctor, Lily? AND your own business? I want to be you when I grow up.

I screen-shot that one, too.

Chapter Twelve

"What are you doing to those poor flowers?" Allysa asks from behind me.

I clamp another silver washer closed and slide it down the stem. "Steampunk."

We both stand back and admire the bouquet. At least . . . I *hope* she's looking at it with admiration. It turned out better than I thought it would. I used florist dip dye to turn some white roses a deep purple. Then I decorated the stems with different steampunk elements, like tiny metal washers and gears, and even super-glued a small clock to the brown leather strap that's holding the bouquet together.

"*Steampunk?*"

"It's a trend. Kind of a subgenre of fiction, but it's catching on in other areas. Art. Music." I turn around and smile, holding up the bouquet. "And now . . . *flowers.*"

Allysa takes the flowers from me and holds them up in front of her. "They're so . . . weird. I love them so much." She hugs them. "Can I have them?"

I pull them away from her. "No, they're our grand opening display. Not for sale." I take the flowers from her and grab the vase I made yesterday. I found a pair of old buttonup women's boots at a flea market last week. They reminded me of the steampunk style, and the boots are actually where I got the idea for the flowers. I washed the boots last week, dried them, and then super-glued pieces of metal to them. Once I brushed them with Mod Podge, I was able to line the inside with a vase to hold water for the flowers.

"Allysa?" I place the flowers on the center display table. "I'm pretty sure this is exactly what I was supposed to do with my life."

"Steampunk?" she asks.

I laugh and spin around. "Create!" I say. And then I flip the sign to open, fifteen minutes early.

We both spend the day busier than we thought we'd be. Between phone orders, Internet orders, and walk-ins, neither of us even has time to take a lunch break.

"You need more employees," Allysa says as she passes me, holding two bouquets of flowers. That is at one o'clock.

"You need more employees," she says to me at two o'clock, holding the phone to her ear and writing down an order while ringing someone up at the register.

Marshall stops by after three o'clock and asks how it's going. Allysa says, "She needs more employees."

I help a woman take a bouquet to her car at four o'clock, and as I'm walking back inside, Allysa is walking out, holding another bouquet. "You need more employees," she says, exasperated.

At six o'clock, she locks the door and flips the sign. She falls against the door and slides to the floor, looking up at me.

"I know," I tell her. "I need more employees."

She just nods.

And then we laugh. I walk over to where she's seated and I sit next to her. We lean our heads together and look at the store. The steampunk flowers are front and center, and although I refused to sell this particular bouquet, we had eight preorders for more of them.

"I'm proud of you, Lily," she says.

I smile. "I couldn't have done it without you, Issa."

We sit there for several minutes, enjoying the rest we're finally giving our feet. This was honestly one of the best days I've ever had, but I can't help but feel a nagging sadness that Ryle never stopped by. He also never texted.

"Have you heard from your brother today?" I ask.

She shakes her head. "No, but I'm sure he's just busy."

I nod. I know he's busy.

We both look up when someone knocks on the door. I smile when I see him cupping his hands around his eyes with his face pressed to the window. He finally looks down and sees us sitting on the floor.

"Speak of the devil," Allysa says.

I jump up and unlock the door to let him in. As soon as I open it, he's pushing his way inside. "I missed it? I did. I missed it." He hugs me. "I'm sorry, I tried to get here as soon as I could."

I hug him back and say, "It's fine. You're here. It was perfect." I'm giddy with excitement that he made it at all.

"*You're* perfect," he says, kissing me.

Allysa brushes past us. "*You're* perfect," she mimics. "Hey Ryle, guess what?"

Ryle releases me. "What?"

Allysa grabs the trash can and drops it on the counter. "Lily needs to hire more employees."

I laugh at her constant repetition. Ryle squeezes my hand and says, "Sounds like business was good."

I shrug. "I can't complain. I mean . . . I'm no *brain* surgeon, but I'm pretty good at what I do."

Ryle laughs. "You guys need any help cleaning up?"

Allysa and I put him to work, helping us clean up after the big day. We get everything finished and prepped for tomorrow, and then Marshall arrives just as we're finishing up. He's carrying a bag when he walks inside and drops it on the counter. He begins to pull out huge lumps of some kind of material and tosses them at each of us. I catch mine and unfold it.

It's a onesie.

With kittens all over it.

"Bruins game. Free beer. Suit up, team!"

Allysa groans and says, "Marshall, you made six million dollars this year. Do we *really* need free beer?"

He shoves a finger against her lips, pushing them in opposite directions. "Shh! Don't speak like a rich girl, Issa. Blasphemy."

She laughs and Marshall grabs the onesie out of her hand. He unzips it and helps her into it. Once we're all suited up, we lock the door and head to the bar.

I've never in my life seen so many men in onesies. Allysa and I are the only women wearing them, but I kind of like that. It's loud. So loud, and each time the Bruins make a good play, Allysa and I have to cover our ears from the screams. After about half an hour, a booth on the top floor opens up and we all run upstairs to claim it.

"Much better," Allysa says as we slide in. It's much quieter up here, although still loud compared to normal standards.

A waitress comes over to take our drink order. I order red wine, and as soon as I do, Marshall practically jumps out of his seat. "Wine?" he yells. "You're in a onesie! You don't get free wine with a onesie!"

He tells the waitress to bring me a beer, instead. Ryle tells her to bring me wine. Allysa wants water, and this upsets Marshall even more. He tells the waitress to bring four bottles of beer and then Ryle says, "Two beers, red wine, and a water." The waitress is very confused by the time she leaves our table.

Marshall throws his arm around Allysa and kisses her. "How am I supposed to try and knock you up tonight if you aren't a little wasted?"

The look on Allysa's face changes, and I feel instantly bad for her. I know Marshall only said that in fun, but it has to bother her. She was just telling me a few days ago how depressed she is that she can't get pregnant.

"I can't have beer, Marshall."

"Then drink wine, at least. You like me more when you're tipsy." He laughs at himself, but Allysa doesn't.

"I can't have wine, either. I can't have *any* alcohol, actually."

Marshall stops laughing.

My heart does a flip-flop.

Marshall turns in the booth and grabs her shoulders, making her face him straight-on. "Allysa?"

She just starts nodding and I don't know who starts crying first. Me or Marshall or Allysa. "I'm gonna be a dad?" he yells.

She's still nodding, and I'm just bawling like an idiot. Marshall jumps up in the booth and yells, "I'm gonna be a dad!"

I can't even explain what this moment is like. A grown man in a onesie, standing up in a booth at a bar, yelling to whoever will listen that he's gonna be a dad. He pulls her up and they're both standing in the booth now. He kisses her and it's the sweetest thing I've ever seen.

Until I look at Ryle and catch him chewing on his bottom lip like he's trying to blink back a potential tear. He glances at me and sees me staring, so he looks away. "Shut up," he says. "She's my sister."

I smile and lean over and kiss him on the cheek. "Congratulations, Uncle Ryle."

Once the parents-to-be stop making out in the booth, Ryle and I both stand up and congratulate them. Allysa said she's been feeling sick for a while, but just took a test this morning before our grand opening. She was going to wait and tell Marshall tonight when they got home, but she couldn't hold it in for another second.

Our drinks come and we order food. Once the waitress walks away, I look at Marshall. "How did you two meet?"

He says, "Allysa tells the story better than I do."

Allysa perks up and leans forward. "I hated him," she says. "He was Ryle's best friend and he was always at the house. I thought he was so annoying. He had just moved to Ohio from Boston and he had that Boston accent. He thought it made him so cool but I just wanted to slap him every time he spoke."

"She's *so* sweet," Marshall says, sarcastically.

"You were an idiot," Allysa replies, rolling her eyes. "Anyway, one day Ryle and I had a few friends over. Nothing big, but our parents were out of town, so of course we had a little get-together."

"There were thirty people there," Ryle says. "It was a party."

"Okay, a party," Allysa says. "I walked into the kitchen and Marshall was standing there pressed up against some floozy."

"She wasn't a floozy," he says. "She was a nice girl. Tasted like Cheetos, but . . ."

Allysa glares at him so he shuts up. She turns back to me. "I lost it," she says. "I started yelling at him to take his whores to his own house. The girl was literally so terrified of me, she ran for the door and didn't come back."

"Cock blocker," Marshall says.

Allysa punches him in the shoulder. "Anyway. After I cock blocked him, I ran to my room, embarrassed that I did that. It was out of pure jealousy, and I didn't even realize I liked him that way until I saw his hands on some other girl's ass. I threw myself on my bed and started crying. A few minutes later, he walked into my room and asked me if I was okay. I rolled over and yelled, 'I *like* you, you stupid fuck-face!' "

"And the rest is history . . ." Marshall says.

I laugh. "Awe. Stupid fuck-face. How sweet."

Ryle holds up a finger and says, "You're leaving out the best part."

Allysa shrugs. "Oh yeah. So Marshall walked over to me, pulled me off the bed, kissed me with the same mouth he was just kissing the floozy with, and we made out for half an hour. Ryle walked in on us and started screaming at Marshall. Then Marshall pushed Ryle out of my bedroom, locked the door, and made out with me for another hour."

Ryle is shaking his head. "Betrayed by my best friend."

Marshall pulls Allysa to him. "I like her, you stupid fuck-face."

I laugh, but Ryle turns to me with a serious look on his

face. "I didn't speak to him for an entire month, I was so mad. I eventually got over it. We were eighteen, she was seventeen. Wasn't much I could do in the way of keeping them apart."

"Wow," I say. "I sometimes forget how close in age you two are."

Allysa smiles and says, "Three kids in three years. I feel so sorry for my parents."

The table grows quiet. I see an apologetic look pass from Allysa to Ryle.

"Three?" I ask. "You have another sibling?"

Ryle straightens up and takes a sip of his beer. He sets it back down on the table and says, "We had an older brother. He passed away when we were kids."

Such a great night, ruined by a simple question. Luckily, Marshall redirects the conversation like a pro.

I spend the rest of the evening listening to stories about them growing up. I'm not sure I've ever laughed as hard as I have tonight.

When the game is over, we all walk back to the shop to retrieve our cars. Ryle said he caught an Uber over earlier, so he'll just ride with me. Before Allysa and Marshall leave, I tell her to hold on. I run inside the store and grab the steampunk flowers and run them back to their car. Her face lights up when I hand them to her.

"I'm happy you're pregnant but that's not why I'm giving you these flowers. I just want you to have them. Because you're my best friend."

Allysa squeezes me and whispers in my ear. "I hope he marries you someday. We'll be even better sisters."

She climbs inside the car and they leave, and I just stand

there watching them because I don't know that I've ever had a friend like her in my whole life. Maybe it's the wine. I don't know, but I love today. Everything about it. I especially love how Ryle looks, leaning against my car, watching me.

"You're really beautiful when you're happy."

Ugh! This day! Perfect!

.   .   .

We're making our way up the stairs to my apartment when Ryle grabs my waist and pushes me against the wall. He just starts kissing me, right there in the stairwell.

"Impatient," I mutter.

He laughs and cups my ass with both of his hands. "Nope. It's this onesie. You really should consider making this your business attire." He kisses me again and doesn't stop kissing me until someone passes us, heading down the stairs.

The guy mumbles, "Nice onesies," as he squeezes past us. "Did the Bruins win?"

Ryle nods. "Three to one," he responds, without looking up at the guy.

"Nice," the guy says.

Once he's gone, I step away from Ryle. "What is this onesie thing? Does every male in Boston know about this?"

He laughs and says, "Free beer, Lily. It's free beer." He pulls me up the stairs, and when we walk in the door, Lucy is standing at the kitchen table taping up a box of her stuff. There's another box she hasn't taped up yet and I could swear I see a bowl that I bought at HomeGoods sticking out of the top. She said she'd have all her stuff out by next week, but I have a feeling she'll conveniently have some of *my* stuff out, too.

"Who are you?" she asks, looking Ryle up and down.

"Ryle Kincaid. I'm Lily's boyfriend."

Lily's boyfriend.

Did you hear that?

Boyfriend.

It's the first time he's confirmed it, and he said it so confidently. "My boyfriend, huh?" I walk into the kitchen and grab a bottle of wine and two wineglasses.

Ryle comes up behind me as I'm pouring the wine and snakes his arms around my waist. "Yep. Your boyfriend."

I hand him a glass of wine and say, "So I'm a girlfriend?"

He holds up his glass and clinks it against mine. "To the end of trial runs and the beginning of sure things."

We're both smiling as we take a drink of our wine.

Lucy stacks the boxes together and walks toward the front door. "Looks like I got out right in time," she says.

The door closes behind her and Ryle raises an eyebrow. "I don't think your roommate likes me very much."

"You'd be surprised. I didn't think she liked me, either, but yesterday she asked me to be a bridesmaid in her wedding. I think she's just hoping for free flowers, though. She's very opportunistic."

Ryle laughs and leans against the refrigerator. His eyes fall to a magnet that says "*Boston*" on it. He pulls it off the refrigerator and raises an eyebrow. "You'll never get out of Boston purgatory if you keep souvenirs of Boston on your fridge like a tourist."

I laugh and grab the magnet, slapping it back on the fridge. I like that he remembers so much about the first night we met. "It was a gift. It only counts as touristy if I bought it myself."

He steps over to me and takes my glass of wine from my hands. He sets both of our glasses on the countertop, and then leans in and gives me a deep, passionate, drunken kiss. I can taste the tart fruitiness of the wine on his tongue and I like it. His hands go to the zipper on my onesie. "Let's get you out of these clothes."

He pulls me toward the bedroom, kissing me while we both struggle out of our clothes. By the time we make it to my bedroom, I'm down to my bra and panties.

He shoves me against the door, and I gasp at the unexpectedness of it.

"Don't move," he says. He presses his lips to my chest, then begins to kiss me slowly as he makes his way down my body.

Oh, Lord. Can this day seriously get any better?

I run my hands through his hair, but he grabs my wrists and presses them against the door. He climbs back up my body, squeezing my wrists tightly. He raises an eyebrow in warning. "I said . . . don't move."

I try not to smile, but it's hard to disguise. He drags his mouth back down my body. He slowly lowers my panties to my ankles, but he told me not to move, so I don't kick them off.

His mouth slides up my thigh until . . .

Yeah.

Best.

Day.

Ever.

Chapter Thirteen

Ryle: Are you at home or still at work?

Me: Work. Should be done in about an hour.

Ryle: Can I come see you?

Me: You know how people say there is no such thing as a stupid question? They're wrong. That was a stupid question.

Ryle: :)

Half an hour later, he's knocking at the front door of the floral shop. I closed the shop almost three hours ago, but I'm still here, trying to get caught up on the chaos that was the first month. The store is still too new to get an accurate projection of how well or how bad it's doing. Some days are great and some are so slow I send Allysa home. But overall, I'm happy with how it's gone so far.

And happy with how things are going with Ryle.

I unlock the door to let him in. He's in light blue scrubs again, and he still has a stethoscope around his neck. Fresh from work. Very nice touch. I swear, every time I see him straight off a shift, I have to hide the stupid grin on my face. I give him a quick kiss and then turn back toward my office. "I have a few things to finish up and then we can go back to my place."

He follows me into my office and closes the door. "You got a couch?" he asks, looking around my office.

I've spent some of this week putting the finishing touches

on it. I bought a couple of lamps so I don't have to turn on the overpowering fluorescent lights. The lamps give the room a soft glow. I also bought a few plants to keep here permanently. It's no garden, but it's as close as it gets. It's come a long way since this room was being used as storage for vegetable crates.

Ryle walks over to the couch and falls down onto it, face-first. "Take your time," he mumbles into the pillow. "I'll just nap until you're finished."

I sometimes worry about how hard he pushes himself with work, but I don't say anything. I've been sitting in my office going on twelve hours now, so I don't have much room to talk when it comes to being too ambitious.

I spend the next fifteen or so minutes finalizing orders. When I'm finished, I close my laptop and look over at Ryle.

I thought he'd be asleep, but instead he's on his side with his head propped up on his hand. He's been watching me this whole time, and seeing the smile on his face makes me blush. I push my chair back and stand up.

"Lily, I think I like you too much," he says as I make my way over to him.

I scrunch up my nose as he sits up on the couch and pulls me onto his lap. "Too much? That doesn't sound like a compliment."

"That's because I don't know if it is," he says. He adjusts my legs on either side of him and then wraps his arms around my waist. "This is my first real relationship. I don't know if I'm supposed to like you this much yet. I don't want to scare you away."

I laugh. "Like that could ever happen. You work way too much to smother me."

He rubs his hands up my back. "Does it bother you that I work too much?"

I shake my head. "No. I worry about you sometimes because I don't want you to burn yourself out. But I don't mind that I have to share you with your passion. I actually really like how ambitious you are. It's kind of sexy. It might even be my favorite thing about you."

"You know what I like the most about you?"

"I already know this answer," I say, smiling. "My mouth."

He leans his head back against the couch. "Oh yeah. That does come first. But do you know what my second favorite thing about you is?"

I shake my head.

"You don't put pressure on me to be something I'm incapable of being. You accept me exactly how I am."

I smile. "Well, in all fairness, you're a little different from when I first met you. You aren't so anti-girlfriend anymore."

"That's because you make it easy," he says, sliding a hand inside the back of my shirt. "It's easy being with you. I can still have the career I've always wanted, but you make it ten times better with the way you support me. When I'm with you, I feel like I get to have my cake and eat it, too."

Now both of his hands are beneath my shirt, pressed against my back. He pulls me toward him and kisses me. I grin against his mouth and whisper, "Is it the best cake you've ever tasted?"

One of his hands moves to the back of my bra and he unfastens it with ease. "I'm pretty sure, but maybe I need another taste of it to be positive." He pulls my shirt and bra over my head. I begin to push myself off of him so I can pull off my jeans, but he pulls me back onto his lap. He grabs his stethoscope and puts it in his ears, then presses the diaphragm against my chest, right over my heart.

"What's got your heart so worked up, Lily?"

I shrug innocently. "It might have a little to do with you, Dr. Kincaid."

He drops the end of the stethoscope and then lifts me off of him, pushing me back onto the couch. He spreads my legs and kneels down on the couch between them, placing the stethoscope against my chest again. He uses his other hand to hold himself up as he continues listening to my heart.

"I'd say you're at about ninety beats per minute," he says.

"Is that good or bad?"

He grins and lowers himself on top of me. "I'll be satisfied when it reaches one forty."

Yeah. If it reaches 140, I'm thinking I'll be satisfied, too.

He lowers his mouth to my chest and my eyes fall shut when I feel his tongue slide across my breast. He takes me in his mouth, keeping the stethoscope pressed against my chest the entire time. "You're at about one hundred now," he says. He wraps the stethoscope around his neck again and then pulls back, unbuttoning my jeans. Once he slides them off of me, he turns me over until I'm on my stomach, my arms draped over the arm of the couch.

"Get on your knees," he says.

I do what he says and before I'm even adjusted, I feel the cold metal of the stethoscope meet my chest again, this time with his arm snaked around me from behind. I remain still as he listens to my heartbeat. His other hand slowly begins to find its way between my legs and then inside my panties and then inside of me. I grip the couch but try to keep the noises to a minimum while he listens to my heart.

"One hundred and ten," he says, still unsatisfied.

He pulls my hips back to meet him and then I can feel him freeing himself from his scrubs. He grips my hip with one hand while shoving my panties aside with the other. Then he pushes forward until he's all the way inside of me.

I'm grasping the couch with two desperate fists when he pauses to listen to my heart again. "Lily," he says with mock disappointment. "One twenty. Not quite where I want you."

The stethoscope disappears again and his arm curls around my waist. His hand slides down my stomach and settles between my legs. I can no longer keep up with his rhythm. I can barely even stay on my knees. He's somehow holding me up with one hand and destroying me in the best possible way with his other hand. Right when I start to tremble, he pulls me upright until my back meets his chest. He's still inside me, but now he's focused on my heart again as he moves his stethoscope around to the front of my chest.

I let out a moan and he presses his lips to my ear. "Shh. No noises."

I have no idea how I make it through the next thirty seconds without making another sound. One of his arms is wrapped around me with the stethoscope pressed to my chest. His other arm is tight against my stomach as his hand continues its magic between my legs. He's still somehow deep inside me and I'm trying to move against him, but he's rock solid as the tremors begin to rush through me. My legs are shaking and my hands are at my sides, gripping the tops of his thighs as it takes every ounce of my strength not to scream out his name.

I'm still shaking when he lifts my hand and places the diaphragm against my wrist. After several seconds, he pulls the stethoscope away and tosses it to the floor. "One fifty," he says with satisfaction. He pulls out of me and flips me onto my back and then his mouth is on mine and he's inside me again.

My body is too weak to move and I can't even open my eyes and watch him. He thrusts against me several times and then holds still, groaning into my mouth. He drops on top of me, tense, yet shaking.

He kisses my neck and then his lips meet the tattoo of the heart on my collarbone. He finally settles against my neck and sighs.

"Have I already mentioned tonight how much I like you?" he asks.

I laugh. "Once or twice."

"Consider this the third time," he says. "I like you. Everything about you, Lily. Being inside of you. Being outside of you. Being near you. I like it all."

I smile, loving how his words feel against my skin. Inside my heart. I open my mouth to tell him I like him, too, but my voice is cut off by the sound of his phone.

He groans against my neck and then pulls out of me and reaches for his phone. He pulls his scrubs back into place and laughs as he looks at his caller ID.

"It's my mother," he says, leaning over and kissing the top of my knee that's resting against the back of the couch. He tosses the phone aside and then stands and walks over to my desk, grabbing a box of tissues.

This is always awkward, having to clean up after sex. But I can't say it's ever been this awkward before, knowing his mother is on the other end of that ring.

Once all my clothes are back in place, he pulls me against him on the couch and I lie down on top of him, resting my head on his chest.

It's after ten now and I'm so comfortable I debate just sleeping here for the night. Ryle's phone makes another noise, alerting him to a new voice mail. The thought of seeing him interact with his mother makes me smile. Allysa talks about their parents some, but I've never really talked to Ryle about them before.

"Do you get along with your parents?"

His arm is stroking mine gently. "Yeah, I do. They're good people. We hit a rough patch when I was a teenager, but we worked through it. I talk to my mother almost daily now."

I fold my arms over his chest and rest my chin on them, looking up at him. "Will you tell me more about your mother? Allysa told me they moved to England a few years ago. And that they were in Australia on vacation, but that was like a month ago."

He laughs. "My mother? Well . . . my mother is very over-bearing. Very judgmental, especially of the people she loves the most. She's never missed a single church service. And I have never heard her refer to my father as anything other than Dr. Kincaid."

Despite the warnings, he smiles the whole time he talks about her.

"Your father is a doctor, too?"

He nods. "Psychiatrist. He chose a field that also allowed him to have a normal life. Smart man."

"Do they ever visit you in Boston?"

"Not really. My mother hates flying, so Allysa and I fly to England a couple of times a year. She does want to meet you, though, so you might be going with us on the next trip."

I grin. "You've told your mother about me?"

"Of course," he says. "This is kind of a monumental thing, you know. Me having a girlfriend. She calls me every day to make sure I haven't screwed it up somehow."

I laugh, which makes him reach for his phone. "You think I'm kidding? I guarantee she somehow brought you up in the voice mail she just left." He presses a few keys and then begins to play the voice mail.

"Hey, sweetheart! It's your mom. Haven't spoken to you since yesterday. Miss you. Give Lily a hug for me. You do still see her, right? Allysa says you can't stop talking about her. She is still your girlfriend, right? Okay. Gretchen's here, we're having high tea. Love you. Kiss kiss."

I press my face against his chest and laugh. "We've only been dating a few months. How much do you talk about me?"

He pulls my hand up between us and kisses it. "Too much, Lily. Way too much."

I smile. "I can't wait to meet them. Not only did they raise an incredible daughter, but they made you. That's pretty impressive."

His arms tighten around me and he kisses the top of my head.

"What was your brother's name?" I ask him.

I can feel a slight stiffness in him after I ask that. I regret bringing it up, but it's too late to take it back.

"Emerson."

I can tell by his voice that it's not something he wants to talk about right now. Instead of pressing it further, I lift my head and scoot forward, pressing my mouth to his.

I should know better. Kisses can't seem to stop at just kisses when it comes to me and Ryle. In a matter of minutes, he's inside of me again, but this time it's everything the other time wasn't.

This time we make love.

Chapter Fourteen

My phone rings. I pick it up to see who it is and I'm a little taken aback. It's the first time Ryle has ever called me. We always just text. How odd to have a boyfriend for over three months that I've never once spoken to on the phone.

"Hello?"

"Hey, girlfriend," he says.

I smile cheesily at the sound of his voice. "Hey, boyfriend."

"Guess what?"

"What?"

"I'm taking the day off tomorrow. Your floral shop doesn't open until one o'clock on Sundays. I'm on my way to your apartment with two bottles of wine. You want to have a sleepover with your boyfriend and have drunken sex all night and sleep until noon?"

It's really embarrassing what his words do to me. I smile and say, "Guess what?"

"What?"

"I'm cooking you dinner. And I'm wearing an apron."

"Oh yeah?" he says.

"*Just* an apron." And then I hang up.

A few seconds later, I get a text message.

Ryle: Pic, please.

Me: Get over here and you can take the picture yourself.

I'm almost finished preparing the casserole mixture when the door opens. I pour it into the glass pan and don't turn around when I hear him walk into the kitchen. When I said I was just wearing an apron, I meant it. I'm not even wearing panties.

I can hear him suck in a rush of air when I reach over to the oven and stick the casserole inside. I might reach a little too far for show when I do it. When I close the oven, I don't face him. I grab a rag and start wiping down the oven, making sure to sway my hips as much as possible. I squeal when I feel a piercing sting on my right butt cheek. I spin around and Ryle is grinning, holding two bottles of wine.

"Did you just *bite* me?"

He gives me an innocent look. "Don't tempt the scorpion if you don't want to get stung." He eyes me up and down while he opens one of the bottles. He holds it up before he pours us a glass and says, "It's vintage."

"*Vintage*," I say with mock impression. "What's the special occasion?"

He hands me a glass and says, "I'm going to be an uncle. I have a smoking hot girlfriend. And I get to perform a very rare, possibly once-in-a-lifetime craniopagus separation on Monday."

"A cranio-*what*?"

He finishes off his glass of wine and pours himself another one. "Craniopagus separation. Conjoined twins," he says. He points to a spot on the top of his head and taps it. "Attached right here. We've been studying them since they were born. It's a very rare surgery. *Very* rare."

For the first time, I think I'm genuinely turned on by

him as a doctor. I mean, I admire his drive. I admire his dedication. But seeing how excited he is about what he's doing for a living is seriously sexy.

"How long do you think it'll take?" I ask.

He shrugs. "Not sure. They're young, so being under general anesthesia for too long is a concern." He holds up his right hand and wiggles his fingers. "But this is a very special hand that has been through almost half a million dollars' worth of specialty education. I have a lot of faith in this hand."

I walk over to him and press my lips to his palm. "I'm a little fond of this hand, too."

He slides the hand down to my neck and then spins me so that I'm flush against the counter. I gasp, because I wasn't expecting that.

He pushes himself against me from behind and slowly slides his hand down the side of my body. I press my palms into the granite and close my eyes, already feeling the rush of the wine.

"This hand," he whispers, "is the steadiest hand in all of Boston."

He pushes on the back of my neck, bending me further over the counter. His hand meets the inside of my knee and he glides it upward. Slowly. *Jesus.*

He pushes my legs apart, and then his fingers are inside me. I moan and try to find something to hold on to. I grip the faucet, just as he begins to work magic.

And then, just like a magician, his hand disappears.

I hear him walking out of the kitchen. I watch as he passes the front of the counter. He winks at me, downs the rest of his glass of wine and says, "I'm gonna take a quick shower."

What a tease.

"You asshole!" I yell after him.

"I'm not an asshole!" he yells from my bedroom. "I'm a highly trained neurosurgeon!"

I laugh and pour myself another glass of wine.

I'll show him who the tease really is.

•   •   •

I'm on my third glass of wine when he walks out of my bedroom.

I'm on the phone with my mother, so I watch him from the couch as he makes his way to the kitchen and pours himself another glass.

That is some seriously good wine.

"What are you doing tonight?" my mother asks.

I have her on speakerphone. Ryle is leaning against a wall, watching me talk to her. "Not much. Helping Ryle study."

"That sounds . . . not very interesting," she says.

Ryle winks at me.

"It's actually very interesting," I say to her. "I help him study a lot. Mostly reviewing fine-motor control of the hands. In fact, we'll probably be up all night studying."

The three glasses of wine has made me frisky. I can't believe I'm flirting with him while I'm on the phone with my mother. *Gross.*

"I gotta go," I tell her. "We're taking Allysa and Marshall out to dinner tomorrow night, so I'll call you on Monday."

"Oh, where are you taking them?"

I roll my eyes. The woman can't take a hint. "I don't know. Ryle, where are we taking them?"

"That place we went to that one time with your mom," he says. "Bib's? I made reservations for six o'clock."

My heart feels like it slinks down my chest. My mother says, "Oh, good choice."

"Yeah. If you like stale bread. Bye, Mom." I hang up and look at Ryle. "I don't want to go back there. I didn't like it. Let's try something new."

I fail to tell him why I *really* don't want to go back there. But how do you tell your brand-new boyfriend that you're trying to avoid your first love?

Ryle pushes off the wall. "You'll be fine," he says. "Allysa's excited to eat there, I told her all about it."

Maybe I'll get lucky and Atlas won't be working.

"Speaking of food," Ryle says. "I'm starving."

The casserole!

"Oh shit!" I say, laughing.

Ryle rushes to the kitchen and I stand up and follow him in there. I walk in just as he pulls the oven door open and waves away the smoke. *Ruined.*

I get dizzy all of a sudden from standing up too fast after having three glasses of wine. I grab the counter beside him to steady myself, just as he reaches in to pull the burnt casserole out.

"Ryle! You need a . . ."

"Shit!" he yells.

"Pot holder."

The casserole falls from his hand and lands on the floor,

shattering everywhere. I lift up my feet to avoid broken glass and mushroom chicken splatter. I start laughing as soon as I realize he didn't even think to use a pot holder.

Must be the wine. *This is some seriously strong wine.*

He slams the oven shut and moves to the faucet, shoving his hand under the cold water, muttering curse words. I'm trying to suppress my laughter, but the wine and the ridiculousness of the last few seconds are making it hard. I look at the floor—at the mess we're about to have to clean up—and the laughter bursts from me. I'm still laughing as I lean over to get a look at Ryle's hand. I hope he didn't hurt it too bad.

I'm instantly not laughing anymore. I'm on the floor, my hand pressed against the corner of my eye.

In a matter of one second, Ryle's arm came out of nowhere and slammed against me, knocking me backward. There was enough force behind it to knock me off balance. When I lost my footing, I hit my face on one of the cabinet door handles as I came down.

Pain shoots through the corner of my eye, right near my temple.

And then I feel the weight.

Heaviness follows and it presses down on every part of me. So much gravity, pushing down on my emotions. Everything shatters.

My tears, my heart, my laughter, my *soul*. Shattered like broken glass, raining down around me.

I wrap my arms over my head and try to wish away the last ten seconds.

"Goddammit, Lily," I hear him say. "It's not funny. This hand is my fucking career."

I don't look up at him. His voice doesn't penetrate through my body this time. It feels like it's stabbing me now, the sharpness of each of his words coming at me like swords. Then I feel him next to me, his *goddamn hand* on my back.

Rubbing.

"Lily," he says. "Oh, God. *Lily.*" He tries to pull my arms from my head, but I refuse to budge. I start shaking my head, wanting the last fifteen seconds to go away. *Fifteen seconds.* That's all it takes to completely change everything about a person.

Fifteen seconds that we'll never get back.

He pulls me against him and starts kissing the top of my head. "I'm so sorry. I just . . . I burned my hand. I panicked. You were laughing and . . . I'm so sorry, it all happened so fast. I didn't mean to push you, Lily, I'm sorry."

I don't hear Ryle's voice this time. All I hear is my father's voice.

"I'm sorry, Jenny. It was an accident. I'm so sorry."

"I'm sorry, Lily. It was an accident. I'm so sorry."

I just want him away from me. I use every ounce of strength I have in both my hands and legs and I force him *the fuck* away from me.

He falls backward, onto his hands. His eyes are full of genuine sorrow, but then they're full of something else.

Worry? Panic?

He slowly pulls up his right hand and it's covered in blood. Blood is trickling out of his palm, down his wrist. I look at the floor—at the shattered pieces of glass from the casserole dish. *His hand.* I just pushed him onto glass.

He turns around and pulls himself up. He sticks his

hand under the stream of water and starts rinsing away the blood. I stand up, just as he pulls a sliver of glass out of his palm and tosses it on the counter.

I'm full of so much anger, but somehow, concern for his hand still finds its way out. I grab a towel and shove it into his fist. There's so much blood.

It's his right hand.

His surgery Monday.

I try to help stop the bleeding, but I'm shaking too bad. "Ryle, your hand."

He pulls the hand away and, with his good hand, he lifts my chin. "*Fuck* the hand, Lily. I don't care about my hand. Are you okay?" He's looking back and forth between my eyes frantically as he assesses the cut on my face.

My shoulders begin to shake and huge, hurt-filled tears spill down my cheeks. "No." I'm a little in shock, and I know he can hear my heart breaking with just that one word, because I can feel it in every part of me. "Oh my God. You *pushed* me, Ryle. You . . ." The realization of what has just happened hurts worse than the actual action.

Ryle wraps his arm around my neck and desperately holds me against him. "I'm so sorry, Lily. *God*, I'm so sorry." He buries his face against my hair, squeezing me with every emotion inside of him. "Please don't hate me. *Please.*"

His voice slowly starts to become Ryle's voice again, and I feel it in my stomach, in my toes. His entire career depends on his hand, so it has to say something that he's not even worried about it. *Right?* I'm so confused.

There's too much happening. The smoke, the wine, the

broken glass, the food splattered everywhere, the blood, the anger, the apologies, *it's too much.*

"I'm so sorry," he says again. I pull back and his eyes are red and I've never seen him look so sad. "I panicked. I didn't mean to push you away, I just panicked. All I could think about was the surgery Monday and my hand and . . . I'm so sorry." He presses his mouth to mine and breathes me in.

He's not like my father. He can't be. He's nothing like that uncaring bastard.

We're both upset and kissing and confused and sad. I've never felt anything like this moment—so ugly and painful. But somehow the only thing that eases the hurt just caused by this man *is* this man. My tears are soothed by his sorrow, my emotions soothed with his mouth against mine, his hand gripping me like he never wants to let go.

I feel his arms go around my waist and he picks me up, carefully stepping through the mess we've made. I can't tell if I'm more disappointed in him or myself. Him for losing his temper in the first place or me for somehow finding comfort in his apology.

He carries me and kisses me all the way to my bedroom. He's still kissing me when he lowers me to the bed and whispers, "I'm sorry, Lily." He moves his lips to the spot on my eye that hit the cabinet, and he kisses me there. "I'm so sorry."

His mouth is on mine again, hot and wet, and I don't even know what's happening to me. I'm hurting so much on the inside, yet my body craves his apology in the form of his mouth and hands on me. I want to lash out at him and react like I always wish my mother would have reacted when my father hurt her, but deep down I want to believe that it really was an accident. Ryle isn't like my father. *He's nothing like him.*

I need to feel his sorrow. His regret. I get both of these things in the way he kisses me. I spread my legs for him and his sorrow comes in another form. Slow, apologetic thrusts inside of me. Every time he enters me, he whispers another apology. And by some miracle, every time he pulls out of me, my anger leaves with him.

.   .   .

He's kissing my shoulder. My cheek. My eye. He's still on top of me, touching me gently. I've never been touched like this . . . with such tenderness. I try to forget what happened in the kitchen, but it's everything right now.

He pushed me away from him.

Ryle pushed me.

For fifteen seconds, I saw a side of him that *wasn't* him. That wasn't *me*. I laughed at him when I should have been concerned. He shoved me when he should have never touched me. I pushed him away and caused him to cut his hand.

It was awful. The whole thing, the entire fifteen seconds it lasted, was absolutely awful. I never want to think about it again.

He still has the rag balled up in his hand and it's soaked with blood. I push against his chest.

"I'll be right back," I tell him. He kisses me one more time and rolls off of me. I walk to the bathroom and close the door. I look in the mirror and gasp.

Blood. In my hair, on my cheeks, on my body. It's all his

blood. I grab a rag and try to wash some off, and then I look under the sink for the first aid kit. I have no idea how bad his hand is. First he burned it, then he sliced it open. Not even an hour after he was just telling me how important this surgery was to him.

No more wine. We're never allowed vintage wine again.

I grab the box from under the sink and open the bedroom door. He's walking back into the bedroom from the kitchen with a small bag of ice. He holds it up, "For your eye," he says.

I hold up the first aid kit. "For your hand."

We both smile and then sit back down on the bed. He leans against the headboard while I pull his hand to my lap. The whole time I'm dressing his wound, he's holding the bag of ice against my eye.

I squeeze some antiseptic cream onto my finger and dab it against the burns on his fingers. They don't look as bad as I thought they might be, so that's a relief. "Can you prevent it from blistering?" I ask him.

He shakes his head. "Not if it's second-degree."

I want to ask him if he can still perform the surgery if his fingers have blisters on them come Monday, but I don't bring it up. I'm sure that's on the forefront of his mind right now.

"Do you want me to put some on your cut?"

He nods. The bleeding has stopped. I'm sure if he needed stitches, he'd get some, but I think it'll be fine. I pull the ACE bandage out of the first aid kit and begin wrapping his hand.

"Lily," he whispers. I look up at him. His head is resting against the headboard, and it looks like he wants to cry. "I feel terrible," he says. "If I could take it back . . ."

"I know," I say, cutting him off. "I know, Ryle. It was

terrible. You pushed me. You made me question everything I thought I knew about you. But I know you feel bad about it. We can't take it back. I don't want to bring it up again." I secure the bandage around his hand and then look him in the eye. "But Ryle? If anything like that ever happens again . . . I'll know that this time wasn't just an accident. And I'll leave you without a second thought."

He stares at me for a long time, his eyebrows drawn apart in regret. He leans forward and presses his lips against mine. "It won't happen again, Lily. I swear. I'm not like him. I know that's what you're thinking, but I swear to you . . ."

I shake my head, wanting him to stop. I can't take the pain in his voice. "I know you're nothing like my father," I say. "Just . . . please don't ever make me doubt you again. Please."

He brushes hair from my forehead. "You're the most important part of my life, Lily. I want to be what brings you happiness. Not what causes you to hurt." He kisses me and then stands up and leans over me, pressing the ice to my face. "Hold this here for about ten more minutes. It'll prevent it from swelling."

I replace his hand with mine. "Where are you going?"

He kisses me on the forehead and says, "To clean up my mess."

He spends the next twenty minutes cleaning the kitchen. I can hear glass being tossed into the trash can, wine being poured out in the sink. I go to the bathroom and take a quick shower to get his blood off of me and then I change the sheets on my bed. When he finally has the kitchen cleaned up, he comes to the bedroom with a glass. He hands it to me. "It's soda," he says. "The caffeine will help."

I take a drink of it and feel it fizz down my throat. It's actually the perfect thing. I take another drink and set it on my nightstand. "What's it help with? The hangover?"

Ryle slides into bed and pulls the covers over us. He shakes his head. "No, I don't think soda actually helps anything. My mom just used to give me a soda after I'd had a bad day and it always made me feel a little better."

I smile. "Well, it worked."

He brushes his hand down my cheek and I can see in his eyes and in the way he touches me that he deserves at least one chance at forgiveness. I feel if I don't find a way to forgive him, I'll somewhat be placing blame on him for the resentment I still hold for my father. *He's not like my father.*

Ryle loves me. He's never come out and said it before, but I know he does. And I love him. What happened in the kitchen tonight is something I'm confident won't happen again. Not after seeing how upset he is that he hurt me.

All humans make mistakes. What determines a person's character aren't the mistakes we make. It's how we take those mistakes and turn them into lessons rather than excuses.

Ryle's eyes somehow grow even more sincere and he leans over and kisses my hand. He settles his head into the pillow and we just lie there, staring at each other, sharing this unspoken energy that fills all the holes the night has left in us.

After a few minutes, he squeezes my hand. "Lily," he says, brushing his thumb over mine. "I'm in love with you."

I feel his words in every part of me. And when I whisper, "*I love you, too,*" it's the most naked truth I've ever spoken to him.

Chapter Fifteen

I arrive at the restaurant fifteen minutes late. Right when I was about to close tonight I had a customer come in to order flowers for a funeral. I couldn't turn them away because . . . sadly . . . funerals are the best business for florists.

Ryle waves me over to the table and I walk straight to them, doing my best not to look around. I don't want to see Atlas. I tried twice to get them to change the restaurant location, but Allysa was hell-bent on eating here after Ryle told her how good it was.

I slide into the booth and Ryle leans over and kisses me on the cheek. "Hey, girlfriend."

Allysa groans. "God, you guys are so cute, it's sickening." I smile at her, and her eyes immediately go to the corner of my eye. It doesn't look as bad as I thought it might today, which is probably due to Ryle forcing me to keep ice on it. "Oh my God," Allysa says. "Ryle told me what happened but I didn't think it was that bad."

I glance at Ryle, wondering what he told her. *The truth?* He smiles and says, "Olive oil was everywhere. When she slipped, it was so graceful you'd think she was a ballerina."

A lie.

Fair enough. I would have done the same thing.

"It was pretty pathetic," I say with a laugh.

Somehow, we get through dinner without a hitch. No

sign of Atlas, no thoughts of last night, and Ryle and I both avoid the wine. After we're finished with our food, our waiter approaches the table. "Care for dessert?" he asks.

I shake my head, but Allysa perks up. "What do you have?"

Marshall looks just as interested. "We're eating for two, so we'll take anything chocolate," he says.

The waiter nods, and when he walks away, Allysa looks at Marshall. "This baby is the size of a bedbug right now. You better not encourage bad habits for the next several months."

The waiter returns with a dessert cart. "The chef gives all expectant mothers dessert on the house," he says. "Congratulations."

"He does?" Allysa says, perking up.

"Guess that's why it's called Bib's," Marshall says. "Chef likes the babies."

We all look at the cart. "Oh, God," I say, looking at the options.

"This is my new favorite restaurant," Allysa says.

We pick out three desserts for the table. The four of us spend the time waiting for it to be served discussing baby names.

"No," Allysa says to Marshall. "We're not naming this baby after a state."

"But I love Nebraska," he whines. "Idaho?"

Allysa drops her head in her hands. "This is going to be the demise of our marriage."

"Demise," Marshall says. "That's actually a good name."

Marshall's murder is thwarted by the arrival of dessert. Our waiter places a piece of chocolate cake in front of Allysa, and steps aside to make room for the waiter behind him who is holding the other two desserts. The waiter motions toward the guy placing our desserts down and says, "The chef would like to extend his congratulations."

"How was the meal?" the chef asks, looking at Allysa and Marshall.

By the time his eyes make it to mine, my anxiety is seeping from me. Atlas locks eyes with me, and without thinking, I blurt out, "You're the *chef*?"

The waiter leans around Atlas and says. "The chef. The owner. Sometimes waiter, sometimes dishwasher. He gives a new meaning to hands-on."

The next five seconds go unnoticed by everyone at our table, but they play out in slow motion to me.

Atlas's eyes fall to the cut on my eye.

The bandage wrapped around Ryle's hand.

Back to my eye.

"We love your restaurant," Allysa says. "You have an incredible place here."

Atlas doesn't look at her. I see the roll of his throat as he swallows. His jaw hardens and he says nothing as he walks away.

Shit.

The waiter tries to cover for Atlas's hasty retreat by smiling and showing way too many teeth. "Enjoy your dessert," he says, scuffling off to the kitchen.

"Bummer," Allysa says. "We find a new favorite restaurant and the chef is an asshole."

Ryle laughs. "Yeah, but the assholes are the best ones. Gordon Ramsay?"

"Good point," Marshall says.

I put my hand on Ryle's arm. "Bathroom," I tell him.

He nods as I scoot out of the booth, and Marshall says, "What about Wolfgang Puck? You think he's an asshole?"

I walk across the restaurant, head down, fast paced. As soon as I get into the familiar hallway, I keep going. I push open the door to the women's restroom and then turn around and lock it.

Shit. Shit, shit, shit.

The look in his eye. The anger in his jaw.

I'm relieved he walked away, but I'm half-convinced he's probably going to be waiting outside the restaurant when we leave, ready to kick Ryle's ass.

I breathe in my nose, out my mouth, wash my hands, repeat the breathing. Once I'm more calm, I dry my hands on a towel.

I'll just go back out there and tell Ryle I'm not feeling well. We'll leave and we'll never come back. They all think the chef is an asshole, so that can be my excuse.

I unlock the door, but I don't pull it open. It starts pushing open from the other side, so I step back. Atlas steps inside the bathroom with me and locks the door. His back rests against the door as he stares at me, focused on the cut near my eye.

"What happened?" he asks.

I shake my head. "Nothing."

His eyes are narrow, still ice blue but somehow burning with fire. "You're lying, Lily."

I muster enough of a smile to get me by. "It was an accident."

Atlas laughs, but then his face falls flat. "Leave him."

Leave him?

Jesus, he thinks this is something else entirely. I take a step forward and shake my head. "He's not like that, Atlas. It wasn't like that. Ryle is a good person."

He tilts his head and leans it forward a little bit. "Funny. You sound just like your mother."

His words sting. I immediately try to reach around him for the door, but he grabs my wrist. "*Leave* him, Lily."

I yank my hand away. I turn my back to him and inhale a deep breath. I release it slowly as I face him again. "If it's any comparison at all, I'm more scared of you right now than I've *ever* been of him."

My words make Atlas pause for a moment. His nod starts out slowly, and then gets more prominent as he steps away from the door. "I certainly didn't mean to make you feel uncomfortable." He motions toward the door. "Just trying to repay the concern you've always shown me."

I stare at him for a moment, unsure how to take his words. He's still raging on the inside, I can see it. But on the outside, he's calm—collected. Allowing me to leave. I reach forward and unlock the door, then pull it open.

I gasp when my eyes meet Ryle's. I quickly glance over my shoulder to see Atlas filing out of the bathroom with me.

Ryle's eyes fill with confusion as he looks from me to Atlas. "What the *fuck*, Lily?"

"Ryle." My voice shakes. *God, this looks so much worse than it is.*

Atlas steps around me and turns toward the doors to the kitchen, as if Ryle doesn't even exist to him. Ryle's eyes are glued to Atlas's back. *Keep walking, Atlas.*

Right when Atlas reaches the kitchen doors, he pauses.

No, no, no. Keep walking.

In what becomes one of the most dreadful moments I can imagine, he spins around and strides toward Ryle, grabbing him by the collar of his shirt. Almost as soon as it happens, Ryle forces Atlas back and slams him against the opposite wall. Atlas lunges for Ryle again, this time shoving his forearm against Ryle's throat, pinning him against the wall.

"You touch her again and I'll cut your fucking hand off and shove it down your throat, you worthless piece of shit!"

"Atlas, stop!" I yell.

Atlas releases Ryle forcefully, taking a huge step back. Ryle is breathing heavily, staring at Atlas long and hard. Then his focus moves directly to me. *"Atlas?"* He says his name with familiarity.

Why is Ryle saying Atlas's name like that? Like he's heard me say it before? I've never told him about Atlas.

Wait.

I did.

That first night on the roof. It was one of my naked truths.

Ryle lets out a disbelieving laugh and points at Atlas, but he's still looking at me. *"This* is Atlas? The homeless boy you *pity*-fucked?"

Oh, God.

The hallway instantly becomes a blur of fists and elbows and my screams for them to stop. Two waiters push through the door behind me and shove past me, separating them just as quickly as it started.

They're pushed apart against opposite walls, staring

each other down, breathing heavily. I can't even look at either of them.

I can't look at Atlas. Not after what Ryle just said to him. I also can't look at Ryle because he's probably thinking the absolute worst possible thing right now.

"Out!" Atlas yells, pointing at the door, but looking at Ryle. "Get the hell out of my restaurant!"

I meet Ryle's eyes as he begins to walk past me, scared of what I'll see in them. But there isn't any anger there.

Only hurt.

Lots of hurt.

He pauses as if he's about to say something to me. But his face just twists into disappointment and he walks back out into the restaurant.

I finally glance up at Atlas and can see disappointment all across his face. Before I can explain away Ryle's words to him, he turns and walks away, pushing through the kitchen doors.

I immediately turn and run after Ryle. He grabs his jacket from the booth and walks toward the exit without even looking at Allysa and Marshall.

Allysa looks up at me and holds her hands up in question. I shake my head, grab my purse and say, "It's a long story. We'll talk tomorrow."

I follow Ryle outside and he's walking toward the parking lot. I run to catch up to him and he just stops and punches at the air.

"I didn't bring my fucking *car!*" he yells, frustrated.

I pull my keys out of my purse and he walks up to me and snatches them from my hand. Again, I follow him, this time to my car.

I don't know what to do. I don't know if he even wants to speak to me right now. He just saw me locked in a bathroom with a guy I used to be in love with. Then, out of nowhere, that guy attacks him.

God, this is so bad.

When we reach my car, he heads straight for the driver's side door. He points to the passenger side and says, "Get in, Lily."

He doesn't speak to me the entire time we're driving. I say his name once, but he just shakes his head like he's not ready to hear my explanation yet. When we pull into my parking garage, he gets out of the car as soon as he turns it off, like he can't get away from me fast enough.

He's pacing the length of the car when I get out. "It wasn't what it looked like, Ryle. I swear."

He stops pacing, and when he looks at me, my heart doubles over. There's so much pain in his eyes right now, and it's not even necessary. It was all due to a stupid misunderstanding.

"I didn't want this, Lily," he says. "I didn't want a relationship! I didn't want this stress in my life!"

As much as he's hurting because of what he thinks he saw, his words still piss me off. "Well, then *leave!*"

"*What?*"

I throw my hands up. "I don't want to be your burden, Ryle! I'm so sorry my presence in your life is so *unbearable!*"

He takes a step forward. "Lily, that's not at all what I'm saying." He throws his hands up in frustration and then walks past me. He leans against my car and folds his arms over his chest. There's a long stretch of silence while I wait for what he has to say. His head is down, but he lifts it slightly, looking up at me.

"Naked truths, Lily. That's all I want from you right now. Can you please give me that?"

I nod.

"Did you know he worked there?"

I purse my lips together and wrap my arm over my chest, grabbing at my elbow. "Yes. That's why I didn't want to go back, Ryle. I didn't want to run into him."

My answer seems to release a little of his tension. He runs a hand down his face. "Did you tell him what happened last night? Did you tell him about our fight?"

I take a step forward and shake my head adamantly. "No. He assumed. He saw my eye and your hand and he just assumed."

He blows out a laden breath and leans his head back, looking up at the roof. It looks like it's almost too painful for him to even ask the next question.

"Why were you alone with him in the bathroom?"

I take another step forward. "He followed me in there. I know nothing about him now, Ryle. I didn't even know he owned that restaurant, I thought he was just a waiter. He's not a part of my life anymore, I swear. He just . . ." I fold my arms together and drop my voice. "We both grew up in abusive households. He saw my face and your hand and . . . he was just worried for me. That's all it was."

Ryle brings his hands up and covers his mouth. I can hear the air rushing through his fingers as he releases his breath. He stands up straight, allowing himself a moment to soak in all I've just said.

"My turn," he says.

He pushes off the car and takes the three steps toward me that previously separated us. He puts both hands on my cheeks and looks me dead in the eyes. "If you don't want to be with me . . . please tell me right now, Lily. Because when I saw you with him . . . that *hurt.* I never want to feel that again. And if it hurts this much now, I'm terrified to think of what it could do to me a year from now."

I can feel the tears begin to stream down my cheeks. I place my hands on top of his and shake my head. "I don't want anyone else, Ryle. I only want you."

He forces the saddest smile I've ever seen on a human. He pulls me to him and holds me there. I wrap my arms around him as tight as I can as he presses his lips to the side of my head.

"I love you, Lily. *God,* I love you."

I squeeze him tight, pressing a kiss to his shoulder. "I love you, too."

I close my eyes and wish I could wash away the entire last two days.

Atlas is wrong about Ryle.

I just wish *Atlas* knew he was wrong.

Chapter Sixteen

"I mean . . . I'm not trying to be selfish, but you didn't taste the dessert, Lily." Allysa groans. "Oh, it was *sooo* good."

"We're never going back there," I say to her.

She stomps her foot like a little kid. "But . . ."

"Nope. We have to respect your brother's feelings."

She folds her arms over her chest. "I know, I know. Why did you have to be a hormonal teenager and fall in love with the best chef in Boston?"

"He wasn't a chef when I knew him."

"Whatever," she says. She walks out of my office and closes the door.

My phone buzzes with an incoming text.

Ryle: 5 hours down. About 5 more to go. So far so good. Hand is great.

I sigh, relieved. I wasn't sure if he'd be able to do the surgery today, but knowing how much he was looking forward to it makes me happy for him.

Me: Steadiest hands in all of Boston.

I open my laptop and check my email. The first thing I see is an inquiry from the *Boston Globe.* I open it and it's from a journalist interested in running an article about the store. I grin like an idiot and start emailing her back when Allysa knocks on the door. She opens it and sticks her head in.

"Hey," she says.

"Hey," I say back.

She taps her fingers on the doorframe. "Remember a few minutes ago when you told me I could never go back to Bib's because it's unfair to Ryle that the boy you loved when you were a teenager is the owner?"

I fall back against my chair. "What do you want, Allysa?"

She scrunches up her nose and says, "If it isn't fair that we can't go back there because of the owner, how is it fair that the owner gets to come here?"

What?

I close my laptop and stand up. "Why would you say that? Is he here?"

She nods and slips inside my office, closing the door behind her. "He is. He asked for you. And I know you're with my brother and I'm with child, but can we please just take a moment to silently admire the perfection that is that man?"

She smiles dreamily and I roll my eyes.

"Allysa."

"Those *eyes*, though." She opens the door and walks out. I follow behind her and catch sight of Atlas. "She's right here," Allysa says. "Would you like me to take your coat?"

We don't take coats.

Atlas glances up when I walk out of my office. His eyes cut to Allysa and he shakes his head. "No, thank you. I won't be long."

Allysa leans forward over the counter, dropping her chin on her hands. "Stay as long as you like. In fact, are you looking for an extra job? Lily needs to hire more people and we're looking for someone who can lift really heavy things. Requires a lot of flexibility. Bending over."

I narrow my eyes at Allysa and mouth, *"Enough."*

She shrugs innocently. I hold my door open for Atlas, but avoid looking directly at him as he passes me. I feel a world of guilt for what happened last night, but also a world of anger for what happened last night.

I walk around my desk and drop into my seat, prepared for an argument. But when I look up at him, I clamp my mouth shut.

He's smiling. He waves his hand around in a circle as he takes a seat across from me. "This is incredible, Lily."

I pause. "Thank you."

He continues smiling at me, like he's proud of me. Then he places a bag between us on the desk and pushes it toward me. "A gift," he says. "You can open it later."

Why is he buying me gifts? He has a girlfriend. I have a boyfriend. Our past has already caused enough problems in my present. I certainly don't need gifts to exacerbate that.

"Why are you buying me gifts, Atlas?"

He leans back in his seat and crosses his arms over his chest. "I bought it three years ago. I've been holding on to it in case I ever ran into you."

Considerate Atlas. He hasn't changed. Dammit.

I pick up the gift and set it on the floor behind my desk. I try to release some of the tension I'm feeling, but it's really hard when everything about him makes me so tense.

"I came here to apologize to you," he says.

I wave off his apology, letting him know it isn't necessary. "It's fine. It was a misunderstanding. Ryle is fine."

He laughs under his breath. "That's not what I'm apologizing for," he says. "I'd never apologize for defending you."

"You weren't defending me," I say. "There was nothing to defend."

He tilts his head, giving me the same look that he gave me last night. The one that lets me know how disappointed in me he is. It stings deep in my gut.

I clear my throat. "Why are you apologizing, then?"

He's quiet for a moment. Contemplative. "I wanted to apologize for saying that you sounded like your mother. That was hurtful. And I'm sorry."

I don't know why I always feel like crying when I'm around him. When I think about him. When I read about him. It's like my emotions are still tethered to him somehow and I can't figure out how to cut the strings.

His eyes drop to my desk. He reaches forward and grabs three things. A pen. A sticky note. My phone.

He writes something down on the sticky note and then proceeds to pull my phone apart. He slips the case off and puts the sticky note between the case and the phone, then slides the cover back over it. He pushes my phone back across the desk. I look down at it and then up at him. He stands up and tosses the pen on my desk.

"It's my cell phone number. Keep it hidden there in case you ever need it."

I wince at the gesture. The *unnecessary* gesture. "I won't need it."

"I hope not." He walks to the door and reaches for the doorknob. And I know this is my only chance to get out what I have to say before he's out of my life forever.

"Atlas, wait."

I stand up so fast, my chair scoots across the room and bumps against the wall. He half turns and faces me.

"What Ryle said to you last night? I never . . ." I bring a nervous hand up to my neck. I can feel my heart beating in my throat. "I *never* said that to him. He was hurt and upset and he misconstrued my words from a long time ago."

The corner of Atlas's mouth twitches, and I'm not sure if he's trying not to smile or trying not to frown. He faces me straight on. "Believe me, Lily. I know that wasn't a *pity* fuck. I was there."

He walks out the door, and his words knock me straight back into my seat.

Only . . . my seat is no longer there. It's still on the other side of my office and I'm now on the floor.

Allysa rushes in and I'm lying on my back behind my desk. "Lily?" She runs around the desk and stands over me. "Are you okay?"

I hold up a thumb. "Fine. Just missed my chair."

She reaches out her hand and helps me to my feet. "What was that all about?"

I glance at the door as I retrieve my chair. I take a seat and look down at my phone. "Nothing. He was just apologizing."

Allysa sighs longingly and looks back at the door. "So does that mean he doesn't want the job?"

I've got to hand it to her. Even in the midst of emotional turmoil, she can make me laugh. "Get back to work before I dock your pay."

She laughs and makes to leave. I tap my pen against my desk and then say, "Allysa. Wait."

"I know," she says, cutting me off. "Ryle doesn't need to know about that visit. You don't have to tell me."

I smile. "Thank you."

She closes the door.

I reach down and pick up the bag with my three-year-old gift inside of it. I pull it out and can easily tell it's a book, wrapped in tissue paper. I tear the tissue paper away and fall against the back of my chair.

There's a picture of Ellen DeGeneres on the front. The title is *Seriously . . . I'm Kidding*. I laugh and then open the book, gasping quietly when I see it's autographed. I run my fingers over the words of the inscription.

Lily,

    Atlas says just keep swimming.

    —Ellen DeGeneres

I run my finger over her signature. Then I drop the book on my desk, press my forehead against it, and fake cry against the cover.

Chapter Seventeen

It's after seven before I get home. Ryle called an hour ago and said he wouldn't be coming over tonight. The confusher-cackle (whatever that big word he used was) separation was a success, but he's staying at the hospital overnight to make sure there aren't complications.

I walk in the door to my quiet apartment. I change into my quiet pajamas. I eat a quiet sandwich. And then I lie down in my quiet bedroom and open my quiet new book, hoping it can quiet my emotions.

Sure enough, three hours and the majority of a book later, all the emotions from the last several days begin to seep out of me. I place a bookmark on the page where I stopped reading and I close it.

I stare at the book for a long time. I think about Ryle. I think about Atlas. I think about how sometimes, no matter how convinced you are that your life will turn out a certain way, all that certainty can be washed away with a simple change in tide.

I take the book Atlas bought me and put it in the closet with all my journals. Then I pick up the one that's filled with memories of him. And I know it's finally time to read the last entry I wrote. Then I can close the book for good.

Dear Ellen,

Most of the time I'm thankful you don't know I exist and that I've never really mailed you any of these things I write to you.

But sometimes, especially tonight, I wish you did. I just need someone to talk to about everything I'm feeling. It's been six months since I've seen Atlas and I honestly don't know where he is or how he's doing. So much has happened since the last letter I wrote to you, when Atlas moved to Boston. I thought it was the last time I'd see him for a while, but it wasn't.

I saw him again after he left, several weeks later. It was my sixteenth birthday and when he showed up, it became the absolute best day of my life.

And then the absolute worst.

It had been exactly forty-two days since Atlas left for Boston. I counted every day like it would help somehow. I was so depressed, Ellen. I still am. People say that teenagers don't know how to love like an adult. Part of me believes that, but I'm not an adult and so I have nothing to compare it to. But I do believe it's probably different. I'm sure there's more substance in the love between two adults than there is between two teenagers. There's probably more maturity, more respect, more responsibility. But no matter how different the substance of a love might be at different ages in a person's life, I know that love still has to weigh the same. You feel that weight on your shoulders and in your stomach and on your heart no matter how old you are. And my feelings for Atlas are very heavy. Every night I cry myself to sleep and I whisper, "Just keep swimming." But it gets really hard to swim when you feel like you're anchored in the water.

Now that I think about it, I've probably been experiencing the stages of grief in a sense. Denial, anger, bargaining, depression, and acceptance. I was deep in the depression stage the night of my sixteenth birthday. My mother had tried to make the day a good one. She bought me gardening supplies, made my favorite cake, and the two of us went to dinner together. But by the time I had crawled into bed that night, I couldn't shake the sadness.

I was crying when I heard the tap on my window. At first, I thought it had started raining. But then I heard his voice. I jumped up and ran to the window, my heart in hysterics. He was standing there in the dark, smiling at me. I raised the window and helped him inside and he took me in his arms and held me there for so long while I cried.

He smelled so good. I could tell when I hugged him that he'd put on some much-needed weight in just the six weeks since I'd last seen him. He pulled back and wiped the tears off my cheeks. "Why are you crying, Lily?"

I was embarrassed that I was crying. I cried a lot that month—probably more than any other month of my life. It was probably just the hormones of being a teenage girl, mixed with the stress of how my father treated my mother, and then having to say goodbye to Atlas.

I grabbed a shirt from the floor and dried my eyes, then we sat down on the bed. He pulled me against his chest and leaned against my headboard.

"What are you doing here?" I asked him.

"It's your birthday," he said. "And you're still my favorite person. And I've missed you."

It was probably no later than ten o'clock when he got there, but we talked so much, I remember it was after midnight the next time I looked at the clock. I can't even remember what all we talked about, but I do remember how I felt. He seemed so happy and there was a light in his eyes that I'd never seen there before. Like he'd finally found his home.

He said he wanted to tell me something and his voice grew serious. He readjusted me so that I was straddling his lap, because he wanted me to look him in the eyes when he told me. I was thinking maybe he *was about to tell me he had a girlfriend or that he was leaving even sooner for the military. But what he said next shocked me.*

He said the first night he went to that old house, he wasn't there because he needed a place to stay.

He went there to kill himself.

My hands went up to my mouth because I had no idea things had gotten that bad for him. So bad that he didn't even want to live anymore.

"I hope you never know what it's like to feel that lonely, Lily," he said.

He went on to tell me that the first night he was at that house, he was sitting in the living room floor with a razor blade to his wrist. Right when he was about to use it, my bedroom light went on. "You were standing there like an angel, backlit by the light of heaven," he said. "I couldn't take my eyes off you."

He watched me walk around my bedroom for a while. Watched me lie on the bed and write in my journal. And he put down the razor blade because he said it'd been a month since life had given him any sort of feeling at all, and looking at me gave him a little bit of feeling. Enough to not be numb enough to end things that night.

Then a day or two later is when I took him the food and set it on his back porch. I guess you already know the rest of that story.

"You saved my life, Lily," he said to me. "And you weren't even trying."

He leaned forward and kissed that spot between my shoulder and my neck that he always kisses. I liked that he did it again. I don't like much about my body, but that spot on my collarbone has become my favorite part of me.

He took my hands in his and told me he was leaving sooner than he planned for the military, but that he couldn't leave without telling me thank you. He told me he'd be gone for four years and that the last thing he wanted for me was to be a sixteen-year-old girl not living my life because of a boyfriend I never got to see or hear from.

The next thing he said made his blue eyes tear up until they looked clear. He said, "Lily. Life is a funny thing. We only get so many years to live it, so we have to do everything we can to make sure those years are as full as they can be. We shouldn't waste time on things that might happen someday, or maybe even never."

I knew what he was saying. That he was leaving for the military and he didn't want me to hold on to him while he was gone. He wasn't really breaking up with me because we weren't ever really together. We'd just been two people who helped each other when we needed it and got our hearts fused together along the way.

It was hard, being let go by someone who had never really grabbed hold of me completely in the first place. In all the time we've spent together, I think we both sort of knew this wasn't a forever thing. I'm not sure why, because I could easily love him that way. I think maybe under normal circumstances, if we were together like typical teenagers and he had an average life with a home, we could be that kind of couple. The kind who comes together so easily and never experiences a life where cruelty sometimes intercepts.

I didn't even try to get him to change his mind that night. I feel like we have the kind of connection that even the fires of hell couldn't sever. I feel like he could go spend his time in the military and I'll spend my years being a teenager and then it will all fall back into place when the timing is right.

"I'm going to make a promise to you," he said. "When my life is good enough for you to be a part of it, I'll come find you. But I don't want you to wait around for me, because that might never happen."

I didn't like that promise, because it meant one of two things.

Either he thought he might never make it out of the military alive, or he didn't think his life would ever be good enough for me.

His life was already good enough for me, but I nodded my head and forced a smile. "If you don't come back for me, I'll come for you. And it won't be pretty, Atlas Corrigan."

He laughed at my threat. "Well, it won't be too hard to find me. You know exactly where I'll be."

I smiled. "Where everything is better."

He smiled back. "In Boston."

And then he kissed me.

Ellen, I know you're an adult and know all about what comes next, but I still don't feel comfortable telling you what happened over those next couple of hours. Let's just say we both kissed a lot. We both laughed a lot. We both loved a lot. We both breathed a lot. A lot. And we both had to cover our mouths and be as quiet and still as we could so we wouldn't get caught.

When we were finished, he held me against him, skin to skin, hand to heart. He kissed me and looked straight in my eyes.

"I love you, Lily. Everything you are. I love you."

I know those words get thrown around a lot, especially by teenagers. A lot of times prematurely and without much merit. But when he said them to me, I knew he wasn't saying it like he was in love with me. It wasn't that kind of "I love you."

Imagine all the people you meet in your life. There are so many. They come in like waves, trickling in and out with the tide. Some waves are much bigger and make more of an impact than others. Sometimes the waves bring with them things from deep in the bottom of the sea and they leave those things tossed onto the shore. Imprints against the grains of sand that prove the waves had once been there, long after the tide recedes.

That was what Atlas was telling me when he said "I love you."
He was letting me know that I was the biggest wave he'd ever come
across. And I brought so much with me that my impressions would
always be there, even when the tide rolled out.

After he said he loved me, he told me he had a birthday present
for me. He pulled out a small brown bag. "It isn't much, but it's all
I could afford."

I opened the bag and pulled out the best present I'd ever received.
It was a magnet that said "Boston" on the top. At the bottom in tiny
letters, it said "Where everything is better." I told him I would keep
it forever, and every time I look at it I'll think of him.

When I started out this letter, I said my sixteenth birthday was
one of the best days of my life. Because up until that second, it was.

It was the next few minutes that weren't.

Before Atlas had shown up that night, I wasn't expecting him, so
I didn't think to lock my bedroom door. My father heard me in there
talking to someone, and when he threw open my door and saw Atlas
in bed with me, he was angrier than I'd ever seen him. And Atlas was
at a disadvantage by not being prepared for what came next.

I'll never forget that moment for as long as I live. Being
completely helpless as my father came down on him with a baseball
bat. The sound of bones snapping was the only thing piercing
through my screams.

I still don't know who called the police. I'm sure it was my
mother, but it's been six months and we still haven't talked about
that night. By the time the police got to my bedroom and pulled my
father off of him, I didn't even recognize Atlas, he was covered in
so much blood.

I was hysterical.
Hysterical.

Not only did they have to take Atlas away in an ambulance, they also had to call an ambulance for me because I couldn't breathe. It was the first and only panic attack I've ever had.

No one would tell me where he was or if he was even okay. My father wasn't even arrested for what he'd done. Word got out that Atlas had been staying in that old house and that he had been homeless. My father became revered for his heroic act—saving his little girl from the homeless boy who manipulated her into having sex with him.

My father said I'd shamed our whole family by giving the town something to gossip about. And let me tell you, they still gossip about it. I heard Katie on the bus today telling someone she tried to warn me about Atlas. She said she knew he was bad news from the moment she laid eyes on him. Which is crap. If Atlas had been on the bus with me, I probably would have kept my mouth shut and been mature about it like he tried to teach me to be. Instead, I was so angry, I turned around and told Katie she could go to hell. I told her Atlas was a better human than she'd ever be and if I ever heard her say one more bad thing about him, she'd regret it.

She just rolled her eyes and said, "Jesus, Lily. Did he brainwash you? He was a dirty, thieving homeless kid who was probably on drugs. He used you for food and sex and now you're defending him?"

She's lucky the bus stopped at my house right then. I grabbed my backpack and walked off the bus, then went inside and cried in my room for three hours straight. Now my head hurts, but I knew the only thing that would make me feel better is if I finally got it all out on paper. I've been avoiding writing this letter for six months now.

No offense, Ellen, but my head still hurts. So does my heart. Maybe even more right now than it did yesterday. This letter didn't help one damn bit.

I think I'm going to take a break from writing to you for a

while. Writing to you reminds me of him, and it all hurts too much. Until he comes back for me, I'm just going to keep pretending to be okay. I'll keep pretending to swim, when really all I'm doing is floating. Barely keeping my head above water.

—Lily

I flip to the next page, but it's blank. That was the last time I ever wrote to Ellen.

I also never heard from Atlas again, and a huge part of me never blamed him. He almost died at the hands of my father. There's not much room for forgiveness there.

I knew he survived and that he was okay, because my curiosity has sometimes gotten the best of me over the years and I'd find what I could about him online. There wasn't much, though. Enough to let me know he'd survived and that he was in the military.

I still never got him out of my head, though. Time made things better, but sometimes I would see something that would remind me of him and it would put me in a funk. It wasn't until I was in college for a couple of years and dating someone else that I realized maybe Atlas wasn't supposed to be my whole life. Maybe he was only supposed to be a part of it.

Maybe love isn't something that comes full circle. It just ebbs and flows, in and out, just like the people in our lives.

On a particularly lonely night in college, I went alone to a tattoo studio and had a heart put in the spot where he used to kiss me. It's a tiny heart, about the size of a thumbprint, and it looks just like the heart he carved for me out of the oak tree. It's not fully closed at the top and I wonder if Atlas carved the heart like that on purpose. Because that's how my heart feels every time I think about him. It just feels like there's a little hole in it, letting out all the air.

After college I ended up moving to Boston, not necessarily because I was hoping to find him, but because I had to see for myself if Boston really was better. Plethora held nothing for me anyway, and I wanted to get as far away from my father as I could. Even though he was sick and could no longer hurt my mother, he still somehow made me want to escape the entire state of Maine, so that's exactly what I did.

Seeing Atlas in his restaurant for the first time filled me with so many emotions, I didn't know how to process them. I was glad to see that he was okay. I was happy that he looked healthy. But I would be lying if I said I wasn't a little bit heartbroken that he never tried to find me like he promised.

I love him. I still do and I always will. He was a huge wave that left a lot of imprints on my life, and I'll feel the weight of that love until I die. I've accepted that.

But things are different now. After today when he walked out of my office, I thought long and hard about us. I think our lives are where they're supposed to be. I have Ryle. Atlas has his girlfriend. We both have the careers we'd always hoped for. Just because we didn't end up on the same wave, doesn't mean we aren't still a part of the same ocean.

Things with Ryle are still fairly new, but I feel that same depth with him that I used to feel with Atlas. He loves me just like Atlas did. And I know if Atlas had a chance to get to know him, he would be able to see that and he'd be happy for me.

Sometimes an unexpected wave comes along, sucks you up and refuses to spit you back out. Ryle is my unexpected tidal wave, and right now I'm skimming the beautiful surface.

Part Two

Chapter Eighteen

"Oh, God. I think I might throw up."

Ryle puts his thumb under my chin and tilts my face up to his. He grins at me. "You'll be fine. Stop freaking out."

I shake my hands out and bounce up and down inside the elevator. "I can't help it," I say. "Everything you and Allysa have told me about your mother makes me so nervous." My eyes widen and I bring my hands up to my mouth. "Oh, God, Ryle. What if she asks me questions about *Jesus*? I don't go to church. I mean, I read the Bible when I was younger, but I don't know answers to any Bible trivia questions."

He's really laughing now. He pulls me to him and kisses the side of my head. "She won't talk about Jesus. She already loves you, based on what I've told her. All you have to do is be you, Lily."

I start nodding. "Be me. Okay. I think I can pretend to be me for one evening. Right?"

The doors open and he walks me out of the elevator, toward Allysa's apartment. It's funny watching him knock, but I guess he technically doesn't live here anymore. Over the last few months, he just sort of slowly began staying with me. All of his clothes are at my apartment. His toiletries. Last week he even hung that ridiculous blurry photograph of me up in our bedroom, and it really felt official after that.

"Does she know we live together?" I ask him. "Is she okay

with that? I mean, we aren't married. She goes to church every Sunday. Oh, no, Ryle! What if your mother thinks I'm a blasphemous whore?"

Ryle nudges his head toward the apartment door and I spin around to see his mother standing in the doorway, a layer of shock on her face.

"Mother," Ryle says. "Meet Lily. My blasphemous whore."

Oh dear God.

His mother reaches for me and pulls me in for a hug, and her laughter is everything I need to get me through this moment. "Lily!" she says, pushing me out to arm's length so she can get a good look at me. "Sweetie, I don't think you're a blasphemous whore. You're the angel I've been praying would land in Ryle's lap for the last ten years!"

She ushers us into the apartment. Ryle's father is the next to greet me with a hug. "No, definitely not a blasphemous whore," he says. "Not like Marshall here, who sank his teeth into my little girl when she was only seventeen." He glares back at Marshall, who is sitting on the couch.

Marshall laughs. "That's where you're wrong, Dr. Kincaid, because Allysa was the one who sank her teeth into me first. My teeth were in another girl who tasted like Cheetos and . . ."

Marshall doubles over when Allysa elbows him in the side.

And just like that, every single fear I had has vanished. They're perfect. They're normal. They say *whore* and laugh at Marshall's jokes.

I couldn't ask for anything better.

Three hours later, I'm lying on Allysa's bed with her.

Their parents went to bed early, claiming jet lag. Ryle and Marshall are in the living room, watching sports. I have my hand on Allysa's stomach, waiting to feel the baby kick.

"Her feet are right here," she says, moving my hand over a few inches. "Give it a few seconds. She's really active tonight."

We remain quiet while we both wait for her to kick. When it happens, I squeal with laughter. "Oh my God! It's like an alien!"

Allysa holds her hands on her stomach, smiling. "These last two and a half months are going to be hell," she says. "I'm so ready to meet her."

"Me too. I can't wait to be an aunt."

"I can't wait for you and Ryle to have a baby," she says.

I fall onto my back and put my hands behind my bed. "I don't know if he wants any. We've never really talked about it."

"It doesn't matter if he doesn't want any," she says. "He will. He didn't want a relationship before you. He didn't want to get married before you, and I feel a proposal coming on any month now."

I prop my head up on my hand and face her. "We've barely been together six months. Pretty sure he wants to wait a lot longer than that."

I don't push things with Ryle when it comes to speeding things up in our relationship. Our lives are perfect how they are. We're too busy for a wedding anyway, so I don't mind if he wants to wait a lot longer.

"What about you?" Allysa presses. "Would you say yes if he proposed?"

I laugh. "Are you kidding me? Of course. I'd marry him tonight."

Allysa looks over my shoulder at her bedroom door. She purses her lips together and tries to hide her smile.

"He's standing in the doorway, isn't he?"

She nods.

"He heard me say that, didn't he?"

She nods again.

I roll onto my back and look at Ryle, propped up against the doorframe with his arms folded over his chest. I can't tell what he's thinking after hearing that. His expression is tight. His jaw is tight. His eyes are narrowed in my direction.

"Lily," he says with stoic composure. "I would marry the *hell* out of you."

His words make me smile the most embarrassing, widest smile, so I pull a pillow over my face. "Why, thank you, Ryle," I say, my words muffled by the pillow.

"That's really sweet," I hear Allysa say. "My brother is actually sweet."

The pillow is pulled away from me and Ryle is standing over me, holding it at his side. "Let's go."

My heart begins to beat faster. "Right now?"

He nods. "I took the weekend off because my parents are in town. You have people who can run your store for you. Let's go to Vegas and get married."

Allysa sits up on the bed. "You can't do that," she says. "Lily's a girl. She wants a real wedding with flowers and bridesmaids and shit."

Ryle looks back at me. "Do you want a real wedding with flowers and bridesmaids and shit?"

I think about it for a second.

"No."

The three of us are quiet for a moment, and then Allysa starts kicking her legs up and down on the bed, giddy with excitement. "They're getting married!" she yells. She rolls off the bed and rushes toward the living room. "Marshall, pack our bags! We're going to Vegas!"

Ryle reaches down and grabs my hand, pulling me to a stand. He's smiling, but there's no way I'm doing this unless I know for sure he wants it.

"Are you sure about this, Ryle?"

He runs his hands through my hair and pulls my face to his, brushing his lips against mine. "Naked truth," he whispers. "I'm so excited to be your husband, I could piss my damn pants."

Chapter Nineteen

"It's been six weeks Mom, you gotta get over it."

My mother sighs into the phone. "You're my only daughter. I can't help it if I've been dreaming about your wedding your whole life."

She still hasn't forgiven me, even though she was there. We called her right before Allysa booked our flights. We forced her out of bed, we forced Ryle's parents out of bed, and then we forced them all on a midnight flight to Vegas. She didn't try to talk me out of it because I'm sure she could tell that Ryle and I had made up our minds by the time she made it to the airport. But she hasn't let me forget it. She's been dreaming of a huge wedding and dress shopping and cake tasting since the day I was born.

I kick my feet up on the couch. "How about I make it up to you?" I say to her. "What if, whenever we decide to have a baby, I promise to do it the natural way and not buy one in Vegas?"

My mom laughs. Then she sighs. "As long as you give me grandchildren someday, I guess I can get over it."

Ryle and I talked about kids on the flight to Vegas. I wanted to make sure that possibility was open for discussion in our future before I made a commitment to spend the rest of my life with him. He said it was definitely open for discussion. Then we cleared the air about a lot of other things that might cause problems down the road. I told him I wanted separate checking accounts, but since he makes more money than me, he has to buy me lots of presents all the time to keep me happy. He agreed. He made me promise him I'd never become vegan. That was a simple promise. I love cheese too much. I told him we had to start some kind of charity, or at least donate to the ones Marshall and Allysa like. He said he already does, and that made me want to marry him even sooner. He made me promise to vote. He said I was allowed to vote Democratic, Republican, or Independent, as long as I made sure to vote. We shook on it.

By the time we landed in Vegas, we were completely on the same page.

I hear the front door unlocking so I flip onto my back. "Gotta go," I say to my mother. "Ryle just got home." He closes the door behind him and then I grin and say, "Wait. Let me rephrase that, Mom. My *husband* just got home."

My mother laughs and tells me goodbye. I hang up with her and toss my phone aside. I bring my arm up above my head and rest it lazily against the arm of the couch. Then I prop my leg over the back of it, letting my skirt slide down my thighs and pool at my waist. Ryle drags his eyes up my body, grinning as he makes his way over to me. He drops to his knees on the couch and slowly crawls up my body.

"How's my wife?" he whispers, planting kisses all around my mouth. He presses himself between my legs and I let my head fall back as he kisses down my neck.

This is the life.

We both work almost every day. He works twice as many hours as I do and he only gets home before I'm in bed two or three nights a week. But the nights we actually do get to spend together, I tend to want him to spend those nights buried deep inside me.

He doesn't complain.

He finds a spot on my neck and he claims it, kissing it so hard it hurts. "Ouch."

He lowers himself on top of me and mutters into my neck. "I'm giving you a hickey. Don't move."

I laugh, but I let him. My hair is long enough that I can cover it, and I've never had a hickey before.

His lips remain in the same spot, sucking and kissing until I can no longer feel the sting. He's pressed against me, bulging against his scrubs. I move my hands and shove his scrubs down far enough so that he can slide inside of me. He continues kissing my neck as he takes me right there on the couch.

·   ·   ·

He took a shower first, and as soon as he got out, I jumped in. I told him we needed to wash the smell of sex off of us before we had dinner with Allysa and Marshall.

Allysa is due in a few weeks, so she's forcing as much couple time on us as she can. She's worried we'll stop coming to visit after the baby is born, which I know is ridiculous. The visits will just grow more frequent. I already love my niece more than any of them, anyway.

Okay, maybe not. But it's close.

I try to avoid getting my hair wet as I rinse off, because we're already running late. I grab my razor and press it under my arm when I hear a crash. I pause.

"Ryle?"

Nothing.

I finish shaving and then wash the soap off. Another crash.

What in the world is he doing?

I turn off the water and grab a towel, running it over myself. "Ryle!"

He still doesn't respond. I pull my jeans on in a hurry and open the door as I'm pulling my shirt over my head. "Ryle?"

The nightstand by our bed is tipped over. I move to the living room and see him sitting on the edge of the couch, his head in one of his hands. He's looking down at something in his other hand.

"What are you doing?"

He looks up at me and I don't recognize his expression. I'm confused by what's happening. I don't know if he just got bad news or . . . *Oh, God. Allysa.*

"Ryle, you're scaring me. What's wrong?"

He holds up my phone and just looks at me like I should know what's happening. When I shake my head in confusion, he holds up a piece of paper. "Funny thing," he says, setting my phone on the coffee table in front of him. "I dropped your phone by accident. Cover pops off. I find this number hidden in the back of it."

Oh, God.

No, no, no.

He crumbles the number in his fist. "I thought, '*Huh. That's weird. Lily doesn't hide things from me.*'" He stands up and picks up my phone. "So I called it." He tightens his fist around the phone. "He's lucky I got his fucking voice mail." He chunks my phone clear across the room and it crashes against the wall, shattering to the floor.

There's a three-second pause where I think this could go one of two ways.

He's going to leave me.

Or he's going to hurt me.

He runs a hand through his hair and walks straight for the door.

He leaves.

"Ryle!" I yell.

Why did I never throw that number away?!

I open the door and run after him. He's taking the stairs two at a time, and I finally reach him when he's at the landing of the second floor. I shove myself in front of him and grab his shirt in my fists. "Ryle, please. Let me explain."

He grabs my wrists and pushes me away from him.

· · ·

"Be still."

I feel his hands on me. Gentle. Steady.

Tears are flowing and for some reason, they sting.

"Lily, be still. Please."

His voice is soothing. My head hurts. "Ryle?" I try to open my eyes, but the light is too bright. I can feel a sting at the corner of my eye and I wince. I try to sit up, but I feel his hand press down on my shoulder.

"You have to be still until I'm finished, Lily."

I open my eyes again and look up at the ceiling. It's our

bedroom ceiling. "Finished with what?" My mouth hurts when I speak, so I bring my hand up and cover it.

"You fell down the stairs," he says. "You're hurt."

My eyes meet his. There's concern in them, but also hurt. Anger. He's feeling *everything* right now, and the only thing I feel is confused.

I close my eyes again and try to remember why he's angry. Why he's hurt.

My phone.

Atlas's number.

The stairwell.

I grabbed his shirt.

He pushed me away.

"You fell down the stairs."

But I *didn't* fall.

He pushed me. Again.

That's twice.

You pushed me, Ryle.

I can feel my whole body start to shake with the sobs. I have no idea how bad I'm hurt, but I don't even care. No physical pain could even compare to what my heart is feeling in this moment. I start to slap at his hands, wanting him away from me. I feel him lift off the bed as I curl up into a ball.

I wait for him to try and soothe it out like he did the last time he hurt me, but it never comes. I hear him walking around our bedroom. I don't know what he's doing. I'm still crying when he kneels down in front of me.

"You might have a concussion," he says, matter-of-fact. "You have a small cut on your lip. I just bandaged up the cut on your eye. You don't need stitches."

His voice is cold.

"Does it hurt anywhere else? Your arms? Legs?"

He sounds just like a doctor and nothing like a husband.

"You pushed me," I say through tears. It's all I can think or say or see.

"You fell," he says calmly. "About five minutes ago. Right after I found out what a fucking liar I married." He places something on my pillow next to me. "If you need anything, I'm sure you can call this number."

I look at the crumpled up piece of paper by my head that holds Atlas's phone number.

"Ryle," I sob.

What is happening?

I hear the front door slam.

My whole world comes crashing down around me.

"Ryle," I whisper to no one. I cover my face with my hands and I cry harder than I've ever cried. I am destroyed.

Five minutes.

That's all it takes to completely destroy a person.

•   •   •

A few minutes pass.

Ten, maybe?

I can't stop crying. I still haven't moved from the bed. I'm scared to look in the mirror. I'm just . . . scared.

I hear the front door open and slam shut again. Ryle appears in the doorway and I have no idea if I'm supposed to hate him.

Or be terrified of him.

Or feel bad for him.

How can I be feeling all three?

He presses his forehead to our bedroom door and I watch as he hits his head against it. Once. Twice. Three times.

He turns and rushes at me, falling to his knees at the side of the bed. He grabs both of my hands and he squeezes them. "Lily," he says, his whole face twisting in pain. "*Please tell me it's nothing.*" He brings his hand to the side of my head and I can feel his hands shaking. "I can't take this, I can't." He leans forward and presses his lips hard against my forehead, then rests his forehead against mine. "Please tell me you aren't seeing him. *Please.*"

I'm not even sure I can tell him that because I don't even want to speak.

He stays pressed against me, his hand wrapped tightly in my hair. "It hurts so much, Lily. I love you so much."

I shake my head, wanting the truth out of me so he'll see what a huge mistake he just made. "I forgot his number was even there," I say quietly. "The day after the fight in the restaurant . . . he came to the store. You can ask Allysa. He was only there for five minutes. He took my phone from me and he put his number inside of it, because he didn't believe I was safe with you. I forgot it was there, Ryle. I've never even looked at it."

He breathes out a shaky breath and begins nodding with relief. "You swear, Lily? You swear on our marriage and our lives and on everything that you are that you haven't spoken to him since that day?" He pulls back so he can look me in the eyes.

"I swear, Ryle. You overreacted before giving me the chance to explain," I say to him. "Now get the *fuck* out of my apartment."

My words knock the breath from him. I see it happen. His back meets the wall behind him and he stares at me silently. In shock. "Lily," he whispers. "You fell down the stairs."

I can't tell if he's trying to convince me or himself.

I calmly repeat myself. "Get out of my apartment."

He remains frozen in place. I sit up on the bed. My hand immediately goes to the throbbing in my eye. He pushes himself up off the floor. When he takes a step forward, I scoot back on the bed.

"You're hurt, Lily. I'm not leaving you alone."

I grab one of my pillows and throw it at him, like it could actually do damage. "Get out!" I yell. He catches the pillow. I grab the other one and stand up on the bed and start swinging it at him as I scream, "Get out! Get out! Get out!"

I toss the pillow on the floor after the front door slams shut.

I run to the living room and dead-bolt the door.

I run back to my bedroom and fall onto my bed. The same bed I share with my husband. The same bed he makes love to me on.

The same bed he lays me on when it's time for him to clean up his messes.

Chapter Twenty

I tried salvaging my phone before I fell asleep last night, but it was no use. It was in two completely separate pieces. I set my alarm so I could get up early and stop and get a new one on my way in to work today.

My face doesn't look as bad as I feared it would. Of course, it's not something I could hide from Allysa, but I'm not even going to try and do that. I part my hair to the side to cover up most of the bandage Ryle had placed over my eye. The only thing visible from last night is the cut on my lip.

And the hickey he gave me on my neck.

Fucking irony at its best.

I grab my purse and open the front door. I stop short when I see the lump at my feet.

It moves.

It's several seconds before I realize that lump is actually Ryle. *He slept out here?*

He pulls himself to his feet as soon as he realizes I've opened the door. He's in front of me, pleading eyes, gentle hands on my cheeks. Lips on my mouth. "I'm sorry, I'm sorry, I'm sorry."

I pull back and scroll my eyes over him. *He slept out here?*

I step out of my apartment and pull my door shut. I calmly walk past him and down the stairs. He follows me the entire way to my car, begging me to talk to him.

I don't.

I leave.

•   •   •

It's an hour later when I have a new phone in my hands. I'm sitting in my car at the cell phone store when I turn it on. I watch the screen as seventeen messages appear. All from Allysa.

I guess it would make sense that Ryle didn't call me all night, since he knew what kind of shape my phone was in.

I start to open a text message when my phone begins ringing. It's Allysa.

"Hello?"

She sighs heavily, and then, "Lily! What in the hell is going on? Oh my God, you can't do this to me, I'm pregnant!"

I start my car and set the phone to Bluetooth while I drive toward the store. Allysa is off today. She's only got a few days left before she gets a jump start on her maternity leave.

"I'm okay," I tell her. "Ryle is okay. We got into a fight. I'm sorry I couldn't call you, he broke my phone."

She's quiet for a moment, and then, "He did? Are you okay? Where are you?"

"I'm fine. Heading to work now."

"Good, I'm almost there myself."

I start to protest, but she hangs up before I have the chance.

By the time I make it to the store, she's already there.

I open the front door, ready to field questions and defend my reasons for kicking her brother out of my apartment. But

I stop short when I see the two of them standing at the counter. Ryle is leaning against it and Allysa has her hands on top of his, saying something to him that I can't hear.

They both turn to face me when they hear the door close behind me.

"Ryle," Allysa whispers. "What did you *do* to her?" She walks around the counter and pulls me in for a hug. "Oh, Lily," she says, running her hand down my back. She pulls back with tears in her eyes, and her reaction confuses me. She obviously knows Ryle is responsible, but if that's the case, it seems she would be attacking him, or at least yelling.

She turns back to Ryle and he's looking up at me apologetically. Longingly. Like he wants to reach out and hug me, but he's scared to death to touch me. He should be.

"You need to tell her," Allysa says to Ryle.

He instantly drops his head in his hands.

"Tell her," Allysa says, her voice angrier now. "She has the right to know, Ryle. She's your wife. If you don't tell her, I will."

Ryle's shoulders roll forward and his head is fully pressed against the counter now. Whatever it is Allysa wants him to tell me has him so agonized, he can't even look at me. I clench my stomach, feeling the angst deeper than my soul.

Allysa spins toward me and puts her hands on my shoulders. "Hear him out," she begs. "I'm not asking you to forgive him, because I have no idea what happened last night. But just please, as my sister-in-law and my best friend, give my brother a chance to talk to you."

• • •

Allysa said she'd watch the store for the next hour until another employee comes in for their shift. I was still so upset with Ryle, I didn't want him in the same car with me. He said he'd send for an Uber and meet me at my apartment.

My entire drive home I agonized over what he could possibly need to tell me that Allysa already knows. So many things went through my head. Is he dying? Has he been cheating on me? Did he lose his job? She didn't seem to know the details of what happened between us last night, so I have no idea how this relates to that.

Ryle finally walks through my front door ten minutes after me. I'm sitting on the couch, nervously picking at my nails.

I stand up and start to pace as he slowly walks to the chair and takes a seat. He leans forward, clasping his hands in front of him.

"Please sit down, Lily."

He says it pleadingly, like he can't take seeing me worry. I return to my seat on the couch, but I scoot to the arm, pull my feet up, and bring my hands to my mouth. "Are you dying?"

His eyes stretch wide and he immediately shakes his head. "No. *No.* It's nothing like that."

"Then what is it?"

I just want him to spit it out. My hands are starting to shake. He sees how much he's freaking me out, so he leans forward and pulls my hands from my face, holding them in his. Part of me doesn't want him touching me after what he did last night, but a piece of me needs the reassurance from him. The anticipation of what I'm about to find out is making me nauseous.

"No one is dying. I'm not cheating on you. What I'm about to tell you isn't going to hurt you, okay? It's all in the past. But Allysa thinks you need to know. And . . . so do I."

I nod and he releases my hands. He's the one up and pacing now, back and forth behind the coffee table. It's as if he's having to work up the courage to find his own words and that's making me even *more* nervous.

He sits in the chair again. "Lily? Do you remember the night we met?"

I nod.

"You remember when I walked out onto the roof? How angry I was?"

I nod again. He was kicking the chair. It was before he knew marine-grade polymer was virtually indestructible.

"Do you remember my naked truth? What I told you about that night and what caused me to be so angry?"

I lean my head down and think back to that night and to all the truths he told me. He said marriage repulsed him. He was only into one-night stands. He never wanted to have kids. He was mad about a patient he'd lost that night.

I start nodding. "The little boy," I said. "That's why you were mad, because a little boy died and it upset you."

He blows out a quick breath of relief. "Yes. That's why I was mad." He stands up again and it's like I see his entire soul crumble. He presses his palms against his eyes and fights back tears. "When I told you about what happened to him, do you remember what you said to me?"

I feel like I'm about to cry and I don't even know why yet. "Yes. I told you I couldn't imagine what something like that will do to that little boy's brother. The one who accidentally shot him." My lips start to tremble. "And that's when you said, *'It'll destroy him for life, that's what it'll do.'*"

Oh, God.

Where is he going with this?

Ryle walks over and drops down to his knees in front of me. "Lily," he says. "I knew it would destroy him. I knew exactly what that little boy was feeling . . . because that's what happened to me. To Allysa's and my older brother . . ."

I can't hold in the tears. I just start crying and he wraps his arms tightly around my waist and lays his head on my lap. "I *shot* him, Lily. My best friend. My big brother. I was only six years old. I didn't even know I was holding a real gun."

His whole body begins to shake and he grips me even tighter. I press a kiss into his hair because it feels like he's on the verge of a breakdown. Just like that night on the roof. And while I'm still so angry at him, I also still love him and it absolutely kills me to find this out about him. About Allysa. We sit quietly for a long time—his head on my lap, his arms around my waist, my lips in his hair.

"She was only five when it happened. Emerson was seven. We were in the garage, so no one heard our screams for a long time. And I just sat there, and . . ."

He pulls away from my lap and stands up, facing the other direction. After a long stretch of silence he sits down on the couch and leans forward. "I was trying to . . ." Ryle's face contorts in pain and he lowers his head, covering it with his hands, shaking it back and forth. "I was trying to put everything back inside his head. I thought I could *fix* him, Lily."

My hand flies up to my mouth. I gasp so loudly, there's no way to hide it.

I have to stand up so I can catch a breath.

It doesn't help.

I still can't breathe.

Ryle walks over to me, taking my hands and pulling me to him. We hug each other for a solid minute when he says, "I would never tell you this because I want it to excuse my behavior." He pulls back and looks me firmly in the eyes. "You have to believe that. Allysa wanted me to tell you all of this because since that happened, there are things I can't control. I get angry. I black out. I've been in therapy since I was six years old. But it is not my excuse. It is my reality."

He wipes away my tears, cradling my head against his shoulder.

"When you ran after me last night, I swear I had no intention of hurting you. I was upset and angry. And sometimes when I feel that much emotion, something inside of me just snaps. I don't remember the moment I pushed you. But I know I did. *I did*. All I was thinking when you were running after me was how I needed to get away from you. I wanted you out of my way. I didn't process that there were stairs around us. I didn't process my strength compared to yours. I fucked up, Lily. I fucked up."

He lowers his mouth to my ear. His voice cracks when he says, "You are my *wife*. I'm supposed to be the one who protects you from the monsters. I'm not supposed to *be* one." He holds me with so much desperation, he begins to shake. I have never, in all my life, felt so much pain radiating from one human.

It breaks me. It rips me apart from the inside out. All my heart wants to do is wrap tightly around his.

But even with everything he just told me, I'm still fighting my own forgiveness. I swore I wouldn't let it happen again. I swore to him and to myself that if he ever hurt me again, I would leave.

I pull away from him, unable to look him in the eye. I walk toward my bedroom to try and take a moment to just catch my breath. I close my bathroom door behind me and grip the sink, but I can't even stand up. I end up sliding to the floor in a heap of tears.

This isn't how this was supposed to be. My whole life, I knew exactly what I'd do if a man ever treated me the way my father treated my mother. It was simple. I would leave and it would never happen again.

But I didn't leave. And now, here I am with bruises and cuts on my body at the hands of the man who is supposed to love me. At the hands of my own husband.

And still, I'm trying to justify what happened.

It was an accident. He thought I was cheating on him. He was hurt and angry and I got in his way.

I bring my hands to my face and I sob, because I feel more pain for that man out there, knowing what he went through as a child, than I feel for myself. And that doesn't make me feel selfless or strong. It makes me feel pathetic and weak. I'm supposed to hate him. I'm supposed to be the woman my mother was never strong enough to be.

But if I'm emulating my mother's behavior, then that would mean Ryle is emulating my father's behavior. But he isn't. I have to stop comparing us to them. We're our own individuals in an entirely different situation. My father never had an excuse for his anger, nor was he immediately apologetic. The way he treated my mother was much worse than what's happened between Ryle and me.

Ryle just opened up to me in a way that he's probably never opened up to anyone. He's struggling to be a better person for me.

Yes, he screwed up last night. But he's here and he's trying to make me understand his past and why he reacted the way he did. Humans aren't perfect and I can't let the only example I've ever witnessed of marriage weigh in on my *own* marriage.

I wipe my eyes and pull myself up. When I look in the mirror, I don't see my mother. I just see me. I see a girl who loves her husband and wants more than anything to be able to help him. I know Ryle and I are strong enough to move past this. Our love is strong enough to get us through this.

I walk out of the bathroom and back into the living room. Ryle stands up and faces me, his face full of fear. He's scared I'm not going to forgive him, and I'm not sure that I *do* forgive him. But an act doesn't have to be forgiven in order to learn from it.

I walk over to him and I grab both of his hands in mine. I speak to him with nothing but naked truth.

"Remember what you said to me on the roof that night? You said, *'There is no such thing as bad people. We're all just people who sometimes do bad things.'*"

He nods and squeezes my hands.

"You aren't a bad person, Ryle. I know that. You can still protect me. When you're upset, just walk away. And I'll walk away. We'll leave the situation until you're calm enough to talk about it, okay? You are *not* a monster, Ryle. You're only human. And as humans, we can't expect to shoulder all of our pain. Sometimes we have to share it with the people who love us so we don't come crashing down from the weight of it all. But I can't help you unless I know you need it. Ask me for help. We'll get through this, I know we can."

He exhales what feels like every breath he's been holding in since last night. He wraps his arms tightly around me and buries his face in my hair. "Help me, Lily," he whispers. "I need you to help me."

He holds me against him and I know deep in my heart that I'm doing the right thing. There is so much more good in him than bad, and I'll do whatever I can to convince him of that until he can see it, too.

Chapter Twenty-One

"I'm heading out. You need me to do anything else?"

I look up from the paperwork and shake my head. "Thank you, Serena. See you tomorrow."

She nods and walks away, leaving the door to my office open.

Allysa's last day was two weeks ago. She's due any day now. I have two other full-time employees, Serena and Lucy.

Yes. *That* Lucy.

She's been married for a couple of months now and came in looking for a job two weeks ago. It's actually worked out pretty well. She keeps herself busy, and if I'm here when she is, I just keep my office door shut so I don't have to listen to her sing.

It's been almost a month since the incident on the stairs. Even with everything Ryle told me about his childhood, the forgiveness was still hard to come by.

I know Ryle has a temper. I saw it the first night we met, before we ever even spoke a word to each other. I saw it that awful night in my kitchen. I saw it when he found the phone number in my phone case.

But I also see the difference between Ryle and my father.

Ryle is compassionate. He does things my father never would have done. He donates to charity, he cares about other people, he puts me before everything. Ryle would never in a million years make me park in the driveway while he took the garage.

I have to remind myself of those things. Sometimes the girl inside of me—the daughter of my father—is really opinionated. She tells me I shouldn't have forgiven him. She tells me I should have left the first time. And sometimes I believe that voice. But then the side of me that knows Ryle understands that marriages aren't perfect. Sometimes there are moments that both parties regret. And I wonder how I'd feel about myself had I just left him after that first incident. He never should have pushed me, but I also did things *I* wasn't proud of. And if I'd have just left, would that not be going against our marriage vows? *For better or for worse.* I refuse to give up on my marriage that easily.

I am a strong woman. I've been around abusive situations my whole life. I will never become my mother. I believe that a hundred percent. And Ryle will never become my father. I think we needed what happened on the stairwell to happen so that I would know his past and we'd be able to work on it together.

Last week we got into another fight.

I was scared. The other two fights we'd gotten into did not end well, and I knew this would be a testament to whether or not our agreement for me to help him through his anger would work.

We were discussing his career. He's finished with his residency now and there's a three-month specialized course in Cambridge, England, he applied for. He'll find out soon if he was approved, but that's not why I was upset. It's a great opportunity and I'd never ask him not to go. Three months is nothing with how busy we are, so that wasn't even what got me so upset. I became upset when he discussed what he wanted to do *after* the Cambridge trip was over.

He was offered a job in Minnesota at the Mayo Clinic and he wants us to move there. He said Mass General is rated the second best neurological hospital in the world. Mayo Clinic is number one.

He said he never intended to stay in Boston forever. I told him that would have been a good subject to bring up when we discussed our futures on the flight to get married in Vegas. I can't leave Boston. My mother lives here. Allysa lives here. He told me it was only a five-hour flight and that we could visit as often as we wanted. I told him it was pretty hard to run a floral business when you live several states away.

The fight continued to escalate and both of us were getting angrier by the second. At one point, he knocked a vase full of flowers off the table and onto the floor. We both just stared at them for a moment. I was scared, wondering if I had made the right decision to stay. To trust that we could work on his anger issues together. He took a deep breath and he said, "I'm going to leave for an hour or two. I think I need to walk away. When I get back, we'll continue this discussion."

He walked out the door and, true to his word, he came back an hour later when he was much calmer. He dropped his keys on the table and then walked straight to where I was standing. He took my face in his hands and he said, "I told you I wanted to be the best in my field, Lily. I told you this the first night we ever met. It was one of my naked truths. But if I have to choose between working at the best hospital in the world and making my wife happy . . . I choose you. You *are* my success. As long as you're happy, I don't care where I work. We'll stay in Boston."

That's when I knew that I had made the right choice. Everyone deserves another chance. Especially the people who mean the most to you.

It's been a week since that fight and he hasn't mentioned moving again. I feel bad, like I thwarted his plans in some way, but marriage is about compromise. It's about doing what's best for the couple as a whole, not individually. And staying in Boston is better for everyone in both of our families.

Speaking of families, I look over at my phone right as a text from Allysa comes through.

Allysa: Are you finished up at work yet? I need your opinion on furniture.

Me: Be there in fifteen minutes.

I don't know if it's the impending delivery or the fact that she's not currently working, but I'm pretty sure I've spent more time at her house this week than I have at my own. I close up the shop and head toward her apartment.

· · ·

When I step off the elevator, there's a note taped to her apartment door. I see my name written across it, so I pull it off the door.

Lily,

On the seventh floor. Apartment 749.

—A

She has an apartment here just for extra furniture? I know they're rich, but even that seems a little excessive for them. I get on the elevator and press the button for the seventh floor. When the doors open, I head down the hall toward apartment 749. When I reach it, I have no idea if I should knock or just go inside. For all I know, someone could live here. Probably one of her *people*.

I knock on the door and hear footsteps from the other side.

I'm shocked when the door swings open and Ryle is standing in front of me.

"Hey," I say, confused. "What are you doing here?"

He grins and leans against the doorframe. "I live here. What are *you* doing here?"

I glance at the pewter number plate next to the door and then back at him. "What do you mean you live here? I thought you lived with me. You've had your own apartment this whole time?" I would think an entire apartment would be something a husband would bring up to his wife at some point. It's a little unnerving.

Actually, it's ludicrous and deceptive. I think I might be really angry at him right now.

Ryle laughs and pushes off the doorframe. Now he's filling up the entire doorway as he lifts his hands to the frame over his head and grips it. "I haven't really had a chance to tell you about this apartment, considering I just signed the paperwork on it this morning."

I take a step back. "Wait. What?"

He reaches for my hand and pulls me inside the apartment. "Welcome home, Lily."

I pause in the foyer.

Yes. I said *foyer*. There is a *foyer*.

"You bought an apartment?"

He nods slowly, gauging my reaction.

"You bought an apartment," I repeat.

He's still nodding. "I did. Is that okay? I figured since we live together now we could use the extra room."

I spin in a slow circle. When my eyes land on the kitchen, I pause. It's not as big as Allysa's kitchen, but it's just as white and almost as beautiful. There's a wine cooler and a dishwasher, two things my own apartment doesn't have. I walk into the kitchen and look around, scared to touch anything. *Is this really my kitchen? This can't be my kitchen.*

I look in the living room at the cathedral ceilings and the huge windows overlooking Boston Harbor.

"Lily?" he says from behind me. "You aren't mad, are you?"

I spin and face him, realizing that he's been waiting on me to react for the past several minutes. But I'm completely speechless.

I shake my head and bring my hand up to cover my mouth. "I don't think so," I whisper.

He walks up to me and takes my hands in his, pulling them up between us. "You don't *think* so?" He looks worried and confused. "Please give me a naked truth, because I'm starting to think maybe I shouldn't have done this as a surprise."

I look down at the hardwood floor. It's real hardwood. It's not laminate. "Okay," I say, looking back up at him. "I think it's crazy that you just went and bought an apartment without me. I feel like that's something we should have done together."

He's nodding and it looks like he's about to spit out an apology, but I'm not finished.

"But my naked truth is that . . . it's perfect. I don't even know what to say, Ryle. Everything is so clean. I'm scared to move. I might get something dirty."

He blows out a rush of air and pulls me to him. "You can get it dirty, babe. It's yours. You can get it as dirty as you want." He kisses the side of my head and I don't even say thank you yet. It seems like such a small response to such a huge gesture.

"When do we move in?"

He shrugs. "Tomorrow? I have the day off. It's not like we have a whole lot of stuff. We can spend the next few weeks buying new furniture."

I nod, trying to run through tomorrow's schedule in my head. I already knew Ryle was off tomorrow, so I didn't have anything planned.

I suddenly feel the need to sit down. There aren't any chairs, but luckily, the floor is clean. "I need to sit down."

Ryle helps me to the floor and then he lowers himself in front of me, still holding my hands.

"Does Allysa know?" I ask him.

He smiles and nods his head. "She's so excited, Lily. I've been thinking about getting an apartment here for a while now. After we decided to stay in Boston for good, I just went ahead with it to surprise you. She helped, but I was starting to worry she'd tell you before I had the chance."

I just can't wrap my head around this. I live here? Me and Allysa get to be neighbors now? I don't know why I feel like this should bother me, because I really am excited about it.

He smiles and then says, "I know you need a minute to process everything, but you haven't seen the best part and it's killing me."

"Show me!"

He grins and pulls me to my feet. We make our way through the living room and down a hallway. He opens each door and tells me what the rooms are, but doesn't even give me time to go in any of them. By the time we make it to the master bedroom, I've concluded that we live in a three-bedroom, two-bath apartment. With an office.

I don't even have time to process the beauty of the bedroom as he pulls me across the room. He reaches a wall covered by a curtain and he turns and faces me. "It's not a ground that you can plant a garden in, but with a few pots, it can come close." He pulls the curtain aside and opens a door, revealing a huge balcony. I follow him outside, already daydreaming about all the potted plants I could fit up here.

"It overlooks the same view as the rooftop deck," he says. "We'll always have the same view we had from the night we met."

It took a while to sink in, but it all hits me in this moment and I just start crying. Ryle pulls me to his chest and wraps his arms tightly around me. "Lily," he whispers, running his hand over my hair. "I didn't mean to make you cry."

I laugh between my tears. "I just can't believe I live here." I pull away from his chest and look up at him. "Are we rich? How can you afford this?"

He laughs. "You married a neurosurgeon, Lily. You aren't necessarily strapped for cash."

His comment makes me laugh and then I cry some more.

And then we have our very first visitor because someone begins pounding on the door.

"Allysa," he says. "She's been waiting down the hall."

I run to the front door and swing it open and we both hug and squeal and I might even cry a little more.

We spend the rest of the evening at our new apartment. Ryle orders Chinese takeout and Marshall comes down to eat with us. We have no tables or chairs yet, so the four of us sit in the middle of the living room floor and eat straight out of the containers. We talk about how we'll decorate, we talk about all the neighborly things we'll do together, we talk about Allysa's impending delivery.

It's everything and more.

I can't wait to tell my mother.

Chapter Twenty-Two

Allysa is three days overdue.

We've lived in our new apartment for a week now. We successfully got all of our stuff moved the day Ryle was off, and Allysa and I went furniture shopping the second day we moved in. We were practically settled by the third day. We got our first piece of mail yesterday. It was a utility bill for establishing service, so it finally feels official now.

I'm married. I have a great husband. An awesome house. My best friend just happens to be my sister-in-law and I'm about to be an aunt.

Dare I say it . . . but can my life get any better?

I close my laptop and get ready to leave for the evening. I've been leaving earlier now than I usually do because I'm so excited to get home to my new apartment. Just as I begin to close my office door, Ryle uses his key to open the front door to the store. He lets the door fall shut behind him as he walks in with his hands full.

There's a newspaper tucked under his arm and two coffees in his hands. Despite the frenzied look about him and the urgency in his step, he's smiling. "Lily," he says, walking toward me. He shoves one of the coffees in my hand and then pulls the newspaper out from under his arm. "Three things. One . . . did you see the paper?" He hands it to me. The paper is folded inside-out. He points at the article. "You got it, Lily. You got it!"

I try not to get my hopes up as I look down at the article. He could be talking about something totally different from what I'm thinking. Once I read the headline, I realize he's talking about *exactly* what I was thinking. "I got it?"

I'd been notified that my business was nominated for an award for Best of Boston. It's a people's choice awards the newspaper holds annually, and Lily Bloom's was nominated under the "Best new businesses in Boston" category. The criteria are for businesses that have been open less than two years. I had a suspicion I might have been chosen when a reporter for the paper called me last week and asked me a series of questions.

The title reads *"Best new businesses in Boston. Votes are in for your top ten!"*

I smile and almost spill my coffee when Ryle pulls me in, picks me up, and spins me around.

He said he had three pieces of news, and if he started with that one, I have no idea what the other two could be. "What's the second thing?"

He sets me back down on my feet and says, "I started with the best one. I was too excited." He takes a sip of his coffee and then says, "I got selected for the training at Cambridge."

My face is taken over by a huge smile. "You did?" He nods and then he hugs me and spins me around again. "I'm so proud of you," I say, kissing him. "We're both so successful, it's sickening."

He laughs.

"Number three?" I ask him.

He pulls back. "Oh, yeah. Number three." He casually leans against the counter and takes a slow sip of his coffee.

He gently places his coffee back on the counter. "Allysa is in labor."

"What?!" I yell.

"Yeah." He nods toward our coffees. "That's why I brought you caffeine. We aren't getting any sleep tonight."

I start clapping, jumping up and down, and then panicking as I try to find my purse, my jacket, my keys, my phone, the light switch. Right before we make it to the door, Ryle rushes back to the counter and grabs the newspaper and tucks it under his arm. My hands are shaking with excitement as I lock the door.

"We're gonna be aunts!" I say as I run to my car.

Ryle laughs at my joke and says, "*Uncles*, Lily. We're gonna be *uncles*."

.　　.　　.

Marshall calmly steps out into the hallway. Ryle and I both perk up and wait for the news. It's been quiet in there for the past half an hour. We've been waiting to hear Allysa scream in agony—a sign she delivered—but there were no sounds at all. Not even the cries of a newborn. My hands go up to my mouth and seeing the look on Marshall's face has me fearing the worst.

His shoulders just start shaking and tears pour out of his eyes. "I'm a dad." And then he punches the air. "I'm a DAD!"

He hugs Ryle and then me and says, "Give us fifteen minutes and you can come inside to meet her."

When he closes the door, Ryle and I both release huge sighs of relief. We look at each other and smile. "You were thinking the worst, too?" he asks.

I nod and then hug him. "You're an uncle," I say, smiling. He kisses my head and says, "You too."

Half an hour later, Ryle and I are both standing next to the bed, watching Allysa hold her new baby. She's absolutely perfect. A little too new to tell who she looks like yet, but she's beautiful, regardless.

"You want to hold your niece?" Allysa says to Ryle.

He kind of stiffens up like he's nervous, but then he nods. She leans over and puts the baby in Ryle's arms, showing him how to hold her. He stares down at her nervously and then walks over to the couch and takes a seat. "Have you guys decided on a name yet?" he asks.

"Yes," Allysa says.

Ryle and I both look at Allysa and she smiles, teary eyed. "We wanted to name her after someone Marshall and I both think the world of. So we added an *E* to your name. We're calling her Rylee."

I instantly look back over at Ryle and he blows out a quick breath like he's a little in shock. He looks back down at Rylee and just starts smiling. "Wow," he whispers. "I don't know what to say."

I squeeze Allysa's hand and then walk over and take a seat next to Ryle. I've had a lot of moments when I thought I couldn't love him more than I already do, but once again I'm proven wrong. Seeing the way he looks at his new baby niece makes my heart expand.

Marshall sits down on the bed next to Allysa. "Did you guys hear how quiet Issa was through the whole thing? Not a single peep. She didn't even take drugs." He puts his arm around her and lies down next to her on the bed. "I feel like

I'm in that movie *Hancock* with Will Smith and I'm about to find out I'm married to a superhero."

Ryle laughs. "She's kicked my ass a time or two growing up. I wouldn't be surprised."

"No cussing around Rylee," Marshall says.

"Ass," Ryle whispers to her.

We both laugh and then he asks me if I want to hold her. I make like I have grabby hands because waiting for my turn has been killing me. I pull her into my arms and am shocked by how much love I have for her already.

"When are Mom and Dad coming in?" Ryle asks Allysa.

"They'll be here by lunch tomorrow."

"I should probably get some sleep then. Just got off a long shift." He looks back at me. "You coming with?"

I shake my head. "I want to hang out for a little while longer. Just take my car and I'll catch a cab home."

He kisses me on the side of my head and then rests his head against mine as we both look down at Rylee. "I think we should make one of these," he says.

I glance up at him, not sure if I heard him correctly.

He winks. "If I'm asleep when you get home later, wake me up. We'll start on it tonight." He tells Marshall and Allysa goodbye and Marshall walks him out.

I glance over at Allysa and she's smiling. "I told you he'd want babies with you."

I grin and walk back over to her bed. She scoots over and makes room for me. I hand Rylee back to her and we snuggle together on her bed and watch Rylee sleep, like it's the most magnificent thing we've ever seen.

Chapter Twenty-Three

It's three hours later and after ten o'clock when I make it back home. I stayed with Allysa for another hour after Ryle left and then went back to my office to finish up a few things so that I don't have to go in for the next two days. Whenever Ryle has a day off, I try to coincide my own days off with his.

The lights are off when I walk through the front door, so that means Ryle is already in bed.

The entire drive home I thought about what he'd said. I wasn't expecting this conversation to come up so soon. I'm almost twenty-five, but I had it in my head it would be at least a couple of years before we started trying for a family. I'm still not certain I'm ready for it yet, but knowing it's now something he wants someday has put me in an incredibly happy mood.

I decide to make myself a quick bite to eat before waking him up. I haven't had dinner yet and I'm starving. When I flip on the kitchen light, I scream. My hand goes to my chest and I fall against the counter. "Jesus Christ, Ryle! What are you doing?"

He's leaning with his back against the wall next to the refrigerator. His feet are crossed at the ankles and his eyes are narrowed in my direction. He's flipping something over in his fingers, staring at me.

My eyes fall to the counter to his left and I see an empty

glass that probably recently held scotch. He drinks it on occasion to help him fall asleep.

I look back at him and there's a smirk on his face. My body instantly grows warm at that smile because I know what comes next. This apartment is about to become a frenzy of clothes and kisses. We've christened nearly every room since we moved in here, but the kitchen is one we haven't tackled yet.

I smile back at him, my heart still beating erratically from the shock of finding him here in the dark. His eyes fall to his hand, and I notice he's holding the Boston magnet. I brought it from the old apartment and stuck it on this fridge when we moved in.

He places it back on the fridge and taps it. "Where'd you get this?"

I look at the magnet and then back at him. The last thing I want to do is tell him that magnet came from Atlas on my sixteenth birthday. It would only bring up an already sore subject, and I'm too excited for what's about to come next between us to give him the naked truth right now.

I shrug. "I can't remember. I've had it forever."

He stares at me silently and then straightens up, taking two steps toward me. I back myself against the counter and my breath catches. His hands meet my waist and he slides them between my ass and my jeans and pulls me against him. His mouth claims mine and he kisses me while he begins to lower my jeans.

Okay. So we're doing this right now.

His lips drag down my neck as I kick off my shoes and then he pulls my jeans off the rest of the way.

I guess I can eat later. Christening the kitchen just became my priority.

When his mouth is back on mine, he lifts me and sets me down on the countertop, standing between my knees. I can smell the scotch on his breath, and I kind of like it. I'm already breathing heavily as his warm lips slide across mine. He takes a fistful of my hair and he tugs gently so that I'm looking up at him.

"Naked truth?" he whispers, looking at my mouth like he's about to devour me.

I nod.

His other hand begins to slide slowly up my thigh until there's nowhere left for his hand to go. He slips two warm fingers inside of me, keeping my gaze locked with his. I suck in a rush of air as my legs tighten around his waist. I begin to slowly move against his hand, moaning softly as he stares heatedly at me.

"Where did you get that magnet, Lily?"

What?

My heart feels like it begins beating in reverse.

Why does he keep asking me this?

His fingers are still moving inside of me, his eyes still look like they want me. *But his hand.* The hand that's wrapped in my hair begins to tug harder and I wince.

"Ryle," I whisper, keeping my voice calm, even though I'm beginning to shake. "That hurts."

His fingers stop moving, but his gaze never leaves mine. He slowly pulls his fingers out of me and then brings his hand up around my throat, squeezing gently. His lips meet mine and his tongue dives inside my mouth. I take it, because

I have no idea what's going through his head right now and I pray I'm overreacting.

I can feel him hard against his jeans as he presses into me. But then he pulls back. His hands leave me entirely as he flattens his back against the refrigerator, scraping his eyes over my body like he wants to take me right here in the kitchen. My heart begins to calm down. *I'm overreacting.*

He reaches beside him, next to the stove, and he picks up a newspaper. It's the same newspaper he showed me earlier, with the awards article printed in it. He holds it up, then tosses it toward me. "Did you get a chance to read that yet?"

I blow out a breath of relief. "Not yet," I say, my eyes falling to the article.

"Read it out loud."

I glance up at him. I smile, but my stomach is anxious. There's something about him right now. The way he's acting. I can't put my finger on it.

"You want me to read the article?" I ask. "Right now?"

I feel odd, sitting on my kitchen counter half naked, holding a newspaper. He nods. "I'd like you to take off your shirt first. *Then* read it out loud."

I stare at him, trying to gauge his behavior. Maybe the scotch has made him extra frisky. A lot of times when we make love, it's as simple as making love. But occasionally, our sex is wild. A little dangerous, like the look in his eyes right now.

I set the paper down, pull off my shirt, and then pick the paper back up. I start reading the article out loud, but he takes a step forward and says, "Not the whole thing." He flips the paper over where it starts in the middle of the article and he points to a sentence. "Read the last few paragraphs."

I look down, even more confused this time. But whatever will get us past this and into the bed . . .

"The business with the highest number of votes should come as no surprise. The iconic Bib's on Marketson opened in April of last year, quickly becoming one of the highest rated restaurants in the city, according to TripAdvisor."

I stop reading and look up at Ryle. He has poured himself more scotch and he's swallowing a sip of it. "Keep reading," he says, nudging his head at the paper in my hand.

I swallow heavily, the saliva in my mouth growing thicker by the second. I try to control the trembling of my hands as I continue reading. "The owner, Atlas Corrigan, is a two-time award-winning chef and also a United States Marine. It's no secret what the acronym for his highly successful restaurant, Bib's, stands for: *Better In Boston*."

I gasp.

Everything is better in Boston.

I clench my stomach, trying to keep my emotions under control as I keep reading. "But when interviewed regarding his most recent award, the chef finally revealed the true history of the meaning behind the name. '*It's a long story*,' Chef Corrigan stated. '*It was an homage to someone who had a huge impact on my life. Someone who meant a lot to me. She still means a lot to me*.'"

I put the newspaper on the counter. "I don't want to read anymore." My voice cracks on its way up my throat.

Ryle takes two swift steps forward and grabs the newspaper. He picks up where I left off, his voice loud and angry now. "When asked if the girl was aware he named a restaurant after her, Chef Corrigan smiled knowingly and said, '*Next question*.'"

The anger in Ryle's voice makes me nauseous. "Ryle, stop

it," I say calmly. "You've had too much to drink." I push past him and walk quickly out of the kitchen toward the hallway that leads to our bedroom. There's so much happening right now and I'm not sure I understand any of it.

The article never stated who Atlas was talking about. Atlas knows it was me and *I* know it was me, but how in the hell would Ryle put two and two together?

And the magnet. How would he know that came from Atlas just by reading that article?

He's overreacting.

I can hear him following me as I walk toward the bedroom. I swing open the door and come to a sudden halt.

The bed is littered with things. An empty moving box with the words, "Lily's stuff," written on the side of it. And then all the contents that were inside that box. Letters . . . journals . . . empty shoeboxes. I close my eyes and breathe in slowly.

He read the journal.

No.

He. Read. The. Journal.

His arm comes around my waist from behind. He slides a hand up my stomach and takes a firm hold of one of my breasts. His other hand feathers my shoulder as he moves the hair away from my neck.

I squeeze my eyes shut, just as his fingers begin to trace across my skin, up to my shoulder. He slowly runs his finger over the heart and a shudder runs over my whole body. His lips meet my skin, right over the tattoo, and then he sinks his teeth into me so hard, I scream.

I try to pull away from him, but he has such a tight grip on me he doesn't even budge. The pain from his teeth piercing my collarbone rips through my shoulder and down my arm. I immediately start crying. *Sobbing.*

"Ryle, let me go," I say, my voice pleading. "Please. Walk away." His arms are cutting into mine as he holds me tightly from behind.

He spins me, but my eyes are still closed. I'm too scared to look at him. His hands are digging into my shoulders as he pushes me toward the bed. I start trying to fight him off of me, but it's useless. He's too strong for me. He's angry. He's hurt. *And he's not Ryle.*

My back meets the bed and I frantically scoot back toward the headboard, trying to get away from him. "Why is he still here, Lily?" His voice isn't as composed as it was in the kitchen. He's really angry now. "He's in *everything.* The magnet on the fridge. The journal in the box I found in our closet. The fucking *tattoo* on your body that used to be my favorite goddamn *part of you!*"

He's on the bed now.

"Ryle," I beg. "I can explain." Tears streak down my temples and into my hair. "You're angry. Please don't hurt me, *please.* Walk away, and when you come back, I'll explain."

His hand grips my ankle and he yanks me until I'm beneath him. "I'm not angry, Lily," he says, his voice disturbingly calm now. "I just think I haven't proved to you how much I love you." His body comes down against mine and he takes my wrists with one hand above my head, pressing them against the mattress.

"Ryle, please." I'm sobbing, trying to push him off of me with any part of my body. "Get off me. *Please.*"

No, no, no, no.

"I love you, Lily," he says, his words crashing against my cheek. "More than he *ever* did. Why can't you *see* that?"

My fear folds in on itself, and I become diluted with rage. All I can see when I squeeze my eyes shut is my mother crying on our old living room couch; my father forcing himself on top of her. Hatred rips through me and I start screaming.

Ryle tries to muffle my screams with his mouth.

I bite down on his tongue.

His forehead comes crashing down against mine.

In an instant, all the pain fades as a blanket of darkness rolls over my eyes and consumes me.

·   ·   ·

I can feel his breath against my ear as he mutters something inaudible. My heart is racing, my whole body is still shaking, my tears are still somehow falling and I'm gasping for air. His words are crashing against my ear, but the pain is throbbing in my head too hard for me to decipher his words.

I try to open my eyes, but it stings. I can feel something trickling into my right eye and I instantly know it's blood.

My blood.

His words begin to come into focus.

"Sorry, I'm sorry, I'm sorry, I'm . . ."

His hand is still pressing mine into the mattress and he's still on top of me. He's no longer trying to force himself on me.

"Lily, I love you, I'm so sorry."

His words are full of panic. He's kissing me, his lips gentle against my cheek and mouth.

He knows what he's done. He's Ryle again, and he knows what he's just done to me. To us. To our future.

I utilize his panic to my advantage. I shake my head and I whisper, "It's okay, Ryle. It's okay. You were angry, it's okay."

His lips meet mine in a frenzy and the taste of scotch makes me want to puke now. He's still whispering apologies when the room begins to fade out again.

•   •   •

My eyes are closed. We're still on the bed, but he's no longer fully on top of me. He's on his side, his arm wrapped tightly over my waist. His head is pressed against my chest. I remain stiff as I assess everything around me.

He isn't moving, but I can feel his breaths, heavy with sleep. I don't know if he passed out or if he fell asleep. The last thing I can remember is his mouth on mine, the taste of my own tears.

I lie still for several more minutes. The pain in my head begins to worsen with every minute of consciousness. I close my eyes and try to think.

Where's my purse?

Where are my keys?

Where is my phone?

It takes me a full five minutes to slide out from under him. I'm too scared to move too much at once, so I do it an inch at a time until I'm able to roll onto the floor. When I can no longer feel his hands on me, an unexpected sob breaks from my chest. I slap my hand over my mouth as I pull myself to my feet and run out of the bedroom.

I find my purse and my phone, but I have no idea where he put my keys. I frantically search the living room and kitchen, but I can barely see anything. When he head-butted me, it must have left a gash on my forehead, because there's too much blood in my eyes and everything is blurry.

I slide to the floor near the door, growing dizzy. My fingers are shaking so hard, it takes three tries to get the password right on my phone.

When I have the screen up to dial a number, I pause. My first thought is to call Allysa and Marshall, but I can't. I can't do that to them right now. She just gave birth to a baby a matter of hours ago. I can't do this to them.

I could call the police, but my mind can't even process what all that entails. I don't want to give a statement. I don't know that I want to press charges, knowing what this could do to his career. I don't want Allysa mad at me. I just don't know. I don't completely rule out eventually notifying the police. I just don't have the energy to make that decision right now.

I squeeze the phone and try to think. *My mother.*

I start to dial her number, but when I think of what this would do to her I start to cry again. I can't involve her in this mess. She's been through too much. And Ryle will try to find me. He'll go to her first. Then Allysa and Marshall. Then to everyone else we know.

I wipe the tears from my eyes and then begin dialing Atlas's number.

I hate myself more in this moment than I ever have in my entire life.

I hate myself, because the day Ryle found Atlas's number in my phone, I lied and said I had forgotten it was there.

I hate myself, because the day Atlas placed his number there, I opened it and looked at it.

I hate myself, because deep down inside, I knew there was a chance that I might one day need it. *So I memorized it.*

"Hello?"

His voice is cautious. Inquiring. He doesn't recognize this number. I immediately start crying when he speaks. I cover my mouth and try to quiet myself.

"Lily?" His voice is much louder now. "Lily, where are you?"

I hate myself, because he knows the tears are mine.

"Atlas," I whisper. "I need help."

"Where are you?" he says again. I can hear panic in his voice. I can hear him walking, moving stuff around. I hear a door slam on his end of the phone.

"I'll text you," I whisper, too scared to keep speaking. I don't want Ryle to wake up. I hang up the phone and somehow find the strength to still my hands while I text him my address and the access code for entry. Then I send a second text that says **Text me when you get here. Please don't knock.**

I crawl to the kitchen and find my pants, struggling back into them. I find my shirt on the counter. When I'm dressed, I go to the living room. I debate opening the door and meeting Atlas downstairs, but I'm too scared I won't be able to make it down to the lobby alone. My forehead is still bleeding and I feel too weak to even stand up and wait by the door. I slide to the floor, clenching my phone in my shaky fist and staring at it, waiting for his text.

It's an agonizing twenty-four minutes later when my phone lights up.

Here.

I scramble to my feet and swing open the door. Arms wrap around me and my face is pressed against something soft. I just start crying and crying and shaking and crying.

"Lily," he whispers. I've never heard my name spoken so sadly. He urges me to look up at him. His blue eyes scroll over my face, and I see it happen. I watch the concern vanish as he darts his head up to the apartment door. "Is he still in there?"

Rage.

I can feel the rage come off of him and he starts to step toward the apartment door. I grab his jacket in my fists. "No. *Please*, Atlas. I just want to leave."

I see the pain roll over him as he pauses, struggling to decide whether to listen to me or bust through the door. He eventually turns away from the door and wraps his arms around me. He helps me to the elevator and then through the lobby. By some miracle, we only run into one person and he's on his phone and facing the other direction.

By the time we make it to the parking garage, I start to feel dizzy again. I tell him to slow down, and then I feel his arm wrap under my knees as he picks me up. Then we're in the car. Then the car is moving.

I know I need stitches.

I know he's taking me to the hospital.

But I have no idea why the next words out of my mouth are, "Don't take me to Mass General. Take me somewhere else."

For whatever reason, I don't want to risk the chance of running into any of Ryle's colleagues. I hate him. I hate him in this moment more than I've ever hated my father. But concern for his career still somehow breaks through the hatred.

When I realize this, I hate myself just as much as I hate him.

Chapter Twenty-Four

Atlas is standing on the other side of the room. He hasn't taken his eyes off me the entire time the nurse has been helping me. After taking a blood sample, she immediately returned and began to attend to my cut. She hasn't asked me very many questions yet, but it's obvious my injuries are the result of an attack. I can see the pitying look on her face as she cleans up blood from the bite mark left on my shoulder.

When she's finished, she glances back at Atlas. She steps to the right, blocking his view of me as she turns and faces me again. "I need to ask you some personal questions. I'm going to ask him to leave the room, okay?"

It's in that moment that I realize she thinks Atlas is the one who did these things to me. I immediately start to shake my head. "It wasn't him," I tell her. "Please don't make him leave."

Relief washes over her face. She nods her head and then pulls up a chair. "Are you hurt anywhere else?"

I shake my head, because she can't fix all the parts of me Ryle broke on the inside.

"Lily?" Her voice is gentle. "Were you raped?"

Tears fill my eyes and I see Atlas roll across the wall, pressing his forehead against it.

The nurse waits until I make eye contact with her again

to continue speaking. "We have a certain examination for these situations. It's called a SANE exam. It's optional, of course, but I highly encourage it in your situation."

"I wasn't raped," I say. "He didn't . . ."

"Are you sure, Lily?" the nurse asks.

I nod. "I don't want one."

Atlas faces me again and I can see the pain in his expression as he steps forward. "Lily. You need this." His eyes are pleading.

I shake my head again. "Atlas, I swear . . ." I squeeze my eyes shut and lower my head. "I'm not covering for him this time," I whisper. "He tried, but then he stopped."

"If you choose to press charges, you'll need—"

"I don't want the exam," I say again, my voice firm.

There's a knock on the door and a doctor enters, sparing me from more pleading looks from Atlas. The nurse gives the doctor a brief rundown of my injuries. She then steps aside as he examines my head and shoulder. He flashes a light into both of my eyes. He looks down at the paperwork again and says, "I'd like to rule out a concussion, but given your situation, I don't want to administer a CT. We'd like to keep you for observation, instead."

"Why don't you want to administer a CT?" I ask him.

The doctor stands up. "We don't like to perform X-rays on pregnant women unless it's vital. We'll monitor you for complications and if there are no further concerns, you'll be free to go."

I don't hear anything beyond that.

Nothing.

The pressure begins to build in my head. My heart. My

stomach. I grip the edges of the exam table I'm sitting on and I stare at the floor until they both leave the room.

When the door closes behind them, I sit, suspended in frozen silence. I see Atlas move closer. His feet are almost touching mine. His fingers brush lightly over my back. "Did you know?"

I release a quick breath, and then drag in more air. I start shaking my head, and when his arms come down around me, I cry harder than I knew my body was even capable of. He holds me the entire time I cry. He holds me through my hatred.

I did this to myself.

I allowed this to happen to me.

I am my mother.

"I want to leave," I whisper.

Atlas pulls back. "They want to monitor you, Lily. I think you should stay."

I look up at him and shake my head. "I need to get out of here. *Please.* I want to leave."

He nods and helps me back into my shoes. He pulls off his jacket and wraps it around me, then we walk out of the hospital without anyone noticing.

He says nothing to me as we drive. I stare out the window, too exhausted to cry. Too in shock to speak. I feel submerged.

Just keep swimming.

•   •   •

Atlas doesn't live in an apartment. He lives in a house. A small suburb outside of Boston called Wellesley, where all the homes are beautiful, sprawling, manicured, and expensive. Before we pull into his driveway, I wonder to myself if he ever married that girl. *Cassie.* I wonder what she'll think of her husband bringing home a girl he once loved who has just been attacked by her own husband.

She'll pity me. She'll wonder why I never left him. She'll wonder how I let myself get to this point. She'll wonder all the same things I used to wonder about my own mother when I saw her in my same situation. People spend so much time wondering why the women don't leave. Where are all the people who wonder why the men are even abusive? Isn't that where the only blame should be placed?

Atlas parks in the garage. There's not another vehicle here. I don't wait for him to help me out of the car. I open the door and get out on my own, and then I follow him into his house. He punches in a code on an alarm and then flips on a few lights. My eyes roam around the kitchen, the dining room, the living room. Everything is made of rich woods and stainless steel, and his kitchen is painted a calming bluish-green. The color of the ocean. If I wasn't hurting so much, I would smile.

Atlas kept swimming, and look at him now. He swam all the way to the fucking Caribbean.

He moves to his refrigerator and pulls out a bottle of water, walking it over to me. He takes the lid off and hands it to me. I take a drink and watch as he turns the living room light on, then the hallway.

"Do you live alone?" I ask.

He nods as he walks back into the kitchen. "Are you hungry?"

I shake my head. Even if I was, I wouldn't be able to eat.

"I'll show you your room," he says. "There's a shower if you need it."

I do. I want to wash the taste of scotch out of my mouth. I want to wash the sterile smell of the hospital off of me. I want to wash away the last four hours of my life.

I follow him down the hallway and to a spare bedroom where he flips on the light. There are two boxes on a bare bed and more stacked up against the walls. There's an oversized chair against one wall, facing the door. He moves to the bed and takes off the boxes, setting them against the wall with the others.

"I just moved in a few months ago. Haven't had much time to decorate yet." He walks to a dresser and pulls open a drawer. "I'll make the bed for you." He takes out sheets and a pillowcase. He begins making the bed as I walk inside the bathroom and close the door.

I remain in the bathroom for thirty minutes. Some of those minutes are spent staring at my reflection in the mirror. Some of those minutes are spent in the shower. The rest are spent over the toilet as I make myself sick with thoughts of the last several hours.

I'm wrapped in a towel when I crack the bathroom door. Atlas is no longer in the bedroom, but there are clothes folded on the freshly made bed. Men's pajama bottoms that are too big for me and a T-shirt that goes past my knees. I pull the drawstring tight, tie it, and then crawl into bed. I turn the lamp off and pull the covers up and over me.

I cry so hard, I don't even make a noise.

Chapter Twenty-Five

I smell toast.

I stretch out on my bed and smile, because Ryle knows toast is my favorite.

My eyes flick open and the clarity smashes down on me with the force of a head-on collision. I squeeze my eyes shut when I realize where I am and why I'm here and that the toast I smell is not at all because my sweet and caring husband is making me breakfast in bed.

I immediately want to cry again, so I force myself off the bed. I focus on the hollowness in my stomach as I use the bathroom, and tell myself I can cry after I eat something. I need to eat before I make myself sick again.

When I walk out of the bathroom and back into the bedroom, I notice the chair has been turned so that it's facing the bed now instead of the door. There's a blanket thrown over it haphazardly, and it's obvious Atlas was in here last night while I slept.

He was probably worried I had a concussion.

When I walk into the kitchen, Atlas is moving back and forth between the fridge, the stove, the counter. For the first time in twelve hours, I feel an inkling of something that isn't agony, because I remember he's a chef. A *good* one. And he's cooking me breakfast.

He glances up at me as I make my way into the kitchen.

"Morning," he says, careful to say it without too much inflection. "I hope you're hungry." He slides a glass and a container of orange juice across the counter toward me, then he turns and faces the stove again.

"I am."

He glances back over his shoulder and gives me a ghost of a smile. I pour myself a glass of orange juice and then walk to the other side of the kitchen where there's a breakfast nook. There's a newspaper on the table and I begin to pick it up. When I see the article about the best businesses in Boston printed across the page, my hands immediately begin to shake and I drop the paper back on the table. I close my eyes and take a slow sip of the orange juice.

A few minutes later, Atlas sets a plate down in front of me, then claims the seat across from me at the table. He pulls his own plate of food in front of him and cuts into a crepe with his fork.

I look down at my plate. Three crepes, drizzled in syrup and garnished with a dab of whipped cream. Orange and strawberry slices line the right side of the plate.

It's almost too pretty to eat, but I'm too hungry to care. I take a bite and close my eyes, trying not to make it obvious that it's the best bite of breakfast I've ever had.

I finally allow myself to admit that his restaurant deserved that award. As much as I tried to talk Ryle and Allysa out of going back, it was the best restaurant I'd ever been to.

"Where did you learn to cook?" I ask him.

He sips from a cup of coffee. "The Marines," he says, placing the cup back down. "I trained for a while during my first stint and then when I reenlisted I came on as a chef." He taps his fork against the side of his plate. "You like it?"

I nod. "It's delicious. But you're wrong. You knew how to cook before you enlisted."

He smiles. "You remember the cookies?"

I nod again. "Best cookies I've ever eaten."

He leans back in his chair. "I taught myself the basics. My mother worked second shift when I was growing up, so if I wanted dinner at night I had to make it. It was either that or starve, so I bought a cookbook at a yard sale and made every single recipe in it over the course of a year. And I was only thirteen."

I smile, shocked that I'm even able to. "The next time someone asks you how you learned to cook, you should tell them *that* story. Not the other one."

He shakes his head. "You're the only person who knows anything about me before the age of nineteen. I'd like to keep it that way."

He begins telling me about working as a chef in the military. How he saved up as much money as he could so that when he got out, he could open his own restaurant. He started with a small café that did really well, then opened Bib's a year and a half ago. "It does okay," he says with modesty.

I glance around his kitchen and then look back at him. "Looks like it does more than just okay."

He shrugs and takes another bite of his food. I don't talk after that as we finish eating, because my mind wanders to his restaurant. The name of it. What he said in the interview. Then, of course, those thoughts lead me back to thoughts of

Ryle and the anger in his voice as he yelled the last line of the interview at me.

I think Atlas can see the change in my demeanor, but he says nothing as he clears the table.

When he takes another seat, he chooses the chair right next to me this time. He places a reassuring hand on top of mine. "I have to go in to work for a few hours," he says. "I don't want you to leave. Stay here as long as you need, Lily. Just . . . please don't go back home today."

I shake my head when I hear the concern in his words. "I won't. I'll stay here," I tell him. "I promise."

"Do you need anything before I go?"

I shake my head. "I'll be fine."

He stands up and grabs his jacket. "I'll make it as quick as I can. I'll be back after lunch and I'll bring you something to eat, okay?"

I force a smile. He opens a drawer and pulls out a pen and paper. He writes something on it before he leaves. When he's gone, I stand up and walk to the counter to read what he wrote. He listed instructions for how to set the alarm. He wrote his cell phone number, even though I have it memorized. He also wrote down his work number, his home address, and his work address.

At the bottom in small print, he wrote, *"Just keep swimming, Lily."*

Dear Ellen,

Hi. It's me. Lily Bloom. Well . . . technically it's Lily Kincaid now.

I know it's been a long time since I've written to you. A really long time. After everything that happened with Atlas, I just couldn't bring myself to open up the journals again. I couldn't even bring myself to watch your show after school, because it hurt to watch it alone. In fact, all thoughts of you kind of depressed me. When I thought of you, I thought of Atlas. And to be honest, I didn't want to think of Atlas, so I had to cut you out of my life, too.

I'm sorry about that. I'm sure you didn't miss me like I missed you, but sometimes the things that matter to you most are also the things that hurt you the most. And in order to get over that hurt, you have to sever all the extensions that keep you tethered to that pain. You were an extension of my pain, so I guess that's what I was doing. I was just trying to save myself a little bit of agony.

I'm sure your show is as great as ever, though. I hear you still dance at the beginning of some episodes, but I've grown to appreciate that. I think that's one of the biggest signs a person has matured—knowing how to appreciate things that matter to others, even if they don't matter very much to you.

I should probably catch you up on my life. My father died. I'm twenty-four now. I got a college degree, worked in marketing for a while, and now I own my own business. A floral shop. Life goals, FTW!

I also have a husband and he isn't Atlas.

And . . . I live in Boston.

I know. Shocker.

The last time I wrote to you, I was sixteen. I was in a really bad place and I was so worried about Atlas. I'm not worried about Atlas anymore, but I am in a really bad place right now. More so than the last time I wrote to you.

I'm sorry I don't seem to need to write to you when I'm in a good place. You tend to only get the shit end of my life, but that's what friends are for, right?

I don't even know where to start. I know you don't know anything about my current life or my husband, Ryle. But there's this thing we do where one of us says "naked truth," and then we're forced to be brutally honest and say what we're really thinking.

So . . . naked truth.

Brace yourself.

I am in love with a man who physically hurts me. Of all people, I have no idea how I let myself get to this point.

There were many times growing up I wondered what was going through my mother's head in the days after my father had hurt her. How she could possibly love a man who had laid his hands on her. A man who repeatedly hit her. Repeatedly promised he would never do it again. Repeatedly hit her again.

I hate that I can empathize with her now.

I've been sitting on Atlas's couch for over four hours, wrestling with my feelings. I can't get a grip on them. I can't understand them. I don't know how to process them. And true to my past, I realized that maybe I need to just get them out on paper. My apologies to you, Ellen. But get ready for a whole lot of word vomit.

If I had to compare this feeling to something, I would compare it to death. Not just the death of anyone. The death of the one. The person who is closer to you than anyone else in the whole world. The one who, when you simply imagine their death, it makes your eyes tear up.

That's what this feels like. It feels like Ryle has died.

It's an astronomical amount of grief. An enormous amount of pain. It's a sense that I've lost my best friend, my lover, my husband, my lifeline. But the difference between this feeling and death is the presence of another emotion that doesn't necessarily follow in the event of an actual death.

Hatred.

I am so angry at him, Ellen. Words can't express the amount of hatred I have for him. Yet somehow, in the midst of all my hatred, there are waves of reasoning that flow through me. I start to think things like "But I shouldn't have had the magnet. I should have told him about the tattoo from the beginning. I shouldn't have kept the journals."

The reasoning is the hardest part of this. It eats at me, little by little, wearing down the strength my hatred lends to me. The reasoning forces me to imagine our future together, and how there are things I could do to prevent that type of anger. I'll never betray him again. I'll never keep secrets from him again. I'll never give him reason to react that way again. We'll both just have to work harder from now on.

For better, for worse, right?

I know these are the things that once went through my mother's head. But the difference between the two of us is that she had more to worry about. She didn't have the financial stability that I have. She didn't have the resources to leave and give me what she thought was a decent shelter. She didn't want to take me away from my father when I was used to living with both parents. I have a feeling reasoning really kicked her ass a time or two.

I can't even begin to process the thought that I'm having a child with this man. There is a human being inside of me that we created together. And no matter which option I choose—whether I choose to stay or choose to leave—neither are choices I would wish upon my child. To grow up in a broken home or an abusive one? I've already failed this baby in life, and I've only known about his or her existence for a single day.

Ellen, I wish you could write back to me. I wish that you could say something funny to me right now, because my heart needs it. I have never felt this alone. This broken. This angry. This hurt.

People on the outside of situations like these often wonder why the woman goes back to the abuser. I read somewhere once that 85 percent of women return to abusive situations. That was before I realized I was in one, and when I heard that statistic, I thought it was because the women were stupid. I thought it was because they were weak. I thought these things about my own mother more than once.

But sometimes the reason women go back is simply because they're in love. I love my husband, Ellen. I love so many things about him. I wish cutting my feelings off for the person who hurt me was as easy as I used to think it would be. Preventing your heart from forgiving someone you love is actually a hell of a lot harder than simply forgiving them.

I'm a statistic now. The things I've thought about women like me are now what others would think of me if they knew my current situation.

"How could she love him after what he did to her? How could she contemplate taking him back?"

It's sad that those are the first thoughts that run through our minds when someone is abused. Shouldn't there be more distaste in our mouths for the abusers than for those who continue to love the abusers?

I think of all the people who have been in this situation before me. Everyone who will be in this situation after me. Do we all repeat the same words in our heads in the days after experiencing abuse at the hands of those who love us? "From this day forward, for better, for worse, for richer, for poorer, in sickness and health, until death do us part."

Maybe those vows weren't meant to be taken as literally as some spouses take them.

For better, for worse?

Fuck.

That.

Shit.

—Lily

Chapter Twenty-Six

I'm lying on Atlas's guest bed, staring up at the ceiling. It's a normal bed. Really comfortable, actually. But it feels like I'm on a water bed. Or maybe a raft, adrift at sea. And I scale over these huge waves, each of them carrying something different. Some are waves of sadness. Some are waves of anger. Some are waves of tears. Some are waves of sleep.

Occasionally, I'll place my hands on my stomach and a tiny wave of love will come. I have no idea how I can already love something so much, but I do. I think about whether or not it'll be a boy or a girl and what I'll name it. I wonder if it will look like me or Ryle. And then another wave of anger will come and crash down on that tiny wave of love.

I feel robbed of the joy a mother should have when she finds out she's pregnant. I feel like Ryle took that from me last night and it's just one more thing I have to hate him for.

Hatred is exhausting.

I force myself off the bed and into the shower. I've been in my room most of the day. Atlas returned home several hours ago and I heard him open the door at one point to check on me but I pretended to be asleep.

I feel awkward being here. Atlas is the very reason Ryle was angry at me last night, yet he's the one I ran to when I needed help? Being here fills me with guilt. Maybe even a little bit of shame, as though my calling Atlas lends credibility to Ryle's anger. But there's literally nowhere I can go right now. I need a couple of days to process things and if I go to a hotel, Ryle could track the credit card charge and find me.

He'd be able to find me at my mother's. At Allysa's. At Lucy's. He's even met Devin a couple of times and would more than likely go there, too.

I can't see him tracking down Atlas, though. Yet. I'm sure if I go a week avoiding his calls and texts, he'll look everywhere he can possibly look to find me. But for now, I don't think he would show up here.

Maybe that's why I'm here. I feel safer here than anywhere else I could possibly go. And Atlas has an alarm system, so there's that.

I glance at the nightstand to look at my phone. I skip over all the missed texts from Ryle and open the one from Allysa.

Allysa: Hey, Aunt Lily! They're sending us home tonight. Come see us tomorrow when you get home from work.

She sent a picture of her and Rylee, and it makes me smile. Then cry. Damn these emotions.

I wait until my eyes are dry again before I walk into the living room. Atlas is sitting at his kitchen table, working on his laptop. When he looks up at me, he smiles and closes it.

"Hey."

I force a smile and then look in the kitchen. "Do you have anything to eat?"

Atlas stands up quickly. "Yeah," he says. "Yeah, sit down. I'll get something ready for you."

I take a seat on the couch as he works his way around the kitchen. The television is on, but it's muted. I unmute it and click on the DVR. He has a few shows recorded, but the one that catches my eye is *The Ellen DeGeneres Show*. I smile and click on the most recent unwatched episode and hit Play.

Atlas brings me a bowl of pasta and a glass of ice water. He glances at the TV and then sits down next to me on the couch.

For the next three hours, we watch a full week's worth of episodes. I laugh out loud six times. It feels good, but when I take a bathroom break and come back to the living room, the weight of it all starts to sink in again.

I sit back down on the couch next to Atlas. He's leaning back with his feet propped up on the coffee table. I naturally lean into him and just like he used to do when we were teenagers, he pulls me against his chest and we just sit there in silence. His thumb brushes the outside of my shoulder, and I know it's his unspoken way of saying he's here for me. That he feels bad for me. And for the first time since he picked me up last night, I feel like talking about it. My head is resting against his shoulder and my hands are in my lap. I'm fidgeting with the drawstring on the pants that are way too big for me.

"Atlas?" I say, my voice barely a whisper. "I'm sorry I got so angry at you that night at the restaurant. You were right. Deep down I knew you were right, but I didn't want to believe it." I lift my head and look at him, cracking a pitiful smile. "You can say, '*I told you so*' now."

His eyebrows draw together, like my words somehow hurt him. "Lily, this is not something I wanted to be right about. I prayed every day that I was wrong about him."

I wince. I shouldn't have said that to him. I know better than to think Atlas would ever think something like *I told you so*.

He squeezes my shoulder and leans forward, kissing the top of my head. I close my eyes as I soak up the familiarity of him. His smell, his touch, his comfort. I've never understood how someone can be so rock solid, yet comforting. But that's always how I've viewed him. Like he could withstand anything, but somehow still feels the weight that everyone else carries.

I don't like that I was never fully able to let go of him, no matter how hard I tried. I think about the fight with Ryle over Atlas's phone number. The fight about the magnet, the article, the things he read in my journal, the tattoo. None of that would have happened if I would have just let go of Atlas and thrown it all away. Ryle wouldn't have had anything to be so upset with me about.

I pull my hands up to my face after that thought, upset that there's a part of me trying to blame Ryle's reaction on my lack of closure with Atlas.

There's no excuse. None.

This is just another wave I'm being forced to ride on. A wave of complete and utter confusion.

Atlas can feel the change in my composure. "You okay?"

I'm not.

I'm not okay, because until this moment, I had no idea how hurt I still am that he never came back for me. If he'd have just come back for me like he promised, I would have never even met Ryle. And I would have never been *in* this situation.

Yep. I'm definitely confused. How am I possibly lending blame to Atlas for any of this?

"I think I need to call it a night," I say quietly, pulling away from him. I stand up and Atlas stands up, too.

"I'll be gone most of the day tomorrow," he says. "Will you be here when I get home?"

I cringe at his question. Of course he wants me to get my shit together and find another place to stay. What am I even still doing here? "No. No, I can get a hotel, it's fine." I turn to walk toward the hallway, but he puts a hand on my shoulder.

"Lily," he says, turning me around. "I wasn't asking you to leave. I was just making sure you'd still be here. I want you to stay as long as you need to."

His eyes are sincere, and if I didn't think it would be a little inappropriate, I would throw my arms around him and hug him. Because I'm not ready to leave yet. Just a couple more days before I'm forced to figure out what my next step is.

I nod. "I need to go in to work for a few hours tomorrow," I tell him. "There are some things I need to take care of. But if you really don't mind, I'd like to stay here for a few more days."

"I don't mind, Lily. I'd prefer it."

I force a smile and then head to the guest bedroom. At least he's giving me a buffer before I'm forced to confront everything.

As much as his presence in my life confuses me right now, I've never been more thankful for him.

Chapter Twenty-Seven

My hand is trembling when I reach for the doorknob. I've never once been scared to walk into my own business before, but I've also never been this on edge.

The building is dark when I enter it, so I flip on the lights, holding my breath. I walk slowly to my office, pushing the door open with caution.

He's nowhere, yet he's everywhere.

When I take a seat at my desk, I turn on my phone for the first time since I went to bed last night. I wanted a good night's sleep without having to worry about whether or not Ryle was trying to contact me.

When it powers on, I have twenty-nine missed texts from Ryle. It just so happens to be the same number of doors Ryle knocked on to find my apartment last year.

I don't know whether to laugh or cry at the irony.

I spend the rest of the day like this. Glancing over my shoulder, looking up at the door every time it opens. I wonder if he's ruined me. If the fear of him will ever leave me.

Half a day goes by without a single phone call from him while I catch up on paperwork. Allysa calls me after lunch and I can tell by her voice that she has no idea about the fight Ryle and I had. I let her talk about the baby for a while before I pretend I have a customer and hang up.

I plan on leaving when Lucy returns from her lunch break. She has half an hour left.

Ryle walks through the front door three minutes later.

I'm the only one here.

As soon as I see him, I turn stone cold. I'm standing behind the counter, my hand on the cash register because it's close to the stapler. I'm sure a stapler couldn't do much harm against the arms of a neurosurgeon, but I'll use what I have.

He slowly makes his way to the counter. It's the first time I've seen him since he was on top of me on our bed the other night. My whole body is immediately taken back to that moment, and I'm engulfed in the same level of emotions as I was in that moment. Both fear and anger rush through me when he reaches the counter.

He lifts his hand and places a set of keys on the counter in front of me. My eyes fall to the keys.

"I'm leaving for England tonight," he says. "I'll be gone for three months. I paid all the bills so you won't have to worry about it while I'm gone."

His voice is composed but I can see the veins in his neck as they prove his composure is taking all the effort he has. "You need time." He swallows hard. "And I want to give that to you." He grimaces and pushes the keys to my apartment toward me. "Go back home, Lily. I won't be there. I promise."

He turns and begins walking toward the door. It occurs to me that he didn't even try to apologize. I'm not angry about it. I understand it. He knows that an apology will never take back what he did. He knows that the best thing for us right now is separation.

He knows what a huge mistake he made . . . yet I still feel the need to dig that knife in a little deeper.

"Ryle."

He looks back at me and it's as if he puts a shield up between us. He doesn't turn all the way around and he's stiff as he waits for whatever I'm about to say. He knows my words are going to hurt him.

"You know what the worst part about this whole thing is?" I ask.

He doesn't say anything. He just stares at me, waiting for my answer.

"All you had to do when you found my journal was ask me for a naked truth. I would have been honest with you. But you didn't. You chose to not ask for my help and now we'll both have to suffer the consequences of your actions for the rest of our lives."

He grimaces with every word. "Lily," he says, turning toward me.

I hold up my hand to stop him from saying anything else. "Don't. You can leave now. Have fun in England."

I can see the war waging inside of him. He knows he can't get anywhere with me in this moment, no matter how hard he wants to beg for my forgiveness. He knows the only choice he has is to turn and walk out that door, even though it's the last thing he wants to do.

When he finally forces himself out the door, I run and lock it. I slide down to the floor and hug my knees, burying my face against them. I'm shaking so hard, I can feel my teeth chatter.

I can't believe part of that man is growing inside me. And I can't believe I'll one day have to admit that to him.

Chapter Twenty-Eight

After Ryle left me his keys this afternoon; I debated going back to our new apartment. I even had a cab pull up to the building, but I couldn't force myself out of the car. I knew if I went back there today, I'd probably see Allysa at some point. I'm not ready to explain the stitches on my forehead to her. I'm not ready to see the kitchen where Ryle's harsh words cut through me. I'm not ready to walk into the bedroom where I was completely destroyed.

So instead of returning to my own home, I took the cab back to Atlas's house. It feels like my only safe zone right now. I don't have to confront things when I'm hiding out here.

Atlas has already texted me twice today checking on me, so when I get a text a few minutes before seven o'clock in the evening, I assume it's from him. It's not; it's from Allysa.

Allysa: You home from work yet? Come up and visit us, I'm already bored.

My heart sinks when I read her text. She has no idea what happened between me and Ryle. I wonder if Ryle even told her he left for England today. My thumb types and erases and types some more as I try to come up with a good excuse as to why I'm not there.

Me: I can't. I'm in the emergency room. Hit my head on that shelf in the storage room at work. Getting stitches.

I hate that I lied to her, but it'll save me from having to explain the cut and also why I'm not home right now.

Allysa: Oh no! Are you alone? Marshall can come sit with you since Ryle is gone.

Okay, so she knows Ryle left for England. That's good. And she thinks we're fine. This is good. That means I have at least three months before I have to tell her the truth.

Look at me, sweeping shit under the rug just like my mother.

Me: No, I'm fine. I'll be finished up by the time Marshall could even get here. I'll come by tomorrow after work. Give Rylee a kiss for me.

I lock the screen on my phone and set it on my bed. It's dark outside now, so I immediately see the scroll of the headlights as someone pulls into the driveway. I instantly know that it isn't Atlas, because he uses the driveway to the side of the house and parks in the garage. My heart begins to race as fear rushes through me. Is it Ryle? Did he find out where Atlas lives?

Moments later, there's a loud knock at the front door. More like pounding. The doorbell also rings.

I tiptoe to the window and barely move the curtains over far enough to take a look outside. I can't see who's at the door, but there's a truck in the driveway. It doesn't belong to Ryle.

Could it be Atlas's girlfriend? Cassie?

I grab my phone and make my way down the hallway, toward the living room. The pounding on the door and the chime of the doorbell are still going off simultaneously. Whoever is at the door is being ridiculously impatient. If it is Cassie, I already find her extremely annoying.

"Atlas!" a guy yells. "Open the damn door!"

Another voice—also male—yells, "My balls are freezing up! They're raisins, man, open the door!"

Before I open the door and let them know Atlas isn't home, I text him, hoping he's about to pull in the driveway and deal with this himself.

Me: Where are you? There are two men at your front door and I have no idea if I should let them in.

I wait through more presses of the doorbell and more pounding, but Atlas doesn't immediately text me back. I finally walk to the door and leave the chain bolted, but unlock the deadbolt and open the door a few inches.

One of the guys is tall, about six feet or so. Despite the youthful look to his face, his hair is salt and pepper. Black with a little bit of gray sprinkled in. The other one is shorter by a few inches, with sandy brown hair and a baby face. They both look to be in their late twenties, maybe early thirties. The tall one's face twists into confusion. "Who are you?" he asks, peeking through the door.

"Lily. Who are you?"

The shorter one pushes in front of the taller one. "Is Atlas here?"

I don't want to tell them no, because then they'll know I'm here alone. I don't necessarily hold much trust in the male population this week.

The phone in my hand rings and all three of us jump from the unexpectedness of it. It's Atlas. I swipe the answer button and bring it to my ear.

"Hello?"

"It's fine, Lily, they're just friends of mine. I forgot it was

Friday, we always play poker on Fridays. I'll call them now and tell them to leave."

I look back at the two of them and they're just standing there, watching me. I feel bad that Atlas feels like he has to cancel his plans just because I'm crashing at his house. I shut the door and unlock the deadbolt, then open the door again, motioning them inside.

"It's fine, Atlas. You don't have to cancel your plans. I was about to go to bed anyway."

"No, I'm on my way. I'll have them leave."

I still have the phone pressed to my ear when the two men enter the living room.

"See you soon," I say to Atlas and then end the call. The next few seconds are awkward as the guys assess me and I assess them.

"What are your names?"

"I'm Darin," the tall one says.

"Brad," the shorter one says.

"Lily," I say to them, even though I already told them my name. "Atlas will be here soon." I move to close the door and they seem to relax a little. Darin heads into the kitchen and helps himself to Atlas's refrigerator.

Brad takes off his jacket and hangs it up. "Do you know how to play poker, Lily?"

I shrug. "It's been a few years, but I used to play with friends in college."

Both of them walk toward the dining room table.

"What happened to your head?" Darin asks as he takes a seat. He asks it so casually, like it doesn't even cross his mind that it might be a sensitive subject.

I don't know why I have an urge to give him the naked truth. Maybe I just want to see how someone will react when they find out my own husband did this to me.

"My husband happened. We got into a fight two nights ago and he head-butted me. Atlas took me to the emergency room. They gave me six stitches and told me I was pregnant. Now I'm hiding out here until I figure out what to do."

Poor Darin is frozen, halfway between standing and sitting. He has no idea how to respond to that. Based on the look on his face, I think he's convinced I'm crazy.

Brad pulls out his chair and takes a seat, pointing at me. "You should get some Rodan and Fields. The amp roller works wonders for scarring."

I immediately laugh at his random response. Somehow.

"Jesus, Brad!" Darin says, finally sinking into his seat. "You're worse than your wife with this direct sales shit. You're like a walking infomercial."

Brad raises his hands in defense. "What?" he says innocently. "I'm not trying to sell her anything, I'm being honest. The stuff works. You'd know that if you'd use it on your damn acne."

"Screw you," Darin says.

"It's like you're trying to be a perpetual teenager," Brad mutters. "Acne isn't cool when you're thirty."

Brad pulls out the chair next to him while Darin begins shuffling a deck of cards. "Have a seat, Lily. One of our friends decided to be an idiot and get married last week, and now his wife won't let him come to poker night anymore. You can be his fill-in until he gets a divorce."

I had every intention of hiding out in my room tonight,

but these two make it hard to walk away. I take a seat next to Brad and reach across the table. "Hand me those," I say to Darin. He's shuffling the cards like a one-armed infant.

He raises an eyebrow and pushes the deck of cards across the table. I don't know much about card games, but I can shuffle cards like a pro.

I separate the cards into two piles and scoot them together, pressing my thumbs to the ends, watching as they beautifully intertwine. Darin and Brad are staring at the deck of cards, when there's another knock on the door. This time the door swings open without pause and a guy walks in dressed in what looks like a very expensive tweed jacket. There's a scarf wrapped around his neck, and he begins to unwind it as soon as he slams the door behind him. He nudges his head in my direction as he walks toward the kitchen. "Who are you?"

He's older than the other two, probably in his mid-forties. Atlas definitely has an interesting mix of friends.

"This is Lily," Brad says. "She's married to an asshole and just found out she's pregnant with the asshole's baby. Lily, this is Jimmy. He's pompous and arrogant."

"Pompous and arrogant are the same thing, idiot," Jimmy says. He pulls out the chair next to Darin and nudges his head at the cards in my hands. "Did Atlas plant you here to hustle us? What kind of average person knows how to shuffle cards like that?"

I smile and begin to pass cards out to each of them. "I guess we'll have to play a round to find out."

•　•　•

We're on our third round of bets when Atlas finally walks in. He closes the door behind him and looks around at the four of us. Brad said something funny right before Atlas opened the door, so I'm in the middle of a fit of laughter when Atlas locks eyes with me. He nods his head toward the kitchen and begins walking in that direction.

"Fold," I say, laying my cards flat on the table as I stand up to follow him. When I get to the kitchen, he's standing where he isn't visible to the guys at the table. I walk over to him and lean against the counter.

"You want me to ask them to leave?"

I shake my head. "No, don't do that. I'm actually enjoying it. It's keeping my mind off things."

He nods and I can't help but notice how he smells like herbs. Rosemary, specifically. It makes me wish I could see him in action at his restaurant.

"You hungry?" he asks.

I shake my head. "Not really. I ate some leftover pasta a couple hours ago."

My hands are pressed into the counter on either side of me. He takes a step closer and puts one of his hands over mine, brushing his thumb across the top of it. I know he doesn't mean for it to be anything more than a comforting gesture, but when he touches me, it feels like a whole lot more. A rush of warmth moves up my chest and I immediately drop my eyes to our hands. Atlas pauses his thumb for a second, like he feels it, too. He pulls his hand away and backs up a step.

"Sorry," he mutters, turning toward the refrigerator, pretending to look for something. It's obvious he's trying to spare me from the awkwardness of what just happened.

I walk back to the table and pick up my cards for the next round. A couple of minutes later, Atlas walks over and takes the seat next to me. Jimmy shuffles out a round of new cards to everyone. "So, Atlas. How do you and Lily know each other?"

Atlas picks up his cards one at a time. "Lily saved my life when we were kids," he says, matter-of-fact. He glances over at me and winks, and I drown in guilt for the way that wink makes me feel. Especially at a time like this. *Why is my heart doing this to me?*

"Aw, that's sweet," Brad says. "Lily saved your life, now you're saving hers."

Atlas lowers his cards and glares at Brad. "Excuse me?"

"Relax," Brad says. "Me and Lily are tight, she knows I'm kidding." Brad looks at me. "Your life might be complete crap right now, Lily, but it'll get better. Trust me, I've been there."

Darin laughs. "You've been beat up and pregnant and hiding out at another man's house?" he says to Brad.

Atlas slaps his cards on the table and pushes back in his chair. "What the hell is wrong with you?" he yells at Darin.

I reach over and squeeze his arm reassuringly. "Relax," I say. "We bonded before you got here. I actually don't mind that they're making light of my situation. It really does make it a little less heavy."

He runs a frustrated hand through his hair, shaking his head. "I'm so confused," he says. "You were alone with them for ten minutes."

I laugh. "You can learn a lot about someone in ten minutes." I try to redirect the conversation. "So how do you all know each other?"

Darin leans forward and points at himself. "I'm the sous chef at Bib's." He points at Brad. "He's the dishwasher."

"For now," Brad interjects. "I'm working my way up."

"What about you?" I say to Jimmy.

He smirks and says, "Take a guess."

Based on the way he dresses and the fact that he's been called arrogant and pompous, I'd have to assume . . . "Maître d'?"

Atlas laughs. "Jimmy actually works in valet."

I glance back at Jimmy and raise an eyebrow. He tosses three poker chips down and says, "It's true. I park cars for tips."

"Don't let him fool you," Atlas says. "He works in valet, but only because he's so rich he gets bored."

I smile. It reminds me of Allysa. "I have an employee like that. Only works because she's bored. She's actually the best employee I have."

"Damn straight," Jimmy mutters.

I take a look at my cards when it's my turn and toss in the three poker chips. Atlas's phone rings and he pulls it out of his pocket. I'm raising the pot with another chip when he excuses himself from the table to take the call.

"Fold," Brad says, slapping his cards on the table.

I'm watching the hallway Atlas just disappeared down in a hurry. It makes me wonder if he's talking to Cassie, or if there's someone else in his life. I know what he does for a living. I know he has at least three friends. I just know nothing about his love life.

Darin lays his cards on the table. Four of a kind. I lay down my straight flush and reach forward for all the poker chips as Darin groans.

"So does Cassie not usually come to poker night?" I ask, fishing for more information on Atlas. Information I'm too scared to ask him myself.

"Cassie?" Brad says.

I stack my winnings up in front of me and nod. "Isn't that his girlfriend's name?"

Darin laughs. "Atlas doesn't have a girlfriend. I've known him for two years and he's never mentioned anyone named Cassie." He begins passing out new cards, but I'm trying to absorb the information he just gave me. I pick up my first two cards when Atlas walks back into the room.

"Hey, Atlas," Jimmy says. "Who the hell is Cassie and how come we've never heard you talk about her?"

Oh, shit.

I'm completely mortified. I tighten my grip around the cards in my hands and try to avoid looking up at Atlas, but the room grows so quiet, it would be more obvious if I *didn't* look at him.

He's staring at Jimmy. Jimmy is staring at him. Brad and Darin are staring at me.

Atlas folds his lips together for a moment and then says, "There is no Cassie." His eyes meet mine, but only for a brief second. But in that brief second, I can see it written all over his face.

There never *was* a Cassie.

He lied to me.

Atlas clears his throat and then says, "Listen, guys. I should have cancelled tonight. This week has been kind of . . ." He rubs his hand over his mouth and Jimmy stands up.

He squeezes Atlas on the shoulder and says, "Next week. My place."

Atlas nods appreciatively. The three of them begin to gather their cards and poker chips. Brad pries my cards from my fingers apologetically because I'm unable to move as I clutch them tightly.

"It was lovely meeting you, Lily," Brad says. I somehow find the strength to smile and stand up. I give them all hugs goodbye and after the front door closes behind them, it's just me and Atlas in the room.

And no Cassie.

Cassie's never even been in this room, because Cassie doesn't exist.

What the hell?

Atlas hasn't moved from his spot near the table. Neither have I. He's standing firm with his arms folded across his chest. His head is slightly tilted down but his eyes are boring into me from across the table.

Why would he lie to me?

Ryle and I weren't even an official couple yet when I ran into Atlas at that restaurant the first time. Hell, if Atlas had given me any reason to believe there was a chance between us that night, I know without a doubt that I would have chosen him over Ryle. I barely even *knew* Ryle at that point.

But Atlas didn't say anything. He lied to me and told me he'd been in a relationship for an entire year. Why? Why would he do that unless he didn't want me to think I had a chance with him?

Maybe I've been wrong all this time. Maybe he never even loved me to begin with and he knew that inventing this Cassie person would keep me away from him for good.

Yet, here I am. Crashing at his house. Interacting with his friends. Eating his food. Using his shower.

I can feel the tears begin to sting my eyes and the last thing I want is to stand in front of him and cry right now. I walk around the table and rush past him. I don't make it far when he grabs my hand. "Wait."

I stop, still facing the other direction.

"Talk to me, Lily."

He's right behind me now, his hand still wrapped around mine. I pull it away from him and walk to the other side of the living room.

I spin and face him just as the first tear rolls down my cheek. "Why did you never come back for me?"

He looked prepared for anything to come out of my mouth other than the words I just spoke to him. He runs a hand through his hair and walks to the couch, taking a seat. After blowing out a calming breath, he carefully looks over at me.

"I did, Lily."

I don't allow air to move in or out of my lungs.

I stand completely still, processing his answer.

He came back for me?

He folds his hands together in front of him. "When I got out of the Marines the first time, I went back to Maine, hoping to find you. I asked around and found out which college you went to. I wasn't sure what to expect when I showed up, because we were two different people by then. It had been four years since we saw each other. I knew a lot about both of us had probably changed in those four years."

My knees feel weak, so I walk to the chair next to him and lower myself. *He came back for me?*

"I walked around your campus the whole day looking for you. Finally, late that afternoon, I saw you. You were sitting in the courtyard with a group of your friends. I watched you for a long time, trying to work up the courage to walk over to you. You were laughing. You looked happy. You were vibrant like I'd never seen you before. I had never felt that kind of happiness for another person like I felt when I saw you that day. Just knowing you were okay . . ."

He pauses for a moment. My hands are clenched around my stomach, because it hurts. It hurts knowing I was so close to him and I didn't even know.

"I began walking toward you when someone came up behind you. A guy. He dropped to his knees next to you and when you saw him, you smiled and threw your arms around him. Then you kissed him."

I close my eyes. *He was just a boy I dated for six months. He never even made me feel a fraction of what I had felt for Atlas.*

He blows out a sharp breath. "I left after that. When I saw that you were happy, it was the worst and best feeling a person could ever have at once. But I believed at that point that my life was still not good enough for you. I had nothing to offer you but love, and to me, you deserved more than that. The next day I signed up for another tour in the Marines. And now . . ." He tosses his hand up lazily in the air, like nothing about his life is impressive.

I bury my head in my hands to take a moment. I quietly grieve what could have been. What is. What wasn't. My fingers move to the tattoo on my shoulder. I begin to wonder if I'll ever be able to fill in that hole now.

It makes me wonder if Atlas ever feels like I felt when I got this tattoo. Like all the air is being let out of his heart.

I still don't understand why he lied to me after running into me at his restaurant. If he really felt the things I felt for him, why would he make something like that up?

"Why did you lie about having a girlfriend?"

He rubs a hand over his face and I can already see the regret before I even hear it in his voice. "I said that because . . . you looked happy that night. When I saw you telling him goodbye, it hurt like hell, but at the same time I was relieved that you seemed to be in a really good place. I didn't want you to worry about me. And I don't know . . . maybe I was a little jealous. I don't know, Lily. I regretted lying to you as soon as I did it."

My hand goes to my mouth. My mind starts to race just as fast as my heart is racing. I instantly start thinking about the what-ifs. *What if he would have been honest with me? Told me how he'd felt? Where would we be now?*

I want to ask him why he did it. Why he didn't fight for me. But I don't have to ask him, because I already know the answer. He thought he was giving me what I wanted, because all he's ever wanted for me was happiness. And for some stupid reason, he's never felt I could get that with him.

Considerate Atlas.

The more I think about it, the more difficult it becomes to breathe. I think about Atlas. Ryle. Tonight. Two nights ago. It's too much.

I stand up and make my way back to the guest bedroom. I pick up my phone and grab my purse and go back to the living room. Atlas hasn't moved.

"Ryle left for England today," I say. "I think I should probably go home now. Can you drive me?"

A sadness enters his eyes and when it does, I know that leaving is the right thing to do. Neither of us has closure. I'm not sure we'll ever get it. I'm beginning to think closure is a myth, and being here right now while I'm still processing everything that's happening to my life is just going to make things worse for me. I have to eliminate as much confusion as possible, and right now, my feelings for Atlas top the list of most confusing.

He presses his lips tightly together for a moment, and then he nods and grabs his keys.

.   .   .

Neither of us speaks the entire drive to my apartment. He doesn't drop me off. He pulls into the parking lot and gets out of his car. "I'd feel better if you let me walk you up," he says.

I nod and we wade through even more silence as we ride the elevator up to the seventh floor. He follows me all the way to my apartment. I fish around in my purse for the keys and don't even realize my hands are shaking until my third failed attempt to open the door. Atlas calmly takes the keys from me and I step aside as he opens the door for me.

"Do you want me to make sure no one's here?" he asks.

I nod. I know Ryle isn't here because he's on his way to England, but I'm honestly still a little scared to walk into the apartment by myself.

Atlas walks in before me and flips on the lights. He continues walking through the apartment, flipping on all the lights and walking into each of the rooms. When he makes it back to the living room, he slides his hands in his jacket pockets. He takes a deep breath and then says, "I don't know what happens next, Lily."

He does. He knows. He just doesn't want it to happen, because we both know how much it hurts to say goodbye to each other.

I look away from him because seeing the look on his face right now cuts straight to my heart. I fold my arms over my chest and stare at the floor. "I have a lot to work through, Atlas. *A lot*. And I'm scared I won't be able to do it with you in my life." I lift my eyes back to his. "I hope you don't take offense to that, because if anything, it's a compliment."

He regards me silently for a moment, not at all surprised by what I'm saying. But I can see there's so much he wants to say. There's a lot I wish I could say to him, too, but we both know discussing the two of us isn't appropriate at this point. I'm married. I'm pregnant with another man's baby. And he's standing in the living room of an apartment that another man bought for me. I'd say these aren't very good conditions in which to bring up all the things we should have said to each other a long time ago.

He looks at the door momentarily as if he's trying to decide to leave or speak. I can see the twitch in his jaw right before he locks eyes with me. "If you ever need me, I want you to call me," he says. "But only if it's an emergency. I'm not capable of being casual with you, Lily."

I'm taken aback by his words, but only momentarily. As much as I wasn't expecting him to admit it, he's absolutely right. Since the day we met, there has been nothing casual about our relationship. It's either all in or not in at all. That's why he separated ties when he left for the military. He knew that a casual friendship would never work between us. It would have been too painful.

Apparently, that hasn't changed.

"Goodbye, Atlas."

Saying those words again tears me up almost as much as the first time I had to say them. He winces and then turns and walks to the door like he can't leave fast enough. When the door closes behind him, I walk over and lock it, then press my head against it.

Two days ago I was asking myself how my life could possibly get any better. Today I'm asking myself how it could possibly get any worse.

I jump back with the sudden knock at the door. It's only been ten seconds since he walked out, so I know it's Atlas. I unlock it and open it and I'm suddenly pressed against something soft. Atlas's arms wrap tightly around me, desperately, and his lips are pressed against the side of my head.

I squeeze my eyes shut and finally let the tears fall. I've cried so many tears for Ryle over the past two days, I have no idea how I still have any left for Atlas. But I do, because they're falling down my cheeks like rain.

"Lily," he whispers, still holding me tightly. "I know this is the last thing you need to hear right now. But I have to say it because I've walked away from you too many times without saying what I really want to say."

He pulls back to look down at me and when he sees my tears, he brings his hands up to my cheeks. "In the future . . . if by some miracle you ever find yourself in the position to fall in love again . . . fall in love with me." He presses his lips against my forehead. "You're still my favorite person, Lily. Always will be."

He releases me and walks away, not even needing a response.

When I close the door again, I slide to the floor. My heart feels like it wants to give up. I don't blame it. It's suffered through two separate heartaches in the course of two days.

And I have a feeling it's going to be a long time before either of those heartaches can even begin to heal.

Chapter Twenty-Nine

Allysa drops onto the couch beside me and Rylee. "I miss you so much, Lily," she says. "I'm thinking about coming back to work a day or two a week."

I laugh, a little shocked by her comment. "I live downstairs and I visit almost every day. How can you possibly miss me?"

She pouts as she pulls her legs up beneath her. "Fine, it's not you I miss. I miss work. And sometimes I just want out of this house."

It's been six weeks since she had Rylee, so I'm sure she would be cleared to come back to work. But I honestly didn't think she'd even want to come back now that she has Rylee. I bend forward and give Rylee a kiss on her nose. "Would you bring Rylee with you?"

Allysa shakes her head. "No, you keep me too busy for that. Marshall can watch her while I work."

"You mean you don't have *people* for that?"

Marshall is passing through the living room when he hears me say that. "Shush, Lily. Don't speak like a rich girl in front of my daughter. Blasphemy."

I laugh. That's why I come over here a few nights a week, because it's the only time I laugh. It's been six weeks since Ryle left for England, and no one knows what happened between us. Ryle hasn't told anyone, and neither have I. Everyone, my mother included, believes he simply left for the study at Cambridge and that nothing has changed between us.

I also still haven't told anyone about the pregnancy.

I've been to the doctor twice. It turns out I was already twelve weeks along the night I found out I was pregnant, which makes me eighteen weeks along now. I'm still trying to wrap my head around it. I've been on the pill since I was eighteen. Apparently being forgetful a few times caught up with me.

I'm beginning to show, but it's cold out so it's been easy to hide. No one suspects a thing when you have on a baggy sweater and a jacket.

I know I need to tell someone soon, but I feel like Ryle should be the first one I tell, and I don't want to do that over a long-distance phone conversation. He'll be back in six weeks. If I can somehow keep things quiet until then, I'll decide where to go from there.

I look down at Rylee and she's smiling up at me. I make silly faces at her to make her smile more. There have been so many times I've wanted to tell Allysa about the pregnancy, but it makes it hard when the secret I'm keeping is being kept from her own brother. I don't want to put her in that kind of situation, no matter how much it kills me that I can't talk to her about it.

"How are you holding up without Ryle?" Allysa asks. "You ready for him to come home?"

I nod, but I don't say anything. I always try to brush off the subject when she brings him up.

Allysa leans back into the couch and says, "Is he still liking Cambridge?"

"Yes," I say, sticking my tongue out at Rylee. She grins. I wonder if my baby will look like her. I hope so. She's really cute, but I might be a little partial.

"Did he ever figure out the subway system there?" Allysa laughs. "I swear, every time I talk to him, he's lost. He can't figure out whether to take the A-line or the B-line."

"Yeah," I tell her. "He figured it out."

Allysa sits up on the couch. "Marshall!"

Marshall walks into the living room and Allysa pulls Rylee out of my hands. She hands her to Marshall and says, "Will you change her diaper?"

I don't know why she asks him that. I just changed her diaper.

Marshall scrunches up his nose and lifts Rylee out of Allysa's arms. "Are you a stinky girl?"

They're wearing matching onesies.

Allysa grabs my hands and yanks me off the couch so fast, I squeal.

"Where are we going?"

She doesn't answer me. She marches toward her bedroom and then slams the door once we're both inside. She paces back and forth a few times and then she stops and faces me.

"You better tell me what the hell is going on right now, Lily!"

I pull back in shock. *What is she talking about?*

My hands instantly go to my stomach, because I think maybe she's noticed, but she doesn't look at my stomach. She takes a step forward and pokes a finger in my chest. "There *is* no subway system in Cambridge, England, you idiot!"

"What?" I am so confused.

"I made that up!" she says. "Something hasn't been right with you for a long time. You're my best friend, Lily. And I know my brother. I talk to him every week, and he isn't the same. Something happened between you two, and I want to know what it is right now!"

Shit. I guess this is happening sooner rather than later.

I slowly bring my hands up to my mouth, not sure what to tell her. How *much* to tell her. I had no idea until this moment how much it's been killing me that I haven't been able to talk to her about this. I almost feel a little relieved that she reads me so well.

I walk to her bed and take a seat on it. "Allysa," I whisper. "Sit down."

I know this is going to hurt her almost as much as it hurt me. She walks over to her bed and sits down next to me, pulling my hands to hers.

"I don't even know where to start."

She squeezes my hands, but says nothing. For the next fifteen minutes, I tell her everything. I tell her about the fight. I tell her about Atlas picking me up. I tell her about the hospital. I tell her about the pregnancy.

I tell her about how, for the last six weeks, I cry myself to sleep every night because I have never felt so alone and so scared.

When I'm finished telling her everything, we're both crying. She hasn't responded to what I've told her with anything other than the occasional *"Oh, Lily."*

She doesn't have to respond, though. Ryle is her brother. I know she wants me to take his past into consideration just like the last time it happened. I know she'll want me to work things out with him because he's her brother. We're supposed to be one big, happy family. I know exactly what she's thinking.

She's quiet for a long time as she struggles through everything I've told her. She finally lifts her eyes to mine and squeezes my hands. "My brother *loves* you, Lily. He loves you so much. You have changed his entire life and have made him someone that I never thought he could be. As his sister, I wish more than anything that you could find a way to forgive him. But as your best friend, I have to tell you that if you take him back, I will never speak to you again."

It takes a moment for her words to register, but when they do, I start sobbing.

She starts sobbing.

She wraps her arms around me and we cry over the mutual love we have for Ryle. We cry over how much we hate him right now.

After several minutes of us sobbing pathetically on her bed, she releases me and walks over to her dresser to retrieve a box of tissues.

We're both wiping our eyes and sniffling when I say, "You're the best friend I've ever had."

She nods. "I know. And now I'm gonna be the best aunt." She wipes her nose and sniffles again, but she's smiling. "Lily. You're having a *baby*." She says it with excitement, and it's the first moment I've been able to share any sense of joy over my pregnancy. "I hate to say it, but I noticed you put on weight. I thought you were just depressed and eating a lot since Ryle left."

She walks to the back of her closet and starts pulling things out for me. "I have so many maternity clothes to give you."

We start going through clothes and she pulls down a suitcase and opens it. She begins to throw things toward the suitcase until it starts to overflow.

"I could never wear these," I tell her, holding up a shirt that still has the tag on it. "They're all designer. I'll get them dirty."

She laughs and shoves them into the suitcase anyway. "I won't need them back. If I get pregnant again, I'll just have my people buy me more." She pulls a shirt off a hanger and hands it to me. "Here, try this one on."

I take my shirt off and then pull the maternity shirt over my head. When I get it into place, I look in the mirror.

I look . . . pregnant. Like *you-can't-hide-this-shit* pregnant.

She puts a hand on my stomach and stares in the mirror with me. "Have you found out if it's a boy or a girl?"

I shake my head. "I don't really want to know."

"I hope it's a girl," she says. "Our daughters can be besties."

"Lily?"

We both spin around to find Marshall standing in the doorway. His eyes are on my stomach. On Allysa's *hand* still on my stomach. He tilts his head. He points at me.

"You . . ." he says, confused. "Lily, there's a . . . do you realize you're pregnant?"

Allysa calmly walks to the door and puts her hand on the doorknob. "There are some things you are never, ever to repeat if you want to keep me as your wife. This is one of those things. Understood?"

Marshall raises his eyebrows and takes a step back. "Yes. Okay. Got it. Lily is not pregnant." He kisses Allysa on the forehead and looks back at me. "I am not telling you congratulations, Lily. For absolutely nothing." Allysa shoves him all the way out the door and closes it, then turns back to me.

"We need to plan a baby shower," she says.

"No. I need to tell Ryle first."

She waves her hand dismissively. "We don't need him to plan a shower. We'll just keep it between the two of us until then."

She pulls out her laptop, and for the first time since I found out I was pregnant, I feel happy about it.

Chapter Thirty

It's rather convenient only having to take an elevator to get home from Allysa's, as much as I want to move out of my own apartment at times. It's still strange living there. We only lived there a week before we split up and Ryle left for England. It never even had the chance to feel like home and now it feels a little tainted. I haven't even been able to sleep in our bedroom since that night, so I've been sleeping in the guest room on my old bed.

Allysa and Marshall are still the only ones who know about the pregnancy. It's only been two weeks since I told them, which makes me twenty weeks along now. I know I should tell my mother, but Ryle will be back in a few weeks. I feel like I should tell him first before anyone else finds out. If I can just somehow hide my baby bump from her until he gets back to the States.

I should probably just accept the fact that I'm more than likely going to have to call him and tell him long-distance. I haven't seen my mother face-to-face in two weeks. It's the longest we've gone without seeing each other since she moved to Boston, so if something doesn't happen soon she'll show up at my front door when I'm not prepared.

I swear my stomach has doubled in size these last two weeks alone. If someone sees me who knows me well, it'll be impossible to hide. So far, no one at the floral shop has asked about it. I think I'm still on the cusp of *"Is she pregnant? Or just chubby?"*

I start to unlock the door to my apartment, but it begins to open from the other side. Before I can pull the jacket over to hide my stomach from whoever is on the other side of the door, Ryle's eyes land on me. I'm wearing one of the shirts Allysa gave me and it's kind of impossible to hide the fact that I'm wearing a maternity shirt when he's staring right at it.

Ryle.

Ryle is here.

My heart begins to smash against the walls of my chest. My neck begins to itch, so I bring my hand up and rest it there, feeling the pounding of my heart against my palm.

It's pounding because I'm terrified of him.

It's pounding because I hate him.

It's pounding because I've missed him.

His eyes slowly crawl from my stomach to my face. A hurtful expression takes over him, like I've just stabbed him straight through the heart. He takes a step back into my apartment and his hands come up to his mouth.

He begins to shake his head in confusion. I can see the betrayal all over his face when he barely forces out my name. *"Lily?"*

I stand frozen, one hand on my stomach in protection, the other hand still flat against my chest. I'm too scared to move or say anything. I don't want to react until I know exactly how *he's* going to react.

When he sees the fear in my eyes and the small gasps of breath I'm barely inhaling, he holds up a reassuring palm.

"I'm not going to hurt you, Lily. I'm just here to talk to you." He swings the door open wider and points into the living room. "Look." He steps aside and my eyes fall to someone standing behind him.

Now *I'm* the one who feels betrayed.

"Marshall?"

Marshall immediately holds up his hands in defense. "I had no idea he was coming home early, Lily. Ryle texted and asked for my help. He specifically told me not to say anything to you or Issa. Please don't let her divorce me, I'm simply an innocent bystander."

I shake my head, trying to understand what I'm seeing.

"I asked him to meet me here so you'd feel more comfortable talking to me," Ryle says. "He's here for you, he's not here for me."

I glance back at Marshall and he nods. It gives me enough reassurance to enter the apartment. Ryle is still somewhat in shock, which is understandable. His eyes keep meeting my stomach and then flicking away like it hurts to look at me. He runs two hands through his hair and then points down the hallway while looking at Marshall.

"We'll be in the bedroom. If you hear me get . . . if I start to yell . . ."

Marshall knows what Ryle is asking him. "I'm not going anywhere."

As I follow Ryle into my bedroom, I wonder what that must be like. To have no idea what might set you off or how bad your reaction will be. To have absolutely no control over your own emotions.

For a brief moment, I feel a minuscule amount of sorrow

for him. But when my eyes fall to our bed and I remember that night, my sorrow diminishes completely.

Ryle pushes the door shut, but doesn't close it all the way. He looks like he's aged an entire year in the two months it's been since I've seen him. The bags under his eyes, the furrowed brow, the sunken posture. If regret took human form, it would look identical to Ryle.

His eyes fall to my stomach again and he takes a slow step forward. Then another. He's cautious, as he should be. He reaches out a timid hand, asking for permission to touch me. I nod softly.

He takes one more step forward and then places a steady palm against my stomach.

I can feel the warmth of his hand through my shirt, and my eyes snap shut. Despite the resentment I've built up in my heart toward him, it doesn't mean the emotions aren't still there. Just because someone hurts you doesn't mean you can simply stop loving them. It's not a person's actions that hurt the most. It's the love. If there was no love attached to the action, the pain would be a little easier to bear.

He moves his hand over my stomach and I open my eyes again. He's shaking his head, like he can't process what's happening right now. I watch as he slowly sinks to his knees in front of me.

His arms snake around my waist and he presses his lips against my stomach. He clasps his hands around my lower back and presses his forehead against me.

It's hard to describe what I feel for him in this moment. Like any mother would want for her child, it's a beautiful thing to see the love he already has. It's been hard not sharing this with anyone. It's hard not being able to share this with *him*, no matter how much resentment I hold toward him. My hands go to his hair while he holds me against him. Part of me wants to scream at him and call the police like I should have done that night. Part of me feels for that little boy who held his brother in his arms and watched him die. Part of me wishes I would have never met him. Part of me wishes I could forgive him.

He unwraps his arms from around my waist and presses a hand into the mattress next to us. He pulls himself up and then sits on the bed. His elbows rest on his knees and his hands are drawn up to his mouth.

I sit next to him, knowing we have to have this conversation, but not wanting to. "Naked truths?"

He nods.

I don't know which one of us is supposed to go first. I don't really have much to say to him at this point, so I wait for him to speak first.

"I don't even know where to start, Lily." He rubs his hands down his face.

"How about you start with, *'I'm sorry I attacked you.'*"

His eyes meet mine, wide with certainty. "Lily, you have no idea. I am *so* sorry. You have no idea what I've been through these past two months knowing what I've done to you."

I clench my teeth together. I can feel my fingers as they fist around the blanket beside me.

I have no idea what *he's* been through?

I shake my head, slowly. "*You* have no idea, Ryle."

I stand up, the anger and hatred spilling out of me. I spin, pointing at him. "*You* have no idea! You have *no* idea what it's like to go through what you've put me through! To fear for your life at the hands of the man you love? To get physically sick just thinking about what he's done to you? *You* have no idea, Ryle! *None! Fuck* you! *Fuck* you for doing this to me!"

I suck in a huge breath, shocked at myself. The anger just came like a wave. I swipe at my tears and spin around, unable to look at him.

"Lily," he says. "I don't . . ."

"No!" I yell, spinning around again. "I am not finished! You don't get to say your truth until I've said mine!"

He's grabbing at his jaw, squeezing the stress out of it. He drops his eyes to the floor, unable to look at the rage in mine. I take three steps toward him and drop to my knees. I place my hands on his legs, forcing him to look me straight in the eyes while I speak to him.

"Yes. I kept the magnet Atlas gave me when we were kids. Yes. I kept the journals. No, I didn't tell you about my tattoo. Yes, I probably should have. And yes, I still love him. And I'll love him until I die, because he was a huge part of my life. And yes, I'm sure that hurts you. But none of that gave you the right to do what you did to me. Even if you would have walked into my bedroom and caught us in bed together, you *still* would not have the right to lay a hand on me, you goddamn son of a bitch!"

I push off his knees and stand up again. "*Now* it's your turn!" I yell.

I continue pacing the room. My heart is pounding like it wants out. I wish I could give it a way out. I'd set the motherfucker free right now if I could.

Several minutes pass as I continue to pace. Ryle's silence and my anger eventually just fold together into pain.

My tears have exhausted me. I am so tired of feeling. I fall desperately onto my bed and cry into my pillow. I press my face so hard against my pillow, I can barely breathe.

I feel Ryle lie down next to me. He places a gentle hand on the back of my head, attempting to sooth away the pain he's causing me. My eyes are closed, still pressed into the pillow, but I feel him gently rest his head against mine.

"My truth is that I have absolutely nothing to say," he says quietly. "I'll never be able to take back what I did to you. And you'll never believe me if I promise it won't happen again." He presses a kiss against my head. "You are my world, Lily. *My world*. When I woke up on this bed that night and you were gone, I knew I would never get you back. I came here to tell you how incredibly sorry I am. I came to tell you I was taking that job offer in Minnesota. I came to tell you goodbye. But Lily . . ." His lips press against my head again and he exhales sharply. "Lily, I can't do that now. You have a part of me inside of you. And I already love this baby more than I've ever loved anything in my whole life." His voice cracks and he grips me even harder. "Please don't take this away from me, Lily. *Please*."

The pain in his voice ripples through me, and when I lift my tear-soaked face to look at him, he presses his lips desperately to mine and then pulls back. "Please, Lily. I love you. *Help* me."

His lips briefly meet mine again. When I don't push him away, his mouth comes back a third time.

A fourth.

When his lips meet mine the fifth time, they don't leave.

He wraps his arms around me and pulls me to him. My body is tired and weak, but it remembers him. My body remembers how his body can soothe everything I'm feeling. How his has a gentleness in it that my body has been craving for two months now.

"I love you," he whispers against my mouth. His tongue sweeps softly against mine and it's so wrong and so good and so painful. Before I know it, I'm on my back and he's crawling on top of me. His touch is everything I need and everything I shouldn't.

His hand wraps in my hair and in an instant, I'm transferred back to that night.

I'm in the kitchen, and his hand is tugging my hair so hard it hurts.

He brushes the hair from my face and in an instant, I'm transferred back to that night.

I'm standing in the doorway, and his hand is trailing across my shoulder, right before he bites into me with all the strength in his jaw.

His forehead rests gently against mine and in an instant, I'm transferred back to that night.

I'm on this same bed beneath him when he slams his head against mine so hard I have to get six stitches.

My body becomes unresponsive to his. The anger begins to roll back over me. His mouth stops moving against mine when he feels me freeze.

When he pulls back and looks down on me, I don't even have to say anything. Our eyes, locked together, speak more naked truths than our mouths ever have. My eyes are telling his that I can no longer stand being touched by him. His eyes are telling mine that he already knows.

He begins to nod, slowly.

He backs away from me, crawling down my body until he's at the edge of the bed with his back to me. He's still nodding as he comes to a slow stand, fully aware that he's not getting my forgiveness tonight. He begins heading toward my bedroom door.

"Wait," I say to him.

He half-turns, looking back at me from the doorway.

I lift my chin, looking at him with finality. "I wish this baby wasn't yours, Ryle. With everything that I am, I wish this baby was not a part of you."

If I thought his world couldn't crumble more, I was wrong.

He walks out of my bedroom and I press my face into my pillow. I thought if I could just hurt him like he had hurt me, I would feel avenged.

I don't.

Instead, I feel vindictive and mean.

I feel like I'm my father.

Chapter Thirty-One

Mom: I miss you. When am I going to see you?

I stare at the text. It's been two days since Ryle found out I'm pregnant. I know it's time to tell my mother. I'm not nervous about telling her I'm pregnant. The only thing that scares me is discussing my situation with Ryle with her.

Me: Miss you, too. I'll come over tomorrow afternoon. Can you make lasagna?

As soon as I close out the text to her, I get another incoming text.

Allysa: Come upstairs and eat dinner with us tonight. It's homemade pizza night.

I haven't been to Allysa's in a few days. Since before Ryle came home. I'm not sure where he's staying, but I assume it's with them. The last thing I want right now is to have to be in the same apartment as him.

Me: Who all will be there?

Allysa: Lily . . . I wouldn't do that to you. He's working until 8 tomorrow morning. It'll just be the three of us.

She knows me way too well. I text her back and tell her I'll come over as soon as I finish up with work.

• • •

"What do babies eat at this age?"

We're all seated around the table. Rylee was asleep when I got here, but I woke her up so I could hold her. Allysa didn't mind; she said she doesn't want her wide awake when she's ready to go to bed.

"Breast milk," Marshall says with a mouthful. "But sometimes I stick my finger in my soda and put it in her mouth so she can taste it."

"Marshall!" Allysa yells. "You better be kidding."

"Totally kidding," he says, although I can't tell if he really is.

"But when do they start eating baby food?" I ask. I figure I need to learn this stuff before giving birth.

"Around four months," Allysa says with a yawn. She drops her fork and leans back in her chair, rubbing her eyes.

"You want me to keep her at my place tonight so you guys can get a full night of sleep?"

Allysa says, "No, it's fine," at the same time Marshall says, "That would be awesome."

I laugh. "Really. I live right downstairs. I don't work tomorrow so if I don't get any sleep tonight I can just sleep in tomorrow."

Allysa looks like she's contemplating it for a moment. "I could leave my cell phone on in case you need me."

I look back down at Rylee and grin. "Did you hear that? You get to have a sleepover with Aunt Lily!"

•   •   •

With everything Allysa is throwing in her diaper bag, it looks like I'm about to take Rylee on a trip across the country.

"She'll let you know when she's hungry. Don't use the microwave to heat the milk, just put it in . . ."

"I know," I interrupt. "I've made her like fifty bottles since she's been alive."

Allysa nods and then walks over to her bed. She drops the diaper bag down beside me. Marshall is in the living room feeding Rylee one last time, so Allysa lies down beside me on the bed while we wait. She props her head up on her hand.

"Do you know what this means?" she asks.

"No. What?"

"I get to have sex tonight. It's been four months."

I crinkle up my nose. "I didn't need to know that."

She laughs and falls down on her pillow, but then sits straight up. "Shit," she says. "I should probably shave my legs. I think it's been four months since I did that, too."

I laugh, but then I gasp. My hands move quickly to my stomach. "Oh my God! I just felt something!"

"Really?" Allysa puts her hand on my stomach and we're both quiet for the next five minutes as we wait for it to happen again. It does, but it's so soft, it's almost unnoticeable. I laugh again as soon as it happens.

"I didn't feel anything," Allysa says, pouting. "I guess it'll be a few more weeks before you can feel it from the outside, though. Is this the first time you felt it move?"

"Yeah. I've been scared I was growing the laziest baby in history." I keep my hands on my stomach, hoping to feel it again. We sit quietly for a few more minutes, and I can't help but wish my circumstances were different. Ryle should be here. He should be the one sitting beside me with his hand on my stomach. Not Allysa.

The thought almost takes away all the joy I'm feeling. Allysa must notice because she puts one of her hands on mine and squeezes. When I look at her, she isn't smiling anymore.

"Lily," she says. "I've been wanting to say something to you."

Oh, God. I don't like the sound of her voice.

"What is it?"

She sighs and then forces a gloomy smile. "I know you're sad that you're going through this without my brother. No matter how involved he is, I just want you to know that this is going to be the best thing you've ever experienced in your life. You're gonna be a great mom, Lily. This baby is *really* lucky."

I'm glad Allysa is the only one in here right now, because her words make me laugh, cry, and snot like a hormonal teenager. I hug her and tell her thank you. It's amazing how hearing those words gives me back the joy I was feeling.

She smiles and then says, "Now go get my baby and take her away from here so I can have some sex with my filthy rich husband."

I roll off the bed and stand up. "You sure know how to bring levity into a situation. I'd say it's your strong point."

She smiles. "That's what I'm here for. Now go away."

Chapter Thirty-Two

Of all the secrets I've held over the last few months, I'm the saddest about keeping everything from my mother. I don't know how she'll take it. I know she'll be excited about the pregnancy, but I don't know how she'll feel about me and Ryle splitting up. She loves Ryle. And based on her history with these types of situations, she'll probably find it very easy to excuse his behavior and try and convince me to take him back. And in all honesty, that's part of the reason I've been stalling this, because I'm scared there's a chance she might be successful.

Most days I'm strong. Most days I'm so mad at him that the thought of ever forgiving him is ludicrous. But some days I miss him so much I can't breathe. I miss the fun I had with him. I miss making love to him. I miss *missing* him. He used to work so many hours that when he would walk in the front door at night I would rush across the room and jump in his arms because I missed him so much. I even miss how much he loved it when I would do that.

It's the not-so-strong days when I wish my mother knew about everything that was going on. I sometimes just want to drive over to her house and curl up on the couch with her while she tucks my hair behind my ear and tells me it'll all be okay. Sometimes even grown women need their mother's comfort so we can just take a break from having to be strong all the time.

I sit in my car, parked in her driveway, for a good five

minutes before I work up the strength to go inside. It sucks that I have to do this because I know that in a way, I'll be breaking her heart, too. I hate it when she's sad and telling her I married a man who might be like my father is going to make her really sad.

When I walk through the front door, she's in the kitchen layering noodles in a pan. I don't remove my coat right away for obvious reasons. I'm not wearing a maternity shirt but my bump is almost impossible to hide without a jacket. Especially from a mother.

"Hey, sweetie!" she says.

I walk into the kitchen and give her a side hug while she layers cheese over the top of the lasagna. Once the lasagna is in the oven, we walk over to the dining room table and take a seat. She leans back in her chair and takes a sip from a glass of tea.

She's smiling. I hate it even more that she looks so happy right now.

"Lily," she says. "There's something I need to tell you."

I don't like this. I was coming over here to talk to *her*. I'm not prepared to *receive* a talk.

"What is it?" I ask hesitantly.

She grips her glass of tea with both hands. "I'm seeing someone."

My mouth drops open.

"Really?" I ask, shaking my head. "That's . . ." I'm about to say *good*, but then I grow instantly worried that she's just put herself in a similar situation she was in with my father. She can see the worry on my face, so she grabs my hands in both of hers.

"He's good, Lily. He's so good. I promise."

Relief washes over me in an instant, because I can see she's telling the truth. I can see the happiness in her eyes. "Wow," I say, not expecting this at all. "I'm happy for you. When can I meet him?"

"Tonight, if you want," she says. "I can invite him over to eat with us."

I shake my head. "No," I whisper. "Now's not a good time."

Her hands squeeze around mine as soon as she realizes I'm here to tell her something important. I start with the better part of the news first.

I stand up and remove my jacket. At first, she doesn't think anything of it. She just assumes I'm making myself comfortable. But then I take one of her hands and I press it against my stomach. "You're gonna be a grandma."

Her eyes widen and for several seconds, she's stunned speechless. But then tears begin to form. She jumps up and pulls me into a hug. "Lily!" she says. "Oh my God!" She pulls back, smiling. "That was so fast. Were you trying? You haven't even been married for very long."

I shake my head. "No. It was a shock. Believe me."

She laughs and after another hug, we both sit down again. I try to keep up my smile, but it's not the smile of an elated expectant mother. She sees that almost immediately. She slides a hand over her mouth. "Sweetie," she whispers. "What's the matter?"

Until this moment, I've fought to remain strong. I've fought to not feel too sorry for myself when I'm around other people. But sitting here with my mother, I crave weakness. I just want to be able to give up for a little while. I want her to take over and hug me and tell me it'll all be okay. And for the next fifteen minutes while I cry in her arms, that's exactly what happens. I just stop fighting for myself because I need someone else to do it for me.

I spare her most of the details of our relationship, but I do tell her the most important things. That he's hurt me on more than one occasion, and I don't know what to do. That I'm scared to have this baby alone. That I'm scared I might make the wrong decision. That I'm scared I'm being too weak and that I should have had him arrested. That I'm scared I'm being too sensitive and I don't know if I'm over-reacting. Basically, I tell her everything I haven't even been brave enough to fully admit to myself.

She retrieves some napkins out of the kitchen and comes back to the table. After our eyes are finally dry, she begins to crumple the napkin up between her hands, rolling it over in circles as she stares down at it.

"Do you want to take him back?" she asks.

I don't say yes. But I also don't say no.

This is the first moment since this has happened that I'm being completely honest. I'm honest to her *and* to myself. Maybe because she's the only one I know who has been through this. She's the only one I know who would understand the massive amounts of confusion I've been experiencing.

I shake my head, but I also shrug. "Most of me feels like I'll never be able to trust him again. But a huge part of me grieves what I had with him. We were so good together, Mom. The times I spent with him were some of the best moments of my life. And occasionally I feel like maybe I don't want to give that up."

I wipe the napkin beneath my eye, soaking up more tears. "Sometimes . . . when I'm really missing him . . . I tell myself that maybe it wasn't that bad. Maybe I could put up with him when he's at his worst just so I can have him when he's at his best."

She puts her hand on top of mine and rubs her thumb back and forth. "I know exactly what you mean, Lily. But the last thing you want to do is lose sight of your limit. Please don't allow that to happen."

I have no idea what she means by that. She sees the confusion in my expression, so she squeezes my arm and explains in more detail.

"We all have a limit. What we're willing to put up with before we break. When I married your father, I knew exactly what my limit was. But slowly . . . with every incident . . . my limit was pushed a little more. And a little more. The first time your father hit me, he was immediately sorry. He swore it would never happen again. The second time he hit me, he was even *more* sorry. The third time it happened, it was more than a hit. It was a beating. And every single time, I took him back. But the fourth time, it was only a slap. And when that happened, I felt relieved. I remember thinking, '*At least he didn't beat me this time. This wasn't so bad.*'"

She brings the napkin up to her eyes and says, "Every incident chips away at your limit. Every time you choose to stay, it makes the next time that much harder to leave. Eventually, you lose sight of your limit altogether, because you start to think, '*I've lasted five years now. What's five more?*'"

She grabs my hands and holds them while I cry. "Don't be like me, Lily. I know that you believe he loves you, and

I'm sure he does. But he's not loving you the right way. He doesn't love you the way you deserve to be loved. If Ryle truly loves you, he wouldn't allow you to take him back. He would make the decision to leave you himself so that he knows for a fact he can never hurt you again. That's the kind of love a woman deserves, Lily."

I wish with all my heart that she didn't learn these things from experience. I pull her to me and hug her.

For whatever reason, I thought I would have to defend myself to her when I came over here. Not once did I think I would come over here and learn from her. I should know better. I thought my mother was weak in the past, but she's actually one of the strongest women I know.

"Mom?" I say, pulling back. "I want to be you when I grow up."

She laughs and brushes the hair from my face. I can see in the way she looks at me that she'd trade spots with me in a heartbeat. She's feeling more pain for me in this moment than she ever felt for herself. "I want to tell you something," she says.

She reaches for my hands again.

"The day you gave your father's eulogy? I know you didn't freeze up, Lily. You stood at that podium and refused to say a single good thing about that man. It was the proudest I have ever been of you. You were the only one in my life who ever stood up for me. You were strong when I was scared." A tear falls from her eye when she says, "Be *that* girl, Lily. Brave and bold."

Chapter Thirty-Three

"What am I going to do with three car seats?"

I'm sitting on Allysa's couch, staring at all the stuff. She threw me a baby shower today. My mother came. Ryle's mother even flew in for it, but she's in the guest room sleeping off her jet lag now. The girls from the floral shop came and a few friends from my old job. Even Devin came. It was actually a lot of fun, despite the fact that I've been dreading it for the past several weeks.

"That's why I told you to start a registry, so none of the gifts would be duplicated," Allysa says.

I sigh. "I guess I can have Mom return hers. She's bought me enough stuff as it is."

I stand up and start gathering all the gifts. Marshall already said he'd help me carry them down to my apartment, so Allysa helps me throw everything inside trash bags. I hold them open while she picks everything up from the floor. I'm almost thirty weeks pregnant now, so she doesn't get the easier job of holding open the trash.

We have everything bagged up and Marshall is on his second trip down to my apartment when I open Allysa's front door, prepared to drag a trash bag full of gifts to the elevator. What I'm not prepared for is Ryle, who is standing on the other side of the door looking back at me. We both look equally as shocked to see each other, considering we haven't spoken since our fight three months ago.

This encounter was bound to happen, though. I can't be best friends with my husband's sister and live in the same building as him without eventually running into him.

I'm sure he knew I was having the shower today since his mother flew in for it, but he still looks a little surprised when he sees all the stuff behind me. It makes me wonder if him showing up just as I'm leaving is a coincidence or a suitable convenience. He looks down at the trash bag I'm holding and he takes it from my hands. "Let me get this."

I let him. He takes that bag and another one down to the apartment while I gather my things. He and Marshall are walking back inside the apartment as I'm preparing to walk out.

Ryle grabs the last bag of stuff and begins to head toward the front door again. I'm following behind him when Marshall gives me a silent look, asking me if I'm okay with Ryle going downstairs with me. I nod. I can't keep avoiding Ryle forever, so now is as good a time as any to discuss where we go from here.

It's only a few floors between their apartment and mine, but the elevator ride down with Ryle feels like the longest it's ever taken. I catch him staring at my stomach a couple of times and it makes me wonder how it must feel, going three months without seeing me pregnant.

My apartment door is unlocked, so I push it open and he follows me inside. He takes the last of the stuff to the nursery and I can hear him moving things around, opening boxes. I stay in the kitchen and clean things that don't even need cleaning. My heart is in my throat, knowing he's in my apartment. I don't feel scared of him in this moment. I just feel nervous. I wanted to be more prepared for this conversation because I absolutely hate confrontation. But I know we need to discuss the baby and our future. I just don't want to. Not yet, anyway.

He walks down the hallway and into the kitchen. I catch him looking at my stomach again. He glances away just as quickly. "Do you want me to assemble the crib while I'm here?"

I should probably say no, but he's half responsible for the child growing inside of me. If he's going to offer physical labor I'm going to take it, no matter how angry I still am at him. "Yeah. That would be a big help."

He points toward the laundry room. "Is my toolbox still in there?"

I nod and he heads toward the laundry room. I open the refrigerator and face it so I don't have to watch him walk back through the kitchen. When he's finally in the nursery again, I close the refrigerator and press my forehead against it as I grip the handle. I breathe in and out as I try to process everything that's happening inside of me right now.

He looks really good. It's been so long since I've seen him, I forgot how beautiful he is. I have an urge to run down the hallway and jump into his arms. I want to feel his mouth on mine. I want to hear him tell me how much he loves me. I want him to lie down next to me and put his hand on my stomach like I've imagined him doing so many times.

It would be so easy. My life would be so much easier right now if I would just forgive him and take him back.

I close my eyes and repeat the words my mother said to me. *"If Ryle truly loves you, he wouldn't allow you to take him back."*

That reminder is the only thing that prevents me from running down the hallway.

.   .   .

I keep myself busy in the kitchen for the next hour as he remains in the nursery. I eventually have to walk past it to grab my phone charger from my room. On my way back down the hallway, I pause at the door of the nursery.

The crib is assembled. He even put the bedding on. He's standing over it, gripping the railing, staring inside the empty crib. He's so quiet and still, he looks like a statue. He's lost in thought and doesn't even notice me standing outside the doorway. It makes me wonder where his mind has wandered.

Is he thinking about the baby? The child he won't even be living with when it sleeps in that very crib?

Until this moment, I wasn't sure if he even wanted to be a part of the baby's life. But the look on his face proves to me that he does. I've never seen so much sadness in one expression, and I'm not even facing him straight on. I feel like the sadness he's feeling in this moment has absolutely nothing to do with me and everything to do with thoughts of his child.

He glances up and sees me standing in the doorway. He pushes off the crib and shakes himself out of his trance. "Finished," he says, waving a hand toward the crib. He begins putting his tools back inside the tool case. "Is there anything else you need while I'm here?"

I shake my head as I walk over to the crib and admire it. Since I don't know if it's a boy or a girl, I decided to go with a nature theme. The bedding set is tan and green with pictures of plants and trees all over it. It matches the curtains and will eventually match a mural I plan to paint on the wall at some point. I also plan to fill the nursery with a few live plants from the shop. I can't help but smile, finally seeing it all start to come together. He even put up the mobile. I reach up and turn it on and Brahms's Lullaby begins to play. I stare at it as it makes a full spin and then I glance back at Ryle. He's standing a few feet away, just watching me.

As I stare back at him, I think about how easy it is for humans to make judgments when we're standing on the outside of a situation. I spent years judging my mother's situation.

It's easy when we're on the outside to believe that we would walk away without a second thought if a person mistreated us. It's easy to say we couldn't continue to love someone who mistreats us when we aren't the ones feeling the love of that person.

When you experience it firsthand, it isn't so easy to hate the person who mistreats you when most of the time they're your godsend.

Ryle's eyes gain a little bit of hope, and I hate that he can see that my walls are temporarily lowered. He begins to take a slow step toward me. I know he's about to pull me to him and hug me, so I take a quick step away from him.

And just like that, the wall is back up between us.

Allowing him back inside this apartment was a huge step for me in itself. He needs to realize that.

He hides whatever rejection he's feeling with a stoic expression. He tucks the toolbox under his arm and then grabs the box the crib came in. It's filled with all the trash from everything he opened and put together. "I'll take this to the

Dumpster," he says, walking toward the door. "If you need help with anything else, just let me know, okay?"

I nod and somehow mutter, "Thank you."

When I hear the front door close, I turn back and face the crib. My eyes fill with tears, and not for myself this time. Not for the baby.

I cry for Ryle. Because even though he's responsible for the situation he's in, I know how sad he is about it. And when you love someone, seeing them sad also makes *you* sad.

Neither of us brought up our separation or even a chance at reconciliation. We didn't even talk about what's going to happen when this baby is born in ten weeks.

I'm just not ready for that conversation yet and the least he can do for me right now is show me patience.

The patience he still owes me from all the times he had none.

Chapter Thirty-Four

I finish rinsing the paint out of the brushes and then walk back to the nursery to admire the mural. I spent most of yesterday and all of today painting it.

It's been two weeks since Ryle came over and put the crib together. Now that the mural is finished and I brought in a few plants from the store, I feel like the nursery is finally complete. I look around and feel a little sad that no one is here to admire the room with me. I grab my phone and text Allysa.

Me: Mural is finished! You should come down and look at it.

Allysa: I'm not home. Running errands. I'll come look at it tomorrow, though.

I frown and decide to text my mother. She has to work tomorrow, but I know she'll be just as excited to see it as I was to finish it.

Me: Feel like driving into town tonight? The nursery is finally finished.

Mom: Can't. Recital night at school. I'll be here late. I can't wait to see it! I'll come by tomorrow!

I sit down in the rocking chair and know that I shouldn't do what I'm about to do, but I do it anyway.

Me: The nursery is finished. Do you want to come look at it?

Every nerve in my body springs to life as soon as I hit Send. I stare at my phone until his reply comes through.

Ryle: Of course. On my way down now.

I immediately stand up and begin making last minute touches. I fluff the pillows on the loveseat and straighten one of the wall hangings. I'm barely to the front door when I hear his knock. I open it and *dammit. He's wearing scrubs.*

I step aside as he makes his way in.

"Allysa said you were painting a mural?"

I follow him down the hallway toward the nursery.

"It's taken two days to finish," I tell him. "My body feels like I ran a marathon and all I did was walk up and down a step ladder a few times."

He glances over his shoulder and I can see the concern in his expression. He's worried that I was here doing it all on my own. He shouldn't worry. I've got this.

When we make it to the nursery, he stops in the doorway. On the opposite wall, I painted a garden. It's complete with almost every fruit and vegetable I could think of that grows in a garden. I'm not a painter, but it's amazing what you can do with a projector and transparent paper.

"Wow," Ryle says.

I grin, because I recognize the surprise in his voice and I know it's genuine. He walks into the room and looks around, shaking his head the whole time. "Lily. It's . . . wow."

If he were Allysa, I'd clap and jump up and down. But he's Ryle and with the way things have been between us, that would be a little awkward.

He walks over to the window where I set up a swing. He gives it a little push and it begins moving from side to side.

"It also moves front to back," I tell him. I don't know if he even knows anything about baby swings, but I was pretty impressed by that feature.

He walks over to the changing table and pulls one of the diapers out of the holder. He unfolds it and holds it up in front of him. "It's so tiny," he says. "I don't remember Rylee being this tiny."

Hearing him mention Rylee makes me a little sad. We've been living apart since the night she was born, so I've never been able to see him interact with her.

Ryle folds up the diaper and puts it back in the holder. When he turns to face me, he smiles, lifting his hands to motion around the room. "It's really great, Lily," he says. "All of it. You're really doing . . ." His hands drop to his hips and his smile falters. "You're doing really well."

A thickness seems to form in the air around me. It's suddenly difficult to take in a full breath because for whatever reason, I feel like I need to cry. I just really like this moment and it saddens me that we couldn't spend the entire pregnancy full of moments like these. It feels good sharing this with him, but I'm also scared I might be giving him false hope.

Now that he's here and he saw the nursery, I'm not sure what to do next. It's glaringly obvious that we need to discuss a lot of things, but I have no idea where to start. Or how.

I walk over to the rocking chair and take a seat. "Naked truth?" I say, looking up at him.

He exhales a huge breath and nods, then takes a seat on the sofa. "*Please.* Lily, please tell me you're ready to talk about this."

His reaction eases my nerves a little, knowing he's ready to discuss everything. I wrap my arms around my stomach and lean forward in the rocking chair. "You go first."

He clasps his hands together between his knees. He looks at me with so much sincerity, I have to glance away.

"I don't know what you want from me, Lily. I don't know what role you want me to have. I'm trying to give you all the space you need, but at the same time I want to help more than you possibly know. I want to be in our baby's life. I want to be your husband and I want to be good at it. But I have no idea what's going through your head."

His words fill me with guilt. Despite what has happened between us in the past, he's still this baby's father. He has the legal right to be a father, no matter how I feel about it. And I *want* him to be a father. I want him to be a *good* father. But deep down, I'm still holding on to one of my biggest fears, and I know I need to talk to him about it.

"I would never keep you from your child, Ryle. I'm happy you want to be involved. But . . ."

He leans forward and buries his face in his hands with that last word.

"What kind of mother would I be if a small part of me doesn't have concern in regard to your temper? The way you lose control? How do I know something won't set you off while you're alone with this baby?"

So much agony floods his eyes, I think they might burst like dams. He begins to shake his head adamantly. "Lily, I would never . . ."

"I know, Ryle. You would never intentionally hurt your own child. I don't even believe it was intentional when you hurt me, but you did. And trust me, I want to believe that you would never do something like that. My father was only abusive toward my mother. There are many men—*women* even—who abuse their significant others without ever losing their temper with anyone else. I want to believe your words with all my heart, but you have to understand where my hesitation comes in. I'll never deny you a relationship with your child. But I'm going to need you to be really patient with me while you rebuild all the trust you've broken."

He nods in agreement. He has to know that I'm giving him much more than he deserves. "Absolutely," he says. "This is on your terms. Everything is on your terms, okay?"

Ryle's hands come together again and he begins to chew nervously on his bottom lip. I sense he has more to say, but he's doubting whether or not he should say it.

"Go ahead and say whatever you're thinking while I'm in the mood to talk about it."

He tilts his head back and looks up at the ceiling. Whatever it is, it's hard for him. I don't know if it's because the question is hard to ask or because he's scared of the answer I might give him.

"What about us?" he whispers.

I lean my head back and sigh. I knew this question would come, but it's really difficult to give him an answer I don't have. Divorce or reconciliation are really the only two options we have, but neither is a choice I want to make.

"I don't want to give you false hope, Ryle," I say quietly. "If I had to make a choice today . . . I'd probably choose divorce. But in all honesty, I don't know if I would be making that choice because I'm overloaded with pregnancy hormones or because it's what I really want. I don't think it would be fair to either of us if I made that decision before the birth of this baby."

He blows out a shaky breath and then brings a hand up to the back of his neck, squeezing tightly. Then he stands up and faces me. "Thank you," he says. "For inviting me over. For the conversation. I've been wanting to stop by since I was here a couple of weeks ago, but I didn't know how you'd feel about it."

"I don't know how I would have felt about it, either," I say with complete honesty. I try to push myself out of the rocking chair, but for some reason it's become a lot harder in the past week. Ryle walks over and reaches for my hand to help me up.

I don't know how I'm supposed to last until my due date when I can't even get out of a chair without grunting.

Once I'm standing, he doesn't immediately release my hand. We're just a few inches apart, and I know if I look up at him I'll feel things. I don't want to feel things for him.

He finds my other hand until he's holding both of them down at my sides. He threads his fingers through mine and I feel it all the way to my heart. I press my forehead against his chest and close my eyes. His cheek meets the top of my head and we stand completely still, both of us too scared to move. I'm scared to move because I might be too weak to stop him from kissing me. He's scared to move because he's afraid if he does, I'll pull away.

For what feels like five full minutes, neither of us moves a muscle.

"Ryle," I finally say. "Can you promise me something?"

I feel him nod.

"Until this baby comes, please don't try to talk me into forgiving you. And *please* don't try to kiss me . . ." I pull away from his chest and look up at him. "I want to tackle one huge thing at a time, and right now my only priority is having this baby. I don't want to add any more stress or confusion on top of everything that's already happening."

He squeezes both of my hands reassuringly. "One monumental life-changing thing at a time. Got it."

I smile, relieved that we've finally had this conversation. I know I didn't make a final decision about the two of us, but I still feel like I can breathe easier now that we're on the same page.

He releases my hands. "I'm late for my shift," he says, tossing a thumb over his shoulder. "I should get to work."

I nod and see him out. It isn't until after I've shut the door and am alone in my apartment that I realize I have a smile on my face.

I'm still incredibly angry with him that we're even in this predicament to begin with, so my smile is simply due to making a little headway. Sometimes parents have to work through their differences and bring a level of maturity into a situation in order to do what's best for their child.

That's exactly what we're doing. Learning how to navigate our situation before our child is brought into the fold.

Chapter Thirty-Five

I smell toast.

I stretch out on my bed and smile, because Ryle knows toast is my favorite. I lie here for a while before I even attempt to get up. It feels like it takes the effort of three men to roll me out of bed. I eventually take a deep breath, and then throw my feet over the side, pushing myself up from the mattress.

The first thing I do is pee. It's really all I do now. I'm due in two days and my doctor says it could be another week. I started maternity leave last week, so this is my life right now. I pee and watch TV.

When I make it to the kitchen, Ryle is stirring a pan of scrambled eggs. He spins around when he hears me walk in. "Good morning," he says. "No baby yet?"

I shake my head and put my hand on my stomach. "No, but I peed nine times last night."

Ryle laughs. "That's a new record." He spoons some eggs onto a plate and then tosses bacon and toast on it. He turns around and hands me the plate, pressing a quick kiss to the side of my head. "I gotta go. I'm already late. I'm leaving my phone on all day."

I smile when I look down at my breakfast. *Okay, so I eat, too. Pee, eat, and watch TV.*

"Thank you," I say cheerfully. I take my plate to the

couch and turn on the TV. Ryle rushes around the living room, gathering his stuff.

"I'll come check on you at lunch. I might be working late tonight, but Allysa said she can bring you dinner."

I roll my eyes. "I'm *fine*, Ryle. The doctor said light bed rest, not complete debilitation."

He starts to open the door, but pauses like he forgets something. He runs back toward me and leans down, planting his lips on my stomach. "I'll double your allowance if you decide to come out today," he says to the baby.

He talks to the baby a lot. I finally felt comfortable enough to let him feel the baby kick a couple of weeks ago and since then, he stops by sometimes just to talk to my belly and doesn't even say much to me. I like it, though. I like how excited he is to be a father.

I grab the blanket Ryle slept on the couch with last night and wrap it over me. He's been staying here for a week now, waiting for me to go into labor. I wasn't sure about the arrangement at first, but it's actually been really helpful. I still sleep in the guest bedroom. The third bedroom is now a nursery, which means the master bedroom is available for him to sleep in. But for whatever reason, he chooses to sleep on the couch. I think the memories in that bedroom plague him just as much as they plague me, so neither of us even bothers going in there.

The last several weeks have been really good. Aside from the fact that there's absolutely no physical relationship between us at this point, things feel like they've kind of gone back to how they used to be. He still works a lot, but on the evenings he's off, I've started having dinner upstairs with all of them. We never eat alone as a couple, though. Anything that might feel like a date or a couples thing, I avoid. I'm still trying to focus on one monumental thing at a time, and until this baby is born and my hormones are back to normal, I refuse to make a decision about my marriage. I'm sure I'm just using the pregnancy as an excuse to stall the inevitable, but being pregnant allows a person to be a little selfish.

My phone begins to ring, and I drop my head into the couch and groan. My phone is all the way in the kitchen. That's like fifteen feet from here.

Ugh.

I push myself off the couch, but nothing happens.

I try it again. *Still sitting.*

I grab hold of the arm of my chair and pull myself up. *Third time's the charm.*

When I stand, my glass of water spills all over me. I groan . . . but then I gasp.

I wasn't holding a glass of water.

Holy shit.

I look down and water is trickling down my leg. My phone is still ringing on the kitchen counter. I walk—or waddle—to the kitchen and answer it.

"Hello?"

"Hey, it's Lucy! Quick question. Our order of red roses was damaged in shipment, but we've got the Levenberg funeral today and they specifically wanted red roses for the casket spray. Do we have a backup plan?"

"Yeah, call the florist on Broadway. They owe me a favor."

"Okay, thanks!"

I start to hang up so I can call Ryle and tell him my water broke, but I hear Lucy say, "Wait!"

I pull the phone back to my ear.

"About these invoices. Did you want me to pay them today or wait . . ."

"You can wait, it's fine."

Again, I start to hang up but she yells my name and starts firing off another question.

"Lucy," I say calmly, interrupting her. "I'll have to call you about all this tomorrow. I think my water just broke."

There's a pause. "Oh. OH! GO!"

I hang up right when the first sign of pain shoots through my stomach. I wince and start dialing Ryle's number. He picks up on the first ring.

"Do I need to turn around?"

"Yes."

"Oh, God. Really? It's happening?"

"Yes."

"Lily!" he says, excited. And then the phone goes dead.

I spend the next few minutes gathering everything I'll need. I already have a hospital bag, but I feel kind of gross, so I jump in the shower to rinse off. The second burst of pain comes about ten minutes after the first. I bend forward and clench my stomach, letting the water beat down on my back. Right when I near the end of the contraction, I hear the bathroom door swing open.

"You're in the *shower*?" Ryle says. "Lily, get out of the shower, let's go!"

"Hand me a towel."

Ryle's hand appears around the shower curtain a few

seconds later. I try to fit the towel around me before pulling the shower curtain aside. It's odd, hiding your body from your own husband.

The towel doesn't fit. It covers up my boobs but then opens like an upside-down V over my stomach.

Another contraction hits as I'm stepping out of the shower. Ryle grabs my hand and helps me breathe through it, then walks me into the bedroom. I'm calmly picking out clean clothes to wear to the hospital when I glance over at him.

He's staring at my stomach. There's a look on his face I can't decipher.

His eyes meet mine and I pause what I'm doing.

There's a moment that passes between us where I can't tell if he's about to frown or smile. His face twists into both somehow, and he blows out a quick breath, dropping his eyes back to my stomach. "You're beautiful," he whispers.

A pang shoots through my chest that has nothing to do with the contractions. I realize this is the first time he's seen my bare stomach. It's the first time he's witnessed what I look like with his baby growing inside of me.

I walk over to him and take his hand. I place it on my stomach and hold it there. He smiles at me, brushing his thumb back and forth. It's a beautiful moment. One of our better moments.

"Thank you, Lily."

It's written all over him, the way he's touching my stomach, the way his eyes are looking back at mine. He's not thanking me for this moment, or any moment that came before this one. He's thanking me for all the moments I'm allowing him to have with his child.

I groan, leaning forward. "Fucking hell."

The moment is over.

Ryle grabs my clothes and helps me into them. He picks up all the things I tell him to carry and then we make our way to the elevator. Slowly. I have a contraction when we're halfway there.

"You should call Allysa," I tell him when we pull out of the parking garage.

"I'm driving. I'll call her when we get to the hospital. And your mom."

I nod. I'm sure I could call them right now, but I kind of just want to make sure we make it to the hospital first, because it feels like this baby is being really impatient and wants to make its debut right here in the car.

We make it to the hospital, but my contractions are less than a minute apart when we arrive. By the time the doctor scrubs in and they get me to a bed, I'm dilated to a nine. It's only five minutes later when I'm being told to push. Ryle doesn't even have a chance to call anyone, it all happens so fast.

I squeeze Ryle's hand with every push. At one point, I think about how important the hand I'm squeezing is to his career, but he says nothing. He just allows me to squeeze it as hard as I possibly can, and that's exactly what I do.

"The head is almost out," the doctor says. "Just a few more pushes."

I can't even describe the next few minutes. It's a blur of pain and heavy breathing and anxiety and pure, unequivocal elation. And pressure. Such an enormous pressure, like I'm about to implode, and then, "It's a girl!" Ryle says. "Lily, we have a daughter!"

I open my eyes and the doctor is holding her up. I can only make out the outline of her, because my eyes are full of too many tears. When they lay her on my chest, it's the absolute greatest moment of my life. I immediately touch her red lips and cheeks and fingers. Ryle cuts the umbilical cord, and when they take her from me to clean her up, I feel empty.

A few minutes later she's back on my chest again, swaddled in a blanket.

I can do nothing but stare at her.

Ryle sits on the bed next to me and pulls the blanket down around her chin so we can get a better look at her face. We count her fingers and her toes. She tries to open her eyes and we think it's the funniest thing in the world. She yawns and we both smile and fall even more in love with her.

After the last nurse leaves the room and we're finally alone, Ryle asks if he can hold her. He raises the head of my bed to make it easier for both of us to sit on the bed. After I hand her to him, I lay my head on his shoulder and we just can't stop staring at her.

"Lily," he whispers. "Naked truth?"

I nod.

"She's so much prettier than Marshall and Allysa's baby."

I laugh and elbow him.

"I'm kidding," he whispers.

I know exactly what he means, though. Rylee is a gorgeous baby, but no one will ever hold a candle to our own daughter.

"What should we name her?" he asks. We didn't have the typical relationship during this pregnancy, so the baby's name hasn't been something we've discussed yet.

"I'd like to name her after your sister," I say, glancing at him. "Or maybe your brother?"

I'm not sure what he thinks of that. I personally think naming our daughter after his brother could be somewhat healing for him, but he may not see it that way.

He glances over at me, not expecting that answer. "Emerson?" he says. "That's kind of cute for a girl name. We could call her Emma. Or Emmy." He smiles proudly and looks down at her. "It's perfect, actually." He leans down and kisses Emerson on her forehead.

After a while, I pull away from his shoulder so I can watch him hold her. It's a beautiful thing, seeing him interact with her like this. I can already see how much love he has for her just from the little time he's known her. I can see that he would do anything to protect her. Anything in the world.

It isn't until this moment that I finally make a decision about him.

About us.

About what's best for our family.

Ryle is amazing in so many ways. He's compassionate. He's caring. He's smart. He's charismatic. He's driven.

My father was some of these things, too. He wasn't very compassionate toward others, but there were times we spent together that I knew he loved me. He was smart. He was charismatic. He was driven. But I hated him so much more than I loved him. I was blinded to all the best things about him thanks to all the glimpses I got of him when he was at his worst. Five minutes of witnessing him at his worst couldn't make up for even five years of him at his best.

I look at Emerson and I look at Ryle. And I know that I have to do what's best for her. For the relationship I hope she builds with her father. I don't make this decision for me and I don't make it for Ryle.

I make it for her.

"Ryle?"

When he glances at me, he's smiling. But when he assesses the look on my face, he stops.

"I want a divorce."

He blinks twice. My words hit him like voltage. He winces and looks back down at our daughter, his shoulders hunched forward. "Lily," he says, shaking his head back and forth. "Please don't do this."

His voice is pleading, and I hate that he's been holding on to hope that I would eventually take him back. That's partly my fault, I know, but I don't think I realized what choice I was going to make until I held my daughter for the first time.

"Just one more chance, Lily. *Please.*" His voice cracks with tears when he speaks.

I know I'm hurting him at the worst possible time. I'm breaking his heart when this should be the best moment of his life. But I know if I don't do it in this moment, I might never be able to convince him of why I can't risk taking him back.

I begin to cry because this is hurting me as much as it's hurting him. "Ryle," I say gently. "What would you do? If one of these days, this little girl looked up at you and she said, *'Daddy? My boyfriend hit me.'* What would you say to her, Ryle?"

He pulls Emerson to his chest and buries his face against the top of her blanket. "Stop, Lily," he begs.

I push myself up straighter on the bed. I place my hand on Emerson's back and try to get Ryle to look me in the eyes. "What if she came to you and said, *'Daddy? My husband pushed me down the stairs. He said it was an accident. What should I do?'*"

His shoulders begin to shake, and for the first time since the day I met him, he has tears. Real tears that rush down his cheeks as he holds his daughter tightly against him. I'm crying, too, but I keep going. For *her* sake.

"What if . . ." My voice breaks. "What if she came to you and said, *'My husband tried to rape me, Daddy. He held me down while I begged him to stop. But he swears he'll never do it again. What should I do, Daddy?'*"

He's kissing her forehead, over and over, tears spilling down his face.

"What would you say to her, Ryle? Tell me. I need to know what you would say to our daughter if the man she loves with all her heart ever hurts her."

A sob breaks from his chest. He leans toward me and wraps an arm around me. "I would beg her to leave him," he says through his tears. His lips press desperately against my forehead and I can feel some of his tears as they fall onto my cheeks. He moves his mouth to my ear and cradles both of us against him. "I would tell her that she is worth *so* much more. And I would *beg* her not to go back, no matter how much he loves her. She's worth so much more."

We become a sobbing mess of tears and broken hearts

and shattered dreams. We hold each other. We hold our daughter. And as hard as this choice is, we break the pattern before the pattern breaks us.

He hands her back to me and wipes his eyes. He stands up, still crying. Still trying to catch his breath. In the last fifteen minutes, he lost the love of his life. In the last fifteen minutes, he became a father to a beautiful little girl.

That's what fifteen minutes can do to a person. It can destroy them.

It can save them.

He points toward the hallway, letting me know he needs to go gather himself. He's sadder than I've ever seen him as he walks toward the door. But I know he'll thank me for this one day. I know the day will come when he'll understand that I made the right choice by his daughter.

When the door closes behind him, I look down at her. I know I'm not giving her the life I dreamed for her. A home where she lives with both parents who can love her and raise her together. But I don't want her to live like I lived. I don't want her to see her father at his worst. I don't want her to see him when he loses his temper with me to the point that she no longer recognizes him as her father. Because no matter how many good moments she might share with Ryle throughout her lifetime, I know from experience that it would only be the worst ones that stuck with her.

Cycles exist because they are excruciating to break. It takes an astronomical amount of pain and courage to disrupt a familiar pattern. Sometimes it seems easier to just keep running in the same familiar circles, rather than facing the fear of jumping and possibly not landing on your feet.

My mother went through it.

I went through it.

I'll be damned if I allow my daughter to go through it.

I kiss her on the forehead and make her a promise. "It stops here. With me and you. It ends with us."

Epilogue

I push through the crowds of Boylston Street until I get to the cross street. I pull the stroller to a crawl and then stop at the edge of the curb. I pull the top of it back and look down at Emmy. She's kicking her feet and smiling like usual. She's a very happy baby. She has a calm energy about her and it's addictive.

"How old is she?" a woman asks. She's standing at the crosswalk with us, staring down at Emerson appreciatively.

"Eleven months."

"She's gorgeous," she says. "Looks just like you. Identical mouths."

I smile. "Thank you. But you should see her father. She definitely has his eyes."

The sign flashes to walk, and I try to beat the crowd as we rush across the street. I'm already half an hour late and Ryle has texted me twice. He hasn't experienced the joy of carrots yet, though. He'll find out today just how messy they are, because I packed plenty in her bag.

I moved out of the apartment Ryle bought when Emerson was three months old. I got my own place closer to my work so I'm within walking distance, which is great. Ryle moved back into the apartment he bought, but between visiting Allysa's place and Ryle's days with Emerson, I feel like I'm still at their apartment building almost as much as I'm at mine.

"Almost there, Emmy." We make a right around the corner and I'm in such a rush, a man has to step out of our way and into the wall just to avoid being plowed over. "Sorry," I mutter, ducking my head and making my way around him.

"Lily?"

I stop.

I turn slowly, because I felt that voice all the way to my toes. There are only two voices that have ever done that to me, and Ryle's doesn't reach that far anymore.

When I look back at him, his blue eyes are squinting against the sun. He lifts a hand to shield it and he grins. "Hey."

"Hi," I say, my frenzied brain trying to slow down and allow me to play catch-up.

He glances at the stroller and points at it. "Is that . . . is this your baby?"

I nod and he walks around to the front of the stroller. He kneels down and smiles widely at her. "Wow. She's gorgeous, Lily," he says. "What's her name?"

"Emerson. We call her Emmy sometimes."

He puts his finger in her hand and she starts kicking, shaking his finger back and forth. He stares at her appreciatively for a moment and then stands back up again.

"You look great," he says.

I try not to give him an obvious once-over, but it's hard. He looks as good as ever, but this is the first time seeing him that I'm not trying to deny how gorgeous he turned out to be. A far cry from that homeless boy in my bedroom. Yet . . . somehow still exactly the same.

I can feel the buzz of my text message going off in my pocket again. *Ryle.*

I point down the street. "We're really late," I say. "Ryle has been waiting for half an hour."

When I say Ryle's name, there's a sadness that reaches Atlas's eyes, but he tries to disguise it. He nods and slowly steps aside for us to pass.

"It's his day to have her," I clarify, saying more in those six words than I could in most full conversations.

I see the relief flash in his eyes. He nods and points behind him. "Yeah, I'm running late, too. Opened a new restaurant on Boylston last month."

"Wow. Congratulations. I'll have to take Mom there to check it out soon."

He smiles. "You should. Let me know and I'll make sure and cook for you myself."

There's an awkward pause, and then I point down the street. "We have to . . ."

"Go," he says with a smile.

I nod again and then duck my head and continue walking. I have no idea why I'm reacting this way. Like I don't know how to hold a normal conversation. When I'm several yards away, I glance back over my shoulder. He hasn't moved. He's still watching me as I walk away.

We round the corner and I see Ryle waiting beside his car outside the floral shop. His face lights up when he sees us approaching. "Did you get my email?" He kneels down and begins to unstrap Emerson.

"Yeah, about the playpen recall?"

He nods as he pulls her out of the stroller. "Didn't we buy one of those for her?"

I press the buttons to fold the stroller and then walk it

to the back of his car. "Yeah, but it broke like a month ago. I threw it in the Dumpster."

He pops the trunk, and then touches Emerson's chin with his fingers. "Did you hear that, Emmy? Your mommy saved your life." She smiles up at him and slaps playfully at his hand. He kisses her on the forehead and then picks up her stroller and tosses it in the trunk. I slam the trunk shut and lean over to give her a quick kiss.

"Love you, Emmy. See you tonight."

Ryle opens the back door to put her in the car seat. I tell him goodbye and then I start to head back down the street in a rush.

"Lily!" he yells. "Where are you going?"

I'm sure he expected me to walk to the front door of my store, since I'm already late opening it. I probably should, but the nagging in my gut won't go away. I need to do something about it. I spin around and walk backward. "There's something I forgot to do! I'll see you when I pick her up tonight!"

Ryle lifts Emerson's hand and they wave goodbye to me. As soon as I round the corner, I break out into a sprint. I dodge people, bump into a few and cause one lady to curse at me, but it's all worth it the moment I see the back of his head.

"Atlas!" I yell. He's heading in the other direction, so I keep pushing through the crowd. "Atlas!"

He stops walking but he doesn't turn around. He cocks his head like he doesn't want to fully trust his ears.

"Atlas!" I yell again.

This time when he turns, he turns with purpose. His

eyes meet mine and there's a three-second pause while we both stare at each other. But then we both start walking toward each other, determination in every step. Twenty steps separate us.

Ten.

Five.

One.

Neither of us takes that final step.

I'm out of breath, panting and nervous. "I forgot to tell you Emerson's middle name." I put my hands on my hips and exhale. "It's Dory."

He doesn't immediately react, but then his eyes crinkle a little in the corners. His mouth twitches like he's forcing back a smile. "What a perfect name for her."

I nod, and smile, and then stop.

I'm not sure what to do now. I just needed him to know that, but now that I've told him, I didn't really think of what I'd do or say next.

I nod again, and then glance around me, throwing a thumb over my shoulder. "Well . . . I guess I'll . . ."

Atlas steps forward, grabs me, and pulls me hard against his chest. I immediately close my eyes when he wraps his arms around me. His hand goes up to the back of my head and he holds me still against him as we stand, surrounded by busy streets, blasts of horns, people brushing us as they pass in a hurry. He presses a gentle kiss into my hair, and all of that fades away.

"Lily," he says quietly. "I feel like my life is good enough for you now. So whenever you're ready . . ."

I clench his jacket in my hands and keep my face pressed

tight against his chest. I suddenly feel like I'm fifteen again. My neck and cheeks flush from his words.

But I'm *not* fifteen.

I'm an adult with responsibilities and a child. I can't just allow my teenage feelings to take over. Not without a little reassurance, at least.

I pull back and look up at him. "Do you donate to charity?"

Atlas laughs with confusion. "Several. Why?"

"Do you want kids someday?"

He nods. "Of course I do."

"Do you think you'll ever want to leave Boston?"

He shakes his head. "No. Never. Everything is better here, remember?"

His answers give me the reassurance I need. I smile up at him. "Okay. I'm ready."

He pulls me tight against him and I laugh. With everything that has happened since the day he came into my life, I never expected this outcome. I've hoped for it a lot, but until now I wasn't sure if it would ever happen.

I close my eyes when I feel his lips meet the spot on my collarbone. He presses a gentle kiss there and it feels just like the first time he kissed me there all those years ago. He brings his mouth to my ear, and in a whisper, he says, "You can stop swimming now, Lily. We finally reached the shore."

Note from the Author

. . .

My earliest memory in life was from the age of two and a half years old. My bedroom didn't have a door and was covered by a sheet nailed to the top of the door frame. I remember hearing my father yelling, so I peeked out from the other side of the sheet just as my father picked up our television and threw it at my mother, knocking her down.

She divorced him before I turned three. Every memory beyond that of my father was a good one. He never once lost his temper with me or my sisters, despite having done so on numerous occasions with my mother.

I knew their marriage was an abusive one, but my mother never talked about it. To discuss it would have meant she was talking ill of my father and that's something she never once did. She wanted the relationship I had with him to be free of any strain that stood between the two of them. Because of this, I have the utmost respect for parents who don't involve their children in the dissolution of their relationships.

I asked my father about the abuse once. He was very candid about their relationship. He was an alcoholic during the years he was married to my mother and he was the first to admit he didn't treat her well. In fact, he told me he had two knuckles replaced in his hand because he had hit her so hard, they broke against her skull.

My father regretted the way he treated my mother his entire life. Mistreating her was the worst mistake he had ever made and he said he would grow old and die still madly in love with her.

I feel that was a very light punishment for what she endured.

When I decided I wanted to write this story, I first asked my mother for permission. I told her I wanted to write it for women like her. I also wanted to write it for all the people who didn't quite understand women like her.

I was one of those people.

The mother I know is not weak. She was not someone I could envision forgiving a man for mistreating her on multiple occasions. But while writing this book and getting into the mind-set of Lily, I quickly realized that it's not as black and white as it seems from the outside.

On more than one occasion while writing this, I wanted to change the plotline. I didn't want Ryle to be who he was going to be because I had fallen in love with him in those first several chapters, just as Lily had fallen in love with him. Just as my mother fell in love with my father.

The first incident between Ryle and Lily in the kitchen is what happened the first time my father ever hit my mother. She was cooking a casserole and he had been drinking. He pulled the casserole out of the oven without using a pot holder. She thought it was funny and she laughed. The next thing she knew, he had hit her so hard she flew across the kitchen floor.

She chose to forgive him for that one incident, because his apology and regret were believable. Or at least believable enough that giving him a second chance hurt less than leaving with a broken heart would have.

Over time, the incidents that followed were similar to the first. My father would repeatedly show remorse and promise to never do it again. It finally got to a point where she knew his promises were empty, but she was a mother of two daughters by then and had no money to leave. And unlike Lily, my mother didn't have a lot of support. There were no local women's shelters. There was very little government support back then. To leave meant risking not having a roof over our heads, but to her it was better than the alternative.

My father passed away several years ago, when I was twenty-five years old. He wasn't the best father. He certainly wasn't the best husband. But thanks to my mother, I was able to have a very close relationship with him because she took the necessary steps to break the pattern before it broke us. And it wasn't easy. She left him right before I turned three and my older sister turned five. We lived off beans and macaroni and cheese for two solid years. She was a single mother without a college education, raising two daughters on her own with virtually no help. But her love for us gave her the strength she needed to take that terrifying step.

By no means do I intend for Ryle and Lily's situation to define domestic abuse. Nor do I intend for Ryle's character to define the characteristics of most abusers. Every situation is different. Every outcome is different. I chose to fashion Lily and Ryle's story after my mother and father's. I fashioned Ryle after my father in many ways. They are handsome, compassionate, funny, and smart—but with moments of unforgivable behavior.

I fashioned Lily after my mother in many ways. They are both caring, intelligent, strong women who simply fell in love with men who didn't deserve to fall in love at all.

Two years after divorcing my father, my mother met my stepfather. He was the epitome of a good husband. The memories I have of them growing up set the bar for the type of marriage I wanted for myself.

When I finally did reach the point of marriage, the hardest thing I ever had to do was tell my biological father that he wouldn't be walking me down the aisle—that I was going to ask my stepfather.

I felt I had to do this for many reasons. My stepfather stepped up as a husband in ways my father never did. My stepfather stepped up financially in ways my father never did. And my stepfather raised us as if we were his own, while never once denying us a relationship with my biological father.

I remember sitting down in my father's living room a month before my wedding. I told him I loved him, but that I was going to be asking my stepfather to walk me down the aisle. I was prepared for his response with every rebuttal I could think of. But the response he gave me was nothing I expected.

He nodded his head and said, "Colleen, he raised you. He deserves to give you away at your wedding. And you shouldn't feel guilty about it, because it's the right thing to do."

I knew my decision absolutely gutted my father. But he was selfless enough as a father to not only respect my decision, but he wanted *me* to respect it, too.

My father sat in the audience at my wedding and watched another man walk me down the aisle. I knew people were wondering why I didn't just have both of them walk me down the aisle, but looking back on it, I realize I made the choice out of respect for my mother.

Who I chose to walk me down the aisle wasn't really about my father and it wasn't even really about my stepfather. It was about her. I wanted the man who treated her how she deserved to be treated to be given the honor of giving away her daughter.

In the past, I've always said I write for entertainment purposes only. I don't write to educate, persuade, or inform.

This book is different. This was not entertainment for me. It was the most grueling thing I have ever written. At times, I wanted to hit the Delete button and take back the way Ryle had treated Lily. I wanted to rewrite the scenes where she forgave him and I wanted to replace those scenes with a more resilient woman—a character who made all the right decisions at all the right times. But those weren't the characters I was writing.

That wasn't the story I was telling.

I wanted to write something realistic to the situation my mother was in—a situation a lot of women find themselves in. I wanted to explore the love between Lily and Ryle so that I would feel what my mother felt when she had to make the decision to leave my father—a man she loved with all her heart.

I sometimes wonder how different my life would have been if my mother had not made the choice she did. She left someone she loved so that her daughters would never think that kind of relationship was okay. She wasn't rescued by another man—a knight in shining armor. She took the initiative to leave my father on her own, knowing she was about to embark on a completely different kind of struggle with added stress as a single mother. It was important to me that Lily's character embody this same empowerment. Lily made the ultimate decision to leave Ryle for the sake of their daughter. Even though there was a slight possibility that Ryle could have eventually changed for the better, some risks are never worth taking. Especially when those risks have failed you in the past.

Before I wrote this book, I had a lot of respect for my mother. Now that I've finished it and was able to explore a tiny fraction of the pain and struggle she went through to get to where she is today, I only have one thing to say to her.

I want to be you when I grow up.

Resources

If you are a victim of domestic violence or know someone who could use assistance in leaving a dangerous situation, please visit: www.thehotline.org.

For a list of resources for homeless individuals, please visit: www.homelessresourcenetwork.org.

To listen to music created specifically for this novel, visit: https://www.colleenhoover.com/portfolio/it-ends-with-us/.

Acknowledgments

There may only be one name listed as the author of this book, but I couldn't have written it without the following people:

My sisters. I would love you both just as much if you weren't my sisters. Sharing a parent with you is just an added bonus.

My children. You are my biggest accomplishment in life. Please never make me regret saying that.

To Weblich, CoHorts, TL Discussion Group, Book Swap, and all the other groups I can turn to online when I need some positive energy. You guys are a huge part of the reason I can do this for a living, so thank you.

The entire team at Dystel & Goderich Literary Management. Thank you for your continued support and encouragement.

Everyone at Atria Books. Thank you for making my release days memorable and some of the best days of my life.

Johanna Castillo, my editor. Thank you for supporting this book. Thank you for supporting me. Thank you for being the biggest supporter of my dream job.

To Ellen DeGeneres, one of only four people I hope I never meet. You are light where there is darkness. Lily and Atlas are grateful for your shine.

Thank you to Marion Archer and Karen Lawson for the valuable feedback. My beta-readers and early supporters of each and every book. Your feedback, support, and constant friendship are more than I deserve. I love you all.

To my niece. I will get to meet you any day now, and I've never been so excited. I'm going to be your favorite aunt.

To Lindy. Thank you for the life lessons and the examples of what it is to be a selfless human. And thank you for one of the most profound quotes that will stick with me forever. *"There is no such thing as bad people. We are all just people who do bad things."* I'm grateful my baby sister has you for a mother.

To Vance. Thank you for being the husband my mother deserved and the father you didn't have to be.

My husband, Heath. You are good, all the way to your soul. I couldn't have chosen a better person to father my children and spend the rest of my life with. We are all so lucky to have you.

To my mother. You are everything to everyone. That can sometimes be a burden, but you somehow see burdens as blessings. Our entire family thanks you.

And last but not least, to my damned ol' daddy, Eddie. You aren't here to see this book come to life, but I know you would have been its biggest supporter. You taught me many things in life—the greatest being that we don't have to end up the same person we once were. I promise not to remember you based on your worst days. I will remember you based on the best, and there were many. I will remember you as a person who was able to overcome what many cannot. Thank you for becoming one of my closest friends. And thank you for supporting me on my wedding day in a way that many fathers would not have. I love you. I miss you.

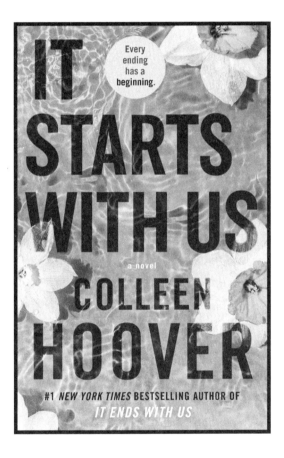